CAVEAT EMPTOR

A Novel of the Roman Empire

RUTH DOWNIE

BLOOMSBURY

New York Berlin London Sydney

Published by Bloomsbury USA, New York

All papers used by Bloomsbury USA are natural, recyclable products made
from wood grown in well-managed forests. The manufacturing processes
conform to the environmental regulations of the country of origin.

Library of Congress Cataloging-in-Publication Data

Downie, Ruth, 1955–
Caveat emptor : a novel of the Roman Empire / Ruth Downie. — 1st U.S. ed.
p. cm.
ISBN 978-1-59691-608-1 (hardback)
1. Physicians—Rome—Fiction.   2. Romans—Great Britain—Fiction.
3. Treasure troves—Fiction.   4. Great Britain—History—Roman period,
55 B.C.-449 A.D.—Fiction.   I. Title.
PR6104.O94C38 2011
823'.92—dc22
2010034525

First published in Great Britain in 2011 by Penguin UK under the name
Ruso and the River of Darkness.

First published in the United States by Bloomsbury USA in 2011
This paperback edition published in 2012

Paperback ISBN: 978-1-60819-707-1

1 3 5 7 9 10 8 6 4 2

Typeset by Westchester Book Group
Printed in the United States of America by Quad/Graphics, Fairfield, Pennsylvania

nec aliud adversus validissimas gentes pro nobis utilius quam quod in commune non consulunt. rarus duabus tribusve civitatibus ad propulsandum commune periculum conventus: ita singuli pugnant, universi vincuntur.

Nothing has been more useful to us against powerful tribes than the fact that they do not act together. Only seldom do two or three states unite to repel a common danger. So, fighting separately, all are conquered.

Tacitus, "Agricola," on the Britons.

CAVEAT EMPTOR

A NOVEL

IN WHICH our hero, Gaius Petreius Ruso, will be ...

Employed by

> The procurator, appointed by the emperor to run the finances of Britannia
> Firmus, the assistant procurator
> Caratius, a chief magistrate of Verulamium
> Gallonius, the other chief magistrate of Verulamium
> Metellus, the governor's head of security

Perplexed by

> Julius Asper, the tax collector for Verulamium
> Julius Bericus, brother and assistant of Asper
> Camma, mother of Asper's baby
> Paula, a young lady whose name he cannot remember

Lied to by

> Innkeeper, a resident of Londinium who does not deserve a name
> The Innkeeper's wife, who does but is not given one
> A number of others not so easily identified

Set straight by

> Tilla, his wife
> The doctor, Verulamium's local medic

Guarded by
> Dias, captain of Verulamium's guard
> Gavo, one of Dias's men

Informed by
> Publius, manager of the mansio (official inn) in Verulamium
> Satto, Verulamium's money changer
> Tetricus, a boatman on the River Tamesis
> Lund, a farmer
> Grata, housekeeper to Asper and Bericus
> Nico, the quaestor (finance officer) of Verulamium
> Rogatus, overseer of the official stables in Verulamium

Assisted by
> Albanus, his former clerk, now a teacher
> Valens, his friend and former colleague
> Valens's apprentices, the tall one
> > the short one

Attacked by
> A mysterious man wearing a hood

Surprised by
> Caratius's mother
> Serena, Valens's wife

Disapproved of by
> Pyramus, Firmus's personal slave
> The clerks in the finance office

Barked at by
> Cerberus, a dog with three legs (not to be confused with the Cerberus who has several heads, and who appears in other books but not this one)
> A landlady's terrier

Overlooked by
> The emperor Hadrian

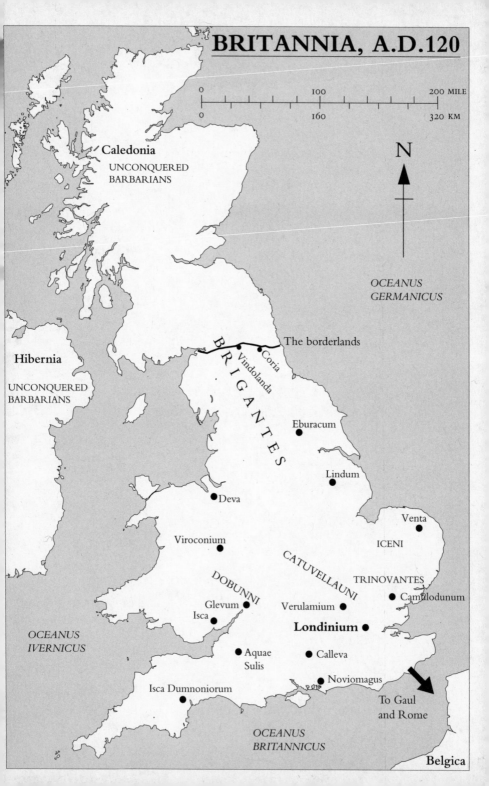

1

THIS CLOSE, EVEN Firmus could see that she was the sort of woman his mother had warned him about. Six feet tall, red hair in a mass of rats' tails, and a pregnant belly that bulged at him like an accusation. The only thing that separated them was a folding desk, and even that wobbled when he placed both hands on it. He sensed a movement behind him. Pyramus's breath was warm on his ear.

"Shall I call the guards, master?"

Firmus opened his mouth to say yes, then realized what a fool he would look if she proved to be harmless. He gestured the slave back to his place. Perhaps, beyond the boundaries of Londinium, this was what all the Britons looked like. He squinted at the sweat-stained folds of her tunic and hoped the guards had at least checked her for weapons.

"Are you the procurator?" she repeated.

Of course not, he wanted to say. *Do you really think Rome would send a short-sighted seventeen year old to look after all the money in Britannia?* Instead, he straightened his back, pushed aside the wax tablet on which he had been compiling a list of Things To Ask Uncle, and said, "I'm his assistant."

"I must talk to him."

Firmus swallowed. "The procurator's not available."

She took another step forward so that her belly protruded over the desk. He forced himself not to flinch. She smelled hot and stale.

"I have traveled twenty miles to ask for his help," she announced. "Where is he?"

Outside, the relentless clink of chisel on stone rang around the courtyard. Someone was whistling. The world was carrying on as normal, but the woman was between him and the door that led to it. Pyramus, crippled with rheumatism, would be no help at all. Should he have called the guards? How fast could a woman in that condition move?

"The procurator won't be here all day," he said. This was not strictly true, since his uncle was only two rooms away, but the thought of interrupting him while he was with the doctor was even more terrifying than facing the woman.

She said, "All day?"

"All day," he said, wondering how he was supposed to manage if the Britons were all like this, and why no one except his mother had warned him.

"If you put your request in writing," he tried, "I'll pass it on to the—"

"Writing is a waste of time. I must talk to him."

"But he isn't here," Firmus insisted, ignoring a roar of pain from the direction of the procurator's private rooms.

"I will go to find him."

"He's ill." It sounded better than admitting the great man had fallen off his horse. "You can talk to me."

He could see her eyes narrow as if she were assessing him. She glanced around the chilly little room, taking in the one cupboard and the triangular blur on the back of the door that was his cloak, hung on a rusty nail. "You are very young to be Assistant Procurator."

It was what they all said. Usually he explained about his eyesight and the army and how grateful he was to his uncle for finding him a post where he could get some overseas experience, but after a taste of that experience, Firmus was not feeling grateful at all. His uncle gave the impression of being perpetually annoyed with him and the staff seemed to think he was a joke. That one with the front teeth missing had practically laughed out loud when Firmus had explained that, as part of the emperor's tightening up on the Imperial transport service, he had personally been put in charge of the Survey of British Milestones. They were probably listening in the corridor now, and sniggering.

Firmus decided he might as well tell the truth. "I'm only here because the procurator is my uncle."

To his surprise, this seemed to reassure her. "So, you really are his assistant?"

"Yes."

"And you will help me?"

"I don't know," he said. "Who are you?"

Her breasts lifted in a distracting fashion as she took a deep breath to launch into her speech. "I am Camma of the Iceni," she announced, "I am wife of . . ."

Firmus had no idea who she was the wife of, because although he tried to pay attention, all he could see was the swell of the magnificent breasts, and all he heard was one word.

Iceni.

Several of the things he had read about Britannia before leaving Rome had turned out to be misleading—where were the woad-painted wife swappers?—but he was fairly certain that the last time a tax official had annoyed an Iceni woman, it had been a very big mistake indeed. Especially since his own grandfather had been one of the officers killed in the ill-starred attempt to rescue the settlers of Camulodunum.

The books said that the Iceni had been crushed years ago, but this one did not look crushed. This one looked tall and fierce and none too clean: exactly how he imagined the raging queen Boudica at the head of her savage hordes.

When future histories were written about Britannia, Firmus did not want to appear in them as the man who had been fool enough to upset the Iceni *again.*

He cleared his throat. She stopped talking.

"Sorry," he explained, making an effort to look her in the eye. "I'm having trouble following your accent." He reached for the stylus and picked up the tablet. "Could you say all that again, a bit slower?"

"I said," she repeated, louder rather than slower, "something has happened to my husband."

"We don't deal with husbands and wives here. This is the finance office."

"I know it is the finance office! I am not stupid!"

Firmus gulped. "No! No, of course not." He recalled the advice of a distant cousin who had served here as a tribune: Half the challenge of dealing with the natives was working out what the problem was, and the other half was deciding what poor bugger you could pass it on to.

"This is why I have come to you," the woman was explaining. "My husband is a tax man."

"Your husband works in the tax section?" he asked, wondering how that had been allowed to slip through security.

"His name is Julius Asper."

"Julius Asper," he repeated, scraping the name into the wax. "What's happened to him?"

"He is missing."

"Missing," he repeated, then looked up. "I see. Thank you for coming to tell us. We'll look into it. If you could leave your details with the clerk . . ."

She folded her arms and rested them on top of her belly. "How can a boy like you assist the procurator when you do not know anything?"

"I've only been here a week," he said. "You'll have to explain a bit more."

"My husband collects the taxes in Verulamium."

"Ah!" Firmus felt a sudden wave of relief. He was on safer ground now. According to his research, Verulamium was a relatively civilized town just a few miles up the North road. For reasons he could not begin to guess, this Camma had married a tax collector in one of the places her tribal ancestors had burned down. "If he works for the Council at Verulamium," he said, seeing a way out, "you should go to them."

"I spit on the Council!" To his relief, she did not demonstrate. "They will lie to you," she said. "That is why I am here. Whatever they tell you about stealing the money is lies."

"Stealing the money?"

"The tax money."

"Your husband has gone missing with the tax money?"

"No, that is a lie."

Firmus put down the stylus and got to his feet. "Wait here," he ordered. "I'll be back in a—" He stopped, because the woman was no longer paying him any attention. Instead, she had pressed both hands into the small of her back and was staring at the floor with an air of intense concentration.

As he watched, her mouth formed a soft *Oh*. She stepped to one side and slid a hand down to lift her skirt. He followed her gaze, peering around the desk in an attempt to make out what she was looking at.

Pyramus was at his side, whispering, "There is liquid trickling down the inside of her leg onto the floor, master."

For a moment Firmus had no idea what his slave was talking about. Then he said, "You can't start that in here, madam! This is an Imperial Office!"

2

GAIUS PETREIUS RUSO stepped over a coil of rope, leaned on the starboard rail of the ship, and wondered, not for the first time, if he was making a very big mistake.

Britannia would only ever be a province. Careers were made by men who visited these damp green islands at the edge of the world and then went back to somewhere more civilized, telling tales of survival. Ruso, on the other hand, was returning without any intention of going home again. In fact he had no plans at all, beyond a keen desire to arrive safely and practice his profession in a place where his wife was not considered a dangerous barbarian.

He moved farther along the rail, keeping out of the way as orders were shouted and the crew scurried about, preparing to bring the ship into port.

Over on the bank the scatter of dumpy thatched round houses began to give way to the red roofs of modern buildings squared up along the street grid of Londinium. He felt his usual sense of detachment when he arrived somewhere by river: gliding into town like a ghost, able to see and hear what was going on but not able to participate.

The breeze carried the tang of stale beer across the water. He could even make out the dingy waterfront bar it was coming from, and catch the strains of native music. It was one of those long, swirly tunes he had first overheard a slender blond woman singing up in Deva, in the days when he had thought that no sensible man would choose to live here.

His doubts were interrupted by the woman's arrival. She placed a hand over his own and took up the tune in a husky voice. At what seemed to be the end of a section she paused and said with obvious delight,

"They sing this at home in the North!"

"I remember."

Very softly, she began to sing again.

Tilla had plans, of course. Women always did. It seemed almost every conversation on the journey had begun with, "When we are home . . ." He had stifled the desire to point out that it might be her home, but it was not his.

He only hoped Valens had remembered the promise to find him a job, because he suspected that now they were here, "When we are home," would turn into "When we have somewhere to live," and then they would be back to, "When we have children," and there was only so much planning a man could stand.

He blamed the crockery. Despite Tilla's unfortunate origins, there was a clear expectation from the female side of the Petreius family that any man who had been presented with a matching set of tableware as a wedding present would hurry to provide a table to put it on, and somewhere to put the table, and a brood of little Petreii to eat at it.

Evidently Tilla's thoughts were not far from his own. As the sailors positioned themselves to throw the mooring ropes, she said, "I want to watch them unload. I am not bringing all those cups and bowls this far to have them dropped on the dockside."

"Good idea," he agreed. "I'll go and tell Valens we've arrived."

The side of the ship bumped gently against the massive planking of the wharf. Ruso felt a surge of energy at the thought of getting back to work. He would have something useful to do at last.

3

THE TROUBLE WITH you, Ruso," said Valens, glancing to check that the door was closed before propping his feet on one of the polished tables in his remarkably ornate dining room, "is that you're never satisfied. Look at me. Here am I, burdened with a massive rent to pay, two children and a dissatisfied wife to support, an endless round of demanding patients, two of the dimmest apprentices in Londinium—and do you hear me complaining?"

"What you promised to do," said Ruso, guessing that Valens's patients must be not only demanding but also wealthy, "was to keep an eye open for a surgical job."

"Exactly!" exclaimed Valens. "Throw me one of those cushions, will you, old chap? You wouldn't believe what she paid for this couch and it's the most uncomfortable—Thanks. You're much better off on the chair, believe me."

Ruso tossed over one of his cushions, removed the pull-along wooden horse that explained the lumpiness of the other, and placed it on the floor.

"Sometimes I think she chose it to keep me awake while I listen to her. Anyway, where was I? Oh, yes. Knowing how desperate you always are for cash, I assumed the operative word in your letter was *job*." The handsome grin that had once charmed his dissatisfied wife reappeared. "And on the very morning you turn up, I've found you a job. Not only for you, but one for your lovely wife as well. You didn't warn me you were going to be picky."

"I'm not being picky," pointed out Ruso. "I'm being realistic. I don't know the first thing about finding missing—" He stopped as a cry of pain echoed down the stairs. "Should one of us go up and have a look at her?"

Valens shook his head. "I saw her just before you got here. The apprentices will call me if anything happens, but she'll probably be hours yet. It's a first baby. What was it you were saying?"

"I said, I don't know anything about finding missing tax collectors."

"Don't worry. You'll get the details this afternoon."

"I haven't said I'll do it."

The brown eyes widened. "You aren't going to let me down, are you? That would be horribly embarrassing. I've just been telling the procurator's assistant what a marvelous chap you are."

"Why would he employ a medic to conduct a manhunt?"

"Well, you wouldn't be anyone's first choice, obviously." Valens glanced at the slave in the corner and nodded toward his cup. The boy stepped forward and poured more wine. "But I said you helped me work out who murdered that soldier up on the border, and—"

"*I* helped *you*?"

Valens shook his head. "There you go again, being picky. And I told him you'd had a good go at finding out what happened to those bar girls in Deva—"

"I did find out."

Valens paused. "Really? I don't remember. Anyway, I managed to convince him that you're just what he's looking for."

"A surgeon."

"If it would have helped to tell him you were a surgeon, I would have. But he wanted an investigator. And you can't resist poking your nose into things, so you are a sort of investigator, aren't you? Admit it, Ruso. Find something that intrigues you and you're like a dog with a bone."

There was another wail from upstairs. Valens frowned. "Shouldn't the lovely Tilla be here by now? I promised the woman a midwife would be here any moment."

Ruso had barely finished saying, "They must be taking a long time to unload," when there was a commotion out in the hall and the door crashed open. Valens removed his feet from the table and swung around to see a figure stagger into the room carrying a jumble of bags and bundles.

"Tilla!" Valens sprang up from the couch. Tilla, evidently not wanting to drop the luggage, was unable to move until he released his embrace. "Dear girl, you shouldn't be carrying all that. Didn't he get you some help?"

Ruso said, "I thought you'd get the driver to bring it in."

"That driver is a clumsy oaf," explained Tilla. Ruso guessed that he had not treated the crockery with sufficient respect.

Valens stepped back and gestured to his slave. "Give her a hand, will you? Into the guest room."

As the boy began to ferry the bags back into the expanse of the hall, Valens turned to Tilla. "You have no idea how glad we are to see you. The young woman upstairs will be even happier. I'm sorry to ask you to take over the moment you arrive, but we chaps aren't much good at this delivery business. And you speak the language."

Tilla looked both weary and confused. "Your wife is having a baby?"

"Emergency patient," Valens explained. "A long way from home, can't find her husband, and her waters popped in the middle of the tax office. I'm sure she'd rather see you than any of us."

The tone of Tilla's *yes* suggested she had more to say but she was saving it for later.

"Still a bit thin," Valens observed after she had gone, "but charmingly freckled. The Gaulish sunshine's done her good." He flung himself back onto the couch. "I practically dropped the letter when I read that you'd married her, you know."

Ruso could hardly believe it himself at times. He was still not sure how a destitute British slave with a broken arm had managed to slip past the defenses of an educated and civilized man—especially a man who had been determined not to repeat the mistake of his first marriage. It was not as if Tilla had deliberately set out to lure him. She had consistently refused to embrace the qualities one might seek in either a slave or a wife. She showed neither obedience nor respect, and both he and Valens had given up hoping that she would ever learn to cook properly. Yet he had found that he was much happier with her than without her. Back at home, with their relationship under the dubious scrutiny of his family, marriage had seemed the natural—even the honorable—thing to do.

"But then I thought," Valens continued, "what harm can it do? And I'm delighted to see you both. Not to mention that rather promising amphora

I notice has arrived with you. You, me, Tilla—it'll be just like the old days in the Legion."

Ruso, noting the absence of mold on the walls and beer stains on the furniture, said, "Not quite."

"Well, no, we've come up in the world since then. At least, I have. Did you notice my rather lovely consulting rooms on the way in? Once word gets around that you're a personal physician to the famous . . ." He smiled and spread his hands in a gesture that was somewhere between a modest shrug and an attempt to demonstrate the enormity of the good things that had come his way since they both left the army. "Anyway, let's hope young Firmus likes you. Then who knows how high you might go?"

Ruso frowned. "Who's Firmus?"

"Some sort of junior relative who's in charge while the procurator's laid up." It was not a ringing endorsement of Firmus's competence as an employer. Ruso suspected that Valens, having failed to find him a job despite all the breezy assurances in his letters that it would be no problem, had now offered his services to the first person who looked open to persuasion.

"Tell me about him."

"Looks as though he's cracked a couple of ribs, and he's seriously shaken up. Not to mention embarrassed. Between you and me, I'd imagine that when the governor's away on tour he's supposed to be sitting in his office running the province, not gallivanting around chasing wild boar. Especially a man of his age."

"I meant Firmus," explained Ruso, who was not interested in the accident that had temporarily disabled one of Hadrian's two top men in Britannia.

Valens shook his head. "Frighteningly young, Ruso. As they all are these days. He came trotting in while I was strapping his uncle up and said he had a mad native ranting about a missing husband and stolen money, and now she was about to give birth on the floor of his office and what should he do?" The grin reappeared. "Unfortunately I'd just filled the procurator with poppy juice, so he wouldn't have cared if Juno herself was giving birth in the office. Young Firmus was looking a bit desperate, and I'd just heard that your ship was coming in on the next tide, so everything fell into place rather neatly."

"You told him I'd rush all over Britannia for the tax office, hunting down this woman's missing husband?"

"From what I can gather, all he needs is someone to nip up the road to

Verulamium—which is a pleasant enough place, by the way—chat to the locals, and confirm whether this fellow's really abandoned his wife and run off with all their money. Just come back with a report the lad can hand over when the procurator gets back to work. What could be simpler?"

"If it's so simple, why can't he find someone else to do it?"

Valens sighed. "He could, Ruso. Frankly, I should think the next-door neighbor's dog could do it. But you're the one with no money and no job. I've solved your problem and his at the same time, you see? You might try and be grateful."

Ruso said, "I'll do my best."

Another cry from upstairs penetrated the room. Valens winced. In the silence that followed he said, 'I hope she doesn't go on too long, poor woman. You can hear it all over the house."

Ruso got to his feet. "I suppose if I'm going to look for her husband," he said, "I'd better try to talk to her while she's still listening." It seemed like bad luck to say, *While she's still alive,* although given the number of women who did not survive childbirth despite the best of help, it might have been more honest.

4

UPSTAIRS, EVERYTHING WAS going very well.

He was not sure whether this was true, or whether Tilla was just saying so to keep her patient calm.

The air held the spearmint smell of the pennyroyal Tilla had taken from Valens's medicine shelves. The woman was kneeling on the floor with her back to him, elbows resting on the bed and head bowed in concentration. A thick tail of tangled red hair cascaded down over a cream linen shift that Ruso thought he might have seen before on his wife. A selection of cloths and woolen bandages and sponges had been laid out next to the bowls of water on top of the cupboard. A little figurine of a goddess had been placed on a stool in the corner. In front of it was a lit candle and an offering of some of the olives they had brought from Gaul. Tilla might have started worshipping Christos while they were away, but here she was taking no chances.

He beckoned her out of the room to explain what he wanted, adding, "Don't tell her I'm a doctor."

His wife looked askance at him. "Do not think of behaving like one. It is bad enough managing with no birthing stool and no helpers."

"If you need us to—"

"If I am truly desperate, I will ask you to fetch a neighbor."

Back in the room, the woman was eager to tell him her troubles. The torrent of words tumbled over one another and at times he had difficulty separating them even though her Latin was good. It seemed that her husband and his brother had left Verulamium three days ago, intending to visit a neighbor on the Londinium road. They had not been seen since. Now the Council were accusing them of theft.

"You must listen!" she insisted, gripping a fistful of bedcover. "Something has happened to them. Nobody will listen to me. That is why I came to the procurator."

She stopped talking, lumbered to her feet, and walked around to the window. Clinging onto the sill, she bent forward and cried out. Tilla stood behind her, patiently massaging her back and assuring her she was doing very well.

He waited for the contraction to pass, silently absorbing this fresh evidence that women were very poorly designed. He had, without telling his wife, added a book on pregnancy and childbirth to his collection of medical texts. Yet it still remained a mystery to him why Tilla, who knew more about childbirth than most, was so desperate to go through it. Picturing himself carrying a small son or even a daughter on his shoulders gave him an inexplicable sense of warmth and contentment, but had his own part in the procedure been as troublesome—not to mention dangerous—as this, he might have wondered whether it was worth the bother.

Finally Camma let go of the windowsill and whispered, "Another step closer?"

"Another step closer," Tilla assured her. "Do not worry. My husband will help to look for your man. He is good at this sort of thing."

As the woman began to describe the missing brothers, he could see his wife counting the time to the next contraction on her fingers.

Julius Asper was a tall man with kind eyes. He was thirty-four years old. His hair was short and brown, with some gray at the temples, and he had no beard. To Ruso's relief he also had a scar under his right eye, which might distinguish him from hundreds of other brown-haired tallish men of the same age. As for the kind eyes—that would perhaps depend on whether one was a devoted wife or a defaulting taxpayer. The brother was shorter, with darker hair in the same style and—oh, joy!—part of an ear missing. Now that was a useful description. Both spoke good Latin. She had never noticed an accent, but since she had one herself, that might not mean much.

"Please find him!" She clutched at the sill again. "Everyone is lying to me. Aargh! Oh blessed Andraste, make it stop!" Her voice rose to a shriek. "Why did I let him do this to me?"

Ruso left the room quietly, unnoticed and doubtlessly unmissed.

Downstairs, Ruso conceded that he would be going to Verulamium. "Serena won't mind if Tilla stays here, will she?"

Valens's hesitant "Uh" hinted at complications.

They had never discussed it, but Ruso was aware that despite their own friendship, the two women had never been close. Serena was the daughter of a high-ranking Roman centurion. Tilla was not only a native, but, when they had first met, she had been Ruso and Valens's housekeeper. It was a social distance that neither woman had really managed to bridge. Still, it was surely not so serious that Valens would turn down a request for hospitality. He said, "I don't think an investigator is supposed to have his wife trailing along all over the place."

"Oh, absolutely. But if Serena comes home tomorrow and finds somebody else's wife here with just me, the apprentices, and the kitchen boy, it'll look a bit odd."

"You mean she's not back tonight?"

"Anything's possible," said Valens, whose earlier statement that his wife had gone to visit a relative had, now Ruso thought about it, been unusually vague.

Ruso looked more closely at the room in which they were sitting. It was true that the walls were elegantly painted and there were no beer stains, but there were balls of dust in the corners. He saw for the first time that someone had dribbled oil down the lamp stand and not wiped up the pool on the floor, and recalled the dying flowers on the table in the hall.

"So where—"

"She's bound to be back any day now," Valens assured him. "She left most of her shoes behind."

Ruso decided not to pry. He would leave that to Tilla. Instead he tried, "How are the twins?"

Valens brightened. "Oh, fine little chaps. Coming along very nicely. New teeth and new words practically every time I see them. Sorry about the state of the place, but she's got most of the staff with her. Still, I was thinking we could crack open that amphora tonight and perhaps Tilla might, uh . . ."

"You want Tilla to cook?"

Their eyes met. For a moment neither of them spoke, each perhaps recalling his own selection of Tilla's culinary disasters.

Valens said, "Of course we could always . . ."

"We'll have something brought in," agreed Ruso, anticipating the end of the sentence.

5

LONDINIUM REMINDED RUSO of a child whose mother had dressed it in a huge tunic and announced, "You'll grow into it." Four years after his first visit, there was still no sign of the town expanding to fit the massively ambitious Forum. Its red roofs dominated the skyline on the far side of the marshy brook separating Valens's end of town from the wharves and most of the official buildings.

Joining his own footsteps to the dull thunder of feet on the nearest bridge, he wondered how the hell he could walk away from the tax office without getting Valens into more trouble than he deserved.

He was distracted by snatches of conversation in a blur of languages: words of complaint in Greek, the first half of an old joke in Latin, and something Eastern. As he passed the gaudy bar where he had first discovered that the native brew really did taste as foul as it smelled, he overheard two trouser-wearing slaves arguing in an oddly strangled burble and realized with a shock that it was British. He had spent much of the voyage struggling to wrap his tongue around the complications of Tilla's native speech, but Tilla was from the North. Now it seemed that if his efforts were to be of any use, he was going to have to perform some sort of mental swerve onto a new track.

He passed the timbered workshop of a cobbler who had once repaired his boots. He nodded to some native god at a street altar, resolving to give proper thanks for a safe voyage as soon as he had time. Moments later he was enjoying the simplicity of Latin as he explained himself to the guards at the grand gatehouse of the Official Residence.

It seemed that the governor had ordered improvements to be made to the Residence in his absence. Ruso followed the guard across the court-yard, through the hall of the main building, and out into what should have been a formal garden area where the great man and his guests could enjoy a grand view of the river. The view was intact but the garden had been converted into a temporary builders' yard. Their progress was ac-companied by the musical clink of stonemasons and the crunch and rattle of someone shoveling gravel. A cargo of roof tiles was being unloaded from a vessel moored against the governor's private steps. A chain of slaves was passing them along and the last man was stacking them inside the clipped rectangle of a box hedge as if they were some kind of delicate plant.

The guard escorted him past the fish pool and around a pile of timber blocking one side of the walkway. Ruso ducked under a scaffolding pole to see a makeshift sign that read, "Procurator's Assistant." Beyond it, he was ushered into the dank chill of a room where the plaster was still dry-ing out.

This wing of the complex might be imposing one day but at the mo-ment nothing was quite finished, and that included the official behind the desk. Firmus was indeed frighteningly young. He had the smooth cheeks of a boy, the nose of a patrician, and the tan of someone who had not just spent a winter in the Northwest provinces. These were arrayed beneath what Ruso supposed was the next fashion in haircuts.

As he approached, a bent slave leaned forward to whisper something in one of the aristocratic ears.

"So you're Ruso," the youth began, squinting as he looked him up and down. "I'm told you've done some work for the governor's security chief?"

"Just an isolated case, sir," said Ruso, hoping Metellus was still safely up on the northern border and had not been seconded to the finance office.

"And you've also worked for the Twentieth Legion?"

"Yes."

"I've never met an investigator before," the youth confessed. "At least, not as far as I know." The squint reappeared. "You're not what I ex-pected."

"I was with the Legion as a medical officer," said Ruso, wondering what an investigator should look like.

"Ah," said the youth, nodding slowly. "Very clever. Good cover."

"I'm not a spy," Ruso explained. "To tell you the truth, I'm not really—" He stopped.

"Not what?"

Ruso hesitated. Assuming she survived, Camma would be expecting him to look for her husband. Silently cursing Tilla's eagerness to help and Valens's ability to tell the wrong lies for all the right reasons, he said, "I'm not really here on business."

Firmus's eyebrows rose. "I hope you're not suggesting you have something more important to do than to help the emperor's personally appointed finance administrator?"

Ruso cleared his throat. "No, sir."

"Excellent. So, where do you want to start?"

Ruso scratched one ear with his forefinger. "I've had a word with the Iceni woman already, sir. She says his brother's gone missing as well."

"There are two of them now? Why didn't she say that before?"

"She may have been distracted, sir. Apparently the brother's called Bericus. He only has half of one ear, so he should be easy enough to find."

"I hope we aren't running around chasing the fantasies of a madwoman."

Ruso pondered this for a moment. Tilla had been convinced by the woman's story, but they barely knew her. "We could send a messenger to Verulamium to check," he said, "but we'll lose the rest of the day waiting for an answer. Are we sure the money's missing? What do your staff know about Asper?"

Evidently Firmus had not thought to ask.

"I'll get a description out along the docks in case they try to leave the province." It was a commonsense move that Firmus should have made straightaway, and even then it would probably have been too late.

The youth's eyes widened. "You think they might be here?"

"If they've stolen a lot of money and one of them's abandoned his wife, I'd imagine they've already left on the first ship they could find."

"Ah." Firmus pondered that for a moment. "If they have, we'd better keep it quiet until we check with the procurator. We don't want a big fuss with the natives, especially when we're leading up to the emperor's visit."

"Hadrian's really coming at last?" asked Ruso. There had been unful-
filled rumors about an Imperial tour of Britain for years. "Do we know
when?"

"When he decides," said Firmus, who evidently did not know himself.
"He's on the way to Gaul now. We've already had orders to tighten up on
government transport. I'm personally organizing a survey of milestones.
Whenever it is, we intend to be ready. Now, do you have everything you
need?"

"Almost," said Ruso, wondering what else an investigator should ask
for. "We just need to talk about payment."

Firmus recoiled, as if payment were not a suitable subject to be discussed in a finance office. He left Ruso to listen to the sound of hammering while he went to consult someone else. Moments later he reappeared
with a short balding clerk who lisped through the gap in his teeth, "We
will arrange an official travel warrant, sir."

"And the fee?"

"It's not policy to offer fees in addition to salary, sir." The *sir* was added
in a tone of practiced insolence that suggested years in some division of
military service involving neither danger nor discomfort. "You'll have
the honor of serving the procurator."

"But I'm not on a salary," Ruso pointed out. Another problem occurred
to him. "I'll need a translator if I'm going out into the countryside."

Firmus glanced at the clerk. "You can ask the Council to give you somebody when you get there," he said, seizing the wrong ground to fight over.

"The Iceni woman's saying the Council can't be trusted," Ruso
pointed out. "Their man could lie to me. I wouldn't know."

The youth gave him a look that said he was not sure whether he could
trust Ruso, either. The clerk offered to send a message over to the fort.
"They might be able to spare somebody, sir."

"No need," put in Ruso before they could lumber him with an un-
wanted helper. "I know someone who can do it." Interpreting the local
accent would not only get Tilla out of Valens's house but—with luck—
take her mind off babies and tableware.

The lisping clerk looked doubtful. "I hope his name's on the official
list, sir?"

"It's unlikely."

"But are you sure he's a reliable man?"

"Speaks it like a native," said Ruso, skirting the question. As for reliability—since Tilla viewed Southerners and Romans with equal mistrust, bias would not be a problem.

"It's very unusual, sir," murmured the clerk, managing to invest the word *unusual* with meanings that ranged from "extravagant" to "rash" via "setting a dangerous precedent."

"If you can find somebody who'll do this job cheaper," said Ruso, "go ahead. You'd be saving treasury money."

Firmus glanced at the clerk, who shook his head. "I've inquired about the investigator we usually use, sir. He's not available."

"Why not?"

"Knifed by a farmer who didn't want to pay his corn tax, sir."

Firmus wrinkled his patrician nose.

"But that was up North, sir," the clerk assured Ruso. "The natives have more manners down here."

Ruso, who had spent several years serving up North, hoped he was right.

"Well, we don't have a choice," said Firmus. He turned to the clerk. "Give him ten denarii. Ruso, after that you'll have to send a note of your costs into the office and I'll ask my—I'll ask the procurator if they can be reimbursed."

The clerk leaned closer and murmured, "You'll want to set a maximum sum, sir. A limit beyond which further authorization—"

"Thirty denarii," said Firmus, suddenly decisive.

"Are you quite sure, sir?"

"Yes."

"It's your decision, of course, sir—"

"Yes, it is."

The clerk gave Ruso a hard stare before gliding out of the room.

Firmus's chair scraped back across the concrete as he rose to ask the most intelligent question of the whole meeting. "Am I doing the right thing in hiring you, Ruso?"

"You're doing *something*," Ruso parried.

"But is it the right thing?"

"Nobody ever knows that until later," said Ruso, warming to the youth. "If the first thing doesn't work, you try something else. After that, it's up to fate."

He was glad none of his patients were listening.

6

THE BABY'S SQUASHED features held an expression of puzzlement, as if he would work out what had just happened to him if he lay quietly and thought about it for long enough. Tilla lifted a loose strand of his mother's hair—the same color as his own—from his face without waking her, and bent to kiss the top of his head. Then she tucked the bundle of soiled bedding and washcloths under one arm, picked up the basin of water, and nudged the door open with her foot.

Downstairs, she could hear muffled voices from Valens's consulting rooms. Her husband's was not among them. He had gone out to talk to a man in an office about hunting for the baby's missing father.

Still faintly surprised every time she took a step and found that the floor was not rolling beneath her feet, she made her way to the back of the house. The slave boy rammed the dirty linen into the top of a bag that smelled as though someone should have taken it to the laundry days ago, and then flung the contents of the bowl out the back door into a display of last year's dead plants.

On the way back upstairs, Tilla wondered again what had happened between Valens and Serena. This could not be a planned absence. A grand house like this, with consulting rooms and corridors and more beds than people, was impossible to manage without the staff to run the kitchen and trim the lamps and sweep the floors and beat the mats. Or to open the shutters and let some light into the upstairs rooms so that guests could see to unpack.

Camma was still asleep. The baby's eyes were closed. Tilla watched to make sure he was breathing, then went back to her own room to fold the heap of clothes she had tipped onto the mattress in her hunt for something clean for the woman to wear. She crouched down and shoved the crate of crockery out of sight under the bed. With luck, they would soon have enough money for lodgings where there would be room to use it. She lifted a second box onto the mattress and unbuckled the strap.

Inside was a collection of swaddling bandages and little tunics and soft leather bootees. Cushioned in the middle of a small folded blanket was a pottery feeder with a baby-sized spout. All were items that her new sister-in-law in Gaul hoped never to need again. "They're hardly worn," she had said, insisting Tilla take the box as they were tying the last of the luggage onto the farm cart and countering her objections with, "Oh, I'm sure you'll be needing them soon!"

The words had been spoken with the casual incomprehension of a woman who had five healthy children.

Her husband had also told her that a baby would happen before long, and that he was not worrying. For some reason this was supposed to reassure her. But she did worry, because even though he was a medicus, he did not know the whole of the story.

There were things that a man might think he should be told when a woman agreed to marry him. She had chosen not to mention several of them. But lately one had floated up from the depths of her past like a bloated and long-dead frog surfacing in a pond after the ice had melted. She fingered the sheepskin of a little boot and wondered if the gods were angry with her.

She had not lied to him. Not about that, anyway. She had tried to drop hints, but he had not understood. She was not sorry. Men were unreasonable about that sort of thing. Especially Roman men, who seemed to have one standard for women and another one for wives, as if wives were not women but were creatures that arrived wrapped and packaged straight from the heavens with no past—except perhaps being somebody else's wife, which was respectable enough. Roman females were, it seemed, expected to spend their early years waiting to become wives. After that it was their duty to boss the servants about, make things out

of wool, and produce lots of children. It was perhaps no wonder that they
sometimes lost their tempers and flounced off, taking the servants with
them.

She had spun yet another fleece and made a few braids on the journey—
there was not much else for a passenger to do on board ship—but she
had no servants to boss, and instead of children, she had produced only
a monthly disappointment.

Across the sea in Gaul, she had tried the herbs and charms that worked
for other women. She had prayed to Christos too. It had annoyed the Medicus, and perhaps it had annoyed Christos as well. All through the chill
of winter, the medicines had failed and the prayers had been ignored—
perhaps because she was neither sorry for her sins nor ready to forgive her
enemies.

Now that she was back on her native island, things might be better.
Even if her own goddess could not hear her down among the Southerners, there would be other gods that she could bargain with. Gods who
were not interested in sins or forgiving people. Gods who would not
care what you had done last time you were with child. Gods who would
reward you for helping other women bring new life into the world, and
would perhaps understand how hard it was for you to give their babies
back to them.

The apprentices seemed happy to watch mother and baby for her while
she went out. Valens had promised he would keep an eye on them. He
had politely not mentioned that an hour ago she had told him to get
those boys out of the room right now and clear off himself.

She stepped out into the cool air of a bright spring afternoon. The great
cities of Gaul had smelled dusty and sweaty, but this place smelled of fish
and woodsmoke, sewers and stale beer. She followed an old woman and a
heavily laden donkey down the narrow street to where the breeze was
chopping up the surface of the Tamesis into jewels.

The great river had sunk into the middle of his channel since this
morning. Gulls were perched on the masts of ships that lay beside the
wharf at odd angles, like stranded fish, waiting for the tide to lift them off
the mud. Ahead of her, a slave was positioning a sign above a warehouse
door. She dodged aside as his companion stepped back to see if it was
level. A youth overtook her, trundling an empty handcart that bounced
and boomed with every bump in the road. Over the din, a soldier and a
dark-skinned man were arguing across a stack of barrels. Nobody paid

her any attention. Nobody stared at her blond hair or commented on her clothes. She was home.

Just past the bridge, a woman was dozing beside a fish stall. Tilla watched as a chunk of bread slipped from her hand and fell to the ground. A couple of pigeons pattered toward it, but Tilla got there first. She shook the woman by the shoulder.

The woman jerked to attention and cried in Latin, "Fresh in this afternoon, lovely mackerel! Oysters from Camulodunum!"

Tilla pressed the bread into her hand and said in her own language, "You dropped it."

The woman blew on the bread, examined it, and wiped at the dust with a grimy fist before trying again in British with a strong Southern accent. "Fresh mackerel for you, miss? Oysters? Eels?"

"No fish," said Tilla. "I am a stranger here. I'm looking for three people. The first is a man of thirty-four named Julius Asper. Brown hair and a scar under one eye."

The woman shook her head. "Never heard of him." She had never seen Julius Bericus, either.

"Never mind. Can you tell me of a woman who helps other women?"

The fish seller looked her up and down. "Well, it's not childbirth. Flux? Husband trouble? Abortion?"

When Tilla did not answer, she said, "Barren, is that it?"

"That is between me and the gods."

"There's a centurion's widow beside the bathhouse," suggested the woman, not sounding very confident. "That's where the officers' wives go. But I hear old Emer has powerful medicines."

Tilla wondered briefly what her husband would make of her seeking old Emer's opinion and decided it was another thing he need not know. "Where can I find this Emer?" she asked.

7

THE EXPENDITURE CLERK with no front teeth was of little help, but the clerks of the income department in the procurator's office were clearly delighted to be allowed to discuss the latest scandal instead of sitting hunched in silence over their ink pots. Julius Asper was swiftly confirmed as the tax collector for Verulamium, with a description matching the one Camma had given. The existence of a brother was a matter of some debate, although all were convinced they would have noticed a man with half an ear. What was without doubt was that Verulamium had been due to deliver seven thousand five hundred and thirty-two denarii three days ago. It had not arrived. This was unusual, since the town always paid on time.

"Unlike some," added one of the clerks, eliciting murmurs of agreement. Ruso suspected that complaining about the lateness of tax collectors was a regular office pastime when they did not have the whereabouts of missing ones to ponder.

Nobody had known anything about Julius Asper's wife until she had arrived this morning, which was hardly surprising. There was an enthusiastic discussion about where two men with a lot of money might have gone, but when Ruso probed further it was clear they did not know how Asper might have traveled, or anything about his usual security arrangements. In the past he might have had one, perhaps two, or possibly three henchmen, but nobody had paid much attention and none could recall any names. To the staff's obvious disappointment, Ruso thanked them and declared that he would not take up any more of their time.

The gate guards could not remember anything at all about Julius Asper but confirmed Ruso's impression that no sensible tax collector would wander around with a large sum of money and no proper security. No, they could not remember ever seeing a man with only half of one ear, but if he were guarding the tax money, might he not be wearing a helmet?

Having confirmed at least some of Camma's story, Ruso spent what was left of the afternoon on a fruitless but necessary round of visits to ships and warehouses, offices and inns, a cheerful brothel and a depressing one, and the local baths. Despite the offer of a reward—something he had forgotten to warn Firmus about—nobody could remember a man with graying brown hair and a scar beneath the right eye, who might or might not be calling himself Julius Asper. Nor could they recall Julius Bericus, or his mangled ear.

The sun was beginning to slide down toward the horizon, and Ruso was hungry. For all he knew, the brothers might have avoided the obvious route south and fled in some other direction. He would have to go to Verulamium tomorrow and start again from there.

He turned away from the river and headed back to find out where Valens was thinking of buying tonight's dinner. He hoped it was none of the places he had visited so far.

He would not have noticed the slight figure approaching along the street but for the two small boys who were following and imitating his gait. It was a moment before he realized the figure was calling to him.

"Doctor Gaius Petreius, sir!"

Ruso stopped. "Albanus?"

He blinked in surprise at his former clerk. Neither seemed to know whether to embrace the other. Albanus solved the problem with a snappy military salute that was immediately parodied behind him. Ruso returned the salute and glared at the boys, who fled.

Invalided out of the army, Albanus was attempting to make a living by teaching boys like the ones Ruso had just frightened away. Although, as he observed, most of the boys were even less eager to learn than their parents were to pay: a fact which was borne out by the patches on his tunic. "I get by, sir. But if you need a clerk, I'd be very happy to help."

"Not at the moment, I'm afraid. I've got a temporary job with the procurator's office. They seem to have a clerk in every corner." He explained about the hunt for the missing brothers. "But if I hear of anybody who needs a good man, I'll mention your name."

The smile was pathetically grateful. "Thank you, sir. They can find me at Albanus's School for Young Gentlemen. We're in the southwest corner of the Forum every morning. Reading, writing, and mathematics as standard; Greek, logic, and rhetoric by special arrangement. In the meantime I'll spread the word about your tax men. And if I hear of anybody who needs a good doctor, I'll tell them you'll be available shortly."

Ruso grinned. "Thank you."

"You will be careful, won't you, sir? People can turn very nasty when there's money involved."

Ruso's smile faded as he watched Albanus walk away down the street. He had always felt vaguely responsible for the head injury that had ended Albanus's career in the army, but at the moment he barely had the resources to look after himself and Tilla, let alone employ a clerk he didn't need. It was unlikely they would ever work together again, and he suspected both of them would be the poorer for it.

8

TILLA WAS EATING upstairs with the new mother. Down in the dining room, Valens poked at the wick on the lamp with the sharp end of his spoon. The flame rose higher. He wiped the spoon on the couch, seemingly unaware of the oily streak it left behind. He poured himself another generous helping of Ruso's wedding-present wine while Ruso helped himself from the platter of salmon that the boy had just fetched from the inn around the corner.

"This is the life!" Valens observed, adjusting the cushions behind him before lifting his feet onto the couch. "Just us chaps together. It's a pity you've got to rush off to Verulamium in the morning. You know"—here he took a mouthful of salmon and carried on talking around it—"sometimes I miss the old place back in Deva."

Ruso licked the overspiced sauce from the spoon. "Didn't we spend most of our time in the old place looking for ways to get out of it?"

"Ah, Ruso," said Valens, "how I've missed your delightfully glum presence." He grinned. "I never thought I'd say this, but it's more fun with you around." Seeing Ruso's surprise he added, "It's an honor to tend the great and the powerful, but frankly it's not very entertaining."

Ruso took another swig of wine and marveled at how Valens's life must have changed if this evening was his idea of fun. He said, "I ran into Albanus this afternoon."

"We should have invited him," said Valens. "I didn't think."

Ruso was about to say, "He's looking for a job," and then considered what it might be like to work for Valens and kept quiet.

If Tilla were here, she would be hinting that this was the time to ask about the mysterious absence of Serena.

"So," said Valens in a tone that implied he was about to say something that had been on his mind for a while. "Women, eh?"

"Women," agreed Ruso, hoping Valens would get to the subject of Serena without any embarrassing prompting.

"Tell me, what do your family make of Tilla?"

Perhaps he was approaching the topic by a roundabout route. "Some of them quite like her," he said. "The rest are somewhere between horror and resignation."

"Ah," said Valens. "Well, as long as you're happy."

"Mm." Ruso glanced down at his cup. "Pass the jug over, will you?"

Valens refilled his own cup before complying. Eyeing his old friend over the top of the jug he said, "What *do* women want, exactly?"

Ruso felt a faint twinge of alarm. This was not supposed to happen. Valens had always been the man with the answers. "You're asking me?"

"Well, you married two of them. You must know something."

Ruso watched the stream of wine cascading into the cup and pondered the question. "Tilla wants to settle down and have children," he said. He was about to ask what Serena wanted when Valens said, "And Claudia?"

Ruso pondered that for a moment. "I tried asking her once."

"And?"

"She said it was obvious."

"If it were obvious," said Valens, "surely you wouldn't have been asking?"

"That's exactly what I said."

"And then?"

"She told me I'd just proved her point."

Valens frowned. "So what was her point?"

The wicker chair creaked as Ruso leaned back in it. "I don't know." He made a careful attempt to sound casual as he asked, "What about Serena?"

Valens appeared to ponder this for a moment, then said, "Well, whatever it is, I can't do much about it if she isn't here, can I?"

9

As Ruso lifted the covers and fell into Valens's spare bed, it dawned on him that not only had he eaten too much, but that he and Valens must have drained the amphora deeper than he had realized. From where he lay, his wife now appeared to be clutching a glass vial in one hand and tiptoeing around the bed with the exaggerated gait of a slave about to deceive a master in a silly comedy.

He closed his eyes, told his slithering mind to get a grip, and looked again. Now she was standing with her loosened curls haloed in the lamp, swirling sludgy gray liquid around in the vial and apparently mouthing words to it.

There would be an explanation. There was always an explanation with Tilla, but not necessarily a logical one and not one he wanted to listen to after a long day. He had a vague memory of wanting to ask her something, but whatever it was could wait. He let his eyes drift shut and left her to carry on. Thus he was totally unprepared to be woken by a rush of cold air, a warm body straddling his overfull stomach, and a voice announcing from above, "I am ready for you, husband!"

"Huh?"

"Now. While the medicine is working."

He opened his eyes and surveyed his naked and wild-haired wife with more alarm than desire. "What medicine?"

"It is spring, and the moon is waxing. It is a good time to make a child."

He swallowed. "Right now?"

The eyes that were not blue but were not really green, either, fixed on his own. "Right now," she declared, and reached across him to pinch out the bedside lamp.

Sometime later, vaguely aware that it was still dark despite the screech of a neighbor's cockerel, he heard her say, "And another thing. This bed is too hard."

He mumbled, "Perhaps the beds will be better in Verulamium."

"I hope many things will be better." He guessed this referred to their latest attempt to produce an heir, which had been swiftly concluded and followed—as far as he could remember—by his drifting off to sleep while she was still talking. She said, "I have told Camma she can travel with us tomorrow."

He grunted his assent.

Outside, the cockerel again shrieked the start of a nonexistent dawn. He said, "Somebody ought to put that bloody bird in the pot."

"It is good we are not at home in Brigantia."

In the silence that followed, he wondered what the Brigantes did with poultry.

"Nobody at home will find out I have married a tax man."

Ruso sighed. There was, he decided, a fundamental incompatibility between women and men. Women could not just get on and do things. They had to decide how they felt about doing them, and then they had to tell you how they felt, and then they expected you to do something about it, no matter how irrational their feelings might be. He had tried to explain to her that modern living needed money, that for ordinary people money came from taking a job, and that a job inevitably involved a man going where he was told and doing what he was paid to do when he got there. There were times when the question of whether his wife would approve was not uppermost in his mind.

"I'm not a tax man," he pointed out, deciding it would not help to admit that he could not care less whether the Britons paid their taxes. "I'm an investigator. Besides, you were the one who wanted me to look for the missing husband."

"I have been thinking about that. Do not look too hard."

"What?" He rolled over to face her in the dark. "It's too late now. I've got everybody from the procurator's office downward on the lookout. Even Albanus is spreading the word."

"He does not deserve her, or his beautiful son. What sort of a man leaves his family for a bag of money?"

"She says he hasn't taken the money."

"Of course she says this. He is a tax collector. He has lied to her and run away with his brother. She will be better off without him."

Ruso lay on his back with his eyes closed and marveled at the speed with which his wife could change her mind.

Outside the window there was a soft pattering of rain, followed by the unsteady rhythms of dripping from the eaves. Farther along the landing he could hear the rasping cry of the newborn child keeping its mother awake in the room usually occupied by Valens's children. Tomorrow, he vowed, he would go and find the temple of a suitable god. He would give thanks for a safe journey and offer whatever the priests thought might be appropriate in exchange for an heir. It could do no harm.

He was just beginning to drift back to sleep when the cockerel jolted him awake with another fanfare. He felt a flash of irritation. Somebody ought to wring that feathery neck. He would cheerfully do it himself. But that would mean leaving a warm bed, groping for his boots, creeping down the stairs, and prowling wet lanes and gardens in the dark. Instead he said, "There should be a law against keeping a bird like that in town."

"He should be in a house with a good low roof to keep his head down," said Tilla. "When you find proper work and we have a home, I shall keep hens."

"It'll be easier to get work as a medic now I'm here," he promised her. "I'll start writing to people in a day or two."

"Perhaps they will want a doctor in Verulamium."

He said, "Don't say that to anybody up there, will you?"

"You are proud to work for the tax man and ashamed to be a healer?"

"I can't get on with inquiries if people keep asking me to look at their bunions."

"Be careful, husband. It is bad enough this Julius Asper is a tax collector, but a man who would leave a wife like that will do anything. If they are still around and they know you are chasing them, they will try to stop you."

He slid one arm around her waist, drawing her close so that her hair tickled his nose. "I'll be safe," he promised. "I've got a fierce British warrior-woman to defend me."

Tilla said something that sounded like, "Hmph."

He remembered what he had wanted to ask her earlier. "Has Valens said anything to you about Serena?"

"She was a fool to marry him."

Ruso assumed this insight had originated from Tilla rather than Valens. A worrying thought crossed his mind. "You haven't been talking to him about us, have you?"

"You think I would talk to Valens?"

He had to admit it was hard to imagine. "So where did you get that medicine?"

There was a pause, then, "From somebody I met."

Clearly she was not going to tell him. "And did this somebody tell you what was in it?"

After a moment's hesitation she said, "Ashes of hare's stomach in wine."

"Ah." He had heard hare recommended as a treatment for barrenness. "Anything else?"

"Roast sparrow."

Another cure more often endorsed by rumor than by experience. "Let's hope it works."

"She would not tell me the other things."

"Probably just as well," he said, glad that they would be leaving in the morning. Whoever had sold Tilla that concoction would have to find some other desperate woman to exploit.

10

THE GUARDIANS OF the sunken chamber of Mithras did not
seem to think the god would be overeager to help a man who had
never bothered with him during all his years in the army. In truth, the
officers' favorite god would not have been Ruso's first choice, but he did
not have time to hunt around for another deity this morning. Finally the
guardians sized him up and agreed that an unblemished lamb would be a
sufficient offering to make should the great one grant him a son, although
unless Ruso were to go through the proper initiations, divine assistance
was unlikely. Ruso duly descended into the gloom and made his promise
to the god. Stepping over a wide puddle outside the exit, he crushed the
unholy thought that the guardians might be partial to roast lamb. He had
more important things to think about.

He could not understand why Camma was convinced the Council was
behind her husband's disappearance, nor why they in turn seemed to suspect him and his brother of running off with the money. Tax collection
was a form of licensed theft anyway. It was hard to see what Asper might
gain by becoming a real criminal when he could sit comfortably where
he was, charging over the odds and growing legally rich on a fat percentage of the receipts. It was the only reason for anyone to take on such an
unpopular role in the first place. If the red-haired Iceni wife had been the

problem, he could have divorced her. It was surely far more likely that the men had been attacked by robbers on the road.

He would find out the real story when he got to Verulamium. In the meantime, he needed to collect the warrants and get across to the stables before other travelers booked all the vehicles.

Over at the Residence, the builders were tying another layer onto the scaffold. Behind a stack of poles he found the office of the underclerk whose job it was to issue warrants for the use of official transport. No, the warrants were not ready. Yes, the request had been sent across yesterday. But no permits could be issued to a new user before he turned up in person. Procedures had been tightened up. The emperor had given orders to crack down on abuse. Not that the clerk was suggesting in any way, of course . . . but since the other traveler appeared to be a native woman . . .

"She's my translator," explained Ruso. "I'll vouch for her." He would also pay the fee of a sestertius that might, like the new rules, be official. On the other hand, it might be the clerk's drinking money. He did not have time to argue. He would put the money on his list of expenses for Firmus, along with the name of the man who had demanded it.

As he handed over the cash the man said, "Oh, and there's a message for you from the assistant procurator, sir. He needs to see you urgently."

"Why didn't you tell me that straightaway?"

"You said you wanted your permits immediately, sir."

Crushing the warrants in his fist, Ruso strode across the courtyard. With luck, Firmus was about to tell him that the missing men had turned up, the cash had been delivered, and he could get on with finding somebody who wanted to hire a surgeon.

In fact, what Firmus wanted to tell him was that someone had just reported the discovery of a body that fitted the description of Julius Asper. "He tried to claim some sort of reward, but the staff sent him packing."

"Ah," said Ruso, wishing he had remembered to warn Firmus about the reward.

"But even if the body is one of our men, it seems he didn't have the money with him."

"I see," said Ruso, wondering whether Firmus had really imagined that the finder might hand over the cash.

"Let's hope the other one turns up soon," said Firmus cheerfully. "Verulamium will have to talk to the procurator about the money, but at least our problem will be solved."

"That depends on how he died," said Ruso, hoping it was not Asper at

all. No matter what Tilla said, the wife clearly did not think she would
be better off without him.

"Does it matter how he died?"

"I'll let you know," promised Ruso.

The body was in a narrow and vile-smelling alleyway that ran up from the
docks between the yard of the Blue Moon—the inn he had seen from
the ship yesterday—and the back wall of a stable block. It was indeed that
of a tallish, thirtyish, brown-haired man who was graying at the temples
and had a crescent-shaped scar under his right eye. Apart from a flushed
complexion and the awkward angle of his head, he looked as though he
had chosen this soft patch of mud at the foot of a damp wall to settle
down, close his eyes, and worry about his problems. After shooing off a
gaggle of curious children, Ruso crouched beside him and slid two fingers behind the jaw in what he knew would be a futile hunt for a pulse.
The chill of the clammy skin and the stiffness of the corpse suggested the
man had been dead for hours. Despite that, neither his cloak nor his
sturdy new boots had been stolen.

"Is that him, then, boss?" The innkeeper who had reported the find
was one of the people Ruso had approached during yesterday's search: a
round-shouldered optimist who seemed to think that combing the remains of his hair forward would hide its retreat underneath.

Ruso pulled the thin blanket up again so that only the head was showing. He beckoned to one of the procurator's income clerks, who was standing in the sunshine at the foot of the alley with a couple of porters. The
man picked his way through the mud with obvious reluctance, gave a
quick look, and confirmed that this was the man who had delivered taxes
from Verulamium. Moments later Ruso watched him hurry away with
orders to tell Firmus that Asper had been found, and that a full report
would arrive later. He would give the wife the bad news himself. Then
he would have to resume the hunt for Bericus.

"Glad to be of service, sir," said the innkeeper. "I thought he was a
drunk to start off with, but he looks too good, don't he?"

Good was a relative term. "It was you who found him?"

"First thing this morning, when I come out to empty the slops."

No wonder the alley smelled so bad.

"We sent a message straight off, in case it was your man."

Instead of replying, Ruso bent to examine the pattern of nails in the
victim's boots. Then he checked to remind himself what his own

footprints looked like and surveyed the mud of the alleyway. "Show me your shoes."

"Very clever, sir," observed the innkeeper. "I can tell you're an investigator. Looking for footprints, eh?"

Ruso walked the short distance to the top of the alley, looked both ways along the street, and strolled back again.

"Any luck, sir?"

"Can't say," lied Ruso. Any footprints that might have led to a villain had been obscured, either by himself, the procurator's man, the curious children, or the innkeeper. The innkeeper seemed to have circled the body several times to view it from different angles and run up and down the alleyway, perhaps in search of help.

"Can you get him moved, sir? I got work to do and the wife don't like cooking with a body around the back."

Ruso got to his feet and beckoned to the slaves he had borrowed from the procurator's office. They were carrying one of the builder's ladders, pressed into service as a stretcher. "You found him first thing this morning? So he'd been out here all night?"

"I wouldn't know, sir."

"Did you hear anything out here after dark?"

"Not a thing, sir. Well, no more than usual. Usually something or other sets the dog going, but they clear off once he starts."

"And you've never seen him before?"

"Never, boss. I'd have told you yesterday."

"I see," said Ruso, reaching up to trail one finger along the soft moss growing on the high wall of the inn yard. As he did so, a furious deep-throated barking erupted. He withdrew the hand as something began to scrabble at the wall from the other side.

"It's all right, Cerberus!" shouted the innkeeper. "Settle down!"

The din subsided and Ruso turned to help his stretcher bearers. "Doctor Valens's house," he ordered them. "Go straight to the surgery entrance, not the main door. Tell whoever answers that it's from Ruso and not to say a word to the rest of the house. I'll sort everything out when I get there."

The slaves set off to carry the remains of Julius Asper down the alleyway. Ruso examined the area where he had been lying. It was just as wet as the ground around it.

"Now that you've found him, sir," prompted the innkeeper, "who do I see about the reward?"

Ruso leaned back against the wall and checked that his knife was in place before folding his arms in a deliberately casual stance. "You won't be getting the reward," he said. "It's more likely you'll be tried for murdering him."

"Me, sir? Oh no, you've got that all wrong!"

"What was he doing in your yard?"

The innkeeper opened his mouth to protest further. The only sound that came out was a faint squeak. He gestured toward the mud as if expecting it to answer for him. Finally he exhaled. "It's not how it looks, sir. I swear."

"I hope not."

"It's the wife, sir. I told her not to get involved, but she's softhearted. Three-legged dogs, pigeons with broken wings—you name it, she takes it in. She's soft, see? I keep telling her, it's no good being too soft. Now look what's happened."

"I'll need to talk to both of you."

"Me, I said we should tell you the truth straight off. It was her what said nobody would believe us. And we was only trying to help him, poor bugger."

Whatever their intentions, Asper was beyond help now.

The innkeeper was shaking his head. "I knew it would never work," he continued. "I told her, we don't know nothing about this sort of thing. Footprints and so on. We never thought about footprints."

Ruso said nothing. They had not thought about the man's clothes, either, which had been dry despite the rain in the early hours of the morning. Nor had they noticed that the efforts to heave Julius Asper over their yard wall had scraped off some of the moss, which had landed in the mud beneath him. Since nobody else could have got past the dog, they were the only plausible culprits.

The man ran one hand through his hair, then hastily smoothed it forward over the bald patch. "How much trouble are we in, sir?"

"That depends on what you've done," said Ruso. "And don't waste my time with any more tales, because you're an even worse liar than I am."

11

SINCE COMING BACK to Britannia, Ruso seemed to have discovered an ability to frighten people. Yesterday he had scared off two small boys in the street, and today he had managed to terrify an innkeeper's wife. She now sat opposite him, weeping over a kitchen table still scattered with vegetable peelings and cat hair. The husband sat next to her, grimfaced. His defense for dumping a dead man and then pretending to find him again seemed to be that they were only trying to help and, "We didn't know what else to do."

Privately Ruso felt that this sentence would have been more honest if it had ended, "We didn't know what else to do *to get the procurator's reward*," but for the moment he was more interested in finding out what the elusive Julius Asper had been doing here all alone in the first place.

"One of the boatmen sent him here yesterday morning," said the innkeeper.

"Which boatman?"

The man shook his head. "He weren't looking too well even then. Said he'd got a headache. And he didn't have no luggage." He gestured toward his wife. "If I'd been here I'd have sent him packing, but she felt sorry for him."

The wife sniffed. "He looked awful poorly, sir. I said we'd call a doctor, but he said no. I did ask, sir."

"He wanted a private room so he could lie down till he felt better. And if anybody come calling, we was to say he weren't here. So we did."

"Did he say why?"

The wife shook her head. "I gave him a cold compress for his head, sir. I thought I was doing right."

"Did he mention anyone else? Another man? Or a woman?"

"No, sir." She looked at her husband. "I knew we should have called a doctor."

"He didn't want a bloody doctor!" snapped the husband "He didn't want anybody. We done everything he asked and then he went and died on us."

"So when I came looking for two men yesterday . . ." prompted Ruso.

"If he'd died a bit earlier, you could have had him," said the man. "We wouldn't have had none of this bother."

"You wouldn't have had it if you'd told me the truth in the first place. Somebody might have been able to save his life."

"We didn't know you was official."

"I told you who I was," Ruso pointed out.

"But how did we know you wasn't lying?"

"Perhaps," said Ruso, losing patience, "when I told you that if you saw either of them, to send a message to the procurator's office?"

The man said nothing. The wife wiped her eyes with her apron. Ruso glanced across to where a row of small scraggy creatures had been skewered along a spit and were now shriveling and browning above the fire. In the absence of fur or feathers, it was hard to guess what they were, and probably wiser not to speculate.

"Go back to this headache for a minute," he said. "Did he complain of anything else? Nausea, disturbed vision, fever? How about a slurred voice? Difficulty moving? Nosebleed, ear discharge?"

"He just said it was a headache," said the man. "We don't poke our noses into—"

The wife clutched his arm to stop him. "Not fever, sir," she said. "I know fever when I see it. He did have a bit of a limp, but I didn't see any of them other things."

Ruso nodded. Perhaps the body would reveal more when it was properly examined. "So you found him dead after I'd gone?"

"About the third hour of the night I saw a light under the door," the man explained. "I went in to make sure he weren't asleep with the candle lit. You can't be too careful in a place like this. And there he was, half-way out of bed. Staring at me. Stone dead."

The wife shuddered. "I had to shut his eyes, sir. It was horrible. We didn't know what to do."

Despite this repeated claim, it seemed to Ruso that at least one of them had known exactly what to do.

"So we went through his clothes," said the man, "trying to find out where he come from, see? If he had any family."

Or if he had anything worth stealing. "And what did you find?"

"Nothing, sir. He didn't have a thing except what he was standing up in when he come."

"So, assuming for a moment that you're telling the truth, whose idea was it to dump him in the alley and claim the reward as if you'd never lied to me?"

"Hers," said the husband, just as the wife said, "It was his."

Ruso got to his feet. "Show me his room."

The room was as drab and cramped as he had expected from the state of the kitchen. The door opened outward to avoid collision with the furniture. What looked like an old sail sagged between the rafters, presumably nailed up to keep out drafts but now giving the impression that a heavy shower of dirt would fall onto the guests below if it were moved. The bed itself filled most of the room and was wide enough to accommodate several sleepers huddled for warmth under the single blanket. There was only one pillow, with an unpleasant stain in the dent where a head would have been.

On the floorboards next to the bed a chipped cup was still half full of water. Ruso sniffed it and was none the wiser. The rough wooden box crammed against the far wall contained only a broken comb.

"We haven't touched nothing, sir," said the man.

Ruso did not greatly want to touch anything, either, but forced himself to pick up the pillow and sniff the stain. The smell reminded him of work.

The small window was open. He glanced down into the yard. Whoever had named that dog after the hound guardian of the Underworld—presumably not its owners—had a sense of humor. Unlike its namesake, the Cerberus now lumbering to its feet in the yard had only one head. However, to make up for this, it had a front leg missing. Another ailing stray taken in by the woman whose sniffling was starting to annoy him.

Ruso ducked his head back before the dog decided to bark at him again and surveyed the room. Whatever Julius Asper's reasons for being here, he felt sorry for him. This was a miserable place for a man to spend his final hours.

There was nothing under the blanket, but when the innkeeper and his wife folded back the second half of the mattress for his inspection, he spotted something lying on the floor between the slats of the bed. He lay down on the floor, reached under the bed, and pulled out a writing tablet garnished with gray fluff.

"Ah," said the man. "He did ask for some writing things to do a message."

"Why didn't you tell me that before?"

"I forgot."

Evidently the innkeeper had been hoping to erase the writing tablet and reuse it.

"He never gave us nothing to send, though."

"So you don't know who he was writing to?"

"No, sir."

Ruso turned it toward the light and saw "ROOM XXVII" inked on the outside. He flipped the leaves open. A couple of lines of script trailed over the wax in a gentle curve, as if the letters were running downhill. The straggly squiggles seemed to include parts of an alphabet Ruso had never met before. He snapped the letter shut. He would look at it later. In the meantime he followed the owners back down to the kitchen, reflecting that if they had needed to smuggle the body up these stairs instead of down them, they would have been forced to leave it where it was, treat it with respect, and cause him a lot less trouble.

The thought of having to break the bad news to Camma took away any sense of satisfaction Ruso might have felt at finding the missing man. It seemed that after arriving in Londinium, Asper had made no attempt to deliver the money or to report its theft to the procurator. Perhaps Tilla was right: The man was himself a thief who had abandoned his family. Or perhaps he had been betrayed and murdered by a greedy brother. However he had ended up here, the sorry tale was unlikely to be of much comfort to his widow.

Asper was beyond help, but it might still be possible to trace the cash. "The money that he was carrying with him was marked," he said, improvising. "It can all be identified. So if you have it, or you know what happened to it, I suggest you hand it over now, because if you try to spend it you'll be in even deeper water than you are already."

The man looked at his wife. "Two denarii, weren't it?"

The wife's nod was a little too hasty.

The man reached for the keys dangling from his belt. "I'll fetch it." As he headed off somewhere to find his takings, he called over his shoulder, "I don't suppose there'll be compensation?"

"No," agreed Ruso, who had hoped to flush out considerably more than two denarii, an outrageous overcharge for a very shabby room. "I don't suppose there will."

When the husband had gone, the wife abandoned the small creatures on the spit, placed her reddened face alarmingly close to Ruso, and whispered, "Sir! Sir, please, I beg you—just take two denarii. Take whatever you want. Please."

Ruso loosened her grip on his arm. "I'm not asking for a bribe," he said. "All the procurator wants is the money that Asper had with him when he went missing."

"But it's not there, sir!" She dropped her voice and mouthed almost silently, "He didn't have no money."

"But—"

She nodded toward the door. "I told Grumpy that, just to shut him up. The man said he had a friend what would pay the bill, and he looked honest, and I felt sorry for him, and—"

She broke off as her husband came back into the room carrying a shallow wooden box. He placed it on the table and lifted the lid to reveal a series of compartments for different denominations of coin. "Two denarii, sir," he reminded Ruso. "Taken in good faith by my wife, who has got me and her into all this trouble and caused you a whole lot of bother because she can't bloody say no."

Ruso was conscious of the wife's eyes on him as he scooped up seven or eight small silver coins. He began to flip them over in his palm. He dropped three back into the box, picked one out, then flipped over a couple more before holding a second one up, squinting at it, and pretending to find what he was looking for. Then he tugged open his own purse, found enough coin to make up the value, and placed it in the correct compartments of the box before closing the lid.

"Oh, thank you, sir!" gasped the wife.

"How do you tell?" asked the innkeeper, looking as though he had just seen some sort of magic trick and was not sure he believed it.

"It's confidential," Ruso told him.

"So what happens now?"

"I'll examine the body and report to the office," said Ruso. "They'll have to decide whether they believe your story. Whatever happens, you've lied repeatedly and wasted official time. Do you two have the faintest idea what the penalty is for getting in the way of a procurator's inquiry?"

A tear slid down the woman's cheek. The man was twisting a fistful of tunic into a knot as he said, "No, sir."

"I didn't think so," said Ruso, who had no idea either. "But if you're still lying, it'll be even worse. So is there anything else you want to tell me before it's too late?"

In the silence that followed, Ruso reflected that he was sounding like his father. "The name of the boatman would be a good start."

Finally the woman said, "It was Tetricus, sir."

The innkeeper muttered something under his breath that sounded very much like "Stupid cow."

"Tetricus," repeated Ruso, guessing Tetricus would not be bringing them any more business and wondering if he was one of the boatmen who had denied all knowledge of Asper and his brother yesterday. "Where can I find him?"

The woman glanced at her husband, then said, "He'll be out on the river, sir. But after dark he lodges somewhere behind the grain warehouse on the corner." The look the innkeeper gave her suggested she would be sorry for this later.

"Good," said Ruso, adding, "At least one of you has some sense," although he doubted that his approval would offer her any protection once the door had closed behind him. "You'll be hearing from us," he continued. "In the meantime, get that room scrubbed clean, wash the bedding, and air the mattress. It's a disgrace. If the accommodation inspectors see that, they'll close you down."

The man looked up. "What accommodation inspectors?"

"The ones who are about to go around checking lodgings ready for the visit of the Imperial household," invented Ruso. "Who, frankly, wouldn't put their lowliest turd collector in a room like that."

According to the unemployed boatmen whose board game Ruso interrupted, Tetricus had been seen heading upriver just after dawn. Nobody knew where he was going, or indeed whether he had subsequently returned, rowed past, and traveled in the opposite direction. Despite the promise of the cheapest rates on the river, Ruso rejected the offers of a boat trip on which they might be lucky enough to spot him. He left a message instead. He ought to break the news to Camma. And although she was unlikely to care, he would have to ask her if she could read the letter, or if she had ever heard of Room Twenty-seven.

Mulling over his morning's experiences as he strode back up the sunlit street, he decided that being an official investigator was much easier than being a doctor. It was the sort of job where you could impress people without knowing very much about anything at all. On the other hand, it seemed to consist largely of making other people miserable. Tilla was right about one thing: The sooner it was over, the better.

12

RUSO HAD BARELY lifted his hand to knock on Valens's door when it was wrenched open. Glimpsing a pile of luggage in the hallway behind his wife, he did not need to be told that she and the newly widowed Iceni woman had been waiting here for hours with everything packed, that all the transport to Verulamium had gone without them, and that if he wanted any lunch he was too late.

She told him anyway.

"I'm sorry, I got held up." He was ashamed to hear himself adding with guile worthy of Valens, "Didn't you get a message?"

"No." She glanced up the stairs and lowered her voice. "Perhaps the dead man you sent forgot to tell me."

Valens's consulting rooms were separated from the main hallway by a narrow lobby that housed mops and brooms and smelled of vinegar and rising damp. He drew her into the dark space before asking, "How's Camma?"

"She is tired and sore and frightened for her husband. And she wants to go home."

"That's him in there," he murmured. "The dead man. I've found Julius Asper."

He was unable to see Tilla's face, but in the short pause that followed, he hoped she was framing an apology.

Instead she said, "You sent his body here with no message to his wife?"

"I was busy trying to find out what happened to him," he said. "The porters were supposed to tell Valens to keep it quiet till I got here."

"Valens and his apprentices were out. Your men came to the house door and told the kitchen boy that if he did not let them in they would leave the body in the street."

"Oh, hell. Did Camma hear all this going on?"

"She was upstairs."

"Good."

"And now we are not going to Verulamium?"

"Not today at least. I need to talk to someone tonight who might have seen the brother."

"So I must unpack the luggage?"

He groped for the latch of the surgery door. "Keep Camma out of the way a bit longer, will you? We'll get him tidied up before she sees him."

"You are still not going to tell her?"

"Of course I am. As soon as we're ready."

"I see."

"Well, it won't bring him back, will it?"

He ducked inside the consulting room to the sound of, "Wives do not need to be told anything!" and closed the door on, "Wives are not important!"

Turning, he was startled to see Valens and the apprentices watching him across an empty operating table. The tall skinny apprentice looked as though he was about to offer some comment. The short one elbowed him in the ribs.

"Glad you're back," said Valens, tactfully ignoring the argument he must have overheard. "The boys are keen to get a closer look at this body you've so kindly sent us. Ready, chaps?"

The shorter of the chaps looked more apprehensive than keen, but dutifully chorused, "Yes, sir!" with his eager-faced companion.

"You're in luck," Valens assured them. "You're starting with a fresh one. I remember my first corpse when I was about your age . . ." He raised his voice as the youths disappeared into the adjoining storeroom to fetch the body, making sure they did not miss any of the graphic details of his first postmortem.

The short lad reappeared clutching one end of a stretcher with a sheet draped over it. Finally noticing the expression on his face, Valens added, "Don't worry, he's not about to sit up and complain. Bring him in and we'll get him cleaned up.'

As the remains of Julius Asper were maneuvered into the surgery, a thump on the ceiling told Ruso that Tilla had just dropped one of the bags on the bedroom floor. While the body was being unloaded onto the table, a series of smaller thumps and bangs told him she was unpacking. Valens was observing, "Notice the rigidity? You may need to cut the clothes off," when something screeched across the floor above him. Ruso guessed the box of crockery had been rammed back under the bed.

The short apprentice was approaching the body as one might a dangerous animal when a fierce knocking shook the outside door of the surgery. The clothing shears in his hand clattered onto the tiled floor.

Valens sent the tall boy to get rid of the caller.

"Very sorry, sirs," Ruso heard the lad say. "The doctor's—"

The door was flung open with a force that knocked the boy sideways. A voice bellowed, "The assistant procurator of the province of Britannia and Senior Magistrate Caratius of Verulamium!'

After this grand announcement, Firmus's entry was something of a disappointment. He sidled in, shoulders hunched as if he was afraid he might brush against something unpleasant, and squinted at the body. He was followed by a tall man in a deep blue traveling cloak pinned by a magnificent enameled brooch in the shape of a prancing horse. The dusty sandals below and the grim expression above suggested he had come a long way to see this, and he was not impressed. Behind him, a massive native wearing chain mail ducked in under the lintel before Firmus's elderly slave closed the door.

Firmus backed away to stand against the shelves. The grimfaced one who must be Senior Magistrate Caratius approached the table and leaned over the body of Julius Asper. A heavy gold earring glinted through the gray hair that had escaped the braid and straggled around his jaw.

"That's one of them," he confirmed. Despite his appearance, his Latin had no trace of a native accent. "Which of you is the investigator?"

Ruso introduced himself. He was about to offer condolences when the man interrupted with, "No sign of the money, I suppose?"

"Not yet, sir."

"But you have men out looking for it?"

Wishing the magistrate would keep his voice down, Ruso glanced at Firmus for some guidance on how to proceed. The youth's face was pale beneath the tan. He was gazing in the direction of Julius Asper's feet. The elderly slave leaned forward and began to describe the body.

"Not now, Pyramus!" snapped his master. "I can see quite enough."

Their presence made Ruso aware of how the mingling aromas of a doctor's surgery and an unwashed dead body might strike an outsider and what his audience might be making of the saw cuts scarring the sides of the operating table. "We're about to examine him in the hope of confirming what's happened," he explained. "Then if the magistrate could fill me in on—"

"Will that help you find the money?" interrupted Caratius.

"Possibly." Ruso nodded to Valens to get on with it. He was about to usher the spectators to a position where they were no longer obstructing the medics and blocking the light when he caught the expression on Firmus's face. He grabbed him by one arm and swung him around toward the internal door. "I think we're a bit in the way here," he announced, struggling to pull the pin out of the latch and wondering if his spare hand would have been better employed holding a bowl in front of the assistant procurator.

Behind him he heard Valens giving orders and the magistrate saying, "I think we should watch."

"It's very tedious, sir," Ruso assured him, putting one knee to the door and jolting the pin out of place. He dragged Firmus through the lobby into the fresh air of the hallway. "If you could just keep your voices down, gentlemen, there are patients asleep upstairs . . ." Finally, with the door of Valens's dining room safely closed, he continued, "Perhaps you could brief me about what's been going on in Verulamium?"

Sipping a cup of Ruso's wedding-present wine, Caratius sat very upright on one end of Valens's uncomfortable couch and began to explain that he had been on the Council for many years just like his father before him, a man who was a respected leader of his people, eager to blend local tradition with modern ways, and whose own father had been educated in Rome . . .

Ruso supposed that explained the fluent Latin. Firmus, who must have heard this tedious preamble once already, sat on the other end of the couch and appeared to be more interested in keeping his lunch down.

Ruso tried to look as though he cared about the size of the Town Forum and the Council's plans to build a theater and wondered how soon an investigator was allowed to interrupt a man who was the modern equivalent of a tribal chief. He was bracing himself to steer Caratius back to the point when he turned toward it by himself. It seemed the new men on the Council had refused to listen to the voice of experience when they voted to give Julius Asper the contract to collect the town's taxes. They had allowed themselves to be dazzled by Asper's glowing references, which were obviously forged, and—

"You mean that was obvious at the time?" interrupted Firmus, "or just after he'd disappeared?"

"Some of us never trusted him from the start."

Ruso said, "When was the last time anybody saw him alive?"

Caratius's account confirmed much of what Ruso already knew, except that his version of events included Asper removing the tax money from the town strong room before he set out. He had then collected a vehicle from the stables and headed south. The following morning the carriage had been found abandoned and there was no sign of either collector or cash. After the local inquiries had led nowhere, Caratius had come to the procurator's office in the hope of hearing that the tax bill had been paid. "But I was right!" he announced, sounding more satisfied than stricken. "The man's tried to make off with the province's money."

"Verulamium's money," Firmus corrected him.

Ruso said, "Isn't it more likely that he was robbed on the way here? I can't see why he would bother to steal from you. He must have been making a good living."

Caratius gave Ruso a look that he had probably honed on rash young newcomers at Council meetings. "You didn't know him as I did. I knew something was wrong as I soon as I heard he hadn't taken any guards with him."

"There was the brother."

"Bericus was only his clerk." Caratius indicated the chain-mailed native who was standing in the corner looking bored. "Normally he asked for three or four of our trained men to escort him to Londinium. This time, he left himself free to disappear with the money."

"The woman says he didn't have the money," put in Ruso.

Caratius cleared his throat. "I'm afraid the woman is not reliable, investigator." He turned to Firmus. "As I said before, I must apologize for the unfortunate way in which you were informed about the problem."

Ruso pulled the writing tablet from his belt and offered it to Firmus.

"I found this under Asper's bed at the inn, sir," he said. "It's addressed to a Room Twenty-seven, but we don't know where, and the content doesn't appear to make any sense."

Firmus held the wax close to his nose, frowned at it, and angled it to catch more light from the window. As he ran one finger along the squiggles and muttered to himself, Caratius's pale eyes were fixed on the tablet with the gleam of a dog waiting to snatch someone's dinner. Finally Firmus confessed that he could make no sense of it, and handed it over. Caratius held it at arm's length, then turned it upside down. Ruso had been hoping for enlightenment, but all Caratius had to offer was, "It must be a coded message."

Firmus said, "Wouldn't a code be legible numbers and letters?"

"I'll have it looked at," Ruso promised, not wanting to admit his ignorance of spying techniques.

Caratius said, "When you find out what it says, I want to be told straightaway." He swiveled on the couch to address Firmus. "As I said earlier, sir, it's a great relief to know that the procurator's office is already looking into this. If we can help in any way, the Council and the people of Verulamium are at your service."

"And as I said," put in Firmus, tactfully refraining from pointing out that the most helpful thing they could do was to send more cash, "our investigator's already found your missing tax collector for you."

"But not his accomplice, and not the procurator's money."

Ruso got to his feet. He had more important things to do than listen to them sparring over who was going to pay up if the money could not be found. Tilla was right: He should have told Camma about the death straightaway. "Excuse me a moment, will you? I'll go and see if the doctor's found any—"

He stopped. There was a living statue blocking his path. He heard a wine cup shatter on the tiles as the statue glided farther into the room, its long red hair flowing over white drapery. Firmus gave a squeak and dodged around to the far side of the couch. The native guard drew his dagger.

The realization that the statue was Camma and the drapery was a sheet did not lessen Ruso's alarm. This was exactly what he had wanted to avoid. Where was Tilla?

The magistrate was demanding to know what this woman was doing here. The guard stepped between them, dagger leveled at Camma's throat.

Caratius motioned him back. "It's all right, Gavo."

Camma pushed past the guard to stand over the couch. "Where is he?"

The magistrate placed both hands on the couch and got slowly to his feet without taking his eyes off her. Middle-aged man and pale young woman faced each other, their noses almost touching.

"This is a private meeting," he told her. "You have no right to be here."

"I know your voice when I hear it. What have you done to him?"

"What have *I* done? I have done less than I should, woman!"

Only when Ruso seized her by the arm did he realize she was trembling. "Come with me," he urged. "There's something we need to tell you."

Camma looked at him as if she had only just noticed there were other people in the room. "What have they done to him?"

"Come," he repeated.

"What have they done?"

He managed to persuade her to the doorway, where she spun around and stabbed a finger toward the magistrate. "You will be sorry!"

Tilla was hurrying down the stairs, a bundle of swaddled baby clasped against one shoulder and her spare hand reaching for Camma's arm. She said something in British. Camma answered in the same tongue. Ruso did not catch all of the Iceni woman's words as Tilla escorted her back up to her room, but beyond the accent he recognized the repetitive form of a curse.

13

W HAT WE THINK happened, sir—"
 "Stop!" ordered Valens. "Don't start by telling him what we think. Tell him what we know."

The short apprentice's face turned pink. He took a deep breath, glanced at the oddly angled form of Julius Asper lying facedown on the table, and started again. "The patient looks to have been in good health, sir. Well, I mean not that good, obviously, not in the end, otherwise . . ."

Ruso, who had already spotted the damage previously hidden by the hair and the foul mud of the alleyway, wondered how Tilla was coping with the woman who had become a mother and a widow on the same day. Across the hall in the dining room, Firmus and the outraged magistrate were being plied with more wine by Valens's only remaining slave. In here, the apprentice cleared his throat and struggled on. "There are some bruises on his back and his right forearm, and a depressed fracture to the rear of the left temporal bone, sir. We think—" He stopped and looked at Valens, who murmured, "Carry on."

"The injuries look two or three days old, sir, but he hasn't been dead for more than a day. The head injury was—I mean, it could have been—" The youth stammered to a halt.

"Could have been what?" prompted Valens.

"I don't know how to do this, master," the youth confessed. "I mean, we know what it looks like, but we can't be certain, can we? Or am I supposed to say we are?"

"No," said Valens. "Well done. You've said what you can see. Now state your conclusions with enough confidence to show that you know what you're talking about, but not so much that you get the blame if you turn out to be wrong."

The youth looked as if Valens had just addressed him in a foreign language.

"Try *the injuries are consistent with . . .*" suggested Ruso. "I find that's usually a good way to start."

"Yes, sir," said the youth, not obviously reassured. Apparently Asper's injuries were consistent with his having been hit with a "—what did you call it, master?"

"A blunt instrument," Valens prompted.

"We thought it might have been an accident," put in the tall one before anyone could ask. "But then we looked at the bruising across the shoulder here. It's the same shape as the head injury but a different angle. Do you see, sir?"

"Somebody's taken a couple of swipes at him," agreed Ruso, walking around the table and bringing an imaginary weapon down across a long streak of purple flesh with his right hand. Then he tried again with his left.

"Can you tell which hand it was, sir?" asked the tall one.

"No," admitted Ruso.

"The bruising on the forearm would be where he's tried to defend himself," put in Valens. "It's all about the same age."

Ruso tried to picture the way the man and his assailant had moved around each other. The tall apprentice evidently had the same idea. He grabbed his companion, turned him around to face the wall, and said, "Imagine I'm coming at you with a stick." Before the shorter lad could complain, his companion began to wield his imaginary stick with such enthusiasm that the short apprentice dodged and crashed into the table, nearly ending up on top of the victim.

"Not in here!" snapped Valens, grabbing the lad and hauling him to his feet.

"Sorry, sir," put in the tall one cheerfully. "I forgot how clumsy he is."

For a brief moment, Ruso saw an image of Valens as an apprentice.

"Fetch a comb and tell the kitchen boy to find a clean tunic to lay him out in," ordered Valens. "Something respectable. And not one of my new ones."

When they had gone, he sighed. "It's hard work having apprentices, Ruso. They're either fighting like two year olds or drooping around the place like a pair of maiden aunts. You can't tell them to get lost or dump them on somebody else like you can in the army. You have to keep finding things that they can do without killing anybody."

Ruso pulled the illegible letter out of his belt. "Try giving them this to decipher," he suggested. "Tell them it might help us catch a murderer."

"Really?"

"Or it might be deranged gibberish." Ruso bent to examine the injury to the skull. "I'm relieved about the cause of death," he admitted. "I did wonder if his landlord had done away with him because I'd been around offering a reward."

"That would be awkward."

"But this corroborates the story I've been told. And it fits with the seepage stain on his pillow." He straightened up and pulled the sheet back over the body. "If you tell the visitors, I'll explain to the wife."

"With pleasure." Valens plunged his hands into the washbowl and reached for a towel. "By the way, I hope I'm getting a decent fee for this? I'm assuming you can claim it back?"

"I wouldn't assume anything," said Ruso, confident that he needed the remains of the ten denarii more than Valens did. "We're working for the finance office now."

14

THE WINE HAD not softened Caratius's mood. His response to Valens's explanation of the cause of death was, "That makes no sense."

Valens was unruffled. "Let me show you how we know about the times, sirs," he offered. "If we pop across to my consulting room you can take a closer look at the—"

Firmus wrinkled his nose and announced that they did not have time for that sort of thing.

"It makes no sense," repeated Caratius. "If he was hit hard enough to kill him two or three days ago, how can he have been walking around yesterday morning?"

"Oh, you'd be amazed," said Valens, apparently delighted to be asked. "I've shown Ruso this sort of thing several times in the army, haven't I, Ruso? The man has a head injury and seems to recover, but there's some sort of damage inside that's gradually spreading. He complains of headaches, he gets confused . . . sometimes there's paralysis down one side. Anyway, once the brain gets inflamed, there's not a lot you can do. Eventually he passes out and dies. You can try bleeding him, or—"

"Thank you, Doctor," put in Ruso, before Valens could start to explain the difficulties of choosing the right place to bore a hole in the skull.

Valens was undeterred. "If you like, we could open up the brain and see where the—."

"No thanks," said Firmus.

"Absolutely not," said Ruso, wondering where Valens's enthusiasm led him when there was nobody around to keep him under control.

"It doesn't matter anyway," put in Caratius. "Asper and his brother deliberately left town with no guards. It's obvious that they planned to disappear with the money. Perhaps the brother decided to take it all for himself. That's who you need to go after now."

"It's equally possible that somebody else saw them unguarded and stole it from both of them," put in Ruso, determined to establish who was the investigator here. "If we find the brother alive, he may be able to explain the lack of security."

"Hmph! If he was robbed, why hasn't he come forward?"

"Perhaps he's dead too," said Ruso. "If he isn't, the road patrols already have his description, and so does half the town. I'll have that letter looked at, and I'll talk to the boatman who picked Asper up. When we see where that gets us, the assistant procurator will decide how we proceed."

Caratius did not look impressed.

Ruso said, "It would help, sir, if you could tell me where you yourself were three days ago?"

Caratius scowled. "I was at home, and at a Council meeting in Veru-lamium, and going about my own business."

"What sort of business?"

"The business of a loyal, law-abiding, tax-paying citizen of Rome, a senior magistrate and Elder of the Catuvellauni who breeds the best horses north of the Tamesis."

When this did not shame Ruso into apologizing, he turned to Firmus. "The woman is a known liar, sir. Anyone in the town will tell you."

Aware of how irritating it sounded, Ruso said, "It's my job to consider all the possibilities."

"While he's considering, sirs," chipped in Valens, "my staff will have the body dressed and ready to be taken away in a few minutes."

Everyone turned to look at Firmus, who said, "We can't have a body polluting the Official Residence!"

"I can't take him," said Caratius quickly. "I can lend you my guard and a couple of slaves, but I'm staying with a friend who's a priest of Jupiter. He can't be polluted by having a body in the house, either. Besides, the man's a common thief."

"How about the fort?" Firmus suggested.

"You might be able to order it, sir," explained Ruso, "but they won't take any notice of us."

Firmus did not look confident that they would take any notice of him, either. He turned to Valens, who insisted that he would be happy to help, ". . . but we don't have the facilities, sir. I'm afraid the other patients—"

"One night won't hurt, surely?" put in Ruso. "His wife can see to the funeral in the morning."

"Hah!" Caratius seemed to find this particularly irritating. "That's what she calls herself now, is it?"

Ruso's patience was wearing thin. "For all we know, the man could have been killed trying to defend your money."

The magistrate ignored him and spoke to Firmus instead. "Sir, the province has been the victim of an organized gang of thieves."

"Not the whole province," Firmus reminded him.

Caratius sighed, as if he was about to say something distressing for both of them. "My people are loyal subjects of the emperor, sir. They handed over their money in good faith—"

"And now one of your people has pinched it."

"Not one of us, sir. A hired man from the Dobunni tribe. We will do everything we can to help, but—"

"You could have helped by taking the body," Firmus pointed out, getting to his feet. He turned to Ruso. "I'm going to have to talk to the procurator."

"Anything else we can do, sir," Caratius insisted. "My people are outraged. The province has been robbed."

As they were leaving Firmus turned to Ruso and murmured, "Are all the Britons as awkward as this?"

"I've not had many dealings with the Southerners before," Ruso confessed. "I hope not."

15

CAMMA'S WHITE FACE was already blotched with tears when Ruso ushered her and Tilla along the landing past the piles of trunks and boxes topped with Valens's old legionary helmet, still impressively polished.

The apprentices had done a good job. The limewashed store at the end of the corridor above the surgery had been hastily emptied of junk and cleared of dust and spiders. A lamp stand had been fetched from the dining room to provide a living flame at the foot of the bed, which had been propped up at one end to support the body of Julius Asper. The bed, as Valens had pointed out when he insisted that the tall apprentice surrender it, was not necessary for the comfort of its occupant, but for the consolation of the bereaved.

Ruso had braced himself for a howl of native grief, but Camma entered the little room in silence.

With his face washed, his hair tidied, and the damage to his skull out of sight, Julius Asper looked almost peaceful.

Camma began to speak in British. Her voice failed. She tried again.

"She is asking for a comb," translated Tilla, confirming what Ruso thought he had understood. "I will fetch it."

When she had gone Camma knelt on the rough boards of the floor and reached out. She flinched as her hand made contact with the cold fingers.

"He wouldn't have known what was happening at the end," Ruso assured her in Latin, glossing over the horrors Asper must have suffered before that. "He would have been in a deep sleep."

She whispered, "If I had known it would end this way . . ."

"Who do you think did this, Camma?"

Instead of answering the question, she began to say, "My husband . . ."

Through the open window he could hear someone whistling out in the street. It was not the right time to be asking the widow questions, but there might not be another opportunity. "Your husband . . . ?" he prompted.

"Nothing." She shook her head. "Nothing at all."

"What do you think happened?"

She ran a forefinger along the back of Asper's hand. "This is what happened. He is dead."

"Where should I look for Bericus?"

"Poor Bericus." She sighed "I suppose they killed him too."

"Did the brothers ever argue?"

"Bericus would never do this!"

"I'm sorry. I have to ask."

When she did not reply he said, "Do you know why he would have been on the river?"

She shook her head.

"Or anything about—"

"I do not know!" She buried her face in her hands. "I do not know anything!"

Tilla, returning at that moment, glared at him. Behind Camma's back she mouthed "Not now!" and motioned to him to get out of the way. Watching her kneel beside Camma and put an arm around her shoulders, he felt like an intruder. But somehow between now and tomorrow morning, he needed to extract whatever information the woman could offer.

Tilla handed over the comb. Camma reached forward. "There," she whispered, gently teasing Asper's hair back from his forehead. "That is better." She turned to Tilla. "You see? He is a fine man."

Tilla passed her a cloth to wipe her eyes. "I will go with you to take him home in the morning, Sister."

Camma shook her head. "I cannot go home."

It was not the right moment to tell her she could not stay here, either.

"I will take him to Verulamium."

Ruso supposed that if they were all like Caratius, it was hardly surprising that she did not think of Verulamium as home. He said, "Did your husband know people down here?" Catching Tilla's warning glance, he added, "I mean, is there anyone else in town we should fetch to mourn him?"

"Only the tax men," Camma said. "I do not want them here. I will keep vigil alone."

He said, "You should get some rest. I'll stay with him tonight."

A small rasping cry sounded from farther along the landing. She sighed. "That is the cause of all this."

"I will go," said Tilla. "We will leave you to speak with your man."

As they left the room, Camma called out something to her husband in British. Moments later, with the door closed, Tilla hissed, "This is not the time for questions!"

"It's my job."

"I know," she said. "But it is a very bad job."

At that moment, he was inclined to agree.

In the nursery she scooped up the angry baby and laid him against her shoulder.

"I can't escort a body to Verulamium," Ruso told her over the din of the crying. "I'm supposed to be tracking down the brother and the money."

With one hand supporting the baby's wobbly ginger head, Tilla began to croon the song they had heard from the riverside bar yesterday morning. She was swaying to the rhythm of the music. Despite the terrible squalling in her ear, she looked more contented than Ruso could remember seeing her for a long time.

To his relief, the frantic cries began to fade. The small red face relaxed back into human shape. His wife kissed the baby's head before finally returning her attention to him. "I did not say you would go."

"But—"

"We will be quite safe without you," she continued. "We are two married ladies escorting each other, and it is not far. I knew you would say yes."

"But—"

"You always say yes in the end."

She ignored his protest of, *No I don't.* "I will try and ask her your questions later. But she has enough troubles. Let her grieve for a fine husband who was attacked and robbed by bandits."

He said, "I'm beginning to have doubts. Why did he leave town with only a clerk to guard him? And if he'd been robbed, why not ask for help instead of hiding away at the Blue Moon?"

When Tilla looked blank, he realized nobody had told her what he had been doing all morning. When he had explained he added, "Obviously I didn't tell Camma about the back alley. She can think he died in his bed and stayed there."

"I shall say nothing," Tilla promised, resting her head against the baby's. Then she said, "Perhaps when you have finished being a tax man in Verulamium you can stay and be a doctor."

"So you can stay and help look after the baby?" Out on the landing, he lowered his voice in case the woman could hear. "This isn't more of that Christos business, is it? Finding widows and orphans to look after?"

"You think without Christos I would leave a woman to give birth in the street?"

"Of course not." He gestured to her to go first down the stairs. "But you do seem very attached. You barely know the woman."

"If I was living with the Catuvellauni and my husband was killed—"

"I know. But be careful how much help you promise."

"There is a housekeeper to look after her when she gets home."

"Good. You can't fight her battles for her, Tilla."

The silence that followed was punctuated by the eerie sound of wailing from the storeroom. To his surprise, Tilla paused at the foot of the stairs and kissed him on the cheek. "You and I should never part in anger," she said. "Hear how it is for her now, begging his forgiveness."

He said, "I'll raid Valens's medicines. See if I can find something to calm her."

"She should not be left alone with the baby."

"Did I really hear her say he was the cause of all this?"

"That," said Tilla, running a finger along the crinkled curl of the baby's ear, "is why she should not be sent home alone with you, little one. There is a storm inside her mind. Whoever caused this, it was not you, was it?"

16

THE EVENING CHILL was creeping up from the river as Ruso went in search of Tetricus the boatman. He was the only person who might know what had happened to Julius Asper between his leaving Verulamium with a brother and possibly seven thousand denarii, and his lone arrival, destitute and fatally injured, at the Blue Moon.

Valens was busy seeing patients. He had offered Ruso an escort of apprentices as if he were doing him a favor, insisting that nobody in his right mind would wander the passages behind Londinium's riverfront when the workshops and warehouses were closing for the evening. Thus it was a group of three that picked its way along the deserted wharf just after sunset and turned left into a narrow street. Forty paces farther and a right turn took them into the gloom of the weed-fringed alleyway leading to the home of Tetricus the boatman.

A couple of urchins who were bouncing a ball off the high wall of the grain warehouse fled at the sight of them. Ruso could make out several doorways opening onto the alley. The nearest was a patched construction with a heavy plank nailed across the rotten section at the bottom. He was about to knock when he was startled by the tall apprentice whispering, "Sir!" in his ear.

"What?"

"Sir, I think we've been followed."

Ruso glanced back along the empty alleyway, wondering if the body and the coded letter had overexcited the youths' imaginations. "Really?"

"He looked suspicious, sir. He was wearing a hood."

To be wearing a hood on a clear spring evening was certainly unusual, but whoever it was had gone about his business elsewhere by the time Ruso and his escort retraced their steps to the street. The only people now in sight were an old man hobbling toward them on two sticks and a heavily made-up girl in a doorway. The girl had not seen anyone in a hood, but it was a pleasure to meet three such handsome men, and would they like to come and join her friends for a drink?

Ruso told her they were busy and drew the apprentices out of earshot. The tall one looked disappointed. The short one looked relieved. It occurred to Ruso that any sensible boatman seeing these three handsome men arriving at his front door would lock up and hide under the bed.

"Stay here on the corner and keep a lookout for your man in the hood."

The tall boy nodded. "We'll get him for you, sir."

"I don't want you to get him," explained Ruso. "Just watch where he goes. Stand well away from that girl, stay together, don't wander off, and don't talk to anybody while I'm gone. Understood?"

"Will you be all right without us, sir?" The short one was evidently taking his duties seriously.

"Make a note of the door I go into," said Ruso, who felt a more pertinent question was whether they would be all right without him. "If I'm in trouble, I'll whistle for you."

The tall one looked delighted. The short one said, "Then what do we do, sir?"

"I want both of you to run and fetch Valens," said Ruso, who could imagine what their parents would say if he got them involved in some sort of fracas. "And if you're in trouble, come and get me."

He made sure they were stationed up on the street corner before rapping on the door in the alley.

Nothing happened. He knocked again. This time the voice of an old woman shouted something in British that he was fairly sure translated as, "Bloody kids! Clear off!"

He explained who he was. The second reply was even shorter than the first: a summary of the woman's views on men who worked for the tax office.

The only reply from the second building was the yapping of a small dog. He was about to knock on the third when a scrawny man appeared from a door farther along. His gait reminded Ruso of rolling waves and swaying ships.

"You're the procurator's man, right?"

Ruso nodded.

"You want to have a word with them clerks of yours, boss. I told 'em it was the one with the pot outside."

Ruso glanced past him and saw that a fat olive oil amphora had been half-buried outside a doorway to house a straggly bush. "Tetricus?"

The man jerked his head toward the door. "Best get inside, boss, eh?"

Ruso followed him into a drab room with a table, a couple of stools, and a sagging curtain hiding what he assumed was a bed against the far wall. Most of this faded into darkness as the door crashed shut, a bar clunked into place, and the room was lit by only the faint yellow square of a window covered with oiled cloth.

"Can't be too careful 'round here, boss," explained the boatman, striking a flint and eventually managing to light a smelly candle. "So, I'm getting it after all, eh?"

"Getting what?"

"You're the one who was looking for him, right? Offering money for *information leading to the finding of*? Well I come back specially to hand in the information, like a good citizen, and a fat lot of thanks I get for it. It weren't my fault he went and died later on."

Ruso frowned. "You've already talked to the office about this?"

"This afternoon," explained the boatman. "Jupiter's balls, didn't they tell you anything? Useless buggers. You want to sack the lot of 'em. Specially that snotty one with the lisp."

The unlucky Tetricus must have arrived at the office to claim his reward while Firmus had been out observing the postmortem. "So," he said, "you came back specially from somewhere today to report a sighting of Julius Asper—"

"Yesterday, it was," explained the man. "I seen him yesterday morning, but I didn't hear you was looking till today. Then I come downriver as quick as I could and I went straight to the Forum to hand in *information leading to the finding of*, and that bunch of tight arses made out they didn't know nothing about a reward. Then I go for a bite to eat and find out he's gone and died and you lot have been down to the Blue Moon. You're not giving them the money, are you?"

"No," said Ruso. Avoiding the wavering light of the candle, he was trying to assess where the man might have hidden any stolen coins.

"None of that moving the body business had nothing to do with me, right? All I did was find him on the river and give him a tow down to the wharf."

"Where did you find him?"

"In the marshes on the north bank, about seven or eight miles up past the double-span bridge. Saw him at first light. Looked like a loose boat was drifted into the reeds. I went in after it, and there he was. He weren't looking too well. Kept telling me to go away. I thought to start with he was just sleeping it off, like, then he started saying he'd got to get to Londinium to meet a friend. But he didn't have no oars. Just a couple of planks. So I said, you don't want to go down there in that thing with the tide and the currents and just them planks. Daft bugger. You can't get a proper hold on a plank, see? Not like you can with oars. I gave him a tow down to the bridge and he asked for a cheap place to stay. Somewhere nobody would bother him."

"So you told him to try the Blue Moon," said Ruso.

"Well, it's cheap," said the man defensively. "And nobody I know would stay there."

"They charged him two denarii for the night."

"Greedy bastard!" muttered the man, confirming Ruso's view of the innkeeper. "I never did know what she saw in him."

"Are you sure he was alone?" asked Ruso. "There was another man missing as well."

"Him with half an ear? I'd have remembered."

"Did he say anything else? Any suggestion of why he was in the boat, or where he'd come from, or who the friend was?"

"Like I said, he wasn't looking too well. Said his head was hurting."

"He had a fractured skull."

"Really?" The whites of the boatman's eyes showed up in the dim light. "He didn't say. He didn't have nothing with him, either."

"What makes you say that?"

"'Cause you lot wouldn't be bothering with him unless he had something worth taking."

"Some money was stolen," Ruso conceded.

"Not by me it weren't. Wait a minute: There's still a bit of light. I'll open the door. Then you can have a good look at everything a man has to show for twenty-four years in the navy."

"The money I'm looking for should have been delivered to the tax office," said Ruso. "It's marked. So if you know anything about it, you'd be wise to say so before we find it."

"Not a thing, boss," announced the man, scraping the bar up out of its socket. "Not a thing. Go on, take the candle and search if you don't believe me."

Ruso, who did believe him, stepped forward to grope under the bed. He stifled the urge to apologize for the intrusion. Real investigators, he was certain, neither apologized nor explained.

"You lot are all the same." The man dragged the door open and Ruso caught sight of the tall apprentice ducking back out of sight outside.

"You want to know if I'm honest?" demanded the boatman. "I could've sold that boat, but I didn't. I went and put word out that I found it. You know why? I don't want some poor sod out of work just 'cause Headache Man helped himself to it."

"You don't think it was Asper's boat?"

"Course it wasn't. He'd have had the oars, wouldn't he?"

Ruso held the candle up. Long shadows from the rafters shifted around sooty cobwebs dangling from the thatch. He walked back and forth across the floor, kicking the rushes aside. There was no sign of disturbance in the packed mud beneath. Then he crouched in the doorway and prodded the soil in and around the pot that held the straggly bush. "There's nothing here," he agreed.

The boatman cleared his throat. "Have I done enough for the reward, then?"

"Any idea where he might have got the boat?"

The man's eyes narrowed. "I'm giving you a lot of help here, boss. I only picked him up to do him a favor. I never got paid for it and now it's causing me all this bother."

Ruso reached for his purse and the man shut the door again. The candle-lit smile revealed a set of black teeth. They disappeared when he realized the large volume of coins he was being given only added up to three denarii.

"I was told forty."

"Never believe rumors," said Ruso, who had not mentioned a figure. The light glinted on the edges of two silver coins as he placed them on the table. "My employer would very much like to know where the boat came from."

The man sucked in air through the black teeth. "You wouldn't believe how many miles of river join up to here. There's whole towns. That's before you count all the farms with land fronting the water."

Ruso placed his forefinger on one of the denarii and slid it back toward his purse. It was less than an inch from the edge of the table when Tetricus said, "I did hear a rumor."

The coin came to a halt.

"It might be nothing. People are always losing boats. And it don't make much sense. I wouldn't waste your time with it, only I heard he come from Verulamium and so does the rumor."

"Just tell me," said Ruso, to whom little of this Asper business was making sense at the moment.

"Farmer by the name of Lund, lives a couple of miles downstream from the town. Going round telling people that a river monster stole his boat."

"Could Asper have traveled by boat from there to where you found him?"

Tetricus shrugged. "I said it didn't make sense. He'd have been a lot quicker by road."

"But it could be done?"

The man frowned, considered it, and agreed that the craft was light enough for the trip to be possible. Ruso slid the money across the table toward him. Tetricus gathered it up and got to his feet. "That's it, then, is it?"

"That's it," Ruso agreed.

Tetricus grinned. "Glad to be of service, boss."

Back in the street, the two apprentices were standing where Ruso had left them as if they had never moved. The impression of innocence was spoiled by a female giggle from a doorway and a call of, "Another time, eh, lads?"

It was difficult to tell in the poor light, but Ruso was fairly sure the short apprentice was blushing. "Wipe that silly grin off your face!" he snapped at the tall one, and was alarmed to find himself again sounding like his father.

17

WHEN RUSO FINALLY returned the apprentices to the safety of Valens's house, he could hear the ominous strains of Tilla singing the sort of song she sang to relieve the boredom of cooking.

He found her disemboweling a plucked fowl by lamplight while the baby lay in a wicker crib in the shadows under the kitchen table. A cauldron was bubbling over the coals and the mixture of steam and chopped onion assaulted his eyes and his lungs. No wonder the kitchen boy had taken himself off to tidy up the dead flowers and sweep the hall.

"Your medicine worked," said Tilla, wiping the back of her hand across her forehead in a vain attempt to push a damp curl out of her eyes. "Camma went to sleep."

He reached across the table and tucked the hair out of the way. "It's late to be starting dinner. We could get something brought in."

"I will boil it very fast," she promised. "So. Have you found out what you wanted to know?"

"I'm not sure." He explained about the boatman.

The bird's leg joint made a sucking noise as Tilla disarticulated it. She sliced it away with a couple of deft strokes. "Camma does not know why he was on the river," she said, holding the leg between finger and thumb to examine both sides before dropping it into a bowl. "How near is it to the road?"

"Miles away. Apparently they diverge just out of Verulamium."

Tilla pondered this as the second leg hit the side of the bowl and slithered down to join its mate.

"Did you ask about the letter?"

"She does not know, but two weeks ago she took some of his letters to the stables for the southbound carriage to pick up, and she thinks one of them had the number of that room written on the outside."

The southbound carriage would have been heading here. "She can't remember any more of the address?"

"Numbers are easy. Words are hard to read." Tilla, who could not read herself, sliced something away from the bird's tail end and tossed it into the waste bucket in the corner.

It occurred to Ruso that his wife seemed to have a particular talent for anything involving a knife. She would probably have made a far better surgeon than she was a cook.

"It wasn't a planned escape," he mused. "If it had been, he wouldn't have needed to steal the boat. It's looking more and more as if they both took the money and then the brother murdered him for it."

Tilla sniffed, either from disdain or from onion: It was hard to tell. "She says Caratius is lying."

"We've been round this already. They looked to me like old enemies."

"She says he must be lying because Asper was not on the way to Londinium, he was only going to visit a neighbor just outside town. And the neighbor was Caratius."

"What? Why didn't she say so?" Why had the magistrate himself not mentioned it? He considered the problem while Tilla hacked the torso of the bird into quarters. He was going to have to question the man again. "Maybe Asper lied to her about where he was going."

"Or else Camma is right and that magistrate is not telling the truth." The cauldron hissed and spat as she upended the contents of the bowl into it. "What is funny?"

"Last night you were convinced Asper was the villain because he was a tax man."

"But now I have seen the magistrate and I do not trust him, either."

"You hardly met him."

"I have met men like him before."

"That's more or less what he said about Asper." No wonder Albanus was reduced to dinning letters and numbers into small boys: The art of logic did not seem much prized among the Britons. Ruso leaned back against the wall, folded his arms, and watched as she wiped the table clean and wrung out the cloth.

She said, "You can tell Valens that dinner will not be long."

Her words reminded him of another mystery. "Has he said anything about Serena coming back?"

"If you really want to know, why do you not ask yourself?"

"You know what Valens is like."

"Hm. I expect Serena has found out what he is like too."

Fond as he was of Valens, he had to admit that she had a point.

"I think we should listen to Camma," Tilla continued. "She is not a fool. When we get to Verulamium I will try and find out the truth."

"I'd rather you concentrated on looking after your patients," he said, alarmed by the prospect of Tilla arriving in a strange town and confronting the chief magistrate. "I'll be there as soon as I can, but get the driver to take you right to the door and be careful who you talk to. If Camma's neighbors think her husband's stolen their money, I don't think you'll be getting a warm welcome."

Tilla raised her chin. "The Catuvellauni have always been a tribe that likes to rule over others," she said. "A warm welcome in their hometown is not something to be proud of."

"Stay out of trouble, Tilla."

"I am not going there to make trouble," she said. "I am going there to—oh!"

The Iceni woman was standing in the doorway. Even in a creased mud-colored tunic that was too short, one hand rubbing sleep out of her eyes and her hair wilder than usual, she was beautiful. She said, "There is something you must know before we go to Verulamium."

Tilla pointed to the chair by the fire. "Come and sit while I cook."

Camma did not move. "When I tell you, you may not want to come with me." She paused, as if she was hoping Tilla might promise to come no matter what she said. When the silence grew awkward, Ruso offered to leave.

"No, you must know this too. I am to blame for what has happened."

Tilla looked up from stirring the pot and assured her that nothing was her fault.

Camma took no notice. "It was my husband," she said. "My husband put a curse on him."

Ruso had very little faith in that sort of irrational nonsense himself, but for people who believed in its power, a curse could stir up an untold amount of trouble. "Your husband put a curse on Caratius?" he said. "What for?"

"No!" She was sounding impatient. "My husband was the one doing the cursing. He cursed Julius Asper."

For a few seconds it made no sense. Then Tilla said, "So Asper was not—"

"Julius Asper is the father of my baby," explained Camma. "My husband . . ." She stopped to clear her throat. "My husband is Chief Magistrate Caratius."

18

R USO WAS STILL considering the implications of Camma's confession as he stretched his legs out across the floorboards and leaned back against the rough wall of Valens's storeroom. At least he would not be bored during the long hours of the night. Watching over the remains of the man who was not Camma's husband after all, he was going to have to go back over his conversations with Caratius. The ground had shifted beneath his feet. He understood now why she had said the baby was "the cause of all this." He understood too why the magistrate had insisted that Asper was a crook and Camma a liar. Camma, in one simple sentence, had transformed Caratius from outraged victim to chief suspect.

She had also shaken Ruso's confidence. What sort of an investigator did he think he was? How the hell had he failed to see it when the two of them had confronted each other in Valens's dining room? Come to that, why had neither of them admitted it? He supposed neither had thought their complaint would be taken seriously if they told the truth.

It was possible—understandable, in fact—that the magistrate would want revenge. But a man planning to do away with his wife's lover would surely keep the matter within his own family, or at least his own tribe. Why involve a large sum of public money and attract the attention of the procurator's office? As for Camma's claim that Asper had not been on the

way to deliver the tax at all, but had disappeared after announcing a visit
to Caratius—he would follow it up, but that would make the magistrate
a fool as well as a murderer. Caratius did not seem like a fool. Still, it was
obvious that he was glad to see the back of Julius Asper.

Maybe there was something in this curse business after all.

The room was growing chilly. Ruso reached for his cloak and threw it
around his shoulders, wondering if Tilla would complain about the
limewash making white marks on the wool and then reminding himself
that he should be concentrating on praying for the spirit of Julius Asper.
After all, hardly anyone else was likely to bother.

In the feeble yellow glow of the lamps he gazed at the shell of a human
being laid out on the bed. This man had chosen to steal someone else's
wife, and possibly someone else's money. He had then been murdered,
dumped in an alley, haggled over, and jovially threatened with having
his brain opened up.

There would be no more choices for Julius Asper.

The silence in the room felt thick enough to reach out and touch. Even
the rogue cockerel seemed to be asleep. Ruso stood up to light the grains
of incense in the bowl, recited what he hoped was a suitable prayer and
began to run through the things he must do in the morning. He would
probably have to pay handsomely for the women's transport to Verulamium, since he could not transfer his travel warrant and he could hardly
ask the grieving widow if she had brought any spare cash with her. Before they left, he would sit Tilla down and make it absolutely clear that
the wife of a Roman citizen and a government investigator must not take
sides in local disputes. Especially disputes between politicians and their
wives.

Then he was going to find Caratius and ask the questions he should
have asked today instead of listening to all that pompous speechifying.
This time he would concentrate on asking him . . . Ruso yawned. On
asking him . . .

He must stay awake and concentrate. He tried to frame some probing
questions, but it had been a long day. A soft fog was drifting across his
brain. He found the same phrases were repeating themselves, circling lazily
around his mind. He felt his eyes drift shut. He would think about it later.

Something made him stumble on the threshold of sleep.

He tried to repeat the sound in his mind. The more he thought about
it, the more convinced he was that he had heard the scrape of the street
door opening downstairs.

It could not have been the door. He could not recall the corresponding scrape of it being closed again, and nobody would leave it open at this hour of the night. Besides, everyone was asleep. If Valens had received a night call, half the house would have heard the messenger arrive.

Shut in a dimly lit room with a dead body, he was starting to imagine things. Julius Asper's spirit had not just slipped out of the room and left the house. Such things did not happen.

Probably.

He must think about something else. Pleasant, daytime thoughts. Where would he want to settle after this was over? There would be plenty of work in the North, mopping up the medical discharges who did not want to go home. Tilla would be near to what remained of her family. On the other hand, tensions would still be high after the recent troubles. He was not sure he wanted to have his domestic life punctuated by arguments about the governor's latest peacekeeping policy.

Perhaps Tilla had a point about Verulamium. Of course it would depend on how the investigation went, but the Catuvellauni were friendly to Rome, aspired to civilization, and were close enough for him to keep in touch with Valens and Albanus.

His backside was going numb. He put both palms flat on the floor, and lifted himself a couple of inches. As soon as he relaxed, the numbness returned.

He closed his eyes and tried to picture himself in his consulting rooms in Verulamium, just a short stroll from proper baths and a decent wine shop. While he chatted about the latest play at the theater with his grateful patients, Tilla would be looking after their scrubbed and smiling children and doing things to food in the kitchen.

He was jolted awake by a sound like someone dropping a spoon on a tiled floor downstairs.

The lamp in the hallway had gone out. The foot of the stairs was even darker than the landing where he stood peering over the banister. The only sound was the soft sigh of his own breath: the only movement the thump of his heart. He shook his head. He was getting jumpy. He had slept badly last night. His imagination was not listening to reason. It was probably just the kitchen boy knocking something over on his way to the night bucket. Maybe the tall apprentice was wandering about in the dark, unable to sleep with a mind full of murder and prostitutes.

He picked his way back along the chilly corridor, seeking the solace of the lamp flame.

A dog was barking in one of the neighbors' houses. The distant blare of the fort trumpet sounded the next watch, and he remembered that he had promised to get the unfinished letter looked at by a code expert. He had no idea how to find one, but Albanus had spent years as a medical clerk charged with deciphering doctors' handwriting. It would be a start.

He stepped across to take a deep breath of air at the window, then stood at the foot of the bed and began to count backward from one hundred to keep himself awake.

He was trying to remember the rhyme for the causes and cures of gout when he heard something smash downstairs. It sounded as though it was in Valens's surgery.

Perhaps he should call out. On the other hand, if he woke the whole house and it turned out to be a clumsy apprentice, or Valens indulging some nocturnal inspiration, he would look a fool.

He eyed the body on the bed. What if Asper's spirit . . .

No. He was not going to think about that.

Perhaps he should just take a look downstairs.

He slid one finger along the latch. It lifted without a sound. Out in the corridor, he closed the door so he was not silhouetted against the lamp. He crept along the rough boards in his bare feet, praying the stairs would not creak beneath him.

He paused just above ground level. As his eyes adjusted to the darkness, he froze. A sinister figure was watching him from along the wall in the hallway. There was a dog crouching at its feet. Neither Ruso nor the figure moved. Gradually, the figure resolved itself into a collection of cloaks on a hook. The dog was a pile of boots. He let out a long breath and forced himself not to gasp for air as he replaced it.

He was moving toward the entrance to Valens's surgery, careful to avoid knocking over the hall table, when he sensed a cool draft wafting around his feet. Something smelled wrong. He spun around.

He could see now that the street door was very slightly ajar.

Instinctively, he flattened himself against the wall and held his breath. He should have brought a weapon. He should have woken Valens. What had he been thinking?

Nothing was moving. He let out his breath and began to edge slowly down the corridor again.

Gods above, what was—?

As he glimpsed it, the shape exploded from the shadows of the alcove. He made a grab for it and ducked just before something crashed into the wall where his head had been. Shouting for Valens, he snatched at a passing flurry of fabric, lost his grip on an oily arm, and felt a blow to his shoulder as he hooked one foot behind the intruder's knee. They both landed on the floor in a messy tangle of limbs and fists, Ruso still yelling as the intruder slithered out of his grasp, threw the table at him, and ran for the door.

Flinging the table aside, Ruso caught enough breath to bellow, "Stop, thief!" as he raced out into the starlit street. The hooded figure was barely ten paces away, heading down toward the river. He was gaining on it when it dissolved into the shadows of the buildings on the right.

Moments later he found himself staring into a narrow black gap between two shops and trying to listen for the sound of footsteps over the pounding of blood in his ears. He could see nothing. The alleyway might be empty. It might contain one man, or ten.

Alone and unarmed, he was not going in there to find out.

He glanced over his shoulder several times as he made his way back to the house, suddenly aware of shadowy hiding places all around him. He paused in the middle of the street and looked around, but as far as he could tell, there was nobody else out here.

A gaggle of bleary-eyed people in various states of undress had gathered in Valens's hall to ask each other what was going on. Ruso locked the door, counted to make sure everyone was safe, and explained that he had chased off a man who had been trying to break into the house.

The confession that the man had succeeded, and that Ruso had allowed him to spend a long time sneaking around downstairs while most of them were asleep, could wait for daylight.

19

SOMEONE WAS SHAKING his shoulder. Tilla wanted him to know that the sun had risen, everyone else was up, and she had prepared breakfast.

"Uh," said Ruso, rolling over and closing his eyes to catch the last tail of sleep as it fled.

"It was a busy night."

"Uh." He had a feeling there was something he should remember, and it was connected with the ache in his ribs. "Thanks for taking over."

After all the excitement of the burglar, Tilla had helped him rub salve into his bruises and volunteered to take over the vigil.

"Valens has been looking around the house," she said, "We are all lucky you did not give that man a chance to steal anything."

Ruso wondered how thoroughly Valens had checked. It was difficult to gauge the passage of time at night, but the prowler must have been creeping around for at least half an hour after he had scraped open the front door ready to make his getaway.

"I am glad you have had a good sleep." Tilla was smiling down at him. It seemed his efforts to protect the household had aroused an unusual degree of wifely devotion.

He rubbed his eyes and wondered if there was time for a further attempt to create an heir before breakfast. "I've got some bruised ribs you could kiss better."

The kiss was perfunctory. Instead of drawing closer, Tilla sat up and started chattering about next door's cockerel. "He has stopped crowing at night now: Did you notice?"

He agreed without thinking, and reached for her. "I'm well rested. Come here."

She dodged his hand and stood up, still looking more cheerful than anyone who had been awake half the night had any right to be. Only slowly did it dawn on him that there might be a link between the silence of the cockerel, Tilla's smile, and the rather stringy meat in last night's stew.

He was not going to ask. Instead he rolled over and grabbed her. Breakfast could wait.

An hour later, the morning traffic came to a halt in the street as the occupants of Valens's house stood to watch a shrouded body being loaded onto the floor of a carriage. Camma was pale and tight lipped, her grief marked only by the damp patches on the shawl wrapped around her fatherless baby.

Ruso, who had paid the driver well with Firmus's money, accompanied the carriage to the edge of town. When it reached the gates to the North road he bade the women good-bye and reminded the driver of his duty to deliver them to their door. The carriage passed under the arch and out toward the cemetery under an overcast sky, picking up speed as the driver urged the horses into a trot. Ruso lifted one hand in a last farewell, but if there was any response, it was hidden by an oxcart coming toward him.

They were gone.

Yesterday Ruso had been an object of interest to the procurator's staff, providing relief from the daily routine. Today he had sunk to being just another nuisance, making annoying requests and placing demands upon their time. They had indeed suffered a visit from Tetricus the boatman yesterday afternoon, and the expenditure clerk seized his chance to point out that if Ruso planned to go around the town announcing rewards, it would help if he warned the office first.

"Sorry," said Ruso, and meant it.

The resigned tone of, "Never mind, sir," suggested that the staff was used to being uninformed and underappreciated. Ruso's attempts to improve things did not seem to help. They did not look at all pleased to be told that others might be arriving to report sightings of the missing Julius Bericus.

"I'll clear all this with Firmus," said Ruso, correctly guessing that this would not impress them either.

"He's in a meeting with the procurator, sir."

"Any idea how long he'll be?"

The expenditure clerk's, "No, sir," somehow also conveyed the information that since nobody in authority ever told the office anything, only a fool would have asked such a stupid question.

"You don't happen to know where the Catuvellauni magistrate's staying, do you?"

"That would be the one who turned up yesterday, sir?"

"Caratius. Yes."

"I believe he lodges with a friend opposite the west gate of the Forum when he's in town, sir."

"Excellent!" said Ruso, pleasantly surprised. "Thank you."

He was almost out of the door when the man added, "But he's not there now, sir."

Apparently the magistrate had been summoned to meet the procurator first thing in the morning, and left for Verulamium immediately afterward.

Ruso left Firmus a note explaining that he needed to question Caratius again. He would have tried to catch him on the road, but he had promised to have that incomprehensible letter looked at, and in all the confusion, he had forgotten to retrieve it from the apprentices this morning.

"Would you care to tell us when you'll be back, sir?"

Ruso looked the clerk in the eye. "Later," he said, then relented. He had suffered from enough unreliable colleagues to know how aggravating it was to work with someone who might or might not turn up at any moment. "I'll drop by for messages when I get here," he promised.

The smirk on the face of the expenditure clerk suggested his concession had been seen as a sign of weakness.

He headed back to Valens's house to collect the letter, glancing around occasionally to see who else was in the street. The events of last night had left him uneasy. While everyone else had been reassuring themselves that no harm had been done, nothing had been stolen, and the only damage was a serious fright, Ruso had been mulling over the identity and the intentions of the intruder. Pausing to lean on the rail of the footbridge while an elderly man and a dog ushered four sheep across the stream, he wondered if he should have taken the tall apprentice's sighting of a hooded man more seriously. What if they really had been followed? Whoever it was must know where they lived—although why anyone should care was a mystery. Besides, any sensible burglar would try to disguise himself. A hood was the easiest way to do it.

There was no answer to Ruso's knock at Valens's street door. After last night's events he was not surprised to find it firmly locked. Three patients were lined up on the bench outside the surgery entrance. That was closed too.

He walked along the side of the building and turned into the back lane. From here he could see into the garden, but his plans to vault over the wall were thwarted by a group of figures outside the kitchen window. The figure in the middle with the toga draped untidily over his head was Valens. He was lifting a cup into the air and speaking to it while the apprentices and the kitchen boy looked on, wide eyed. Then he tipped the cup and a pale stream of wine cascaded down into the scrubby undergrowth. Evidently he had taken the break-in seriously enough to seek divine protection.

Distracted by the sight of this unusually diligent appeal to the household gods, Ruso was startled to hear a heavy sigh beside him. A pair of muscular arms leaned on the wall. They were attached to solid shoulders encased in plate armor. Above the armor a thick neck led to a square jaw, a broken nose, and an army haircut.

Valens finished his devotions and looked up. "Can I help, sir?"

"I'm a friend of the landlord," said the centurion. "Saw the address on the night watch report. Any damage?"

Valens unwrapped his toga and rolled it into an untidy bundle as he made his way through the weeds to the garden wall. "Just a downstairs window forced. Ruso there chased him off before he could take anything."

The gaze was aimed at Ruso while the broken nose veered slightly off to the left. "Don't suppose you got a description?"

"It was dark," Ruso said. "I tried to stop him getting past me, but I couldn't get hold of him. He was covered in something slippery, he was wearing a hood, and he'd left the door open to make a quick escape."

"Greased himself to avoid capture," said the centurion, as if it was something Ruso should have expected. He glanced at the apprentices and the kitchen boy. "Any of you lot see anything?"

The taller lad looked delighted to be asked. "I'm almost sure there was a man with a hood following us down behind the wharf last night, sir."

"I meant here."

"No, sir. We were asleep till we heard all the crashing around and the ladies calling out, sir."

The man grunted. "I'll submit a report." He gestured toward the window, said, "Get some bars put on it," and walked away.

While Valens was dealing with his patients, the short apprentice emerged from the surgery with a small box of broken pottery. Part of the disturbance Ruso had heard last night was a jar of bear grease smashing on the tiled floor.

"He took the hall lamp in there, sir," the lad observed. "He must have been clever not to wake anybody. But he wasn't much of a burglar. Doctor Valens's equipment was all laid out in there, but nothing's been taken."

"Good," said Ruso, his unease growing. Quality medical instruments were precision made, portable, and costly, and a thief as intelligent as this one seemed to be should have stolen them. He had been prowling around the house for longer than Ruso cared to remember. What had he been doing?

It was a mystery he did not have time to ponder.

"That letter I gave you,' he said. 'Did you have any luck deciphering it?"

They had not, but both apprentices had spent a couple of hours trying. Oblivious to how happy this must have made Valens, the short apprentice went back into the surgery to fetch the wax tablet on which it was written.

While he was waiting, Ruso gathered up a couple of chunks of fallen plaster almost the size of his fist from the foot of the hall wall. He tried to fit them, painted side out, into the hole made by whatever weapon had narrowly missed his head. More dry plaster crumbled away from the lath and showered onto his feet. The hall table, presumably broken, had been removed. Serena was not going to be pleased when—if—she returned.

Ruso unfastened his left boot and shook out a piece of plaster grit. Then he leaned back against an intact stretch of wall, folded his arms, and began to make a mental list of the new questions he was going to ask Caratius.

He was interrupted by the reappearance of the short apprentice, pink in the face and clearly agitated. "It must be in our room, sir," he declared, scuttling away toward the back of the house. "Won't be a moment."

There followed a series of muffled crashes, thumps, and screeches that suggested the flinging open of cupboards and the shifting of heavy furniture. After a brief silence in which Ruso wondered if he should offer to help, the noises recommenced with increased vigor. Finally the youth reemerged, his face even pinker and shiny with sweat. "Sorry about this, sir. He's put it somewhere."

"He" was presumably the tall apprentice. Moments later both youths were in the hallway denying having moved the letter from the surgery shelf and blaming each other for its disappearance.

"It was probably Doctor Valens," suggested Ruso, not wanting to voice a growing suspicion that it was none of them. "You two get back to work. I'll have a word with him in between patients."

As they headed back through the surgery lobby, the tall apprentice voiced Ruso's own thoughts. "Perhaps the burglar took it."

"Huh," said his companion. As the door closed Ruso overheard, "That'll be the same thief as took the only decent pen I had, and gave you one just like it."

Ruso went into the dining room. Since the apprentices were not allowed to use the room, there was no reason why the letter should be in it, but he might as well do something while he was waiting.

Shifting cushions and peering under the couch produced several small coins, a wooden whistle, a child's shoe, a crust of bread hardened to the consistency of concrete, a green hair ribbon that must belong to Serena . . . and a writing tablet. His brief moment of elation was destroyed by the words *Pharmacy List* inked on the outside. Idly curious, he took it across to the window to read.

What it contained was not a list but a message.

Scrawled in a large and badly formed hand were the words, *"When you finally notice that we are not here, you may want to know that I have taken the boys and gone to live with my cousin."* The message was scraped so deep into the wax that it had scored the wood underneath.

So that was it.

Ruso was more saddened than surprised. He wished he had found the note before Tilla had gone. She would have known what to say. In fact it would have been better not to have found it at all, or at least to have left it unopened. Now he felt like the woman in the old Jewish tale: the one who ate the fruit from the tree and knew too much. He should say something helpful to Valens, but what? How could a man interfere in his friend's marriage? Especially since he was not supposed to have read the note, anyway.

He pushed the message back under the couch. When the apprentices reappeared with orders from Valens to question the kitchen boy and search the rest of the house, he closed the door of the dining room and told them he had already checked it. There was nothing there.

He entered the surgery just in time to see a middle-aged man stagger out into the street with a poultice clutched to his face and a message for the next patient that he would be called in a moment.

"Splendid abscess," said Valens, describing the departed patient rather than the space beside a stack of rolled bandages to which he now pointed. That was where he had seen the letter late last night. He had almost called one of the boys to put it away until he realized it was not a patient record after all. "Somebody must have come in here after me."

Ruso waited until the patient had shut the door before suggesting, "The burglar was in here."

Valens's eyes widened. "Ruso, you don't think you're taking this investigation business a little too seriously? I know it must have been a shock finding this chap in the house, but really—what sort of burglar steals somebody's letters?"

"The sort who wants to know what's in them?" Ruso suggested, remembering Caratius's eagerness to see the letter. "Or the sort who already knows and doesn't want other people to find out." He glanced around at the neatly stacked shelves. "If it was here last night and it's not here now, where is it?"

"I don't know," Valens admitted.

"The women wouldn't have taken it. Neither of them can read."

"Nor can the kitchen boy, much."

"Which leaves only the burglar."

"I'm sure it'll turn up," Valens assured him. "You can let the lads carry on hunting for a while. I'm running late for house calls, and it's much quicker in here without them. Don't fancy seeing a few patients yourself, do you? Keep your hand in?"

"Sorry," said Ruso, backing out of the room. "I'm only an investigator."

At the far end of the hall there seemed to have been an explosion in the laundry basket. It was the work of the kitchen boy, still delving down and flinging out the contents. As Ruso approached, a blanket unfurled in the air. A sock disengaged from it and sailed past his shoulder. The kitchen boy apologized. He had not found the letter yet. "But we're all looking, sir."

"Thank you," said Ruso, grateful for his efforts even though the bottom of the laundry basket had obviously lain undisturbed since whenever it was Serena had walked out and taken the staff with her. "Let me know if you find anything."

He was not optimistic. If he was right about the burglar, then one question about the letter had been answered: Its contents were important to somebody. Unfortunately, the manner in which he had learned of their importance meant he was not going to be able to find out what they were.

The apprentices had now moved on to the upstairs rooms in their efforts to vindicate themselves. Remembering Tilla's precious crockery, Ruso hurried up to restrain them. The box had been dragged out from under the bed and he deduced from the shape of the legs protruding in its place that the tall apprentice was conducting a thorough search.

"It won't be under there," Ruso pointed out. "Nobody who had it came in here."

"I know, sir," agreed a muffled voice. "But we've tried everywhere else."

The legs began to shuffle back toward Ruso. The tall apprentice's face, when it appeared, was smudged with soot. His hair was sticking up at unintended angles and a cobweb festooned one ear, evidence of his searching in other unlikely places.

"I'm going to have to go out," said Ruso. "If you have to look in here, be careful of that box with "fragile" written on it."

The boy's bewildered glance around the room showed that he had not noticed the warning when he moved it.

"And that trunk has my medical texts and instruments locked in it, so don't bother looking there."

He turned to leave, and found himself facing the short apprentice. He was about to say, "There's no point in two of you wasting time in here," when he noticed a battered piece of parchment cut from a scroll in the youth's hand.

"That's not it," he said. "We're looking for a wax tablet."

"Yes, sir," said the youth, "but is it the actual tablet you want, or just what was written on it?"

Ruso paused. "You mean you can remember what was written on it?"

"No, sir." The youth held out the parchment. "But I've got my notes. It was hopeless with two of us trying to work on it at once, so I copied it out."

Ruso scanned the document and read aloud, "Dearest girl, when your sweet lips meet my eager—" He looked up. "This isn't it, surely?"

"Oh, no, sir! That's a poem. The other side."

He turned it over and flattened the curve against the wall with his thumbs to reveal two lines of text in fresh black ink. As far as he could recall, the shapes echoed those of the original. They even curved down toward the foot of the document at the right-hand end.

The tall apprentice was leaning over his shoulder. "Why didn't you say you'd got that, stupid?"

It was a good question, but not one Ruso was inclined to waste time on. "Young man," he said, placing his hand on the short apprentice's shoulder, "You are a hero."

The blush shot upward. The youth mumbled something about Doctor Valens insisting they always took notes. For a moment Ruso even felt a rush of gratitude toward Valens and his ability to teach by lecture, if not by example.

"Will it do, sir, or do you want us to keep on looking?"

"This will do," said Ruso, tightening the roll of the parchment. "This will do very nicely."

20

A S THE CARRIAGE trundled northward, it occurred to Tilla that before she met her husband she would never have thought of traveling undefended through the territory of a southern tribe. Especially not that of the Catuvellauni, notorious for trampling all over their neighbors until the Romans had come and put them in their place. Naturally the Catuvellauni, untrustworthy as ever, had then switched sides and become staunch supporters of the emperor.

Among all his other warnings this morning, the Medicus had told her not to mention any of this to anybody in Verulamium. As if she would be such a fool! The last thing she wanted to do was remind them that their warriors' resistance to Rome had finally crumbled when a treacherous queen of her own tribe had betrayed their leader. Such shameful deeds were best left unspoken. She was part of a new world now. She was the well-traveled and respectable wife of a man who worked for the procurator.

The vehicle jolted through a pothole. Tilla leaned back against the blanket she had folded to cushion the carriage wall and closed her eyes. No one in her family had ever been south of Eboracum before. She tried to imagine what they would think if they could see her now. What would she say to them about her marriage? They would never understand how

easy it was to drift once you were away from home: how small compro-
mises seemed right at the time, and how you could find yourself on the
far side of a river with no clear idea of when you had crossed it.

Was that what had happened to Camma?

When she had some privacy, Tilla would tell Christos about Camma
and the baby and the missing brother. He was supposed to be able to hear
you no matter where you were, but just in case he had no power here
across the sea, she would find out where the gods of the Catuvellauni
were worshipped and make an offering to them too.

The baby who was not the husband's was asleep in a box tied to the
seat beside his mother, lulled by the steady clop of hooves and the rumble
of the wheels. He was swaddled in the cloths and bandages Tilla had
brought back from Gaul. Camma seemed to think she carried baby clothes
about with her because she was a midwife, and she had not bothered to
explain. Still, if that disgusting gritty medicine had worked, she would
have a use for them herself before long. If the gods were kind, she and
the Medicus would have their own home too. The red crockery gleaming on the table would remind them of Gaul and they would have a pair
of iron fire dogs framing the hearth like the ones in the house where
she grew up. Outside there would be a vegetable patch, and some hens,
and—

"You have been kind to me, sister."

Tilla returned to the present. "Anyone would have done the same."

Camma had pulled a strand of hair forward and was chewing the end
of it. "I was afraid nobody would help. I thought I would die."

"You were in need," Tilla pointed out. "Of course people would help
you, even here in the South."

"And now you are leaving your husband behind to come with me,
when I don't deserve it."

"It's nothing," Tilla assured her, wondering if Camma was about to
explain the rift with her own husband. Instead, the Iceni woman glanced
down at the shrouded figure laid out along the floor of the carriage. "A
man who collects taxes is never liked," she said, "but somebody must
do it."

"Doctors are not much liked, either," offered Tilla. "A few bad ones
and they all get the blame."

It was not until Camma said, "I thought he must be a doctor," that
Tilla remembered she was supposed to be keeping that quiet.

"But now he is an investigator," she added.

"If you say so."

"It is only a job," said Tilla.

"So is collecting taxes."

They were passing a couple of thatched round houses. A woman was working at a loom set up outside one of the doors. Behind her, fat skeins of brown wool were hung to dry on lines slung from one porch to the other. It reminded Tilla of her childhood.

Camma said, "I can't believe he is gone. The medicine makes me sleep, then I wake up and it has all still happened."

"Have you thought about a name for the baby?"

There was no reply.

Whoever was supposed to mend the road after the winter had not done it very well. The carriage lurched as a front and then a back wheel went into the same hole. The baby's eyes opened. Camma checked the cords that held the box onto the seat. Satisfied they were secure, she leaned forward so the driver could not listen. "You will be asking what an Iceni woman is doing among the Catuvellauni."

It would not have been Tilla's first question, but considering the old enmity between the tribes, it was a good one.

"When we get there I expect someone will tell you about my famous ancestor."

There was only one famous family among the Iceni, headed by a woman who had seen her people bitterly wronged by Rome and taken revenge. Tilla realized she was staring at her traveling companion. "You are—"

"She was my great-grandmother," said Camma. "Whatever they tell you about all of my family being hunted down after the battle is a lie."

As Tilla digested this she continued, "What do you do with an ancestor like that? Everyone watches you. Everything you do has meaning."

Tilla gazed out of the carriage. Farm carts and passenger vehicles were going about their business with scarcely a guard in sight. The verges were spattered with primroses and beyond, sheep were grazing with their lambs. A small villa was poised on a southern slope to catch the sun and the occasional drift of smoke marked the site of an isolated farm. She tried to picture Camma's ancestors and their allies thundering up this road with Londinium in flames behind them and Verulamium undefended in front.

They said that Boudica had lost control of her warriors. That her forces had butchered anyone who could not run fast enough. Old people. Women. Children. They said too that the soldiers who should have fought to save Londinium had marched away and abandoned it.

"I was sent to Verulamium in payment of a debt," continued Camma. "I was accepted to show that the past is buried and forgotten. An Iceni princess can marry a Catuvellauni leader. Look, we are all modern Romans now!"

"Not where I come from," said Tilla, understanding at last why Camma had married that angry old man. "Most of my people would rather be who we have always been."

"Do your people know about our Great Rebellion?"

"Everybody knows."

Camma gave a small nod of acknowledgment, like a princess accepting a compliment. "In Verulamium," she said, "mothers tell their children that if they're naughty, Boudica will come and get them."

Nobody had come out of the great rebellion with much glory. Thousands had not come out of it at all.

There had to be better ways. Caratius must have believed that when he married an Iceni woman. Christos believed in loving his enemies. Her own Da had believed that if you ignored the Romans for long enough, they would go away. He had always refused to learn Latin because before long there would be nobody left to speak it to. But Caratius had been betrayed by this beautiful Iceni wife. Nobody here seemed to have heard of Christos. And now Da was in the next world with the rest of her family, and the Romans were still here.

The pace of the horses changed. Looking out, Tilla saw they had reached the crest of a long hill. The driver was slowing the team to walk them down the other side.

Camma said, "You know what it is to have a good man."

"He is the best one I've found," Tilla agreed. "So far."

"Asper was a man who knew what it is to be an outsider," Camma said. "To be part of one thing when everybody around you is part of something else."

"That is a hard way to live," said Tilla, who had often felt the same way herself.

"When he first came to the house I brought him wine from my husband's store. He noticed I was pale. He asked if I was unwell."

"I see," said Tilla. Perhaps Asper had fancied himself a doctor.

"Lots of men only talk to women to show how important they are themselves. But when I met him again, he remembered what I had said before. And he didn't look at me in the way that many men look at women when their families aren't around."

"And how is that?"

"Picturing them with no clothes on."

Tilla had spent long enough living in army lodgings not to argue with that, but it was sad to find a woman so easily impressed.

"You must think me very weak."

Guessing the rest, Tilla said, "I think you were very lonely."

Camma shrugged. "When I knew about the child, I tried to do the right thing. I left the house and went to live in town. I told Caratius we must divorce." She sat back and pulled her shawl tighter around her shoulders. "People talked," she said. "Women said things. Men looked at me in the street. Nobody wanted to be my friend. I wanted to leave, but Asper had a contract and they said he must carry it through."

"I'm surprised."

"He said there might be a way out but it was best for me not to know what it was." She shook her head. "This is all my fault! If I had been stronger—"

"No it is not." Tilla insisted. "Things like this happen all the time. Wrongs are done. People get angry. There is a divorce, compensation is paid, and they marry somebody else. The man who is wronged does not murder other men, and if he does, that's his choice. It is not the fault of the woman."

"Do you think so?"

"I'm sure of it."

"I never liked Caratius," Camma said. "And he never liked me. He talked to me as if he was addressing a meeting, and he was a wilting weed in the bed. But I never thought he was a bad man." She shook her head. "I'm tired. Everything is going round too fast in my mind, and I can't catch hold of it. I never dreamed he would do something like this."

"An old man like that must have had help. Asper and his brother would have fought back, surely?"

"Oh, he would do nothing himself!" Camma looked surprised at the suggestion. "He would just give the order. And many of his people will say he did the right thing."

Tilla said, "I shall ask my husband to speak up against him."

"Your husband must do what the procurator says," said Camma. "The procurator won't care about any of it as long as he gets the tax money."

Tilla felt her spirits sink. It was true: The Medicus would insist on following his orders. "So, she said, wondering if the procurator's orders could be made to serve a better purpose, "if the money is missing, where is it?"

Camma pushed her hair away from her face. "I suppose Caratius said it was stolen to explain why Asper and Bericus disappeared."

"So did he take it himself?"

Instead of answering the question Camma said, "I was awake most of the night waiting for them to come back. When the sun rose and there was no message, I knew something terrible had happened."

This was looking more and more like a planned and vicious murder by a jealous husband. "How can you live in Verulamium with no friends if he is still there?"

"Where else can I go?" Her voice was barely audible above the noise of the carriage. "I sent a message to my family months ago. They told me I had brought shame on them, and not to come back. They said I should have the baby taken away." She looked up. "How could I do that?"

When Tilla did not answer, she said, "I should have been stronger. Everything has slid into a pit."

"You have just brought a new life into the world, sister, and you're very tired. When you are recovered, you will see things differently."

Camma said, "Perhaps. Perhaps Bericus will be found alive and my family will want me back and your husband will make Caratius tell the truth about what he did."

"All this is possible."

"Yes." She sighed. "But Julius Asper will still be dead."

The carriage rolled on northward, carrying home the dead father and the live son.

Suddenly Camma said, "There is one good thing about being in Verulamium."

"Yes?"

"Every time he sees me, Caratius will be reminded of my curse. Even with his fine clothes and his horses and his proud speeches, that man will be afraid!"

They were words of courage. Glad to see Camma so animated, Tilla reached for her hand. "I will curse him as well, sister!" Too late, she remembered that back in Gaul she had promised Christos to give up that sort of thing. "And then I will pray for him to repent," she added.

"We will both make him repent!" agreed Camma, grasping Tilla's hand in both of hers. "We will seek justice from the gods, and together we will make him sorry he is alive!"

For the first time since they had met, she smiled. Even with the purple shadows beneath her eyes, it was easy to see why two men had fought over this woman.

Tilla did not want to stomp on this brief spark of happiness by telling Camma she had not meant that sort of repentance. As the carriage pulled in at the halfway stop, it occurred to her that she had just managed to disobey both Christos and the Medicus at the same time.

21

B Y T H E T I M E Ruso entered the Forum it was approaching midday, but the sky was dark and the air cool. The buildings that surrounded the vast rectangle of open ground on three sides provided little shelter, and a fresh breeze was flapping the covers of a handful of market stalls huddled in a corner by the Great Hall. Ruso had barely begun the search for Albanus's School for Young Gentlemen when he felt a cold splash of rain. Within seconds stallholders and shoppers were rushing to take cover.

Ruso heard the shrill chant of childish voices above the drumming of raindrops on roof tiles. He could not make out the words, but from somewhere among the ragged assortment of sounds rose the indomitable rhythms of poetry.

He found a dozen or so small boys seated cross-legged beneath a colonnade that, in another time and another place, would be there to protect them from the sun. They were facing an expanse of lime-washed board on which Albanus had painted the lines they were supposed to be reciting. Fluency and volume reached a crescendo as Hercules grabbed a half-human monster so tightly that its eyeballs fell out. Once the violence was over, the class lost interest. There was a scuffle at the back.

"Stop!" cried Albanus.

The chant faltered into confusion.

Through the downpour Ruso could make out Hadrian's statue high on its plinth, holding out one dripping hand as if he were commanding the rain to cease. He was having no more effect than Albanus.

"I said, stop!" Albanus stabbed a finger at the board. "Start again from here. Vattus, if you pull his hair again I shall make everyone stay behind while I beat you."

By the time the class was dismissed, the shower had passed. Albanus looked startled as Ruso emerged from behind a pillar. "I'm afraid I haven't found your missing men, sir."

"Never mind," said Ruso. "I can see you've been busy. And one of them's turned up dead, anyway."

Albanus dipped a brush into a bucket of water and began to scrub Virgil and lime wash off the boards. "Frankly, sir, I don't seem to be having much success with anything. My father hardly ever had to resort to beating. He just gave his pupils The Look and they did what he told them."

"The Look?"

"I don't seem to have inherited it, sir." Albanus emptied the bucket into the nearest drain and tossed the brush back inside.

"Never mind," said Ruso. "Recommend a good bar and I'll buy you a drink. I want to show you something."

Albanus, who had downed his wine with remarkable speed, put his wooden cup back on the stained counter of Neptune's Retreat and perused the new copy of the letter with "To Room XXVII" clearly legible at the top. The apprentice had carefully transcribed it onto a fresh tablet: one that bore no references to kissing. "It's a bit messy," he observed.

"The man was on his deathbed when he wrote it," explained Ruso. "And this is a second-generation copy. So if it doesn't make any sense, don't worry. But do you think it's a language, or just gibberish?"

Albanus looked up. "Well, yes, sir. It's certainly a language. It's Latin."

"Latin?" Ruso was incredulous. He had seen some terrible writing in his time, much of it produced by his own hand, but never anything this bad. "Can you make any sense of it?"

Albanus squinted at the wax and held it at the right angle for the light to fall across the surface. "Urgent help needed. Inn of the—" He hesitated. "Something to do with the moon?"

"Blue Moon. How the hell can you read that?"

"Inn of the Blue Moon. I have now seized conclusive and incriminating proof . . . oh dear. That's frustrating, isn't it, sir? That's where it ends. We don't know what he had proof of."

Ruso snatched back the tablet and peered at the lettering. "I still can't see it."

"No, sir. You wouldn't. It's shorthand."

"*Shorthand?*" repeated Ruso, incredulous. In response to Albanus's warning glance, he turned and realized a couple of sailors farther along the bar had paused to listen. "Why," he continued, lowering his voice, "would anyone send a message begging for urgent help in shorthand?"

Albanus looked confused. "I've no idea, sir. And where's Room Twenty-seven, and what did he have proof of?"

"It's not as useful as I'd hoped," admitted Ruso.

"Perhaps if your second man turns up, he'll be able to help us," suggested Albanus. "I did some thinking last night, and while the children were copying their lesson this morning I sent a message around to all the city gates and I've had a notice posted over at the fort."

Ruso swallowed.

"I hope that's all right, sir? It didn't cost much."

"Absolutely," said Ruso, who had forgotten how thorough his former clerk could be when given an order. "Well done. If anybody's seen him, we'll find out."

And even if they had not, the procurator's office would shortly be besieged by members of the local garrison reporting sightings in the hope of extra pay. He needed to get back and warn young Firmus before he had a clerical mutiny on his hands. He downed the rest of his drink and clapped the cup back on the counter. "You've been a great help, Albanus."

The clerk's pinched face creased into a smile. "It's good to be working with you again, sir. If there's anything else I can do . . ."

Ruso said, "You don't happen to know how to sweet-talk the clerks over at the procurator's office, do you?"

"I'm afraid not, sir."

"Never mind. I was just hoping you might know one or two of them."

"I do know them, sir," said Albanus. "I've just threatened to beat one of their sons."

22

IT SEEMED ALBANUS had never learned the first lesson of military life and was continuing to volunteer for things. When Ruso explained the problem, he happily offered to stand at the gate of the Residence and spend the afternoon noting down the details of everyone who claimed to have seen a dark-haired man with part of one ear missing and recording any possible sightings of Julius Asper before yesterday.

Indoors, the tomblike chill of Firmus's room seemed less noticeable this afternoon. Evidently the plaster was drying out. The welcome was warm too. Firmus invited Ruso to sit and offered him an olive from the bowl on the desk.

The reason for his relaxed demeanor became clear when the youth said, "That awful magistrate has pushed off, and my unc— sorry, the procurator, says I was right to hire you. He wants to talk to you straightaway. He did want me to check one thing first, though. You aren't working for Metellus now, are you?"

"Absolutely not, sir," Ruso assured him. "That was just an isolated case." He might have added that the less he had to do with the governor's security man, the happier he would be.

"Good. So have you found the missing brother?"

"Not yet," said Ruso, "but there are other developments. There's a complication with the woman. That's why I need to talk to Caratius."

Complications with women were evidently of little interest to Firmus. "Any luck with the letter?"

Hoping the procurator did not know he was chatting to the assistant instead of obeying the order to report in straightaway, Ruso told him.

Firmus's attempt to conceal his disappointment was not entirely successful. "What does he mean, incriminating evidence? And what's the point of writing in shorthand if any clerk can read it?"

"We don't know. But my man's had a few thoughts about the destination."

Ruso repeated what Albanus had just explained to him on the way over: that the only buildings in town big enough to have twenty-seven rooms were the fort, the Forum, the amphitheater, and possibly the Official Residence. Between them they had eliminated the first three before arriving here, so the only remaining possibility was—

Firmus was out from behind his desk before Ruso had finished the sentence. "The guard room will know where it is."

"I'm supposed to be reporting to—"

"Oh, uncle has plenty of other things to do. And this way you'll be able to tell him the whole story." Ruso hoped Firmus was right. At least locating Room Twenty-seven would not involve another visit to the procurator's clerks.

Firmus was almost in the corridor when the elderly slave who had been hovering beside him managed to catch up and whisper something in his ear. "I know he does," replied the youth, irritated. "Ruso will go and see him as soon as we've finished." He rebuffed the slave's attempt to follow him with, "It's all right, Pyramus—Ruso can tell me everything."

The slave did not look impressed. On the way through to the gatehouse, Firmus said, "Sorry about that. I'm sure Mother made Pyramus promise to write home and tell her everything I get up to."

"Ah," said Ruso, wondering what Firmus's mother imagined she could do about it.

Over at the gatehouse they found five men queuing up to speak to Albanus. He had scrounged a stool from somewhere and was listening to a long diatribe from a man whose hair could only have been squashed into that shape by an army helmet. The man was complaining about a native who had sold him a dud hunting dog in a bar. Albanus stopped writing when the man admitted that he had not noticed anything about the native's ears, but he was definitely a villain.

"We'll be in touch if we catch him," Albanus promised, ever polite.

"How do I know you won't just catch him and not tell me?"

"This is an inquiry on behalf of the procurator's office," put in Ruso. "Are you suggesting the procurator wouldn't honor his promises?"

The man was not. At least, not while anyone official was listening. Ruso put a hand on the clerk's shoulder. "Albanus, I need a word."

Albanus got to his feet and announced, "Back in a moment," to the line, clearly relishing his newfound authority.

Firmus reappeared. The legionary following behind him had a bunch of heavy keys dangling from one hand.

Firmus announced, "It's in the west wing of the courtyard, on the ground floor," then lowered his voice to add, "There's something funny going on. The watch captain had another man asking about it this morning. He said his name was Ruso, and he told them he had authority from me."

This was a new development. "Did they let him in?"

Firmus shook his head. "When they said they had to check with me, he ran off. Apparently he was a medium-sized man in his twenties, but they didn't get much of a look at him because he was wearing a hood."

Ruso said, "That's interesting."

"Not really," said Firmus. "It was raining."

As they crossed the courtyard, Ruso dismissed the idea that this mysterious impostor might be the missing Bericus. An honest man would not be sneaking about. A thief would be on the run. It could not be Caratius, who was too old, nor his guard, who was too big. So who else might be calling himself "Ruso"?

Firmus was enjoying himself. "I must say," he said, "this procurating business is much more fun than I thought. Secret messages and stolen money and mystery men and murders. It must be even better being an investigator."

"It's very dangerous, sir," put in Albanus, speaking from experience.

"And there's a lot of tedious routine," added Ruso, aware that he should have insisted on reporting to the procurator as ordered, instead of feeding young Firmus's craving for excitement.

"I'd be hopeless at it, of course," Firmus confessed. "I'd never see anything unless it were right under my nose. I mean, look at that." He paused, gesturing toward the slab of paving beneath his expensive sandals. "I can see there's something down there, but I can't tell you if it's a coin or a cockroach."

Ruso glanced down at the lump of charcoal that somebody had dropped on the way to a brazier. It gave a satisfying crunch as he stomped on it.

"I was right!" exclaimed Firmus, clearly delighted at the possibility that he was not as shortsighted as he feared. They paused outside a rough wooden door under the west portico. "Is this it? Open up!"

The guard jiggled the iron key in the lock, trying to coax the prongs up into the holes of the mechanism. "Needs greasing," he muttered, in a tone that suggested somebody else should have seen to it.

Albanus's cheeks were pink. It could not have escaped him that this was the chance for a harassed schoolmaster to impress the procurator's office. Ruso wondered if he had noticed the delicate mesh of cobweb joining the edges of the door to the frame.

Finally winning the battle with the lock, the guard was obliged to shoulder the door open. As it gave way he dipped his head, hastily brushing something out of his hair. Stepping inside, Ruso glimpsed a couple of earwigs squirming on the threshold.

Room Twenty-seven smelled musty. Ruso's eyes began to adjust to the gloom. Those vertical shapes were the legs of one table stacked upside down on top of another. A couple of old doors were propped lengthways against the wall. A half-bald broom lay along the top of them. He stepped over a bucket that appeared to be lined with concrete, and maneuvered an arm in between the table legs to release the catch on the window. As the hinge on the nearest shutter squealed in complaint, the movement ripped open a beautifully constructed white tunnel in the corner of the frame. A large spider emerged, scuttled back and forth along the sill in panic, then ran down the wall and vanished somewhere into the gloom.

The new light revealed a worm-eaten wheel with several spokes missing and a two-foot-high statue of Diana with one arm lying at her feet. Farther back was an old window frame complete with glass. Rusty nails were sticking out of the wood. A length of bent lead pipe snaked out from behind it. Everything in here was waiting for the day when it would be needed again.

Ruso pulled the old doors away from the wall to check but found only a mummified mouse. There was nothing else in the room.

Albanus looked like a boy who had just found out he had been up half the night doing the wrong homework. It was plain from Firmus's expression that even he could see they had reached a dead end.

For reasons he did not understand, Ruso felt it was his job to soften the blow. As if there were some point in asking, he tried, "Who's in charge of this room?"

Predictably, the guard did not know. He suggested another name, but Ruso knew it was hopeless. The next man would be unlikely to know either. Room Twenty-seven had obviously lain undisturbed for years while the workmen who had stored their junk in here had moved on and forgotten all about it.

Asper's unknown correspondent remained as elusive as ever.

23

BY THE TIME Ruso, Firmus, and Albanus returned from their un-successful visit to Room Twenty-seven, the procurator had gone into another meeting and would not be free for at least half an hour. Albanus settled down outside the gates to deal with more sightings of missing men. Firmus was accosted by a waiting Pyramus with messages about wheat tallies and milestone surveys, and by a clerk bearing a pile of ingot ledgers for checking.

Ruso, seeing Firmus about to turn Pyramus and the ledgers away, de-clared that he needed some time to think, and he was going to take a lone stroll along the wharf. Firmus looked disappointed. Ruso decided not to tell him it was for his own good.

Unable to serve as an army officer like most young men of his class, Firmus would have to work his way up through the less glamorous back door of the tax office. He would need to make a good impression. Good impressions were made by obeying orders, not by hanging around with investigators. Especially investigators whose every discovery seemed to leave them more baffled than before.

Ruso emerged onto the wharf and turned left, passing a glassblower's workshop and the secure warehouses that were another part of the proc-urator's jurisdiction. If he was going to meet one of the most powerful men in the province, he needed a plan of action. It might be the wrong plan, but Ruso suspected that this was one of those rare occasions when a subordinate was expected to come up with ideas of his own.

Perhaps it was the business of the hooded man that was making him more cautious than usual, but as he was mulling over how Caratius could be connected with the mystery of Room Twenty-seven and the man who had stolen his name, Ruso realized he was being followed along the wharf.

From a distance the suspect seemed an ordinary-looking man. Medium height. Nondescript hair. Sheep brown tunic. Even features that broke into a smile just as Ruso recognized him and realized it was too late to get away.

"Good morning, Doctor."

He paused by a stack of crates. "Metellus."

"I haven't seen you in—how long is it?"

Not long enough. "Two years."

"I heard you went home to Gaul. I must say I was amazed when you came back here."

There was no point in asking how Metellus knew he was back. Metellus knew all sorts of things, largely because people who understood what he was capable of were too frightened to lie to him.

"And now you're heading up an investigation for the procurator."

"Just until I can get work as a medic," said Ruso, wondering where this was leading.

"Very interesting," said Metellus. "Shall we go farther down and talk on the bridge? It's a little more private."

Ruso did not want to talk to Metellus anywhere, especially about anything private, but neither did he want to annoy him.

They were leaning over the rail and watching the gray Tamesis slither toward the sea as the security man said, "I take it the procurator doesn't know why you hurried out of the province last summer?"

"I was on sick leave," said Ruso, trying to look and sound like a man having a casual chat with an old acquaintance. "And then my contract with the Legion ran out."

"Ah," said Metellus. "I must have been mistaken, then. I'd assumed it was because of your young lady having money that could only have come from the missing army pay chest."

Ruso felt something cold clamp itself around his ribs. "Money from the pay chest?" he repeated, while his mind scrambled to separate what he was supposed to know from what he really did know. "Tilla?"

"Obviously, had you known at the time, you would have reported it."

"Of course."

"Good. I'm glad we understand each other." Metellus's voice was smooth as glass. I've had Tilla's name on my list of people to talk to for some months. So when it popped up on a travel warrant . . ."

Ruso gripped the rail to stop his hand trembling. Metellus was still talk-ing, but he was not listening. He had thought they were safe. How had anyone found out? Last summer, Tilla had unwittingly accepted stolen coins a couple of days after native bandits had ambushed the pay wagon. She had refused to tell him the name of the family who had passed them on to her. If he had done his duty and reported her to the army, she would have been arrested and tortured until she revealed it. Instead, he had told her to get rid of the money and they had left for Gaul the next day.

"So," Metellus was saying, "I thought I'd come and renew our acquain-tance. How's your inquiry going?"

Ruso straightened up. "Ask the man you had following me yesterday."

"Has somebody been following you?" Metellus seemed genuinely surprised. "It's nothing to do with me. If I'd wanted to talk to you ur-gently, I would have asked. As I now am."

"And the break-in at Valens's house? And the man using my name this morning? That wasn't your man, either, I suppose?"

"Ruso, I know nothing about any of this. I'm merely interested to know who's been murdering tax collectors."

"The procurator's interested in the money, not the murderer."

A faintly patronizing expression flitted across Metellus's normally in-scrutable face. "I'd imagine they're together, wouldn't you?"

"Personally I'd imagine the money's already melted down and will never be seen again," said Ruso. "But if I'm ordered to look for it, then I'll look."

"Very good," said Metellus. "If you find anything out, I'd be grateful if you'd let me know straightaway."

"I'm not working for you," said Ruso, wondering why Metellus was interested. "I'm working for the procurator."

"I'm not asking for myself, Ruso. The governor needs to be kept in-formed."

"I'm sure the procurator will tell him whatever he needs to know."

Metellus sighed. "That's very disappointing. I was hoping we could help each other. I haven't said a word to anyone about Tilla and the sto-len coins, you know."

In the silence that followed, Ruso tried to find ways of extricating himself from Metellus's grip. He said, "I heard you'd already caught the pay thieves and had them executed."

"Some natives were rounded up and executed, certainly," Metellus agreed. "It was necessary to reassure our men."

"You mean you just rounded up a few random locals and—"

"No, no. Of course not. What do you think we are? They were all on the list already for something or other."

As, it seemed, was Tilla. Ruso doubted that Metellus was interested in catching whoever had ambushed the wagon. It was quite possible that he was lying about the nature of the executions. There was no way of knowing.

Ruso suppressed an urge to tell the man to get lost and take his filthy devious threats with him. Antagonizing him would only put Tilla's name higher up on the list. Something, however, had begun to make sense at last. "Will you be wanting me to send reports to you in Room Twenty-seven, then?"

A slight smile played around Metellus's lips "Well done, Ruso. That won't be necessary. When I need to know, I'll find you."

"Tell me something. What was Asper investigating for you?"

Metellus shook his head. "You're making this far too complicated. If I wanted an investigator, I'd have used somebody properly trained. Asper was just one of a number of loyal Britons recruited to keep their eyes and ears open and alert us to anything interesting. Frankly, there was never much of great use in his reports. It was hardly worth paying him, except that the Catuvellauni are allowed to have their own town guards, so we like to make sure they're as loyal as they claim to be. Since I'll need to recruit a new informer, it would help to know what happened to the last one."

Ruso said, "His last letter said he'd found incriminating evidence of something, and he needed help."

"You've seen his last letter?"

Either Metellus was a very good liar or whoever had been spying for him was not very well informed himself.

"If you know what he was up to," said Ruso, "then tell me. We're on the same side."

"Of course," Metellus agreed. "I don't know at all, but I'd like to. Have you got the letter with you?"

"So it really wasn't your man who stole it from Valens's house?"

The slight crease between the eyebrows was probably the nearest Metellus ever came to looking disconcerted. "I told you. I know nothing about that. One of my men has been murdered, Ruso. A decent, law-abiding man not unlike yourself. I think we owe it to him to find out what's been going on up there, don't you?"

Metellus had once taken Tilla in for questioning over the death of a soldier on the northern border. Ruso had never been entirely sure what had passed between them in that room but she was still waking with nightmares weeks later. He said, "If we do business, I want Tilla kept out of it. And I want your word that if I find out what happened to your man, you'll take her name off that list."

"I knew you would be a good choice," Metellus said, ignoring the re-quest. You've been a great help already. I had no idea there was a final letter."

Ruso did not want to be a great help to Metellus. He wanted Metellus to think he was completely useless. He wanted to be overlooked and ignored. How he longed for the straightforward problems of surgery and sprained ankles and fevers.

"You may want to be careful what you say to the procurator," Me-tellus continued. "It seems that when he was in trouble, Asper felt he couldn't trust his employers in Verulamium, or the procurator's office, either."

"Maybe they'd found out he was working for you."

"Don't be petulant, Ruso."

"Room Twenty-seven isn't a very good system when your men need to contact you urgently."

"I told you, he was merely paid to send reports. Background intelli-gence. The sort that needs to be sifted and assessed before it's passed on."

"This didn't need sifting. He was in trouble and he needed help. He must have been afraid of the message being intercepted because he wrote it in shorthand."

"It should have been in code. Are you sure it was genuine?"

"It was found under the bed he died in. He was probably just doing his best: He wouldn't have been well enough to work out a code. And what-ever evidence he'd found may have been the real reason he was mur-dered, so if you know anything you're not telling me . . ."

Metellus shook his head. "Sorry," he said. "I really have no idea. Do let me know when you find out." He stepped away from the rail, waited for a couple of porters to pass carrying bales of cloth on their heads, and then turned to follow them at a safe distance back toward the north bank. "I'm glad we've been able to renew our acquaintance," he said. "I'm sure you know better than to upset the procurator by mentioning this little chat."

"You think my talking to the governor's security man would upset the procurator?"

Metellus sighed. "Don't be naive, Ruso. Hadrian appoints two men to run a province. Obviously there are going to be tensions. People like you and I are here to—"

"To spy on the one for the other."

"I was going to say, to smooth the path between them. And by the way, if it sets your mind at rest, your wife probably wasn't part of the forward planning for the ambush on the pay wagon."

Ruso raised his voice to be heard over the rumble of approaching wheels. "Of course she wasn't!"

"Even though she would have been in a good position to find out when it was coming."

Did Metellus really think that would frighten him? Ruso waited until the cart had passed before saying, "Everybody knows when the pay wagon's coming. The army gets paid on the same dates every year."

"Fair enough," agreed Metellus, untroubled. "So it's quite possible that she was innocent of any involvement. She may not even have known the money was stolen until you told her."

Ruso saw the real trap just in time. "Are you sure she had stolen money?"

"I'm afraid so," said Metellus. "And she must know who gave it to her." He smiled. "Don't look so worried, doctor. As long as you and I have an understanding, nobody else needs to be told."

It was like being locked up with a tiger who promised not to eat you—as long as he wasn't hungry.

24

THE ROOM SMELLED of liniment. The procurator's portly middle-aged form was propped up on a couch instead of sitting at the desk, but the crisp white tunic suggested he was of the no-nonsense school that believed it was necessary to dress properly even when in pain.

"So," the man said, "you're my nephew's investigator."

"Yes, sir." But not, if he could find an escape route, for much longer.

The man's breathing was shallow and quick, as if he did not dare take a full-size breath for fear of splitting open his cracked ribs. Ruso guessed that he too had been awake for much of the night.

The procurator's gray eyes moved to his nephew. "Thank you, Firmus. I'll have you called if I need you."

"But sir, I—"

"Have you finished looking through the ingot ledgers?"

Firmus had not.

The man shifted slightly and gasped. Ruso guessed he was waiting for the pain to subside before continuing. "I understand the local magistrate's blaming the dead man for everything."

"Yes, sir."

"And what do you make of that?"

"The magistrate has a personal grudge against Asper," said Ruso, real-

izing that in all the excitement over Room Twenty-seven he had failed
to tell Firmus about Caratius's broken marriage. "So it's hard to say. He
claims Asper left town with only his brother for security. The brother's
still missing and so is the money. Perhaps they were both robbed, or the
brother turned on him. The woman says he never had the money in the
first place, but if he was planning to leave her and run off with it, he'd
hardly tell her beforehand."

"It's an odd business altogether," said the procurator. "We've never
had any trouble with Verulamium before. They usually pay up straightaway. They're more enthusiastic about being Roman than most of Rome
is. Firmus tells me you have a codes man tackling a mystery letter?"

Ruso explained. To his relief, the procurator was not impressed. "Sounds
like his mind was going. Don't waste any more time on it. I want you to
concentrate on helping the magistrate track down the money."

Ruso realized he had also failed to tell Firmus that someone thought
the letter worth stealing. With luck, it would be quietly forgotten.
Metellus's name would never need to be mentioned.

The procurator extended one arm at an awkward angle, then winced as
he lifted the drink off the table. "Tastes disgusting," he observed after a
long drink. "Wretched medic says I'll be like this for weeks. Not much
he can do except strapping up and doping, he says. When I asked how
much I was paying him for doing nothing, he said he was saving me from
all the other quacks who'd make it worse."

Ruso could imagine that conversation. "There's not much else can be
done for ribs, sir."

"Ah. Yes. Young Firmus tells me you were working undercover as a
medic."

There it was. The escape route. If he were dismissed by the procurator,
he would be of no use to Metellus. The security man would lose interest
in him, and in Tilla. Ruso took a deep breath and fixed his gaze on a
point on the far wall just above the procurator's head. "I think there's
something you should know, sir," he said. "I'm not really an investigator.
I'm just a medic who happens to have gotten involved in a few things by
mistake. This has all been a misunderstanding."

To his surprise, the procurator did not react. Ruso was baffled. Had he
not made it plain enough? The combination of pain and medicine must
be slowing the man's brain. He stood at attention and tried again. "I'm
not an investigator at all, sir," he repeated. "I never have been. I accepted
the job under false pretenses."

The procurator downed the last of the drink, then put both hands on the edge of the couch and gasped as he lifted himself into a slightly different position. "So have you worked for Metellus, or not?"

Ruso cleared his throat. "Only as a medical officer when he was dealing with an incident up on the border, sir." It was near enough to the truth. "I'm sorry to have wasted your time."

"So you should be." There was a pause while the procurator seemed to be considering what to do next. Finally he said, "Strictly speaking, none of this is our problem. We could insist that the Catuvellauni pay up. The magistrate knows that as well as I do, but he's pretending he doesn't. And frankly, I'd rather pretend I don't too. We have enough trouble with the difficult tribes without upsetting the ones who are supposed to like us."

Ruso waited. He had expected to be punished, or dismissed in disgrace. He had not expected to be offered the procurator's views on fiscal politics.

"I hear you did a good enough job with the body. Just go up there, look helpful, and try not to annoy them or make me look a fool."

Ruso swallowed. "You still want me to carry on, sir?"

The man frowned. "Am I not making myself plain? I've promised them an investigator. I don't have anyone else to offer, so you'll have to do. Consider yourself seconded to the Council at Verulamium."

"Yes, sir." He was available, cheap—and expendable.

"Ask some sensible questions and see if there's any chance of getting their money back. It's probably long gone, but while you're there you can take a discreet look at this connection with the Iceni. I take it that having worked alongside Metellus, you do know what 'discreet' means?"

"Yes, sir," said Ruso, his spirits sinking even further.

"Last time there was trouble around here," continued the procurator, "one of my esteemed predecessors got the blame for stirring up the Iceni with unreasonable tax demands."

So that was it. The man was trying to find out how hard he could push the natives if the money didn't turn up.

"Of course," he continued, "all that business was sixty years ago. I doubt there's anyone alive up there who remembers it."

Ruso wondered about the quality of the briefing the procurator had received before taking up his post. Evidently nobody had suggested that he spend time listening to the locals. If he had, he would know that a lack of living witnesses made little difference to the Britons. If Camma's people were anything like Tilla's, the tale of How We Nearly Chased

Off The Roman Oppressors would be lovingly polished, embellished, and passed around the tribal hearths for many generations to come.

"The natives have long memories, sir," he ventured. "But the Iceni woman who came here wasn't hostile to Rome."

The Procurator grunted. "Hooking up with the local tax collector could have given her access to a lot of information. I'm told the first one seemed friendly enough till some idiot upset her."

"Boudica?"

The bushy eyebrows met again. "We don't mention that name here, Ruso. And you'd be wise not to mention it in Verulamium, either."

"Yes, sir."

"Our people learned a lot of lessons after that little fracas," observed the procurator. "It pays to keep the locals sweet. Give them money to put up a few grand buildings and let them run their own affairs. That way they do their falling out with one another, not with us."

Ruso reflected that the tribes down here must be very different from those in the North, with its dreary cycle of native raids and vicious crackdowns by the army.

"Honor the gods, obey the law, and pay the emperor," observed the procurator. "The three secrets of success. Although since Hadrian generously made a bonfire of all the old unpaid tax bills, some of the tribes seem a little hazy over the last one. Any questions?"

"I don't think so, sir."

"Good. Keep in touch and watch your back. The Britons are a tricky bunch. Even the ones who speak Latin and know how to use a bathhouse. You can never tell what they're thinking."

"Yes, sir," agreed Ruso, remembering last night's chicken dinner. "I will."

25

Firmus must have been waiting for Ruso to leave the procurator's office, because he appeared from somewhere and latched on to him as soon as he emerged. "So, what do we do now?"

He seemed to have decided they were a team. Ruso said, "I'm going straight up to Verulamium to try and track down the money." And to find a way of keeping Tilla out of this business without mentioning Metellus. If there was even the slightest chance that she might be pregnant, he did not want to frighten her.

Firmus was insisting on knowing what his uncle had said about the letter.

Ruso said, "All it shows is that Asper was ill and confused."

"I don't agree. With all respect to my uncle, of course. I think Asper was about to expose some sort of crook who had him murdered."

Ruso loyally defended the procurator's position, aware that he was talking too much and it must be obvious that he was lying. Aware too that he should never have allowed Firmus to get so deeply involved in this. The lad had been sent here by his mother to work in an office, not to chase thieves and murderers, and certainly not to get within the striking range of vipers like Metellus.

Finally Firmus gave up. "So what do we do now?"

"While I'm away, I'd be grateful if you'd forward any news that comes into the office."

The aristocratic nose wrinkled. "That sounds boring."

"Most investigating is boring, sir," Ruso assured him, adding the "sir" to try and reestablish the distance that he should have had the sense to keep between them all along. "It's just collecting detailed information, and most of what you find out turns out to have nothing to do with what you want to know."

They were almost at the gatehouse now. Seeing them approach, Albanus raised one hand and hurried toward them, cramming his official writing tablets into his satchel. "Sirs!"

"I was just explaining to the assistant procurator that investigating isn't as exciting as it sounds," said Ruso, noticing to his discomfort that Albanus's eyes were bright and he was shifting his weight from one foot to the other as if he was eager to say something. "For example, you've just spent the afternoon recording—how many sightings of the missing brother?"

"Twenty-four, sir. Sir, I—"

"Twenty-four. And how many of them are credible?"

"Probably about three, sir. And even those contradict one another."

Ruso fixed him with what he hoped was a meaningful stare. "So would you say investigating was exciting, Albanus?"

"It was a tedious afternoon, to be honest, sir."

"Exactly," said Ruso.

"Until I found out what Room Twenty-seven really means," continued Albanus, unable to resist beaming with pride as he destroyed all Ruso's good work in a sentence.

"Oh, well done!" cried Firmus. "I knew you were wrong, Ruso!"

At Albanus's suggestion, they moved across to stand by the hitching rail on one side of the courtyard. Horses might hear, but they would not talk.

Apparently as he sat listening to the various accounts of sightings of men with mangled ears, Albanus had watched the stream of people going in and out of the Residence. Among them had been several couriers, most of whom delivered their items to the guard house at the gates to be distributed.

"And that's when I thought again about the letter, sir. And about the way my aunt's letters got forwarded on to me after I left the army, and that's when it dawned on me. It doesn't matter what you write on the outside. What matters is that the person who receives it knows what to do with it."

Albanus paused here, perhaps waiting for his listeners to catch up.

"So where's the real Room Twenty-seven?" demanded Firmus.

"We saw it earlier," Albanus said. "But that's not the point. The point is, when the men in the sorting room here get letters with addresses that don't make sense, they put them all in the bottom right-hand pigeon-hole. And there they stay, until somebody comes to look for them."

So that was how Metellus did it. It was ridiculously simple.

"Or until there's a clear-out, whichever happens sooner."

"But that doesn't prove that Room Twenty-seven means anything," said Ruso, attempting to head them off. "It could just be a mistake by a dying man."

"It could, sir," agreed Albanus, "but the post room clerk says some-body's been writing to it every week. And the pigeonhole hasn't been cleared for a month, but there aren't any Room Twenty-seven letters in there."

"Somebody's been collecting them!" exclaimed Firmus. "Oh, well done, Albanus! So all we have to do now is keep a watch on the post room—"

This was like trying to stop a runaway horse. "If the collector knows that Asper's dead, he won't come back for any more," said Ruso, hoping the youth would not stumble over someone seeking messages from other in-formers. Would Metellus use the same system for several people? He had no way of knowing, nor any way to contact him and warn him.

Holy gods. He was starting to think in terms of warning Metellus now.

"Anyway," he continued, "I'm supposed to be finding the money, not tracking down missing correspondence."

"You are," agreed Firmus, "but I'm not. I'm supposed to be learning about administration." His smile was triumphant. "Administration in-cludes post."

Ruso restrained an urge to grab the front of his tunic and shake some sense into him. He sent a disappointed Albanus back to the gate to see if there were any more sightings of men with only one and a half ears before continuing, "Listen to me, Firmus. This isn't a game. I don't know what Asper was caught up in, but it might well be the business that got him murdered. Whoever follows the trail is going to run into the same people, and you're not . . ." He hesitated.

"I'm not what?"

"You're not supposed to be involving yourself in this sort of thing."

"You were going to say, *You're not suitable because you can't see past the tips of your fingers.*"

"That too," said Ruso, who wasn't.

Firmus drew himself up to his full height, which was at least half a head shorter than Ruso despite the fancy hairstyle. "I am the assistant procurator," he announced. "You have been given your orders. While you're in Verulamium, I shall take whatever steps I consider to be necessary."

Ruso sighed. That was the trouble with the upper classes. They were very friendly until you tried to cross them. Then they pulled rank on you.

This was going to be painful, but it was necessary. "Firmus," he said, "I have a job to do. If I think someone—anyone—is compromising my investigation, not to mention getting himself into danger, then I won't hesitate to report him to the procurator."

The shortsighted eyes narrowed, as if the youth were trying to assess whether he was joking.

"I'm grateful for all the help you've given me, but it's got to stop. Straightaway."

"But I thought . . ." There was a tremor in the youth's voice. "Ruso, I thought you were my friend."

Ruso felt his stomach clench, just as it used to in the early days when he was about to amputate a limb in the hope of saving the owner's life. "I'm sorry, sir," he said, seeing hurt and bewilderment in the lad's eyes. "I hope I've served you well. But we can't ever be friends."

Firmus's chin rose. "Of course," he said. "Thank you for reminding me. I am the assistant procurator of Britannia and you are a man who chases criminals for money." He turned to peer around the courtyard and then strode off in the direction of Pyramus, who was waving at him from a doorway.

There was a bitter taste in Ruso's mouth as he watched him go. No matter how often he told himself he had done that for the youth's own good, he knew there would still be a whisper suggesting that he had done it to get himself out of trouble. And the whisper would have the smooth tones of Metellus.

26

"THIS IS IT," Camma said.

Tilla stretched, stiff from the long journey, and shifted her balance on the seat as the carriage began to descend another slow incline. Nearer the town, the road was lined on both sides by graves and grand carved wooden memorials. It occurred to her that Asper would not be allowed such an honor even if Camma could afford it. In a town where she had no friends and a powerful enemy, she would be lucky if she were allowed a stick to mark his place. Tilla watched as she gathered up her shawl and the remains of the bread that neither of them had felt hungry enough to finish, and wondered whether she had thought of that. If the people here really believed Asper had betrayed the town, his remains might not be welcome here at all.

How did you honor a disgraced man? It was one of the many questions the Druids would have been able to answer, but Rome had seen to it that Druids were hard to find these days. Tilla was not sure she had ever met one. Nowadays ordinary people had to muddle along with only memory and tradition and guesswork, while the leaders of the tribes squabbled over whatever power the governor was prepared to give them. With no one to settle the dispute over his wife, Caratius had been left to take his revenge. The whole thing had led to this dreadful mess—and it was not finished yet.

There was a shout from the roadside. The carriage drew up beside the deep ditch and gatehouse that marked the edge of the town. Someone was asking the driver if he had seen a man called Bericus on the road. Camma whispered, "They have still not found him."

The driver denied all knowledge of the missing man and the carriage jerked into motion again.

Camma leaned forward to direct the driver. They passed a triangular temple precinct that smelled of incense and a grand inn that boasted glass windows and entered a busy street full of bars and shops and lodging houses—all, Tilla supposed, placed to tempt the travelers passing through. A couple of local men with chain mail over their scarlet tunics were lounging against a wall as if they had nothing better to do. Tilla peered into a bone worker's shop and was startled when the workman glanced up and winked at her. Farther along, a woman dressed in gold and green plaid shouted at a tethered donkey while one of her children howled and clutched at his foot.

Tilla rejoiced in the unfussy hairstyles, the bright jewelry, and, among the plain workaday browns, the bold stripes and cheerful colors that spoke of a people not afraid to enjoy themselves. After the pale and washed-out drapery that the Medicus's people thought was tasteful, it was like a feast for the eyes. Yet oddly, instead of having ordinary round houses, this southern tribe dressed in their no-nonsense tunics and trousers seemed to live like foreigners. Straight-sided buildings were crammed in precise rows. Beyond them rose the dome of a bathhouse and the red roofs of a Forum and a Great Hall like the one they had left behind.

She had not expected a tribal gathering place to look like this. Londinium was a town of soldiers and merchants, created by Rome in its own image—but she had expected Verulamium to look more like home. How could you roast an ox over a good fire in the middle of all those buildings? Where could you all sit in a circle around the embers with the soft grass beneath you and your backs to the dark and children falling asleep in their mothers' arms, listening to the stories of your people? The Catuvellauni had turned their meeting place into something that was more welcoming to strangers from across the sea than to the people of their own island.

Out in the street, progress slowed to a crawl and then stopped altogether. A man rapped on the back of the carriage and cried, "Looking for a bed, travelers?" before glancing in at the shrouded body and hastily backing away. The driver reached into his bag for the remains of his lunch.

Tilla stood up and peered past him. A string of pack ponies had somehow spread themselves across the road and got tangled up with a flock of sheep. Passersby were making futile grabs as woolly brown shapes leapt between shying ponies, parked vehicles, and a man trying to deliver barrels. A terrier had decided to join in the fun and was rushing about snapping at the sheep, ignoring the whistles of its frantic owner. A couple of men in chain mail arrived and began to shout orders, but nobody seemed to be listening.

By the time there was a clear route through the chaos, a manure cart had drawn up behind them. "Take the first on the left, up by the bakery," Camma called, grimacing at the stench.

"I hope you ladies aren't wanting to stop near the Forum."

"No, go on past, by the meat market."

They were moving again. Mumbling something that ended in, "after a bloody market day," the driver swung the vehicle around and urged the horses forward in the shadow of the Great Hall that made up one end of the Forum. Vehicles were parked on both sides of the road in such a way that there was barely room to fit another carriage in between. To Tilla's disgust, the manure cart followed them. She lifted her overtunic and inhaled through the fabric. It made no difference.

Beyond the hall the driver called over his shoulder, "I'll have to drop you ladies and move on."

"But we need help to unload!" Tilla insisted, careful not to announce to the girl scuttling past with a basket of eggs and her nose pinched shut that they had brought a body with them. "My friend has just had a baby. She should not be lifting things."

Especially that sort of thing.

Instructed by Camma, the carriage passed a meat market on the right and then drew up in the middle of the street outside a row of narrow timber-framed houses and workshops. The driver jumped down. "I can't wait here, missus."

"You must help!" insisted Tilla. "My husband paid you extra."

The driver's eyes, red with the dust of travel, met her own. "They'll have me for blocking the traffic."

"The housekeeper should be home from market," put in Camma,

handing the box containing the sleeping baby out to the driver. He lifted it above the inquiring muzzle of a tethered mule and placed it in the door-way. "Grata will help us," she said, accepting the man's offer of a hand as she climbed down from the carriage. "She will be waiting for us."

The complaints from the drivers jammed behind them fell silent as Julius Asper was unloaded onto the pavement. Even so, when their own man looked as though he might be stopping to help, there was a roar of, "If you don't get a move on, sunshine, we'll bury you and all!"

"Don't stir yourself to help, will you?" retorted the driver, jabbing his middle finger into the air just to make sure his point was clear.

A voice from farther back yelled, "She don't need no help taking his weight. She's been doing it for months!"

Camma's face was blank. With the shrouded body set down at the side of the street, the driver clambered back into his seat and urged the horses into a trot. The carriage jolted away down the street and the queue of traffic began to move at last.

Camma turned to one of the house doors with her hand raised ready to knock, and froze. "What's this?"

Tilla frowned at the dribbly limewash letters slapped across the wood and decided it was probably just as well neither of them could read. She wrinkled her nose. Now that the cart had gone, there was a sharp stink of urine around the front of the house.

"Grata should have done something about this." Camma bunched her fist and raised her arm, ready to thump on the lettering.

Tilla seized her wrist before she could make contact. "Wait!" There were pale gashes of freshly splintered wood where the lock met the up-right of the door frame. "Don't go in there." She pushed the door ajar with the tip of her forefinger and drew back.

"But Grata is—"

"There is somebody inside," murmured Tilla, hearing a crash from somewhere inside the building, "but I don't think it's your housekeeper. Who else is allowed in there?"

"Nobody," said Camma, frowning. "Unless—" She stopped. "No, Bericus would have a key."

Tilla turned back toward the street and called to the nearest driver, "We need help!"

"Sorry, missus. Can't stop here."

The next one said the same. The workshop next door was shuttered and padlocked. The guards who had been directing the traffic had disappeared. The only pedestrians in the street were a wizened old lady and a boy being pulled along by a goat.

Camma said, "We could try to find that guard."

"Did you see where he went?"

"No."

Tilla eyed the two bodies laid out at the foot of the wall: father and son, dead and alive.

"We can't leave them lying here in the street." She fingered the hilt of her knife. "We shall have to help ourselves."

27

TILLA PICKED HER way past a patch of leeks and cabbages and bean seedlings in the back garden. The shutters of the back window were open. She crouched under the rough sill to listen. Indoors, heavy footsteps were clumping about. Someone whistled a snatch of a dancing tune that pipers played at feasts. Whoever was in there was making no effort to keep quiet.

She risked a quick glance through the window. The embers beneath the fancy cooking grill were dead. The table held a bowl whose contents were now a sunken and congealed brown mass. Whatever had been poured into the delicate cup next to it had a thick skin on the top and there was a smell of rancid milk. Camma's housekeeper had not been there for some time.

She ducked back out of sight as the footsteps grew louder. A deep voice shouted to someone in British to get a move on. Another man replied that he couldn't manage by himself.

The first intruder gave a heavy sigh. The fading sound of footsteps suggested he had gone to help.

So. There were only two of them. She had the advantage of surprise, but that would not last long. If she cornered them, they might try to fight their way out. If she did not, they would run out of the front door and if Camma had still not found a guard to help by then, they would escape with whatever they could carry.

Tilla crouched on the hard earth between the bean patch and the wall and silently cursed the driver. If he had done the job he had been paid for, the intruders could have been dealt with by now. She was wondering what had happened to the housekeeper when she heard the shuffling and grunting that accompanies men carrying something heavy through an awkward space.

Back on her feet, she pressed herself flat against the wall and peered around the edge of the window again. She could see into the corridor, where two men were busy maneuvering a fancily carved cupboard out of a side room. They did not notice her.

In a moment they would be gone, and so would the cupboard. Tilla reached out an arm to try the latch on the back door. She unsheathed her knife and took a deep breath. Then she flung the door open, shouting loud enough to be heard across the surrounding yards and gardens, "Stop, thief!"

The second man halted.

"Thief!" she cried, turning around to shout across the neighboring gardens, "Help us, they are stealing!"

Hoping help was on its way, she strode into the abandoned kitchen. Any alarm in the thief's dark eyes died when he looked past her and saw that she was alone. She was glad of the open door behind her. Stopping well out of his reach, she demanded, "Who are you?"

He glanced at whoever was holding the other end of the cupboard. One of the doors fell open as they lowered it to the floor.

"Who are you?" repeated Tilla. He was much better looking than a thief ought to be. "What are you doing here?"

"Who am I?" He reached down to close the cupboard door. As the black hair swung forward she saw that he had scarlet braids woven into it. "Who are you, Northerner?"

"I am a friend of Camma, Princess of the Iceni," said Tilla, wondering if there might be something here she had misunderstood. The man did not look like someone who needed to steal. His scarlet tunic was clean and almost new. "What are you doing in her house?"

"Princess of the Iceni, eh?"

Tilla raised her knife to suggest a little more respect.

The man lifted his hands into the air and backed away in mock alarm. "It's all right," he assured her. "There's no need for that."

"You can explain to her. And to the guards."

The man lowered his hands. His grin revealed dimples and even white teeth. "I'm the captain of the guards, miss. Put that knife away, or I'll have to report us both to myself."

A shadow fell across the kitchen. Camma's voice said, "Dias? What are you doing here?"

Tilla, who had not heard Camma making her way past the vegetable patch, slid the knife back into the sheath.

"Where's Grata?" Camma demanded, clutching the baby against her as if she thought Dias might take him away along with the cupboard.

An older man with a furrowed face appeared in the kitchen doorway. Camma said, "Where's Grata? What are you doing here?"

The second man raised large grimy hands to show they were empty before heading off toward the front of the house. "Sorry, miss. I was only doing a mate a favor."

Camma looked around the abandoned kitchen, wrinkling her nose at the smell of sour milk. "What happened to Grata?"

"She left," explained the first man, adding, "She'd had enough." He gestured toward the baby. "I see you've, ah—"

Whatever he might have said was interrupted by a yell of alarm from his companion before the front door slammed shut. Tilla guessed that the second man had found Julius Asper on the threshold.

"But what are you doing with the furniture?" persisted Camma.

Dias shrugged. "Grata's moved on, the place is deserted—"

"But I was only in Londinium! And Bericus may come home any day. What are you thinking?"

"I'm thinking," said Dias, "that your man owed my lads wages for guard duty. I'm sorry for your loss, lady, but somebody was going to clear the place. It might as well be us."

Camma slumped onto a kitchen stool. Seeing tears welling in her eyes, Tilla put an arm around her. "Julius Asper has just arrived home," she said. "This is not the day to be asking for wages."

"We weren't to know."

"Put back what you have taken," said Tilla. "If you help us bring him in, I will try to see that your wages are paid."

Dias's dark eyes widened. "And you are . . . ?"

"I am Darlughdacha of the Corionotatae among the Brigantes," she told him. "Sometimes called Tilla. I have come from Londinium to help."

He eyed her for a moment, then began to retreat toward the front of the house. "Holy Sucellus, this place stinks."

"Julius Asper was robbed and murdered when he was carrying the money from your town," said Tilla, following him. "Why was nobody there to guard him?"

"We weren't asked," said Dias, leaning on the splintered front doorpost. "We only work for him when we're asked. He went with his brother. My lads rode out to help the minute we knew he was missing."

"Bericus is still not found," said Tilla.

"Maybe he did it," suggested Dias. The dark eyes looked into her own. "Maybe he's the one you want to be calling a thief, not me."

"If he is alive," said Tilla, "I will. Now, are you going to help?"

When Asper had been laid out on the pinkish gray floor of the smart front room, Dias nodded to the household shrine in the corner and said, "I'll let the cemetery slaves know. First thing tomorrow morning, all right, ladies?"

Tilla glanced over at Camma, who did not look as though she understood the question. "First thing tomorrow morning," she agreed. The sooner it was over, the better. "Thank you."

Safely inside with the cupboard rammed against the broken street door to keep it closed, Camma slumped against the wall. "He was not attacked for money." She sighed. "He did not take any money. There is nobody left who will listen to me."

"I believe you," said Tilla. She bent down to straighten the rush mat that had been kicked aside as they carried the body in. "But you and I cannot prove anything else yet, and we need that man to help with the burial."

"But—"

"It is always good to speak the truth, sister," said Tilla, wishing she had left the mat hiding the pair of man-sized house shoes that she had just revealed, "but sometimes it is wiser to say what is useful."

28

A S THE OSTLER had promised, the ginger mare was keen to
go—but not necessarily forward. After winning the argument over
which of them was steering, Ruso urged it out under the archway and
onto the wide expanse of the North road. The rhythm of its gait changed
instantly as a clear run stretched out ahead. He sat deep in the saddle,
relishing the rush of speed. They pounded past a crawling train of supply
wagons and he grinned at the envious glances as he overtook a column
of legionaries slogging along at the military pace. At this rate he would
be in Verulamium by late afternoon.

As he passed the first milestone, more native houses started to appear.
It occurred to him that Londinium had been an easy place to be a foreigner: a place run by the army and full of veterans and merchants. Beyond the safety of its walls people like himself were vastly outnumbered
by the Britons, and Tilla was right: Whatever his intentions, he was
venturing out into the province in the role of a tax collector.

Still, in other ways it was a relief to be heading out of town. Valens
seemed to be suffering from an uncharacteristic and worrying urge to be
helpful. While Ruso had been in a hurry to leave, Valens had been flapping about asking whether he was sure he had everything he needed and
insisting on lending him even more money than he asked for.

For someone who had known Valens as long as Ruso had, it was all deeply disturbing. Most disturbing of all was their parting conversation. It began, "If you should happen to run into Serena and the children . . ." and trailed off into, "no, it doesn't matter." Valens had slapped him on the shoulder with something of his old bravado. "She's bound to be back before long. Have a good trip, old chap. Don't worry about me. I'll be fine. You've got far more important things to think about."

Ruso squinted at the road ahead, where a rapidly expanding shape became an official dispatch rider. He had one hand raised in greeting before he remembered he was a civilian now. The rider flashed past without acknowledging him, hurrying south with whatever the governor had to say concealed in the leather pouch strapped to his side. Perhaps there were messages in there for Metellus.

One of the unsettling things about Metellus was that you never knew how far his influence extended. He seemed to have no idea why Asper had been killed, which suggested he had no other source of information in Verulamium. If that were true, Ruso could do whatever kept the Council and the procurator happy, and as long as he produced a plausible report at the end, Metellus would be none the wiser. On the other hand, Metellus could be lying. It would be just like him to have somebody watching the watcher. But if he still had another spy in Verulamium, why had he bothered to recruit Ruso? Did he have doubts about the loyalty of this hypothetical second man?

Ruso shook his head. Once you began to believe in hypothetical spies, you began to jump at the movement of your own shadow. You stopped trusting anybody. He glanced back over his shoulder, just to confirm that there was no hooded man behind him. The mare, sensitive to his movement, shifted sideways. He nudged her back onto the soft verge, barely conscious of the mule train he was overtaking as he wondered where a man who did not know whom to trust would turn for help if he had been attacked. Instead of doing the sensible thing and asking the nearest person to fetch a doctor, he might just flee to another town.

Asper's assailant must have left him truly terrified. He had not even dared to seek help when he arrived in Londinium, probably miles away from the scene of the attack. Confused or frightened or both, he had been convinced that an urgent message to Metellus was his best hope.

Ruso put both reins in one hand and loosened his neckerchief to let in some air. Nine milestones gone: He must be almost halfway by now.

The horse was tiring. He was in need of a break himself. He was starting to get confused. If Asper had needed help from Metellus, then the murderer was definitely not some random robber. Besides, if Camma was right, Asper had taken no cash with him and would not be worth robbing. On the other hand, the tax money was missing . . .

This whole business seemed to be as slippery as the burglar he had chased out of Valens's entrance hall. He hoped it would make more sense when he got to Verulamium.

There was a cluster of buildings farther up the hill. As he drew closer a carriage pulled out from among them and began to head south. He shifted in the saddle, already beginning to relax muscles he had not realized were tense. This was what he was looking for: the official posting station.

He handed the ginger mare's reins to a groom and ordered a fresh horse, then headed for the awning of a roadside snack bar. A few paces away, a large carriage with polished surfaces still visible through the dust had parked up on the scrubby gravel beside the road. Its cavalry escort seemed to have scattered in search of fodder and latrines, its driver was busy tending to the horses, and three faces were peering out the window. The woman was saying something to the children. Ruso caught the end of her sentence: something about, "No. It might be dirty."

He commandeered a bar stool, refused the stew, and was wondering how rough the really cheap wine might be, if this was the medium, when the door of the carriage opened and a servant stepped down followed by the three he had seen just now. The small girl was shifting from foot to foot in a manner that betrayed their purpose. The bartender leaned out and pointed to the left. "Round the back behind the empties, missus."

"Officer's family?" Ruso speculated as they hurried away.

"Just in off the ship, I'll bet," observed the barman. "Too frightened to come out and eat with the barbarians."

Having smelled the stew, Ruso did not blame them. As the bartender moved away to serve the family's escort, he wondered how the woman would cope when she reached her destination. Probably she would dictate letters home with news of a terrifying journey and only leave the safety of her husband's fort for escorted trips to visit other officers' wives.

The voice of his own first wife echoed from the depths of his memory. *You never take me anywhere nice, Gaius.*

I've tried. You won't go.

But how can I? The whole of Antioch is full of those dreadful people!

The barman returned, ostensibly to see if he had changed his mind about the stew. It seemed the cavalrymen were disinclined to gossip and the lone customer was a better bet. "You hear about that tax man being murdered?"

Ruso nodded.

"Used to stop here regular," said the man. "Him and that brother they can't find, and the guards."

"Did you know him well?"

"Not what you'd call a big spender. Jug of wine, bread, and a bit of cheese. Always the same." The man shook his head, as if the crime had deprived him not only of trade but of words. "Makes you think, don't it? Him setting out thinking it was just a normal trip and he'd be home next morning."

Ruso balanced the cup on the uneven planks that made up the bar and shrugged the stiffness out of his shoulders. "Do they know who did it?"

"Northerners," said the bartender confidently, then, "Or it might be the Iceni, or some of their friends. But most likely Northerners. More and more of them hanging around these days."

Ruso wondered if Tilla had stopped by for refreshment. "Do you get much trouble around here?"

"You don't want to worry, boss. You got a fine day. Plenty of folk on the road. Just make sure you're settled in somewhere before it gets dark."

Ruso downed the rest of his drink and stood up. "I need to find a farmer called Lund."

"Oh, everybody knows Lund." The bartender chuckled. "Lives a couple of miles this side of Verulamium. Turn left at the split oak before the bridge and watch out for the monster. I hear it gets bigger every time he tells it."

29

THE BARTENDER WAS right. According to the eager farmer who dragged the gate open and ushered Ruso into his yard, the river monster was at least eight feet tall and broad as a bull. It had snatched the family's boat from its mooring and hurled it into the middle of the river before chasing the terrified children into the woods. To Ruso's relief, the farmer was able to explain all this in reasonably fluent Latin.

His children, whose ages ranged between about four and ten, were neatly lined up beside him. Their skinny frames were clothed in tunics that were patched but clean and their hair was combed. The girl, who was the eldest, wore a chain of fresh daisies around her neck. All three nodded enthusiastically every time they heard, "Ain't that right, kids?"

They escorted Ruso down a muddy track to where the monster's footprints could be seen across the open grass leading up from the empty mooring post at the river. The prints were marked by wilting clumps of wild garlic, which had miraculously sprung up the day after the visitation.

"Remarkable," said Ruso, noting a swathe of similar plants growing under the trees on the far side of the clearing.

Lund and his group of witnesses led him around a curve in the bank to a freshly hollowed tree stump where a pinch of incense could be burned to appease Ver, the life-giving river. There was no charge for this service as long as you brought your own incense: Ver did not approve of exploiting his followers. He did, however, look especially kindly on those who left gifts glistening in his gravelly shallows. If the officer cared to look closely, he could see the sorts of offerings left by earlier visitors. Did he see the way the sun caught that gold coin over on the left, behind the big red pebble? The man who left that coin went straight home and found news of a legacy waiting for him when he got there. "Ain't that right, kids?"

It seemed several visitors had reason to thank the native god. Another donor had been promoted to centurion. A third had been healed of a broken arm.

"Remarkable," repeated Ruso, shielding his eyes with one hand and peering into the water to admire the shiny trinkets scattered there, one or two of which were already showing spots of rust. Behind him the eldest child observed in British, "He don't look very rich, Da."

"Shut up and keep smiling," replied the father in the same tongue. "You can never tell with these foreigners."

Ruso, who had truthfully told the man that he had only been in the province a few days, suppressed a smile of his own and wondered how best to deal with this. There was no malice in the harmless nonsense about the river monster. Clearly the family was not wealthy, and if they managed to make a little money out of gullible travelers, it was probably no worse than the followers of—

He curtailed that thought, just in case Mithras was able to read men's minds. He was conscious of the family watching as he delved into his purse and pulled out one of Valens's silver denarii. It would be worth more than all the rubbish in the river put together. "Does the god answer questions?"

The children looked at their father, who hesitated. It seemed nobody had made this request before. "What sort of questions?"

"I'm trying to find out what happened to a man who came from Verulamium," Ruso explained. "He was badly injured and he ended up a long way down the river in a small flat-bottomed boat that seems to have been stolen. I'm wondering if the river god might have seen what happened to him."

In the silence that followed, he was conscious of the gurgle of the water in the shallows and the distant cry of a drover on the North road.

"I don't want to get anybody into trouble," he said, flexing the base of his thumb so the coin on his palm lifted and tipped over. The sun glinted on the squat profile of Vespasian. "And I wouldn't want to upset the monster. But perhaps one of you could have a word with the god and see if he could give me a few pointers."

The father sent the younger children back to the house in the care of the oldest girl. When they had disappeared around the bend in the river, he said, "Please don't be angry, sir. They are just kids. He frightened them."

"And he grew into a monster?"

"Just a bit of fun. With the taxes and a sick wife and the price of seed corn, we need money."

Ruso flipped the denarius over again, then held out his hand for the man to take it. "Tell me," he said.

Soon afterward Ruso's horse was picking its way back along the shady track toward the main road and its rider was deep in thought.

Very early on the morning after Asper had disappeared, Lund's children had gone down to the river to fetch water. A terrifying figure with blood on his face and mud all over his clothes rose from the reeds farther along the riverbank and demanded to know where he was. The first Lund knew of it was when he heard them running toward the house screaming about a monster. By the time he reached the bank, the boat had been loosed from its mooring and was drifting out of sight around the bend in the river. He could not see if there was anyone in it.

He had accused the children of untying it and inventing the monster to avoid a beating, but they all told the same story and passed it on to the neighbors' children. Within a couple of days the tale had grown and spread along the course of the river. It was some time before Lund heard about the disappearance of Julius Asper and began to wonder if the monster—who might originally have fit his description—had something to do with it.

"Are you sure there was just the one man? Could there have been somebody with him?"

"Just the one," insisted the man. "We did him no harm, sir."

"There were two men went missing."

"If the brother was here, the dogs would find him," said the man, grasping his meaning.

Ruso paused, distracted. "Is that your wife coughing?"

"The same all through the winter, sir."

Most people suffered from coughs and chilblains through the damp British winter, but generally those who survived had recovered by now. "Has she seen a doctor?"

"They all try something different. Now she is thin as a stick and brings up blood."

There was no point in offering a further prognosis. It would not be good. "Leek juice with frankincense might help a little," he suggested, wishing he had brought his supplies with him. "And whatever they tell you, don't let them bleed her more than once every three weeks."

Before he left he remembered to tell the man where his boat was. It was not much consolation. Turning the horse's head north, he rode past an elderly couple shuffling along carrying a basket full of cabbages and leeks between them. He wondered what sort of welcome Tilla had received in Verulamium. With luck he would sort out this Julius Asper business to Metellus's satisfaction and her name would be erased from the list. If not, as soon as it was over he would suggest they pack up the red crockery and the baby clothes and take the next ship back to Gaul.

30

THESE DAYS HADRIAN'S reforming zeal had seen to it that all lodging houses for traveling officials were centrally administered. The majority of every mansio's staff, however, were bound to be locals. Ruso suspected there would still be a wide variation, not only in style, but in the guests' confidence that nobody might have spit in the soup. However, he was optimistic about Verulamium. It was a major town on one of the busiest routes in the province. The governor must travel this way regularly on his trips to the troubled North. If the natives here were the sort who wanted a theater, they would also want to impress with the size of their bathhouse, the jingle of coins at their market—and, hopefully, the welcome they afforded to the representatives of Rome.

Before he could sample that welcome, he found himself held up outside the town gates. Easing the sweating horse past a couple of vehicles whose drivers were obliged to wait in line, he saw that the delay was being caused by a couple of natives sporting military-style chain mail and red tunics. One of them was the strapping youth who had been escorting Caratius around Londinium. They were equipped with daggers and their spears looked like standard army issue, but in the place of swords they wore stout wooden clubs. He recalled his conversation with Metellus: presumably the routine wearing of swords would have indicated that the local guards had ideas above their station.

Today they were stopping everyone to ask in both British and heavily accented Latin whether anyone had seen a man named Bericus. They were looking very bored with the job until Ruso asked whether a carriage with two women, a baby, and a body had arrived from Londinium. The big one glanced across at the sound of his voice and announced, "It's the investigator!"

His arrival seemed to straighten their shoulders and brighten their eyes. After confirming that his wife had arrived safely, Ruso followed the guard's directions though a grid of busy streets and introduced himself to the bandy-legged overseer of the mansio stables. The man put down the bridle he was inspecting and shouted what sounded like "He's here, lads!" in British before ordering one man to lead the horse away across the yard, a second to carry the investigator's luggage around to reception—"Is that all you've got, sir?"—and a third to fetch a drink. "I'm Rogatus, sir," he said, adding, "We've been expecting you," as if Ruso might not have guessed. He glanced around, evidently looking for something. "Just you at the moment, is it, sir?"

"Just me."

"I'll take you across to your rooms right away. When your men arrive we'll tell them—"

"There aren't any men. It's just me."

"Ah! Well, not to worry. You'll find everyone very willing to help. We're all loyal to the emperor here."

"Good," said Ruso, wondering why it was necessary to say so.

"Always the first to send in our taxes, sir. Famous for it."

Ruso refrained from pointing out that the town was known less for enthusiastic taxpaying than for being ravaged by people who wanted to pay no taxes at all. "Is everyone expecting me, or were you told in confidence?"

The man looked surprised, as if it had never struck him that an investigator might want to be discreet. "No, sir. The chief magistrates had a notice read out in the Forum this morning. You've been announced in both languages, just in case."

Ruso suppressed a sigh and grasped the welcome cup of cool water. As he drank, the man stepped aside to deal with a question about a damaged axle before returning to say, "They said anyone with information was to come forward and tell you, sir."

Clearly the Council had given up any idea of keeping the loss a secret. Now the whole town would be waiting to see what the procurator's man would do about it. He had escaped from a small gang of willing helpers only to be confronted with a large one.

"You can be the first," he said. "Tell me about Asper's transport. Was it one of the public vehicles?"

"Asper had a warrant, sir. He made official journeys."

Evidently they thought he was here to inspect the transport arrangements too. He handed his cup to the hovering servant and indicated that they could talk as they walked. "Did he always drive himself?"

"We didn't have a man available, sir. It was pouring rain, and he was late starting out. His brother could drive."

"So you did him a favor by letting him take a decent carriage."

"The tax had to be delivered, sir."

Asper had not given a reason for the late start, and Rogatus had not felt it was his place to ask.

They passed between gateposts where deep gouges at axle level bore witness to overoptimistic steering, and turned into the street. Rogatus explained that the carriage had been found the following morning, abandoned by the side of the road two or three miles out of town.

"Still with all the horses?"

"We were very lucky, sir." Perhaps in case this sounded too cheerful, he added, "Not like that Julius Asper."

Shooing a couple of children aside with a cry of "Make way for the procurator's man!" he led Ruso toward a long low building. Its pristine white limewash gleamed, its glass windows glittered, and it seemed to occupy most of the rest of the block. Ruso's hopes rose.

"Tell me something," he said. "Asper was on a busy road: Do you think a carriage could be ambushed without anybody seeing it happen?"

Rogatus raised a grimy hand to scratch the back of his neck. "Hard to say, sir. It was a wet old afternoon. Nobody would be out if they could help it, and if they were, they'd be trying to keep under cover."

Ruso paused at the foot of the low stone steps leading up to the reception doors of the mansio and tried not to be distracted by the smell of frying chicken. "If the horses were spooked, how far do you think they might bolt?"

This appeared to be some sort of insult. "We got our animals well trained here, sir."

"I'm just wondering where the men and the carriage actually parted company."

Rogatus, mollified, confirmed that it was "a heavy old vehicle" and was unlikely to have gone far without a driver.

Ruso said, "I'll need to look at it."

Rogatus looked at him as if he had just suggested interviewing the horses. "It's out at the moment, sir. I'll tell the boys you'll be needing to see it."

"I'll need to talk to his, ah—where can I find a woman named Camma?"

The stable overseer's face brightened. "She's just turned up this afternoon, sir. I hear she's back at Asper's house with another young lady." Ruso supposed the man was well placed to hear all the gossip of comings and goings. Reassured, he decided there was no need to rush across there.

"It's a bad old business, sir."

Ruso agreed. His foot was on the bottom step when he heard, "What do you think the procurator will do about it?"

"I couldn't tell you," he said. He had a feeling he was going to be repeating that many times over the next few days.

31

THE MANAGER OF the mansio, a lean and gray-haired retired cavalry officer called Publius, was also expecting the investigator. In fact he brought his young wife out to greet him as well. The wife looked refreshingly bored at the prospect of meeting a tax man and disappeared as soon as the formalities were over. Ruso dismissed a vague feeling that he had seen her somewhere before and followed her husband through the reception area and out under a covered walkway that led around a series of rooms forming three sides of a formal garden.

"You'll have to make the most of us as we are, I'm afraid, sir." Ruso noted the encouraging smells and clattering sounds from the kitchens as Publius was waving his walking stick toward the garden wall and explaining about the improvements he had hoped to put in place in time for the emperor's visit. "I can't see them being agreed until the missing money turns up, sir."

"I'll do my best," agreed Ruso, who had never been called "sir" by a cavalry officer before and decided he liked it.

"You're in Suite Three, sir." Publius paused under the walkway to unlock a door that led into a dim corridor. "That leads out to the alley by the stables," he said, aiming the stick at the streaks of light that outlined an exit straight ahead. "The key's on the hook, so you can come and go as you please."

Ruso was less interested in the hefty iron key hung above the lintel than in seizing the chance to talk while there were no servants or wife around to overhear. "Tell me," he said, "what do you make of the locals?"

"They're a fine bunch of people, sir. Good to work with."

Ruso sighed. "Not the official line, Publius. If I'm going to find this money, I need to know the truth. What do you make of the locals?"

The cavalryman paused, then said, "Ambitious. The emperor allows them to run their own Council and town guard. The town's on a junction of two main roads, so there's a lot of lucrative trade comes through here. They're talking about building a theater."

"Friendly?" prompted Ruso hopefully.

"When it suits them."

Ruso suspected that if he asked too many difficult questions, it would not suit them for long. "Who would you trust?"

Publius cleared his throat. "I'm probably not the best person to ask, sir."

"Because?"

"Because, sir, you work for the procurator's office, and the procurator's office is in charge of mansiones and transport, and if I tell you what really goes on, I'll be getting myself and a lot of other people into trouble."

"I'm not inspecting anything," Ruso promised him. "Just hunting for the money."

The stick clunked against the wall as Publius leaned back and folded his arms. "I'm appointed by Londinium," he said, "but I've got to get along with the suppliers who are near enough to deliver. So I'm not going to tell you about the councillor who overcharges us for the horses he breeds, or how the stable overseer declares them unfit two years later even when they aren't and sells them at a nice profit to himself. I'm certainly not going to tell you that the same overseer takes bribes to slip ordinary letters in with the official post, because doing that would be illegal."

"Absolutely," said Ruso, recognizing the descriptions of Caratius and Rogatus. "It's best that I don't know about any of that. Anything else you're not going to mention?"

"There's the other important councillor whose country estate supplies us with wildly overpriced meat for the kitchens and animal feed that we could get a lot cheaper twenty miles up the road. I won't be telling you about him."

"No, don't."

"Because if I do, then to be fair I'll have to complain about the number of jumped-up officials who come through here demanding services they don't have the warrants for and threatening to report me if they don't get them. And then I'll be in trouble with everybody for not clamping down on it, as if they think I'm some sort of miracle worker."

"I can see that."

"Frankly, sir, once you've been in this job awhile you stop trusting anyone. But from what I can gather, it's no worse here than anywhere else."

"What do you think's gone on with Asper and the tax money?"

"I haven't a clue, sir. But if I were you, I'd watch my back." Publius reached for his stick. "Now that I haven't told you anything, sir, if you'd like me to show you your rooms?"

Publius resumed his well-practiced introduction about keys and bathing and arrangements for dinner. "Your dining room and kitchen are through this door on your right, sir. Since you haven't brought your staff, we'll serve your meals from the main kitchen."

His dining room?

Staff?

"I'm afraid at this hour we can't really make changes to the menu—"

"As long as there's plenty of it," Ruso assured him.

"And this—" The man flung open a door on his left with a flourish. "This is the rest of Suite Three."

Ruso had been surveying the rest of Suite Three for some time before he remembered to close his mouth.

While Publius was saying something about notifying reception of any guests, Ruso was gazing across the expanse of scrubbed floorboards to the open door beyond and wondering how many cavalrymen Publius would have billeted in a space that size in his former career. Even in the civilian world there would be room for a doctor, his wife, several putative children, and as much crockery as any respectable citizen could accumulate.

His reverie was interrupted by a question about his men.

"I've allocated a room just across the garden, sir, unless you'd like some bedding moved into here?"

"I haven't brought any men," he confessed. The surprise on Publius's face recalled the disappointment of the stable overseer. "I prefer to work alone."

"Well, you know best, sir. I'll have some water brought over for washing. If there's anything you want, you just have to ask."

"Thank you. I'll try not to demand any services I'm not entitled to."

The cavalryman grinned. "Oh, demand away, sir. We've got orders to give you every assistance. The Council wants you kept sweet."

Several minutes later, Publius's confidence that Ruso knew best might have been dented by the sight of him throwing his traveling clothes into the corner, standing on tiptoe with his fingers stretched toward the plastered ceiling, and then giving a "Hah!" of delight as he flung his naked form across the bed.

The sheets smelled of lavender. The water in which the slave had just washed his feet smelled of roses, and he himself would cease to smell of horse just as soon as he had finished testing the bed, consuming the drinks and pastries thoughtfully laid out on the table in his reception room, putting on the clean tunic provided, and taking himself out through his own private exit to visit the public baths. He wasn't even going to have to pay. The foot-washing slave had just trotted off to fetch a baths token.

He was deciding that there was, after all, something to be said for being the procurator's man, when he heard the slave tapping on the reception room door.

"It's open," he called, not bothering to move. He heard the hinges of the outer door creak as he took another sniff of the sheets. A man could get used to this. "Just leave it on the table."

There was no reply. Instead of retreating, whoever was out there was striding across the floorboards toward the bedroom.

If I were you, I'd watch my back.

What if it wasn't the servant?

Someone lifted the latch.

Where the hell was his knife?

Ruso was off the bed, across the room, and flattened against the wall just as the door opened to hide him.

A broad-shouldered figure entered the room, looked around, then closed the door and said, "So it is you, Ruso."

"Serena!" His hands clamped over his groin as his eyes met the piercing gaze of a woman, who, had she been male, would have been considered handsome. He swallowed. "What are you doing here?"

"My cousin thought she recognized you." The thick brows met in puzzlement. "Why are you hiding behind the door?"

"I thought you were a slave," he explained with a lack of clarity that he felt was excusable in a man who had just found himself naked in a bedroom with his best friend's wife. "Then I thought you might not be. Uh—how are you?"

Serena looked him up and down and gave a sigh that suggested the weariness of a woman who was used to dealing with naughty boys. "Put some clothes on, Ruso."

As he fumbled his way gratefully into the clean tunic, he heard, "I suppose he's sent you to ask me to come home." Before he could reply she said, "Well, don't bother. I shan't listen."

Finally emerging into daylight, he said, "To be honest, I didn't know you were here."

She pondered that for a moment. "But he knew you were coming?"

"Valens?"

"Who else?"

Ruso, seeing where this was heading, tried, "Possibly."

"Possibly," she repeated, as if she was trying the word to see whether or not she liked it. "Well, did he, or didn't he?"

Ruso straightened a crease across his shoulder. "Yes."

"So," concluded Serena, raising the eyebrows and arching her neck in a way that reminded him of an intelligent horse, "my husband knew you were coming here, and he knows I am here, but he didn't even trouble himself to send a message."

Ruso reached for his belt. "I wouldn't say he didn't trouble himself, exactly . . ."

"No," said Serena, seizing the door handle. "I don't suppose you would. But then, what do you know about it?"

Before he could answer, the door slammed shut. "Not a lot," he confessed, gazing past the space where she had just been standing and wondering if that crack in the plaster had been there before.

32

CLUTCHING HIS BATH token, Ruso stepped out of his private exit and into the alley that separated the mansio's accommodation from its transport yard. The smell of hot metal and horse dung grew stronger, and the clang of hammer on iron signaled that even this late in the day, the stable workshops had a repair job under way. He locked the door behind him, dropped the key into his purse, and turned left. He must set aside for the moment the awkward and embarrassing coincidence of Serena's cousin being married to the mansio manager. He must restrain the urge to scrawl a rude note to Valens, who should have warned him. He must get himself cleaned up, make an attempt to report to the Council—with luck it would be too late today—and then find Tilla.

He was approaching the doors of a bathhouse that would not have disgraced a small town at home when he heard a pair of studded boots striding up behind him. A voice said, "Investigator?"

It was another of the local guards. This one not only had the red tunic, the chain mail, and a silver-buckled belt, but also flamboyant scarlet braids woven through dark hair that hung below his shoulders. No attempt to emulate Rome here, then.

"Dias." The man, slightly out of breath, was holding out a hand.

"Captain of the town guard. We've been looking into the theft of the tax money. When do you want me to brief you?"

Ruso need not have worried about translation. The locals' grasp of Latin was as impressive as their eagerness to cooperate. "I was going across to the baths," he explained, "but if there's somewhere we can talk . . ."

Dias assured him that the baths would be fine. Ruso handed his token to the attendant on the door and entered the echoing din of the entrance hall. The guard captain sauntered past with a nod. Moments later Ruso was seated beneath the high window of a private and overscented warm room. The other occupants had grabbed their towels and clattered out in their wooden bath shoes as soon as they saw Dias enter. Ruso felt his skin begin to prickle with sweat. Since the native was sitting upright on the bench opposite without so much as loosening his belt, it did not seem appropriate to undress.

Dias turned out to be the exact opposite of Caratius. His hairstyle might be unmilitary but his summary was professional and concise, and it confirmed what the magistrate and the stable overseer had already told him. Asper had collected the tax money from the town strong room without requesting a guard, and set off in the rain. He and his brother had last been seen driving out through the gates on the Londinium road. Next morning, the carriage had been found abandoned just off the main road between the second and third milestones. "I'm told Asper got to Londinium by boat," he said. "My men searched the area where the carriage was found and we had a look downriver, but we still can't find Bericus."

"No, I haven't traced him, either." Ruso unpeeled his tunic from his back. "Asper was already alone when he took the boat, though, so they must have parted near here." The dark eyes widened as Ruso explained about his inquiries into the river monster a couple of miles away.

Ruso hoped he had not just wrecked Lund's moneymaking activities. "Your men don't need to bother with the farmer," he said. "He's told everything he knows and he's harmless." He wiped a trickle of sweat from his forehead before venturing into more difficult territory. "I gather one of your magistrates had a personal grudge against Asper?"

Dias nodded as if he had been expecting the question. "Asper got Chief Magistrate Caratius's wife pregnant. She left, or Caratius kicked her out, I don't know which—but Asper had to take her in."

"Do you think it's relevant?"

"You mean, did the chief magistrate have a reason to have Asper murdered? Or did Asper have a reason to get out of town with no woman, no guards, and a big bag of somebody else's money?"

"It certainly doesn't seem to be a random theft," said Ruso, deciding not to mention the claim that Asper had really been on the way to visit the chief magistrate when he vanished. For all he knew, Dias would be reporting the conversation back to the Council.

"We think the brother turned on him," said Dias. "They used to argue a lot."

As Ruso was considering this nugget of fresh information, Dias said, "I hear you haven't brought any men with you. I'll assign you a couple of guards."

"If this whole thing was engineered by a dead man and a brother on the run, I doubt I'll be in much danger."

Dias grinned. "True," he said, "but I don't want your pals in Londinium thinking the natives don't know how to make a man welcome. I served in the army too: I know the sort of things that get said about us. Besides, my lads can help you find your way around."

The military service explained the Latin. "I was with the Twentieth for a while," said Ruso, realizing Dias had noticed his old army belt, now adapted for civilian use. "You?"

"Five years with the Third Brittones over in Germania," said Dias, adding, "Medical discharge" to explain the short duration of a service that would normally last a couple of decades. "Back trouble."

Ruso eyed the lithe form, the good bone structure that meant Dias would grow old still handsome, and the colorful native hairstyle. "There's a lot of back trouble in the army," he observed. Much of it was completely unprovable, but he was not going to insult the man by saying so.

"It's settled down now," said Dias. "How about you?"

Clearly Ruso did not look like an aristocrat who had served briefly on the way to greater things, and he was not going to admit that he was a doctor with a short-term contract. He lifted one leg and said truthfully, "Broke my foot."

Dias gestured toward it. "All right now, is it?"

"Fine."

The native stood up, apparently satisfied that they had established some sort of connection.

Ruso said, "I'll need to report to the Council."

"No chance at this hour," said Dias. "But there's a few of them hanging around here. Don't worry, they'll find you."

His visit to Tilla would have to be postponed.

"I'll have a couple of lads waiting by the time you've finished cleaning up," Dias said, adding as if he had only just noticed, "Hot in here, isn't it?"

Half an hour later Ruso was cleaner but no more enlightened. He had been offered opinions by glistening men with rats' tail hair in the hot room, by fat old men playing board games in the hall, by a masseur with a large mole on his nose, and by a couple of weightlifters with thick necks and veins bulging around the outsides of their oiled muscles.

Several were off-duty councillors. One or two suggested that Asper might have been the victim of a robbery, but most were convinced that he had stolen their money himself. There were dark mutterings about That Woman. The fact that he had been murdered was explained as divine vengeance. He had insulted the emperor, the chief magistrate, the Council, and the whole tribe. When they realized the money was missing, the magistrates had sacrificed a ram to Jupiter and a dog to Sucellus— whoever he was—and the thief had gotten what he deserved.

It was further evidence for Albanus's view that the Britons were not interested in logic.

Most people, though, were less interested in the fate of Julius Asper than in knowing what the procurator would do if the money did not turn up. Would he insist that the councillors make good the loss? Would everyone have to pay their taxes twice?

Ruso's refusal to speculate did nothing to allay their fears. He had picked up his towel and was fending off requests from opposite sides to champion one design for the new theater over another when the word *Investigator!* boomed and echoed around the exercise hall.

Ruso gave his hair one final rub and dropped the towel onto the changing bench. A large expanse of exposed flesh was approaching with one pudgy bejeweled hand outstretched. The flesh tapered up into a fashionable beard and neatly trimmed hair framing a broad smile. "Gallonius," it introduced itself. "Chief Magistrate."

"Joint Chief Magistrate," chimed in a second voice over the sound of footsteps. Ruso looked over the shoulder of the first speaker to see Caratius striding across the hall with his cloak billowing out behind him.

"Please excuse the informal welcome, investigator," continued the large man, pumping Ruso's arm up and down with one hand and making a grab for his slithering towel with the other. "They've only just told me you're here. I hope they're looking after you over at the mansio. This has all come as a bit of a shock."

"I've already told the investigator the facts," put in Caratius.

"Your guard captain's briefed me on the inquiries so far," said Ruso, "but I've got a few questions. I'll need to talk to you both separately."

While Gallonius nodded approval, Caratius said, "Of course. You'll have to question everyone involved."

Ruso said, "Did Asper have any trouble collecting the taxes?"

Both men looked taken aback. "No more than anyone else would," Gallonius told him. "Collecting the corn tribute is always a slow business, but we get there in the end."

"It's a matter of honor," said Caratius. "Verulamium always pays on time."

This impressive show of unity and loyalty was followed by an awkward silence. Ruso said, "Perhaps we could talk at a more convenient—"

"Dinner tonight," said Caratius.

Taken by surprise, Ruso cast about for an excuse. He had barely slept last night and it had been a long day with a tiring ride, but he could hardly say he had been looking forward to an early acquaintance with the scented sheets of Suite Three.

"I insist," said Caratius.

Gallonius's expression might have been indigestion, or it might have been the effort of holding back an opinion.

"I'll send a man to escort you out to the house in an hour," said Caratius, promising a private conversation with "a few details there wasn't time to explain yesterday."

Ruso supposed he wanted to give his side of the marriage story. Meanwhile Gallonius was still looking as though his internal workings were badly out of balance.

Ignoring the complaints from his own stomach that an hour was a long time to wait, Ruso accepted. "There's no need for an escort," he said. "I've already been assigned a couple of guards."

Was that annoyance on the magistrate's hard features? Finally he said, "I'll call in at the stables and tell Rogatus to give you one of my horses," as if Ruso had just bargained him down. "You can use it for as long as you're here."

He did not much want the horse, either, but it seemed churlish to refuse.

Caratius gave his fellow magistrate a look of triumph before departing with, "Good! I'll see you later."

When he had gone, the big man beckoned Ruso back toward the stifling room in which he had already endured the conversation with the guard captain. "A word in private, Investigator."

Ruso, wishing he had not just put all his clothes back on, was obliged to follow.

Gallonius threw his towel along the bench under the window. His lips made the sound of a deflating bladder as he slowly collapsed himself to a seated position. "Sorry about Caratius," he said. "Still thinks he's in charge of the place."

Ruso, feeling overdressed, said, "I gather he comes from a long line of influential men?"

Gallonius chuckled. "On one side only. His other grandfather was an ordinary craftsman like mine. And the famous one with the Roman education is nothing to be proud of. He failed to organize any defenses for the town and then ran off as soon as there was trouble."

Ruso had the word *Boudica?* on the tip of his tongue when he remembered the procurator's injunction.

"Things are much better organized these days," Gallonius continued. "These days we elect our Council in the Roman way."

"So I see," said Ruso, noting that Caratius's family seemed to be at the top no matter what system was in place. "Asper didn't have any other duties, did he?"

"Such as?"

"I don't know," said Ruso, not wanting to explain about the reference to evidence in the unfinished letter. "Security? I've been told about the woman, but I wondered if there was any other way he might have made enemies."

"His contract was to collect the taxes, which wouldn't make him popular. Are you suggesting it wasn't a robbery?"

"Just trying to get the full picture."

"Our own guards deal with security. Within the limits of the Constitution, of course. For anything else we consult the governor."

It was a speech designed to reassure visiting officials. "So what do you think happened to your money?"

Gallonius's forefinger sank into the soft flesh of his chin as he stroked his beard. "You could say it was taken by robbers," he said. "Or you could say that Julius Asper realized he had made a foolish mistake over the woman, tried to run off with the money, and chose the wrong accomplice."

None of this was anything new. Ruso noted that the indigestion look had reappeared. "What else could you say?" he prompted.

Gallonius lifted a towel from the stack farther along the bench and wiped his forehead. "I wouldn't say it," he said. "And I wouldn't even want to think it. Not of a fellow magistrate."

"If you have any proof that—"

"If I had any proof, Investigator, I would offer it for the good of the town. As it is, we're relying on you."

When Ruso escaped to the relative cool of the exercise hall, he found two burly guards in the familiar red tunics waiting by the main door. One of them was the big youth again. He introduced himself as Gavo and announced that they were at the investigator's service. Neither showed any surprise when he asked them to escort him to Julius Asper's house, where he intended to make sure they were out of earshot when he told Tilla he had just agreed to dine with Camma's estranged husband.

33

TILLA KNEW PEOPLE were lying to her. She knew because she would have done the same if a Catuvellauni woman had turned up at home and started asking questions about one of her own neighbors: even one as distinctive as this Grata seemed to be. She wished she had thought to ask Dias where the housekeeper had gone. Instead she had hoped that if she hung around near the water-pipe on the corner for long enough, she could strike up a conversation with somebody who could tell her. But the Catuvellauni townsfolk had come and gone, shaking their heads as they splashed water into their jars and buckets and sometimes over their feet. Several people knew who Grata was, but none admitted to knowing where to find her.

Tilla glanced around the streets that had been busy when they arrived. Most of the carts had gone now, taking their owners home from market. There was still plenty of light but the evening chill was beginning to creep in, and there was hardly anyone about. People who needed water had already been to fetch it. Now they were in their homes preparing their dinner. She should get back. Camma should not be left too long on her own. She bent to heave up the two buckets she had taken from the deserted kitchen.

At that moment she saw a small brisk woman in her midtwenties hurrying from the direction of the Forum. The woman was dressed in the fine-woven plaid of a local, but her coloring spoke of ancestors in one of those impossibly hot and dry places across the sea. Tilla lowered the buckets to the ground.

The woman walked straight up to her and said in British, "Who are you, and why are you asking for me?"

Tilla explained, adding, "Camma was expecting to find you at the house."

Grata tilted up her chin. "The master and his brother disappeared," she said. "*She* went off to Londinium, and I'm left with people banging on the door at all hours shouting "where's our money?" And they were the polite ones. The council came around wanting to know where he was and searching the house and then I woke up in the middle of the night with a bunch of drunks outside trying to piss through the window."

Tilla said, "When we got there, people were stealing the furniture."

"I told them to clear off," Grata said, as if that might have kept everyone out once she had left. "More than once."

"I am sorry for you. But now she is back, your mistress needs you. She has a man to mourn and a new son to look after."

The woman hitched the basket up her arm. "He was my master, but she was never my mistress. I'm not a slave, you know."

The refusal to call Camma by name or show any interest in the baby was not promising, but Tilla pressed on. "I did not mean to insult. But she needs help, and I will be gone in a day or two."

"I've got a job in a bakery now. You'll have to find somebody else."

"Do you know anybody?"

The silence suggested that no one else would want the job, either. "She should go back where she came from."

Tilla said, "She can't."

"It's no good you looking at me like that. She made her choice. Ask anyone: They'll tell you the same."

Tilla tried again. "I can't pretend that Camma did a wise thing," she said. "But I'm asking you—"

"Look, it was a job. I kept house and I got paid for it. It was all fine till she came along causing trouble. I tried to tell him, and so did his brother, but he wouldn't listen."

Tilla tried a different approach. "Do you know what happened to them?"

"What's it to you?"

"Nothing," admitted Tilla. "But it is to Camma. Who do you think would want to hurt them?"

Grata shrugged. "How should I know?"

"I heard there was trouble about the baby."

The dark eyes narrowed. "You've been hearing a lot. For a Northerner."

"Northerners have ears too. Do you think that magistrate she married—"

Grata's slender hand clutched at her arm. "I don't think things about magistrates," she hissed, "and if I did I wouldn't be fool enough to talk about them with strangers in the street. They were asking for trouble, and they got it."

"I'm sorry. I am only a midwife trying to help a patient."

Grata released her grip. "I've no quarrel with you. You don't know what you're meddling in."

"I have a husband to go back to. I promise there will be money to pay you if—"

"How many times? I have another job!"

Tilla shook her head. "I am sad to find this is how things are in the South."

"Hah! Well, maybe it's all very friendly up where you come from, but round here if you want to fit in, you have to behave like a decent woman."

There was something about the words that recalled Tilla's own loneliest moments in faraway Gaul. "It is not easy being different," she said. "I am sorry to have wasted your time."

Grata shifted awkwardly. "Yes. Well, I'm sorry I can't help. But—"

"I know," said Tilla, crouching to heave up the buckets. "You have a new job."

34

GAVO AND HIS companion led Ruso along a street that ran past the back of the Great Hall, a building so huge that he found himself counting paces as he walked alongside it.

He must stop doing that. He was not in the army now.

The natives here had a hall nearly as big as the one down in Londinium. They had their own baths, and he had passed a decent-looking temple on the way in. There wasn't a round house in sight, and instead of a rabble of painted warriors they had a well-disciplined militia and elected politicians. Now these long-haired men with their jewelry and their trousers were squabbling over the design of their theater. Gods above.

Ahead of him, a couple of women were chatting by a trough. The natives also had clean running water piped to the middle of town. It was a foreign innovation that even Tilla would have to admit was an improvement. In fact—that woman just heaving up a couple of buckets and walking away was Tilla herself.

He recognized the purposeful stride his wife adopted when she was annoyed. As he fell into step and seized a bucket handle, he was greeted with, "I am glad you are here. How can anyone live among these people?"

With some foreboding, he said, "Problems?"

Apparently Tilla's problem was that the Catuvellauni were a lazy and selfish tribe who knew nothing about honor or decency.

A silversmith closing up his workshop across the road turned to see who was speaking. Ruso glanced back at Gavo, who was a couple of paces behind him. "I suppose it's too much to hope that they might be deaf, as well."

"Why are those men following us?"

"They're my guards."

As she marched him past a covered market with a couple of dogs sniffing around the entrance, Tilla explained her attempt to persuade the housekeeper back to her old job. "She says nobody else will do it, either, and how can I leave Camma on her own?"

The situation was beginning to sound as bad as he had feared back in Londinium. "How is she?"

"She is tired and upset and the neighbors want to rob her. She says Asper was trying to get them both out of here but he never told her how."

He glanced at his wife, noting the delicate lines of strain around her eyes. This was definitely not the right time to tell her about Metellus.

He felt a surge of anger with Camma. If he had known the full story at the beginning, he might have been able to sort this business out before Metellus got involved. Now the best he could hope for was to extricate them both without Tilla ever knowing her name had been on that list.

As they passed an expanse of weedy gravel being grazed by a tethered goat, he gave her a version of events in Londinium that gave no hint of Metellus's involvement. Finally they stopped outside a two-story house where a carpenter was measuring up to replace a splintered door jamb. The man responded to Tilla's greeting with a grunt of, "It's a job," as if he was justifying himself to someone who was not there.

Ruso told his guards to wait outside. Tilla led him down a gap between the house and a bronzesmith's workshop. "That man should not complain," she said as he followed her out into a garden where a few scraps of laundry were dripping onto the vegetable patch. "I paid him double to work late so we can lock up when we go to the funeral." She paused with one hand on the back door. "I told you, nobody wants to help."

The kitchen smelled of cabbage, which must be what was bubbling under a layer of scum in the pot. Ruso looked around in vain for a more appetizing snack, then pulled a stool up to the table and tried to imagine what it must be like to be the owner of this comfortably appointed house. The chair by the hearth was elegantly carved and the walls had a fresh coat of cream paint with no signs of damp. Asper had done well for himself here.

He had then undermined his success by seducing the wife of a powerful man. Instead of fleeing town with her, he had stayed and carried on his business under the husband's mustached nose while the unfaithful wife grew large with his own illegitimate child. What sort of man did a thing like that? He couldn't imagine. Nor could he imagine any innocent reason why the husband might invite Asper to visit him, nor why Asper might take the tax money with him if he were bold enough to accept.

Tilla returned and closed the door quietly. "They are both sleeping in the front room." She gave the pot a stir and then sat down heavily in the chair by the fire. "She does not want to go to an empty bed."

"Is she helping, or are you doing all the work?"

Tilla shrugged. "She needs to rest. She has many problems and a baby to look after. Perhaps she will be better after the funeral."

"You aren't arranging that as well, are you?"

She stifled a yawn as she said, "The captain of your guards said he would do it in the morning."

"I'm glad one person's helping."

Tilla said, "He is helping because he is embarrassed. We caught him stealing the furniture."

"Dias?" Ruso wondered if she had misunderstood something. The guard captain was supposed to arrest thieves, not act as one.

"He says Asper owed him money."

There was a lot here he did not understand himself. "I really need to talk to Camma again."

"Not now," she said. "But I have tried to ask her some questions for you."

It seemed that on the day they disappeared, Asper and his brother had been to work as usual in the morning. A message had arrived just before midday asking them to visit Caratius, and later on they had changed into their best clothes and set off with no luggage and no mention of taxes or guards. As far as Camma knew, they had been planning a trip to Londinium the day after.

"She told him not to go," Tilla said before he could interrupt, "but he thought it was to agree on a price to pay for the dishonor. He had been waiting for Caratius to ask. She offered to go with him, but he said seeing her would make Caratius even more angry."

That made sense.

"At home when something like this happens, there is a . . .' She paused. "What is the word? Someone who comes in between who does not take sides."

"Arbiter?" he suggested.

"Yes. He thought there would be somebody there with Caratius. He took Bericus to represent him."

He said, "Who brought the message?"

Tilla paused. "I think the housekeeper took it. I should have asked her."

"We can do that later. I want to ask her how the brothers got along, as well. I've been told that they argued."

Tilla nodded. "Bericus said he should stay away from Camma."

His wife had certainly been busy. He said, "Is it possible the brother took a bribe to attack Asper and then run away?"

Tilla shrugged. "Camma says no, but I do not know the man."

"And if he did," he said, "where did the tax money go?"

"Perhaps it was the brother's reward."

"Really? How much do you imagine it costs to get someone murdered in a place like this?"

"At home it can be done for two cows. If you know the right person." She might have been discussing the price of a loaf of bread.

"Here, they are greedy. And a brother would cost a lot more."

"Even so," he said, "it can't possibly run to seven thousand denarii."

"Who knows?" She shrugged. "Perhaps Caratius and the brother shared it. Perhaps both brothers are dead and Caratius has it."

"Or it's gone to someone else entirely. This is getting us nowhere."

There was a thump and the rasp of a saw from the front of the house. The carpenter had cheered up. He was whistling.

Tilla gestured toward the pot of cabbage. "I spent most of the money getting the door mended, but there is food. Will you stay for supper?"

He shook his head, feeling guilty about the luxury of Suite Three while his wife was struggling to run a house, comfort the bereaved, and boil cabbage. He said, "I'll ask the manager at the mansio if his wife knows a housekeeper." He paused, realizing he had almost failed to pass on a major piece of news. "You won't believe this, but Serena's here."

"I know this."

"Her cousin's married to the chap who runs the—what?"

"Valens told me this morning. He asked me to talk to her. I said he must talk to her himself."

"You might have warned me!"

She said, "I forgot. But when there is time I will go and say hello."

At the moment, they both had bigger things to worry about. Digging into his purse for some of the money Valens had loaned him earlier this afternoon, he tipped it onto the table and then got to his feet. "I have to go."

"So soon?"

He bent and kissed her on the forehead. He wondered if she really was carrying his child this time. It was too soon to tell. "Get an early night," he told her. "It'll be a difficult day tomorrow."

"Will you come to the funeral?"

"I'll try," he promised. "You never know, I might have some answers by then. Caratius has invited me to dinner."

"Caratius? I will pray to Christos and his father to keep you safe."

"If you must. But he's not going to do anything to a procurator's man."

"If he thinks you suspect—"

"He won't," he promised. "Besides, I've got two guards and the other magistrate knows I'm going there."

She called across the kitchen, "What if the guards are working for him?"

"Of course they aren't," he assured her as he stepped out into the garden, not wanting her to worry.

When he emerged into the street, the guards stationed themselves one on each side of him. It occurred to him that these men worked for the Council of which Caratius was a senior member. There was no need for Tilla to worry, because he could do enough worrying for himself.

35

PUBLIUS'S WIFE WAS on duty in the reception area of the mansio. She seemed unexpectedly pleased to see Ruso, declaring, "I knew I'd met you somewhere before!"

He mumbled something conciliatory. It was not the time to reminisce. It had been a long day, his hunger had overwhelmed the temporary relief of the pastries, and he was probably already late for his meal with Caratius.

"You were one of the doctors stationed at Deva. Don't you remember me? I'm Paula. You and Valens came to our house for dinner."

"I do," agreed Ruso, not adding that he remembered this elegantly coiffed young woman as one of a pair of giggly girls. The dinner invitation had been part of Valens's campaign to impress Serena, a campaign that had unfortunately succeeded.

"I always liked you best," she said. "I told Serena, but she wouldn't listen. You can't trust a man who's too good looking. He's had other women down there while she's been away, you know."

Women? In the plural? He said, "Are you sure?"

"Oh, yes."

It seemed Valens had been busy in the short space between Serena's leaving and his own arrival. In the face of such certainty, his "I didn't see any women" made it sound as though he had failed to notice them hiding under the beds.

"We know everything that goes on, you know," the cousin assured him. "We're only twenty miles away and we have friends. Why don't you join us for dinner and we can all hear one another's news?"

Verulamium was a remarkably hospitable town. He had been in the place only a few hours and this was his third invitation to dinner. Sadly none of them was as appealing as his original plan to wolf down something tasty and filling before catching up on last night's lost sleep in the comfort of Suite Three.

He explained that he had been invited out this evening. He was almost at the door when he paused and turned to ask her how late the staff would be on duty. "I'm told Caratius lives out of town," he explained, "so I may be late back from dinner, but I'll definitely be sleeping here tonight and I'd like an early breakfast."

Her promise to alert the night porter and the kitchen staff was doubly reassuring. Not only were several people now expecting him back this evening, but his guards, waiting out on the steps, would have overheard him telling her.

Had Julius Asper been trying to protect himself in the same way when he told Camma where he was going? Or had he been lying to confuse any pursuers while he escaped with the money?

When Ruso emerged from the mansio he found the big guard lounging against the wall by himself. Gavo snapped to attention, explaining that his comrade had gone next door to check the arrangements for the horses. Ruso was not sorry. He wanted a private word with Gavo. He wanted to know what the young man had seen while he had been escorting the magistrate around Londinium.

Making the excuse of collecting his cloak, Ruso led him back through reception and out past the garden toward Suite Three.

"So, what did you make of being invited into a postmortem?" was perhaps not the best way to start a conversation, but it turned out that Gavo was sorry he'd missed most of it. In fact, he was sorry he hadn't been able to spend longer in Londinium. Freed from the watchful eye of his companion, he turned out to be remarkably talkative. Incredibly, since Londinium was only twenty miles away, it turned out to be his first trip. "As an adult, sir," he added, clearly eager to make sure Ruso did not think he was some sort of unsophisticated bumpkin. "We used to go there when my father was alive."

Ruso concluded with some relief that Gavo on his own was unlikely to be much of a threat. While he gathered up his cloak, the young man explained that his father had been a leatherworker, but he had joined the guards to better himself. "Dias says I might even be able to go for the army in a year or two," he added. "He was on the way to being a centurion himself, sir. Till he got invalided out with his back."

"Sounds as though you're getting good experience," said Ruso, locking the door once more and hoping the youth had not been too busy chatting to notice him checking his knife. "Were you Caratius's sole escort or part of a team?"

"Just me and the magistrate's personal slaves, sir." Gavo looked pleased with himself. "Usually Dias gets all these—" Whatever word he was about to use, he stifled it and said, "All the Londinium duties. But he put me on the roster to go instead."

"I don't suppose you got much of a chance to look round, having to stay with the magistrate and then come straight back."

"Oh, no, sir! Once the magistrate was settled in with his friend, I was off duty."

As they clattered down the mansio steps, Ruso said, "That was very generous of him."

"Yes, sir." Gavo cleared his throat as if there was something he was not supposed to say. "So I went out exploring."

Ruso wondered if he should make inquiries about Caratius's friend. There couldn't be that many priests of Jupiter.

"There's a few good brewers down there, I can tell you." The big face split into a rueful grin. "I had a storming headache on the way home."

"You should be careful," said Ruso, alarmed by the very naïveté he was himself exploiting. "It's not a good idea to go drinking in a strange town on your own."

"Oh, I wasn't on my own, sir," the lad assured him. "Dias showed me round."

Ruso felt his whole body tense. As casually as he could he said, "So your captain was in Londinium as well?"

The youth looked uncomfortable. "It was a personal matter, sir. Nothing to do with the magistrate. You won't mention it to him tonight, will you, sir?"

They turned in at the stable gate. Ruso glimpsed another chain-mailed figure bending to tighten a girth as he chatted to the stable overseer. He said, "Is there a reason you don't want me to mention it to Caratius?"

"Not to Caratius, sir—"

The other guard straightened up and Ruso saw who it was.

"I'd rather you didn't say anything to Dias, sir. He's the other half of your escort tonight."

36

THEY RODE OUT beneath the arch of the south gate, Ruso automatically returning the gatekeeper's salute as they passed. It was a scene that, captured in a painting, would have said all the right things about the benevolent rule of Rome. The procurator's man on a gleaming bay gelding, accompanied by his smart native escort, all riding out of town on a spring evening to enjoy dinner with an influential Briton in his country house.

The painter could not have depicted the thud of Ruso's heart as they left the safety of the town and headed out past the cemetery that would soon hold the remains of the murdered Julius Asper. *Dias had been in Londinium all along.* No picture could have captured the turmoil in his mind as he eyed the lithe form on the horse beside him and tried to recall the shape he had grabbed in Valens's hallway. Was that a bruise just visible under the scarlet sleeve? Had that hood been hiding not a mangled ear but a flamboyant hairstyle shot through with red threads?

Dias was about the right height and build. There was no evidence now of any back problem that might prevent him from climbing in through the kitchen window. Either he had met a good doctor, or he had made one of the miraculous recoveries that disaffected soldiers sometimes enjoyed after medical discharge.

If Dias had been secretly working for the magistrate in Londinium it was not clear why he had bothered to take Gavo out drinking, but perhaps he was genuinely concerned to keep his protégé out of trouble. In any case, the youth's presence might not have restricted him for long. Already flattered at being chosen for the Londinium trip, Gavo must have been thrilled to be offered a tour of the town in the company of his hero. He could have been too drunk to know when the evening ended or what either of them had been up to.

They were topping the gentle rise beyond the cemetery now. The spring sun was still above the trees but he was glad of his cloak: The sky was clear and it would be cold later. Apart from a donkey cart and a shawled woman hurrying along behind it, all of the traffic was heading the other way. Sensible travelers would be settled safely in town before nightfall. Ruso, on the other hand, was following the road out across open fields to visit a suspect who had a motive for murdering Julius Asper. He was in the company of an armed man he could no longer trust and a junior guard who, if the choice came, would follow his leader.

If I were you, I'd watch my back. Publius had warned him. Tilla had warned him. He was an official employee and several people knew where he was going, but none of those things had saved Julius Asper.

He sneaked another glance at Dias, riding easily beside him. Now they were out on the open road, the man had added a long sword to his personal armory, dwarfing the wicked-looking knife he always wore on his belt. Why was the captain of the town guard bothering to perform a simple escort duty? He recalled the confused fight in Valens's hallway, and the crater left in the plaster that might easily have been in his own head. If Dias realized he was under suspicion, then Ruso was in trouble. Besides, with Dias watching his every move, how the hell was he supposed to investigate anything? On the other hand, if he investigated nothing, that would look suspicious too.

He nudged the borrowed gelding over toward Dias's mount. Above the gentle jingling of the fancy bridle trappings, he said, "I'm told Asper owed you money?"

"Not me. The lads. Wages for guard duty. I went to the house to find something to pay them with."

"Any luck?"

"Didn't have time. Some woman thought I was a burglar and went for me with a knife."

Ruso could guess which woman that had been.

Dias carried on scanning the surrounding fields for the trouble that Ruso now suspected he was more likely to cause than to prevent. They were passing an overgrown track that led off to the left when he said, "That's where the carriage was picked up. Stuck on a branch about twenty yards down."

"Where does it lead?"

"A couple of farms. We asked around but nobody saw anything."

Ruso walked his horse slowly forward between the lush grasses bowing in from either side. He stopped where the branch of an oak overhung the track. He could see no evidence of any attack that might have taken place here. The carriage could have been deliberately driven along the track to get it off the road—or the horses, with all night to wander about, could have meandered down here in search of a roadside snack.

Returning to the others he said, "While we're out here, let's see if we can see how Asper ended up on the river."

Dias turned. The dark eyes seemed to be scrutinizing him, as if trying to assess how much he knew. Ruso forced himself to stay relaxed, knowing the horse might react to any tension, and Dias was not a fool.

Finally Dias said, "And what will that tell us, sir?"

Was there a whisper of insolence in the "sir"? Dias had had five years in the auxiliaries to practice being just the right side of insubordination. "Probably not a lot," Ruso admitted. "But it's your money, and you never know."

Dias looked him up and down. "You haven't got a bloody clue where the money is, have you?"

"Neither have you," said Ruso, returning the candor, "or we wouldn't be standing here."

Dias's face relaxed. "Move on!" he called over his shoulder to Gavo, the harness jingling louder as he urged his horse into a trot. "The investigator wants to look at the river."

As the road approached the meandering river, it had been raised to cross flat watermeadows where the lowest patches were dotted with tufts of reed. Apart from the cover of the occasional willow tree, Ruso had to concede that it was a poor site for an ambush. The road was straight in both directions. The drivers of a couple of vehicles in the distance must have a clear and puzzling view of him and his escort, halting on each of the three bridges in turn. They could also be seen from the native farmsteads on the low hills around, most of which had been cleared of trees.

There was a villa beyond a wood on one side of the road and, on the other, a grand stone memorial reminding travelers of some deceased landowner with plenty of money.

On the last bridge he stared into the dark water and watched long green fingers of weeds waving downstream. The river was no more revealing now than it had been when he had paused to inspect it on the way here. Still, on Asper's last journey, it had been raining heavily. The traffic would have been lighter than usual and the visibility poor. If Asper had been attacked by men he recognized, they might have been able to get alongside before he realized he was in danger. There would have been no pursuit or ambush to alert his fellow travelers.

The water would have been higher with the rain too. High enough, perhaps, for a man to float downstream, abandoned for dead by assailants who needed to get away before someone else came along and saw what was happening. Farther along, Asper could have crawled out of the water. By morning he had gathered enough strength to frighten Lund's children and steal his boat.

It was all speculation. The ambush-on-an-open-road theory was just about plausible, but none of it answered the question of what had happened to the missing brother.

The wooden bridge gave a dull boom as Dias's horse stamped with impatience. Its rider said, "Tell you anything, sir?"

"Not really," said Ruso, tossing a very small coin into the water for luck and hoping Christos, if he existed, was listening to Tilla's prayers. "I think I'm ready for some dinner."

They turned right off the main road soon after, Dias leading the way along a narrow unmade lane where grass sprouted between the wheel ruts. The gelding picked up its pace, recognizing the route. Ruso was aware of Gavo drawing up beside him, waving one hand to attract his attention and mouthing, "Sir?"

He slowed the horse, letting Dias draw away in front of them.

"Sir, I should never have said that about Dias. You won't say anything to anybody, will you?"

"I'm sure he can explain," said Ruso. "Don't worry, I'll have a word with him and sort it out."

"But sir—"

"I won't tell him who told me," said Ruso. The youth evidently had no clue that he might be involved in covering up a murder. "With luck, he'll never find out."

The youth glanced at Dias, still a couple of horse lengths in front. He moved closer until his and Ruso's knees brushed against each other and hissed, "Please, sir! It wasn't anything bad. He just went to meet a woman."

"I thought he spent the evening with you?"

Gavo shook his head. "In the end he had to, sir. Her husband was at home."

"Ah," said Ruso, who didn't believe a word of it but could see why Gavo had been impressed.

"Please don't tell anyone, sir. If his girl finds out, I'm dead."

With that, Gavo drew back and left him to ride on alone. The gentle plod of hoofs on dried mud was accompanied by evening birdsong as they followed the track through fresh green woods that would have been an ideal ambush site but were implausibly far from the river.

After a couple of hundred paces the view opened to reveal the villa he had seen from the road: a two-story building with tiles on the roof, paint on the walls, and glass in several of the windows—which by British standards made it a high-class residence. Horses in the surrounding paddocks lifted their heads and trotted up to greet the new arrivals. A gray-headed figure that could only be Caratius appeared on the porch.

He had just raised one arm in greeting when there was a commotion behind them. The alarm calls of startled birds rose above the sound of someone crashing about and shouting. Ruso wheeled the horse around. Where Gavo should have been was an empty track. Dias, spear raised, yelled, "Keep back!" as he thundered past toward the woods. Over the hoofbeats, from somewhere deep in the trees, came a shrill and terrible scream.

It was all over by the time they got there. Gavo was standing triumphant, the tip of his spear pressed into the rough clothing of a prisoner who was lying facedown among the leaves.

"Got her, boss!" he announced proudly to Dias, and then to Ruso, "This woman was following us, sir."

Ruso put both reins into one hand and swung down from the horse. As he knelt beside the prisoner, Dias approached and said something in British.

"Tell your man to stand easy, Dias," said Ruso, relieved to see that the prisoner's expression was one of indignation rather than pain. "There's no danger."

"She's the associate of the Iceni woman," said Dias.

"Yes," said Ruso, sighing. "She's also my wife. Would you mind letting her up, please?"

By the time Ruso emerged onto the track Caratius had arrived with a posse of excited farmworkers clutching pitchforks and horsewhips. His own escort was still wandering about the woods, trying to catch the horse that had fled from Gavo in all the excitement. Ruso jumped the gelding back over the ditch, then turned and leaned down to grab his wife's hand as she leapt across onto the track with her skirts bunched up into the other fist.

The embarrassment of having to explain the arrival of an uninvited dinner guest who was still picking twigs out of her hair was something Ruso would later try very hard to forget. Caratius made an effort to be polite but the tone in which he said, "From the North, I see!" suggested that if Ruso was going to marry a Briton, he might have made a more civilized choice. Indeed, it probably looked as though Ruso had failed to mention her before because he was ashamed of her.

As Caratius showed them around the estate, Tilla seemed to be trying to make up for her bizarre behavior by being unusually sociable. She was busy complimenting their host on the mares and foals grazing in the paddocks when Ruso wandered a few paces farther along the track, which carried on past the house. He stopped. The river had not followed the course he had assumed. Instead it had swept round in a wide curve. Not only did it flow across Caratius's land: down there in the shifting shadows of the willow trees he could make out some sort of planking and mooring posts.

It was difficult to concentrate on the tour of the stables. He barely noticed the tack room, hung with plenty of jingling decorations for Caratius's slaves to polish. He had to force himself to pay attention to the conversation as they paused to watch a very small boy in man-sized boots hold the halter of a gray stallion while a man clamped its nearside hoof between his own thighs and circled it with a pair of long-handled pincers, clipping off a hard crescent of extra growth.

When Caratius finally left them in a hall that smelled of roasting beef and mold and went to warn the cook about the extra guest, he hissed, "What the hell are you doing here?"

"I am here to protect you."

"I thought you couldn't leave Camma on her own?"

"She is not on her own," said Tilla, looking pleased with herself. "The housekeeper came to pay respects to her master. She said she will stay while I am out."

"Well, don't say anything careless. I think the guard captain was Valens's burglar."

"I told you," she whispered, "you cannot trust these people."

She lifted her hands to tuck a solitary primrose into her ruffled hair. She was still flushed after the chase through the woods. How did this woman always manage to be desirable at inconvenient moments?

"Turn round," he ordered her as a slave approached clutching a towel. "Stand still. You've still got pieces of leaf stuck to your back."

37

THE MEN HAD gone into the dining room ahead of her. Tilla
settled herself on the stool, leaned against the wall, and stretched
out one leg so the slave could struggle with the knot in the damp leather
lacing of her boot.

She had made a fool of herself, and the Medicus was embarrassed. Still,
it was better to be a fool than a widow. Better to be embarrassed than to
suffer some "accident" at the hands of the Catuvellauni. He would come
to see that in a day or two. And at least she was getting dinner.

When the slave had finished drying her feet and taken her boots away
to clean, she was ushered into a big room where instead of good beef
there was all sorts of fiddly food set out in red bowls much like their own
on a low table. Her husband and Caratius stopped talking and turned to
look at her as if they had been discussing something important and secret.
Perhaps Caratius had been trying to find out what the Medicus knew
about the murder. Or perhaps he had been giving his own side of the
marriage story that both he and Camma had been too embarrassed to tell
in Londinium.

She sat in the wicker chair, relieved that this house did not have those
terrible dining couches to go with the foreign food. She had never understood how people could eat lying down. It was against all common

sense. A slave poured her watered wine, then offered her olives and oysters. She knew it was an odd combination. She might be a Northerner but she had traveled across the sea to places that most men like Caratius could only dream about. She supposed he was trying to impress.

Perhaps she had been worrying about nothing. Caratius did not know he was under suspicion. Besides, the man had spent money on the dinner. He would not do that if he were planning to attack his guest. He had just brought the Medicus out here to tell him what to think.

She glanced at her husband's bowl. He had stayed with the oysters. She helped herself to a couple of olives. The taste reminded her of Gaul. Caratius was boasting about his wine specially imported "from a man I know in Aquitania" and how their grandfathers had been friends and how he was thinking of inviting him over here to help set up a vineyard. The Medicus very politely did not say that his own family had been making wine back in Gaul for years and that anyone—even a British woman who preferred a good beer—could tell that it was better than the rubbish the grandfather's friend was sending over.

Caratius carried on gulping down oysters and ignoring her. He was too busy explaining why the Council would do well to listen to him in future and how the Medicus ought to go about his investigating. The Medicus was saying very little, perhaps waiting for Caratius to give something away by mistake.

Her hand slipped down to massage her bare toes. She could have outrun that big lad. She had been watching them for most of the journey. Neither of the so-called guards had paid any attention to a woman in a nondescript shawl hurrying along the road to get home before dark. None of them had noticed her slip into the woods. Even when she had startled a magpie and the big one had spun around and spotted her, she could have gotten away. She flexed her toes and rubbed away a sliver of grazed skin. If only she had noticed that tree root.

She shivered. The evening air drifting in through the window was chilly and Grata's shawl was damp after its roll in the leaves. Outside, she could see the Medicus's guards leading the stray horse up the track from the woods.

One of the slaves came in to light the lamps. Caratius stopped talking for long enough to grab another oyster and order the shutters closed. Before he could start again she said, "Have you told the investigator that you invited Julius Asper here to see you on the day he was killed?"

The point of Caratius's spoon skidded off the edge of the oyster and narrowly missed stabbing his thumb. The Medicus glared at her. Later on, no doubt, he would tell her he had a plan and she had wrecked it. When really, he was trying to find a way to ask, and not doing very well at it.

Caratius put the oyster down. "I think you are mistaken."

"I have been told," she said, "that he was not going to Londinium at all. He had a message to come here and see you. I have spoken to the housekeeper who took it."

"Here? No, no, no. I never wanted to go near the man. Absolutely not."

He turned to the Medicus. "This is the sort of thing I was telling you about earlier. False rumors. Cursing in public places. Vindictive behavior. I wasn't even at home that day."

That, of course, meant nothing at all. He could still have sent the message and ordered the murder. She said, "Asper thought you wanted to talk about—" She stopped. Outside in the hall, an old woman was shouting in British for help.

As they all leapt to their feet, Caratius was saying, "Please don't disturb yourselves!" and heading for the door. It burst open before he got there. A little woman with sparse white hair was shouting in a cracked voice, "They are here! Warriors in the woods!"

Caratius moved to put himself between her and his guests. He said in British, "It's all right, mother." He took hold of one thin arm and tried to steer her back out of the room. "They're just guards from town rounding up a loose horse. They won't hurt anybody. Mother, have you been hiding food again?"

"Let go of my bag!" Her hands were like claws, clutching a grimy sack to her chest. "I need my bag!"

The waft of roasting beef from the kitchen mingled with something more pungent.

"Just go to your room, mother. Nobody wants your bag. Where's that dratted girl?"

The woman peered past him. "What are those people doing in my house? Are they the ones who took our silver?"

"They're visiting, Mother. Guests come to share a meal. It's nothing to worry about."

A maid hurried in, flustered, and took the old woman by the arm. As she was led away she was still saying, "There are men in the woods!" and the maid was trying to reassure her.

Caratius turned to the Medicus. "I'm sorry. My mother is having a bad day." He cleared his throat. "You may have understood her talking about stealing. Please don't take offence. She's not well."

Tilla said, "Have you lost some silver?"

Caratius shook his head. "My mother remembers many things, but not in the right order. My grandfather's stock of silver was lost sixty years ago. If it ever existed. I'm sorry you were disturbed." He clapped his hands and a servant stepped out of the corner to stand at his shoulder. "We'll have the beef." He turned back to his guests. "Now, as I was saying . . ."

As he went back to talking about the Council, Tilla was distracted by a whispered conversation in the doorway behind her. The servant who was supposed to be fetching the beef hurried back into the room and murmured something into his master's ear. Caratius hissed in British, "Can't it wait?"

The servant did some more murmuring. Caratius's body jolted as if someone had just shot an arrow into his back. He looked at the Medicus. Suddenly efficient, he said, "Investigator, you need to come with me."

Before she could say anything, the Medicus gave her a look that said if she tried to follow, he would be very angry indeed. On the way out she heard Caratius giving someone orders to bring lanterns. She needed her shoes.

The hall was empty. Behind the farthest door she could hear the mother's anxious voice and the maid still trying to calm her. The main door was open. Servants and farmworkers had clustered out in the yard. All had their backs to the house and were standing looking toward the darkening woods.

What had the servant done with her shoes?

As she entered the kitchen a tabby cat leapt off the table, onto the sill, and out the open window. The steaming joint of beef sat abandoned on the table in a pool of congealing grease. The platter held the small clean wipes of tongue marks.

She found the shoes set back from the fire. The damp leather was cold and clammy around her feet. She had just closed the window shutters to keep the cat out when Caratius's mother wandered into the kitchen. The maid was close behind, looking almost as desperate as her charge. "Your little boy is a man now, mistress. He will make sure you are safe."

"You're lying to me!" insisted the mother. "Everybody lies to me. What have they done with my son? Where's my bag? I saw the warriors!"

"Your bag is here, mistress. You have everything you need. Your son is safe. We're all safe now. Come back and eat."

"Where's Father? Father is still down there. He thinks he can talk to them."

The maid shot Tilla a look of despair across the gloom of the shuttered kitchen.

"Your Da is in the next world with mine, Mother," Tilla assured her.

The woman backed away. "Who are you?"

"A friend," Tilla told her. "Your Da and mine are in the next world talking about the breeding of horses and my brothers are arguing with them and my mother is asking why they always have to shout."

"We don't care about horses. Father is a silversmith. We live behind the workshop. Who are you?"

"She's a friend, mistress," said the maid.

"A friend?"

"Yes."

The old woman's grip was surprisingly strong. "Where are your children?"

Tilla said, "I have no children."

The woman shook her head. "No, no. Always know where your children are. Always have a bag behind the door. See?"

She held out the bag. It did not smell good. "Bread and cheese, a blanket and a—a—"

"A comb," prompted the maid.

Trying to coax her toward the door, Tilla said, "Very good."

"Yes. Somebody will always take you in if you comb your hair and look respectable. Mother says so."

As they passed, the maid murmured in Tilla's ear, "I think it's seeing those men set her off. She thinks she's a child again. Her father was killed when the Iceni raided the town."

"What's that? What is she saying?"

There was nothing wrong with the old woman's hearing. "We are all safe here, Mother," Tilla assured her.

"That's what they told us. The warriors will never come here. The army will stop them."

"The army has stopped them."

"Put your shawl over your nose when you run through the smoke. Hold Mother's hand." The bag fell to the floor as the thin hands went up over her face. "Don't smell the man with his clothes on fire. Don't hear them calling for help."

"It is over now."

"Can you hear the other mothers?" The vein tracks on her hands glistened with tears. "Listen! They are calling for my lost friends who went out to play."

Tilla swallowed. She put an arm around the thin shoulders.

"Always keep a bag by the door," whispered the old woman. "Always know where your children are."

By the time Tilla and the maid had settled the mother with a large cup of strong beer (sometimes, according to the maid, it was the only way), it was dark. Tilla went out onto the porch. She could hear the voices of the men returning from the woods. There were three lanterns bobbing about by the track. A couple of them headed off toward the stables. The third came back toward the house. She unfastened the safety strap on her knife. In all the fuss with the mother, she had forgotten the Medicus altogether. Anything could have happened. "Who is there?"

"It's all right, Tilla."

She relaxed her grip on the knife. "What is happening?"

She could make him out now, on the left of a group of five or six men. Dias was one of the two supporting a stumbling Caratius. Caratius, unusually, seemed to be having trouble with his words. "I still can't believe . . . To think that . . . Out there all this time . . . How terrible this must . . . I never thought anyone would stoop to this!"

The Medicus was talking to him in the way he spoke to his patients. "Don't worry about it tonight," he was saying. "Just go indoors, keep warm, and have a hot drink with some honey in it."

"Whoever did this has no fear. No fear of gods or men. We are all in danger."

As he came into the light, Tilla could see a leaf caught in the long gray hair and mud smeared across his face. All of the men seemed to have muck on their clothes and boots and there was a smell about them that she did not like. The Medicus followed them into the house. As he passed Tilla he murmured, "I'll just get him settled, then we're going straight back to town."

"But what—?"

"While they were rounding up that horse in the woods," he said, "they found the remains of the missing brother."

38

RUSO WOKE TO a sense that there was a heavy burden lurking just beyond the comfort of his bed and that when he opened his eyes he would have to get up and shoulder it. Sooner than he wished, the sound of a horse whinnying in the stables brought back the memory of last night: the ghastly journey to town in the dark, enveloped in the smell that none of them would ever forget. Gavo driving the borrowed cart with a subdued Tilla beside him. Dias riding next to Ruso, quietly taking charge of transporting the body in a manner so professional that Ruso began to wonder if he had been mistaken about him. Maybe Dias was no more than an ambitious young man with an overactive love life.

There had been no thought of taking Bericus's remains to lie indoors next to Asper. The cart had been left in the cemetery all night with a pair of lanterns for company. Dias had observed that nobody was going to steal it, and if anyone but Ruso had felt a slight chill at the thought of ghosts and murderers, or imagined they glimpsed some movement in the darkness as they glanced back over their shoulders, they had not spoken of it. Dias had promised to alert the local doctor and ask him to join them in the morning to see what they could find out before a hasty cremation. Finally, once Tilla had been safely delivered back to Camma's house with the bad news, Ruso had returned to the mansio, dismissed his guard, and made sure the doors of Suite Three were securely locked.

He swung his feet onto the floor and stretched and yawned before splashing his face with water from the bowl. Then he wandered barefoot out onto the wooden walkway and told the passing slave that he would not be needing breakfast after all. Before long he was going to have to face the remains of Bericus in daylight. He leaned out over the rail that separated the walkway from the garden and took a deep breath of chilly air. The sun was not fully up, but the sky was clear. It would be a fine morning.

A servant emerged from the main kitchen, carried a pail across to one of the flowerbeds, and carefully ran a stream of water along a row of seedlings. Another appeared farther along the walkway with a bundle of bedding clutched to her chest and threw it over the rail. Ruso wondered whether Asper's funeral procession had set off yet. Tilla had promised to break the latest bad news to Camma and the housekeeper last night.

He wished Tilla were not caught up in this wretched affair. She was only trying to help, but her presence was a further complication. Her courage was beyond doubt. But courage and loyalty would not be enough. He needed to be impartial, objective, and highly alert if he was to steer a safe course for them both among the procurator's politics, Metellus's scheming, and whatever the hell Caratius—and possibly Dias—had been up to. He did not need the distraction of worrying about his wife.

Ruso frowned at a beetle scurrying along the edge of a flowerbed and tried to order his thoughts. Caratius had strenuously denied any involvement in the murder, but he had no explanation for why Julius Bericus had been found on his land. It must be the work of "some enemy," or "that woman's curse." The servants and laborers whom there had been time to question seemed as shocked as their master.

Camma had been right about Bericus all along. He was not responsible for the death of his brother. Ruso wondered briefly if events might have happened the other way around—if Asper had been injured while murdering Bericus for his share of the money—but digging even Bericus's pathetically shallow grave would have been beyond the strength of a man with a serious head injury.

There seemed to be three versions of events, and not all of them could be true. He pressed his right forefinger onto the rail as if to hold down the first version while he considered the others.

Asper and his brother had taken the money, intending to deliver it to Londinium.
Second finger.
Asper and his brother had taken the money, intending to steal it.
Third finger.
Asper and his brother had not taken the money at all, as they were intending to visit Caratius and then go home.
This led to three possibilities. Left hand.
Asper had lied about his intentions.
Second finger.
Someone was mistaken about what Asper had said and done.
Third finger.
Someone was lying to him.

Perhaps the answer lay in whatever Asper had been trying to tell Metellus in that ill-fated letter to Room Twenty-seven. That was unfortunate because he still had no idea what it was. He was going to have to recheck everyone's story. He also needed to go to a funeral, examine a body, report officially to the Council, get into Asper's office, talk to the local money changer . . .

Farther along the walkway, a door opened. A child's voice was raised in complaint. A slave emerged with both hands full of bags. Behind her he heard the child insisting that she wanted to stay here. Ruso shrugged his shoulders a couple of times to loosen them before he turned and headed back into Suite Three to get properly dressed and face the day.

That was when he noticed the pale rectangular shape lying just inside the street door. He flipped open the thin leaves of wood. Neatly penned across them in a bland script were the words, *Get out of town as fast as you can. From a well-wisher.*

He snatched the key from the hook, sliding it back and forth in the lock with an unsteady hand and swearing as the prongs failed to find the holes. Finally he wrenched the door open.

Dias was leaning against the stable wall opposite. The rest of the alley was empty except for a couple of hens scratching in the dirt.

Ruso forced himself to stay calm. "How long have you been there?"

"I came to take you to the cemetery, sir. The doctor's on his way out there now."

"Why didn't you knock?"

"I did."

"Did you see anybody put a note under my door?"

"No. Is there a problem?"

Ruso retreated. "No. I'll be ready in a minute."

Get out of town as fast as you can.

Why? And how long had Dias been standing there? Had he put the note there himself and then waited calmly for Ruso to find it?

He should have checked the street door as soon as he got up. Instead, he had wandered out to the garden with his mind full of the day ahead. The note could have been there all night.

He was halfway to the reception area when Serena's cousin, whose name he had forgotten again, came out of the door clutching a ring of heavy keys. "Hello Ruso! There's a message for you to pop next door and look at a carriage. How was your dinner party?"

"Short," he said. Evidently the news about Bericus had not reached her yet. "I've had a confidential note pushed under the door," he continued, "but nobody's signed it. Could you ask the staff if anyone saw anything? Has anyone been asking which room I was in?"

"Of course." A furrow appeared between the neatly plucked brows. "Are you all right? You look a bit pale."

"I'm fine," he assured her, backing away and giving what he hoped was a reassuring wave. "Absolutely fine. No problem at all. Fine."

Any illusion that she might have believed him was spoiled as he heard her say, "Oh dear."

39

T HERE WAS NO need to go to the stables to find Rogatus: Outside the mansio the overseer's bandy legs were stationed next to a vehicle whose roof was being loaded with luggage.

"You wanted to see it before it went out, boss."

The carriage was old and much repaired. Ruso walked all around it, conscious that Dias was watching him and wishing he knew what he was looking for. There was a fresh scrape along one side at about the right height for the overhanging oak. Other signs of damage to the woodwork could have been caused by wear and tear. There were no marks that looked like weapon scars. Rogatus, who clearly thought this was a waste of time, said he could see nothing, either.

"Perhaps," said Ruso, crouching to squint along the shadowy line of a mud-spattered axle and wondering who wanted him out of town, "you could remind me exactly what Asper said about where he was going."

"He was on the way to your office, boss," replied the man without hesitation. "He'd got the tax money ready to go."

Noting that he had now become *boss* instead of *sir*, Ruso said, "Did he mention calling on anyone on the way?"

"Not a word, boss."

"And you've no idea why he was setting out so late?"

"I never asked. He could have made it before dark, though."

Ruso moved to the front and eyed the hefty team of four who would pull the carriage to its next destination. "Are these—?"

"That's them," Rogatus confirmed.

One horse was munching thoughtfully on its bit. Another bent its neck to rub its muzzle against an itch on its left foreleg. None looked highly strung. Rogatus had rightly described the carriage as a "heavy old vehicle" and Ruso suspected the weight must be near the limit of their strength. Evidently the overseer did not believe in wasting horsepower. This was not a carriage that could outrun a mounted enemy, and he could see why it had not been stolen for a fast getaway.

He approached the weather-beaten native who was loading the luggage. "Are you the regular driver?"

"It's no good talking to him, boss," put in Rogatus. "He don't know a thing."

The native sniffed, wiped his nose on the back of his hand, and swung a heavy bag up into the carriage. "At least I know how to drive." Continuing in Latin that was effective rather than elegant, he added, "Him over there, he tell me there is no work for the day, then he give my team to some fool who lose them on the road and he think I will not find out."

Rogatus pretended not to have heard. "Like I said before, boss, I was doing the tax man a favor. Most of us around here"—plainly this excluded the sniffing driver—"know how to show a bit of respect to authority."

"Hah!" said the driver before Ruso could answer. "It is himself he is doing the favor to. The tax man drives, and the driver gets no wages."

"The driver might get some wages," said Rogatus, "If he got off his backside a bit more often."

The driver tutted. "It is lucky I am a patient man," he said, shaking his head as if contemplating the horrors that would ensue if he were not. "Without me here, his stables will fall to pieces."

Rogatus gave the smallest of shrugs, as if the driver were not worth the effort of more. "Good luck getting any sense out of that one, boss. I tell you, if the rest of him worked as hard as his mouth, he'd be a wonder."

The driver stabbed a rude gesture toward Rogatus's departing back before bending to lift the next trunk. Ruso could imagine returning in twenty years' time to find the pair of them toothless and shriveled with age, propping up opposite ends of the same bar and still complaining about each other over their beers to anyone who would listen.

The driver gasped a few choice words in British as he heaved up the weight of the trunk. It landed on the floor of the carriage with a crash. "What is it women put in these things?" he demanded.

"Crockery," said Ruso.

The driver stepped back from the door. "You want a look, then? Have a look."

Ruso climbed in, and out, and learned nothing other than the fact that today's passengers had vast amounts of luggage. He was outside on the driver's seat assessing how well he could see approaching robbers when a boy's voice announced, "That's a new driver."

Ruso turned and recognized the officer's family he had seen stopping to use the latrines at the posting station yesterday. He explained his presence with, "I've just finished checking your vehicle."

"He is here to ask questions," the real driver explained. "The last man who take it is murder on the road and the horses run off."

The woman gave a small squeak of terror and clutched at both children.

"No problems, mistress," the driver continued, giving her a grin that displayed a solitary tooth and slapping the nearest horse on the neck as if to show how dependable it was. "All safe with me today."

Ruso climbed down, fixing him with the same look that had frightened Albanus's young followers and the innkeeper's wife. The driver did not seem to notice.

"Was it the natives?" asked the girl, peering wide eyed from behind her mother's skirts.

"Of course it was," the boy said. "I bet they tied him up and stuck a big spike through his—"

"No they didn't!" said Ruso and the mother in unison.

At that moment the riders who had been escorting the family yesterday clattered out of the stables and halted, two in front of the vehicle and two behind. Ruso had just promised the mother that she would be perfectly safe when Serena's voice called out from the top of the mansio steps, "Of course you'll be safe! I hope Ruso hasn't been frightening you with some silly nonsense about the natives?"

The woman was looking up at Serena with the expression of a stray dog begging to be taken in.

"Absolutely not," insisted Ruso.

"Good," said Serena. "There's no need to worry about the natives down here. You'll meet the dangerous tribes in the North." After these words of doubtful comfort, she added, "Have a good journey!"

"You'll be fine," Ruso assured the woman. "You're on the main road and you have a good escort."

"But that poor man who was—"

"He was a native himself," said Ruso, knowing that would reassure her. "He was known to be carrying a lot of money and he had no guards with him."

The woman said, "Why not?"

"That's what I'm trying to work out." He glanced across at Dias, who seemed to be more interested in the maid sweeping the steps, and wondered whether he knew.

Before leaving he stepped back inside the mansio and told Serena and the cousin that if there were any urgent messages, he would be out at the cemetery with Dias to supervise a postmortem examination and then he was going to report to the Council.

Dias, who must have overheard, greeted him with something that might have been a smile. Or a smirk. Without knowing what the man was thinking, Ruso had no way of telling the difference.

40

THE MORNING HAD not started well. Tilla woke to the sound of the baby crying and the pallbearers hammering on a door that bore a damp streak and a fresh tang of urine. Camma looked haggard and smelled unwashed. When Tilla asked if she had slept, she did not seem to know. She had insisted on huddling under some blankets on the couch, sharing the front room for one last night with her lover. Tilla had gone to lie awake in the curtained space just off the kitchen that used to belong to Grata. The second bedroom had a better bed, but it held Bericus's clothes and smelled of his hair oil, and neither of them could face going in there.

The kitchen fire had collapsed into a pile of warm ash. There was no time to revive it. While the men loaded up the bier, Tilla encouraged Camma to wash in the cold water from the bucket and pull on some fresh clothes.

At the last minute Camma decided there should be a coin in Asper's mouth, just in case a man who collected taxes for Rome needed to pay the ferryman, and then decided she could not face placing it there. Tilla searched her purse, took a deep breath, and did it herself.

They set off while the sun was barely more than a red tinge below a streak of cloud in the east. Dias had not only kept his word, but instead of leaving it to the cemetery slaves, he had sent four guards to carry the body, all smartly dressed in their scarlet tunics and chain mail. One of them had brought a torch, which he handed to Tilla.

If the pallbearers were impressive, the party of mourners following Julius Asper on his final journey through the chilly streets of Verulamium was pitifully small. Two women and a baby, only one of whom had known the deceased when he was alive. Several early risers stopped to watch them pass, but none chose to join them. Tilla could not help noticing that the watching faces bore more curiosity than sorrow. She had wondered if Grata might come, but there was no sign of her. Her new job was in a bakery: She was probably at work.

By the time they passed through the town gates and out along the road, the sky was pale and clear. The soft wailing of the small procession blended with the morning birdsong. Almost as if he understood, the baby woke up and began to cry as well.

There was a faint scent of bluebells drifting across from the woods behind the cemetery. The dew soaked into Tilla's boots as they picked their way between the grave markers to the circle of trampled grass that must have seen many Catuvellauni dispatched to the next world. The cemetery slaves had already stacked two pyres. With Asper laid out on the nearest one, they began to place more brushwood and dried holly over the body. Tilla guessed that the second pyre was for Bericus. She hoped Camma had not noticed the cart parked behind the workers' hut at the far end of the cemetery. The two guards who seemed to be responsible were standing well away from it.

More men appeared from the direction of the town. A group of four stationed themselves on the far side of the clearing without acknowledging the widow. One of them, a servant, opened up a folding stool. The fat one with the short hair and close-cropped beard sat facing the pyre and tapping a jeweled forefinger on his knee, as if he was a busy man who was counting the time he was spending here. His smaller companion stood slightly to one side. He was fingering some sort of charm around his neck and looking around warily, as though something might go wrong at any moment and when it did, he expected to get the blame.

She was pleased to see the Medicus arrive with Dias and another of his troop. They too stood facing the pyres. Tilla decided there must be a wondrous number of town guards if four pallbearers, their captain, and a sixth man could be spared to see off Julius Asper and his brother. Perhaps they were embarrassed that a double murder had taken place almost on their doorstep.

There was, of course, no sign of Caratius.

The cemetery staff finished their work and stood back. The wailing fell silent. Nearer to the road, a family of starlings erupted into a noisy squabble over some tidbit in the grass. Around the pyre, there was a foot-shuffling, glance-exchanging pause that suggested somebody was supposed to be doing something, but nobody knew who or what it was. Dias was gazing into the middle distance as if none of this had anything to do with him. Tilla guessed that he had not thought beyond organizing the cremation.

Finally Camma whispered, "Should someone speak?"

Tilla whispered, "Go on."

"What can I say?"

Anything would be better than this lengthening silence. Tilla said, "Give the call and send him on his way. His son is too small to light the flames: You will have to do it."

With some difficulty they exchanged torch and baby, Camma murmuring an unnecessary "Look after him for me" before she stepped forward across the well-trodden ground.

The cry of "Julius Asper, wake up!" silenced the birdsong. As expected, the corpse made no response. The baby began to cry again. Tilla licked the top of her little finger clean and slid it between his lips. She felt the warm wet gums clamp around it. The crying stopped.

Careful to keep the torch away from the wood, Camma reached for the jug one of the slaves had placed at the foot of the pyre. The scent of roses wafted across as the oil dripped down through the brushwood and soaked into the shroud.

Camma stumbled several times as she circled around the pyre with the torch raised. When she came to a standstill she looked white faced and exhausted. Instead of lowering the torch, she looked around the small company. "Someone should speak."

Tilla swallowed. Why did she not lower the torch and light the pyre? Who would be willing to speak on behalf of Julius Asper? From the humblest slave to the wealthy visitor and his flunkies, all the mourners had their eyes fixed anywhere but on the woman who was asking them to honor her man. Tilla no longer believed he was a thief, and she knew the Medicus did not, either, but how could they explain that to everyone in the middle of a funeral?

"Magistrate?" Camma's voice was hoarse.

The fat man stopped tapping and leaned across to mutter something to his companion, who looked even more worried than before.

"Chief Magistrate Gallonius!" Camma was addressing the seated man by name now, still holding the torch away from the pyre. "You represent the Council. This man collected your taxes. Will you speak?"

The magistrate said something else to his companion, who explained, "The magistrate is here to observe in a private capacity, madam. He cannot speak on behalf of the Council without their agreement."

"Can he not speak as a man?"

No reply.

"You, Nico? You worked with him."

The little man raised his palms as if he were trying to fend her off, but she had already turned away.

"Dias?"

No reply.

"Not one of you?" She sighed. "Not a single one of these cowards dares to open his mouth."

Tilla and the Medicus looked at each other. He frowned, giving her a look that said a man working for the procurator should not get involved in tribal affairs, and neither should his wife.

"Just light it, woman!" The rich bass of the magistrate Gallonius was that of a man well used to making himself heard. "We haven't got all day."

Camma bent over the body. The few words she spoke were whispered to Julius Asper. Then at last, to everyone's relief, she lowered the torch. Flames began to lick and crackle around the brushwood. Black smoke rose into the sky as she moved around, touching fuel with fire. Finally she knelt and thrust the torch into the base of the pyre. The oil-soaked logs disappeared behind a curtain of flame.

The baby had drifted off to sleep in Tilla's arms. He would not be aware of the smell of the burning, nor feel the heat that was already wafting toward the mourners.

He would not see the bewildered expressions of those mourners as his mother faced that pyre with her hands raised to the gods.

He would not hear the scream that sent the birds fluttering out of the trees with cries of their own as she shrieked her curse upon Caratius and strode toward the flames. He would not share the horror of the onlookers when they realized what was happening.

Figures were rushing toward the pyre as Tilla lunged for a fistful of

Camma's skirt. The Medicus and the guards grabbed Camma by the arms and the hair and everyone dragged her back from the fire. Tilla thrust the baby into the arms of a bemused cemetery slave and went to help the Medicus and the guards beat at the sparks gleaming in Camma's clothes and frizzling the unruly red hair.

Camma's face was flushed with the heat. She looked confused, as if she had just been woken from a dream.

"I will deal with her," Tilla insisted, shooing the men out of the way. "What is the matter with you?" she hissed, pulling Camma's clothes straight and tutting at the scorch marks in the wool. "How can you get justice if you are dead too?"

"I will die cursing him and be with Asper in the next world!"

"You will not!" Tilla insisted. "I have not gone to all this trouble just so you can die. Now stay there. I will speak, and you will listen." She beckoned to the nearest guard, who stood ready to grab Camma if she made another dangerous move.

Tilla could feel the warmth on her flesh as she stepped toward the pyre. She had no idea what she was going to say. She turned and glanced around at the pitiful collection of mourners. Dias, she realized, had not moved at all during the commotion. The fat magistrate had gotten to his feet but was now seated again and looking exasperated. The flunky that Camma had called Nico was chewing his thumbnail. She did not look at her husband. She was not supposed to get involved. Well, it was too late now.

"This man," she announced in Latin, "was Julius Asper." That was safe enough. "He lived for thirty-four winters." She hoped she had remembered that correctly. "He collected taxes for Rome, and he and his brother were cruelly murdered before he could see the beautiful son who has been born to him." At least the Medicus would approve of that much.

Conscious of the flames at her back, she raised her hands and cried, "Whatever sacred gods may be willing to listen to us, we ask you to guide Julius Asper safely into the next world. Holy Christos, if you are up there sitting at the right hand of your father . . ."—she was deliberately not looking at her husband—"we will be glad if you lean across and ask him to forgive what this man did in this life. Look after him in the next life. Protect his family . . ." She glanced around at the magistrate and the guards and the slaves. It occurred to her that someone would tell Caratius about Camma's fresh curse. They might mention the Northern woman who had come forward to support her, and Caratius would know who it was. She had a feeling the Medicus was going to be very cross indeed.

It was no good worrying about that now. "Give courage to all these people who have come to honor him," she cried. "Make them speak the truth! Make them tell how an enemy lured Julius Asper to his death so that there will be justice!"

The flames were roaring now. She could feel sweat breaking out on her back. The wool of her tunic felt prickly. It was a relief to say "Amen!" and step away. Without waiting to see the reaction, she collected the baby from the slave who was holding it as if it might bite him, and took Camma by the hand.

"Come, sister," she said, leading her away through the cool spring grass. "He is gone, and you have a son to look after."

41

RUSO STRODE THROUGH the cemetery with his fists clenched, ignoring Dias and Gavo, who were hurrying to keep pace with him. Tilla had just flouted all his instructions. Thanks to that bizarre—not to mention illegal—public prayer, the whole town would soon know that the wife of the procurator's man was taking Camma's side in the dispute. She had more or less accused Caratius of murder.

She had undermined the credibility of his investigation. She had put him in an impossible position. She had . . . he was running out of words to describe what she had done. What was more, he knew that when he objected, she would come up with some irrational way of justifying it.

Get out of town as fast as you can.

He would like nothing better than to get out of town, but he had accepted the job, and, besides, if he abandoned the investigation, what would Metellus do?

He didn't want to find out.

Word must have spread about the discovery of Bericus's body: At the far end of the cemetery a gaggle of adults, youths, and even half a dozen scruffy children were gathered just beyond the reach of the guards. There was a murmur of interest as he passed between them on his way to the cart that had been parked well away from the pyres. When he turned they were craning to see what he would do next. He restrained an impulse to tell them that the dead man had not been brought here for their entertainment.

A pot-bellied man with straggly gray hair and a tunic spattered with old blood was crouching in the back of the cart. He was reaching forward with one hand and clutching a cloth over his nose with the other. Ruso paused to tie his neckerchief over his own nose and mouth before swinging up to sit backward on the worn wooden seat, tuck his feet well out of the way, and observe what was happening.

The pot-bellied man was the local doctor, and he was not happy in his work. Yes, he agreed as he put away the bronze probe with which he had been investigating the corpse, the deceased could have been dead for five or six days. Any fool could see that he hadn't died yesterday. Probably being severely battered around the head would have killed him. It tended to do that. Now if that was all, there were live patients waiting back in town.

Having made a courtesy gesture to the local man, Ruso was about to finish the job himself when there was a disturbance among the gawpers. A small dark woman was being manhandled away by one of the guards. Instead of admitting defeat she was shouting, "Let me through!"

Ruso recognized the person Tilla had been talking to by the water fountain yesterday. "Isn't that Asper's housekeeper?"

The doctor ordered Dias to keep her back. "This is no sight for a woman."

"I'd like to talk to her," said Ruso.

"Absolutely not!" said the doctor. "We know who this is. You can still just about make out the damage to the ear. I don't need a fainting female on my hands as well."

Ruso leaned out and beckoned to a cemetery slave who was passing with a basket load of kindling. "Hand me up that sheet over there, will you?"

"I won't allow this!" insisted the doctor. "I am the doctor here, and that woman is one of my patients."

"And I'm the investigator," said Ruso, his respect for the doctor rising. If the roles had been reversed, he would have been just as indignant. He turned to Dias. "Give me a minute and then have her brought over."

"I protest!"

"I'm not enjoying this, either," conceded Ruso, standing up and shaking the folds out of the rough linen sheet. "But I once knew somebody who went to her husband's funeral only to have him turn up alive and well three weeks later." It was an exaggeration: He had never met the apocryphal woman, but it had been one of his uncle's favorite stories. "Let's have her make sure, shall we?"

The doctor clambered down from the cart, still complaining as he left. Ruso flung the sheet over the body. Then he retrieved one of the sandals that had been placed in the corner of the cart, loosened his neckerchief, and jumped down.

Grata wrenched her arm out of Dias's grasp as Ruso approached. Dias said something but if she heard it, she did not reply. Ruso dismissed him and said quietly, "I'm the investigator. We think this is your master."

In a small voice, as if she was not sure it was true, Grata said, "I want to see."

"He is not how you remember him." He produced the sandal from behind his back. One of the thongs had snapped and been retied, the sole needed restitching at the toes, and the whole thing was swollen with damp. "If you can identify this, there's no need for any more."

She put one hand over her mouth.

He had to be certain. "Did this belong to Julius Bericus?"

She nodded.

"I am sorry."

She nodded again, as if she did not know what else to do.

"If there's anything you can tell me that might help me find out—"

"No! No, I know nothing."

She had lived in the same house as the dead man. Perhaps they had been fond of each other. He said, "I heard there was a message from someone inviting the brothers to visit."

"A message for Asper," she said. "From Caratius."

"Who brought that message, Grata?"

She gathered up her skirts. "One of his servants."

"Which one?"

She did not answer. He thought she was about to walk away. Instead she moved toward the cart. The doctor in Ruso wanted to go after her: to head her off with a warning about the dangers of bad air and the news that she could pay her respects at the pyre in a few minutes and . . . and anything that would stop her from seeing what she was about to see.

There was a murmur from the gawpers as she reached the cart and lifted the sheet. The investigator in Ruso left her there—alone, one hand clamped over her mouth and nose, taking in what man and nature had done.

The doctor in him told the investigator he should have stopped her.

Grata turned and walked straight back the way she had come, arms tightly folded, battered boots kicking her skirts out of the way. Her face was set like a wax model.

As she passed him Ruso murmured, "If you think of anything, speak to Tilla. Nobody will know who told me."

His gaze followed her lonely progress between the graves to the road. The investigator in him had done rather well. The doctor in him warned the investigator that he couldn't stand much more of this.

He turned to find Dias at his shoulder. He took a breath and said brightly, "Right. I've finished here."

"You bastard," Dias said, so softly so that no one but Ruso could hear. "You didn't need to do that to her. You evil bastard."

42

THERE WAS NO funeral feast, either at the cemetery or afterward. The women returned to a silent house. No neighbors called to ease the long wait between the burning and the hour tomorrow when the ashes would be cool enough for burial. The empty shoes were still in a pair by the door, ready for a man who no longer needed them.

Camma was still in this world, but her eyes were dull and her mind was filled with dark clouds. She lay slumped on the couch, seemingly unaware of the baby at her breast. Tilla clattered the shutters open and apologized to the household gods for leaving them with the smell that still lingered despite yesterday's efforts with the scrubbing brush, and then apologized to Christos for paying attention to them. Over the sea in Gaul, people would have said she ought to choose one or the other. Here, she was not so sure.

Camma said suddenly, "We should have stayed to say good-bye to Bericus."

"The men will look after him."

"Poor Bericus. I prayed to Andaste, but it was too late. He was already gone."

Tilla said, "The brothers will be together in the next world," and Camma's eyes filled with tears.

When the baby drifted off to sleep, his mother settled him in the box and wandered down the gloomy corridor toward the bedroom. Tilla stood over him, watching the flicker of his eyelids and marking each tiny rise and fall of the blanket with his breathing. She tried to imagine how desperate a woman would have to be to leave a helpless baby in the care of strangers and follow her man to the next world.

He might not sleep for long. She must use the time well. She began to count on her fingers all the jobs that needed to be done. Suddenly overwhelmed, she reached for a darned sock that had fallen behind the couch. It was too big to belong to Camma. She went to the little room where Bericus had slept and added the sock to the loincloths and spare trousers and three tunics and an old belt lying in an untidy jumble on the bed. Asper's clothes must be in the next room with Camma. All of that, like naming the baby, was a problem for later.

She must do one job at a time.

First, water.

She walked down to the corner water pipe clutching the buckets and pretended not to notice the way the conversation died as she approached. In response to her question, the women said they did not know of any followers of Christos in the town. In fact they had never heard of Christos.

Back in Gaul, the brothers and sisters would have seized this chance to share the good news. Tilla, feeling she had enough problems already, decided to leave Verulamium in ignorance for a while longer.

She had let the water fill too high. Trying not to spill any, she crouched to pick up both buckets and made her way slowly back along the uneven cobblestones of the street, all the while wrestling with the problem of how, now that she had gotten herself into this, she was going to get out of it again.

Be careful how much help you promise.

Helping a woman in labor was only natural. Supporting a woman who had been bereaved and wronged—especially by the Catuvellauni—was a good thing to do. But should she have waved Camma and her baby good-bye at the gates of Londinium with good wishes and a blessing and gone back to minding her own business?

You can't fight her battles for her, Tilla.

He was wrong: She had not wanted to get involved. She had wanted to believe that Julius Asper was faithless and that Camma would have a better life without him. Instead, she had somehow ended up demanding justice for him in public and helping to curse the local magistrate.

Once the word spread about Camma and the pyre, it would be even harder to find someone to take on the job of housekeeper. Perhaps a message could be sent to the Iceni about the baby. Maybe if they understood how desperate their princess was, they would relent and allow her back.

In the meantime, the neighbors here were unlikely to be much help. The workshop next door was owned by a pair of elderly bronzesmiths. On the other side, the woman had grudgingly given her a light when she could not find the flint yesterday and insisted on telling her that if anything was wrong next door, it was not their fault. "You tell that woman if she's got any complaints, it's nothing to do with us."

"What sort of complaints?"

"It's not enough we have to put up with the tax man and his fancy woman," the neighbor had said, ramming Tilla's proffered stick of kindling into the fire and waiting for it to catch. "You should have heard the goings-on in there the other night. I never heard anything like it. That other one—what's her name?"

"Grata?" Tilla suggested.

"Voice like a fishwife. Language. They even woke Father up."

"She was all alone and there were frightening people outside."

The woman ignored her and leaned across the hearth to shout at a pile of blankets in the corner, "Didn't they, Father?"

The blankets shifted and a white head emerged. "What?"

"All that shouting next door. They woke you up."

"What's she doing here?"

"Nothing. She's just leaving."

And that was before Camma had tried to join Asper in the next world. It seemed that even if her mind were restored to order, an incomer who had betrayed a local husband and allied herself with a tax collector believed to be a thief would be at the wrong end of any queue for help.

43

R USO KNEW THAT the tongue of the Britons boasted a rich vo-
cabulary of insult. He was unable to translate much of it, since his
wife used it chiefly when she was too exasperated to continue in Latin,
but he recognized it being shouted across Verulamium's Council chamber as the door guards moved aside to let him enter. His arrival went
unnoticed by the thirty or forty quarreling men within, who between
them were wearing more togas than he had seen together for years. It
struck him that, unusually for the Britons, there was not a woman in
sight.

Ruso lingered just inside the entrance, letting the din wash over him
while he waited for a suitable moment to present himself. The air smelled
of hair oil and musty wool. The plain walls around him were adorned with
a series of engraved bronze plaques crammed with what he supposed were
the rules of the Council: presumably the constitution dictated by Rome
when the town had been granted permission to govern itself. It was an
illustration of how far these remote island peoples had come. Or been led
by the nose. He was not sure which.

A pale clerk was standing to one side, stylus poised to note any deci-
sions. It looked as though he would be waiting a long time.

Ruso managed to catch odd phrases about the honor of the magistrates, the honor of the town, and something to do with "when the emperor comes." Finally, "You were there when it was decided!" was followed by a familiar voice shouting, "Against my advice!"

A couple of councillors sat down in disgust, allowing him to see Caratius seated in a metal-framed chair at the front. His expression was grim. Gallonius, less exposed and more authoritative than he had been at the baths, rose from a seat beside him and clambered up onto a small podium. His rich voice was impressive but his words were drowned by the furore, and under the circumstances a toga had not been the best choice of garment. In fact, a toga was not the best garment for anything that Ruso could immediately think of, and Gallonius was having trouble keeping his under control. Every time he forgot it and raised both hands to emphasise his point, the heavy wool slid over his arm toward the floor and he had to grab it to maintain some dignity. Someone had attached it to his elegant cream tunic with a secret pin, but the pin was now exposed as the fulcrum of a lopsided tangle of fabric hanging off one shoulder. As he tried to wrench it back into position, someone shouted, "Just take it off, man! You're only a butcher!"

So Gallonius must be the councillor whose country estate supplied overpriced meat to the mansio. He raised both arms again and bellowed, "Silence!" but nobody took any notice.

"The question is," insisted someone else above the confusion, "What are we going to do?"

"Silence!" shouted Caratius, leaping out of his chair to intervene at last. "This is—"

His voice was drowned beneath a cacophony of shouts and jeers. He gesticulated to the clerk, who reached behind the podium and produced a horn. Finally a blast of noise cut through the babble. "I insist we wait for the procurator's man," declared Caratius.

"Why?" someone demanded, adding something that sounded like, "What does he know that we don't?"

Ruso, who had no idea, took a deep breath and stepped forward.

Moments later, he was regretting it. Under the guise of introducing him, Caratius had seized him by the arm, led him up onto the podium, and abandoned him there with the whispered words, "Tell them it wasn't me!"

Ruso looked around the hall. He was surrounded by Britons whose ancestors must have been barbarian chiefs and druids and rabble-rousing warriors. Now they were arrayed on their benches, many of them draped in the garb of Roman citizens, all watching him and waiting for him to speak on behalf of the Imperial procurator. Not only that, but Caratius was demanding to be defended.

He cleared his throat. The sound died away into an unnerving silence. Inside his head, a small voice urged him to say . . . *something*. Gods above, he had heard enough speeches! Why could he not remember anything from any of them?

Caratius was sitting very upright in his seat. Gallonius was standing with his arms held wide while a slave struggled to restore some dignity to his toga. He recognized one or two faces from yesterday's trip to the bathhouse.

His mouth was dry.

Say something.

"Speak in Latin!" urged someone at the back who had misunderstood the problem.

Dias was standing in the open doorway, listening.

What would Cicero do?

Perhaps he should start by declaring how venerable and wise this assembly was and how, despite being inexperienced and feeling daunted by the magnitude of the task that lay before him . . .

Perhaps not. Gazing out at the expectant faces of the Catuvellauni, Ruso had the feeling that a man who tried that sort of smooth talking here would very soon regret it. He was conscious of an awkward shuffling among his audience: of sidelong glances and whispers. *Say something.*

He opened his mouth.

Even as the words came out, he knew that "If only Julius Caesar could see this" was not the most tactful way to start. There was a tense silence. Then someone at the back called out, "We'd show him!"

There was a roar of agreement. The Britons were cheering. He let out his breath. They seemed to think he had given them the cue for a joke.

Encouraged, he squared his shoulders and told himself that this was just like giving a report on a patient. He had to tell the truth while avoiding the parts the relatives didn't need to know. "I'm sorry to have to confirm," he said, "that your tax collector and his brother have both been killed. Asper was found dead in Londinium two days ago. Last night the body of his brother was—"

"We know all that!" called a voice from the back while someone else yelled, "And we know who did it!" and one or two shouted, "Where's our money?"

"I haven't found it yet," said Ruso.

"Who's going to pay if you don't?" demanded a lone voice over shouts of "Ask Caratius!" At least one of the men now accusing Caratius had insisted to Ruso only yesterday that the money had been stolen by Asper.

His voice rose to penetrate the din. "The question of who's going to pay is up to the procurator to answer, not me. I'll be trying to trace the money—"

There was a shout of "So are we all!" and "Ask Caratius!" and one ominous "Ask your wife, man, she knows more than you do already!"

Gallonius roared something in British which sounded like, "Shut up and let the man speak! Do you want him thinking we're barbarians?"

There followed more confusion during which everyone seemed to be telling everyone else to be quiet. Gallonius made another attempt to impose order and was shouted down. The clerk's desperate blasts on the horn only added to the cacophony. Anyone listening outside would think a riot was in progress.

Ruso stood his ground, folding his arms and surveying the rabble with what he hoped was conspicuous impatience. If he could identify him, the man who had made that remark about Tilla would soon be one very sorry Briton.

Finally the din died away. He let the silence build for a moment before starting again, his voice deliberately quiet. "I've already spoken to Chief Magistrate Caratius," he said, "and I've examined the bodies of Asper and Bericus. I advise you not to make any hasty judgments about what happened to your tax collector or where the money went." That was as much defense as he was willing to offer Caratius, and neither the magistrate nor the rest of the Council looked satisfied with it. "I'll be trying to trace the money from the moment it was last seen, so I'll be asking plenty of questions. I need to talk to anybody who knows anything about the movements of Asper and his brother on that last day or who saw anything suspicious. If you can help, don't leave the Forum today before you've spoken to me."

He had reached the end without interruption. It had gone better than he had feared. He was about to thank them and step down when Caratius said, "What about Asper's letter?"

"Asper's letter," repeated Ruso. "Ah, yes. Thank you for reminding me." Damn. He should have expected this. Even if it was Caratius who had arranged for the Room Twenty-seven letter to be stolen, the man needed to pretend that he didn't know anything about it. He would probably have asked last night if dinner had not been interrupted.

The men on the benches remained silent, waiting to hear something new. "Some of you may have heard that Asper wrote a letter before he died." He paused, fingering one ear. If he told them it had been stolen, it would make him—and by implication, the procurator—look careless. If he didn't, they would want to see it. "We had it decoded," he announced, "but it was no help at all."

"What did it say?" Caratius again.

Did he already know? Perhaps he was pushing to find out how much had been deciphered before it was stolen. The last thing Ruso wanted at the moment was for anyone here to suspect that Asper had been in touch with the governor's security service and tried to alert Metellus to some sort of crime.

Get out of town as fast as you can. He looked around at the expectant faces. Was the wellwisher among them?

Say something. "It was just a couple of unfinished lines," he said, "scribbled when Asper was on the verge of death."

"But what did it say?"

"Nothing of any use."

He was stalling for time, and they all knew it.

"Tell us, man!" urged a voice.

Caratius said, "It might mean something to us, if not to you." His acting, if that was what it was, was impressive.

Say something. Ruso cleared his throat. "It said," he began, "Dearest girl. When your sweet lips meet my eager—"

There was a fresh shout of laughter. Caratius looked as though someone had just slapped him across the face.

Gallonius stepped up and stopped chuckling for long enough to call for order. When he could make himself heard, he thanked the absent procurator for his understanding, congratulated the investigator on his work so far, and urged everyone to cooperate as fully as possible in the hunt for the money. Then he called upon the clerk to remind them of the rest of the business for the meeting.

Ruso retreated to the sound of the clerk reciting, "The continuing problem of flooding behind the market halls. The behavior of unruly youths on market days. The appointment of ambassadors fit to represent this Council."

"I object!" shouted Caratius, who had come back to life.

Stepping out into the fresh air of the Forum, Ruso decided that the leaders of the Catuvellauni might be accused of many things, but being dull was not one of them.

44

SHE HAD SWEPT the floors and filled the lamps with the last of the oil. Back in the kitchen, Tilla wrapped a cloth around one hand, steadying the steaming pot over the fire. Then she hooked a tangle of dripping cloths out of the first rinsing bucket with a stick and lowered it at arm's length into the hot water. She could hear someone moving about and chased away a fleeting sense of dread. Camma's behavior at the funeral had been caused by grief and shock. Time and kindness and the favor of the right gods would restore her.

Moments later she heard footsteps in the corridor. Camma was disheveled but bright eyed. She was clutching a wooden box with fancy metal hinges. It could have been a funeral cask for a newborn child.

She said, "I caused trouble for everyone this morning."

"Yes." Tilla was eyeing the box.

"I was wrong."

"It is forgotten." There was no sound from the baby in the front room. "What is that?"

"I think Andaste sent you to save me so that I can see Asper and Bericus avenged."

"Sister, what do you have in that box?"

Camma placed it on the table and wiped dust off the lid with one hand before lifting it. "We have money."

Relieved, Tilla gave the cloths a final poke with the stick and went to stand beside her. Inside, three small leather bags were resting on some sort of burned tile. Camma undid one of the drawstrings and tipped the bag over. Silver coins tumbled and rolled onto the table.

Tilla's eyes widened. "This is the money all the trouble is about?"

"Oh, no!" Camma seemed shocked at the suggestion. "This is not stolen."

Hoping she was right, Tilla ran one forefinger along the table, leaving a wake through the pile of coins. "This is a miracle!"

"No, it's his savings. Hidden under the bedroom floor. This is what those thieves were looking for."

The heaviest bag contained bronze and the third, the smallest of the three, a few more silver denarii.

When they had all been emptied, Tilla lifted out the fat tile. "And this?"

Camma frowned. "I don't know."

There was something odd about the feel of the underside. She turned it over. The surface was pocked with a series of holes arranged in rows. She ran her finger across, counting them. Six rows, seven holes in each. Each hole about big enough to hold the top joint of her little finger.

Camma said, "I have never seen that before."

"It's been burned," said Tilla, turning it sideways and peering at the rounded edges to see if there was anything that looked like writing. The tile was clumsily made. "Why is it in the treasure box?"

Camma sat down and reached for one of the empty bags. "I don't know."

Watching her, Tilla felt a sense of relief. Money was a nuisance that her own people had not needed before the Romans came, and greed for it was a curse, but she had to admit that the discovery of Asper's savings was useful. Not only that, but seeing Camma seated at the table calmly counting forty-seven silver coins back into a bag was a comfort. The frightening events of the funeral seemed a long way away, and perhaps best forgotten. She said, "I made porridge."

"In the middle of the day?"

"That was before you told me there was plenty of money."

A small wail from the front room announced that the baby would be joining them for lunch.

★ ★ ★

Tilla placed the bowl of porridge on the corner of the table so Camma could reach it without moving and glanced across at the baby with approval. "He is feeding well."

Camma picked up the spoon without having to be persuaded. It was a good sign. She said, "What will happen to Caratius?"

Tilla reached for her own bowl and began to drizzle an uneven golden spiral of honey around the surface. She said, "Tell me about him."

"He is the son of chiefs," Camma said, "but he has no sons of his own. He is old and angry, and he is not interested in women."

"Why did he marry?"

Camma shrugged. "I think because having friends among a neighboring tribe might give him a stronger voice here. But instead of living in the grand town he told my people about, I had to stay out in that house miles from anywhere with the servants and the horses and his terrible old mother."

"His mother's mind is going."

"Some days she knew who I was. Other days I had to keep away from her because she was frightened of me."

It could not have been easy to avoid her in that lonely house. In such a place, with such a husband, why would any wife have wanted to stay?

Camma said, "I tried to be friends, but it made her worse. Did she talk about the silver?"

"She thought we'd come to steal it."

"She thinks that of everyone. She thinks her father's savings were buried under the floor when his workshop burned down." She pointed with her spoon toward the door. "It was just along the street, near where the market halls are now. From the way Caratius likes to stand and watch whenever the men dig up the drains, I think he half believes her himself."

Tilla cut into the honey spiral with the edge of her spoon. She shifted the spoon sideways to make a half-moon crater in the porridge and watched as the milk flowed in. As the morning wore on, she had grown increasingly uncomfortable about her speech at the cemetery. "Caratius was not how I expected," she said.

Camma's smile was bitter. "If he looked like the man he really is, I would never have married him. Now, I curse him!"

Tilla busied herself blowing ripples across the milk. "I hope you're right, Sister."

"You have doubts?"

"If he wanted revenge, it would have been easier to catch Asper alone in town."

"Of course. But if his enemies could say Caratius had killed a tax man, they might throw him off the Council. So he sent a secret message and invited him to his death and everyone thought the brothers had run away."

It was a good reply. "Somebody sent a message," Tilla agreed. "Caratius says it wasn't him."

"Of course he does! He thought he was safe because nobody here would believe what I told them. He never thought I would dare go to the procurator."

At that moment the outside door opened. A small figure stepped into the kitchen. "*She* said you wanted me back," announced Grata, pointing an accusing finger at Tilla. Her bag landed on the table with a thud, making the treasure box and the porridge bowls bounce. Before anyone could speak she added, "I never liked working in that bakery anyway."

Whatever she had thought of the bakery, returning to housekeeping seemed to give Grata no pleasure, either.

Silent and tight lipped, she threw a faded old tunic over her clothes. Then she crashed the kitchen stools up onto the table, grabbed the broom, and began to sweep the floor as if it had just insulted her.

Camma said, "I am sorry about Bericus."

Tilla said, "And so am I."

"You never met him," snapped Grata.

Camma said, "You were not to know Caratius's message was a trap."

Grata carried on sweeping the floor as if she had not heard.

Camma and Tilla exchanged a glance over the legs of the upturned stools. Camma said, "I am feeling stronger now. There is money, and I would like to go out in the sunshine and buy food. Come with us, Grata."

"She needs the right food to make her strong again," put in Tilla, pleased to see Camma taking an interest in someone else's troubles. "Eggs and lentils and honey and butter and bread. And pigs' feet to thicken the milk, and while we are out I want to find a scribe to write a letter."

Camma said, "Grata, I shall need your help to carry everything."

"I'm busy."

"The stalls will close soon. The floor will still be here when we get back."

Grata flung the broom back into the corner with a cry of exasperation.

It bounced off the wall and clattered down against the table. Camma retrieved it and put it away. "I did not know you were so fond of Asper and Bericus."

"I wasn't."

"Come with us."

"What for?"

"Because we need more vegetables and meat and cheese."

Grata snorted. "Nobody will talk to us, you know."

"Are you afraid of them?"

Grata straightened up. "A few gossiping women?" She wiped her hands on the old tunic. "No. There are far worse things to be afraid of, believe me."

45

SAFELY OUTSIDE THE chaos of the Council chamber, Ruso turned to Dias. "I appreciate the personal escort," he said, "but you must have more important things to do."

If the guard captain suspected that Ruso was trying to get rid of him, he did not show it. Instead he appeared to be thinking about the idea. Finally he gestured toward one of the offices that opened onto the walkway around the Forum. "I could do with some time over at headquarters," he said. "We caught a sheep stealer last night, so there's a flogging to organize. We've only got twenty-nine lads and a couple of clerks on the books here, so I'd rather not waste men keeping him locked up till market day."

It sounded like a speech designed to allay the fears of visiting officials. As a former soldier, Dias must be well aware that Rome kept an eye on native militias. Ruso said, "I'm sure you could have done without extra escort duties."

"We've had two murders already, sir," said Dias equably. "We don't want anything happening to you."

"Do you think it's likely?"

"I'd say the closer you get to finding out who did it, the more danger you'll be in." When Ruso did not answer, he continued, "That note you found this morning. You seemed a bit shaken up."

Unable to think of a plausible lie, Ruso said, "Someone wants me out of town."

Dias frowned. "If you've been threatened, we need to know. Did you bring it with you?"

"I burned it," said Ruso, knowing a sensible investigator would do no such thing, but if the writer really was a well wisher, the last thing he deserved was a visit from Dias.

"What did it say, exactly?"

"Get out of town," said Ruso, getting into the stride of the lie.

"That's it?"

"That's it." As if assessing anonymous warnings was all part of an investigator's daily grind, he said, "With everything else going on, I forgot to mention it. The threat wasn't very specific." He promised to keep any further notes and Dias agreed to assign some new men to "keep an eye on him" for the next few hours.

It was an interesting choice of words.

"That little man who turned up at the funeral with Gallonius," Ruso said. "The woman said he used to work with Asper?"

"Nico." Dias gestured toward the Great Hall. "He's got an office in there. Good luck."

Ruso crossed the Forum toward the Great Hall followed by the rhythmic tramp of his new guards. Ahead, above the entrance, was a grand plaque honoring the long-dead emperor Titus Vespasian and some departed governor. As he drew closer he could make out a rough patch in the middle of the engraving. That must be the scar of Titus's brother Domitian, officially obliterated from memory and now messing things up in death just as he had in life.

The locals had certainly made an effort to keep up. He wondered how many of them could read it. Sadly, since it seemed to have been put up at about the same time that Mount Vesuvius exploded and buried several complete towns much nearer to Rome, he doubted whether Titus had cared what the Britons were building on their remote little island.

Beneath the plaque was a pair of open doors conveniently designed for the entry of a man fifteen feet tall. Inside, the hall was high enough to humble the mere mortals clustered below. The clack of the guards' studded boots on the concrete sounded like the cracking of whips as they led Ruso across to a range of side rooms stretching into the distance beyond a row of columns.

They passed the town money changer—another man Ruso intended to meet—and three doors farther down one of the guards pointed out Julius Asper's office. This was firmly padlocked, although damage around the lock suggested someone had already broken in and resealed it. Ruso would need to look around in there later. For now, his target was the man named Nico.

Nico turned out to be not some humble clerk as he had supposed but the finance officer of Verulamium, with an office near the shrine over the underground strong room.

Nico did not seem to be happy in his work. Long after the door marked "Quaestor" in spindly red letters was closed, the little man was still scuttling about putting away documents and muttering to himself, occasionally glancing at the new problem that was standing before him in the shape of Ruso and repeating, "Yes, yes," in answer to a question Ruso could only imagine. His voice was small, his movements quick and light, and his eyes seemed to be permanently on the lookout for predators.

Ruso helped himself to a folding stool. He sat very still, deciding it must be the recent strain of losing the money that had reduced the man to this state. It was hard to imagine what kind of outfit would put a mouse in charge of large sums of cash.

Eventually Nico had cleared away everything except an abacus, which he set on the windowsill, retrieved, placed on the desk beside his inkstand, and then retrieved yet again. Finally he stood between window and desk clutching it and looking lost. Ruso reached across, took it from him, and put it back on the windowsill. Then he said as gently as he could, "Why don't you sit down and I'll see what I can do to help?"

After a final check around for danger, Nico settled behind his desk and began to nibble the top of his thumb. Ruso explained why he was here, not because he thought the man was listening but in the hope that it might calm him down. When he moved on to explain that he didn't know how a quaestor's office worked and he needed someone to explain it to him, Nico's eyes brightened.

As Ruso had suspected, once the man started talking, there was no stopping him. This was largely because every statement of fact had to be followed by a partial retraction and several long qualifications to cover differing circumstances, a pause for consultation as Ruso was asked to confirm whether that was his interpretation of the law also, and then a conjunction consisting of either, "Oh dear, where was I?" or, "Now what else is there?" and occasionally an alarming, "But I'll tell you about that later on. Don't let me forget." No wonder he had so much work to do here that he barely found the time to attend Council meetings.

It was a far cry from Firmus's fantasy of an exciting investigation. Ruso wished he had brought Albanus, who might have understood some of this. Albanus took an arcane pleasure in the workings of officialdom. He made a genuine effort to listen but found his mind wandering off to the key question of whether or not Asper and Bericus had taken the money with them. Given the complexity of the system Nico was explaining, it was clear that the Council kept thorough records. That meant there was one thing about this business that could be easily proved or disproved. The tax money was either under guard in the strong room (he had listened that far) or it wasn't. Once he had established that fact, he could tether his theories to it while he tried to untangle them.

"I'm impressed," he said when Nico seemed to have come to an end.

"Really?" Nico looked nervous again, as if he was afraid his visitor was being sarcastic.

"Really," said Ruso, and meant it. "You've obviously got a thorough grip on the job. Now if you could just show me the strong room records for the day Asper disappeared . . ."

Nico hurried straight to the relevant box, drew out an exceptionally long writing tablet and flipped it open. Ruso suspected he had been staring at it in despair for much of the last few days. The black squiggle at the bottom apparently showed that the money had been signed out. "There's a parallel record in Asper's office," Nico volunteered before Ruso thought to ask.

"You've got his records too?"

Nico looked worried again as he explained how the Council had arranged for Asper's home to be searched and his office to be broken into. "Just in case he hadn't taken the money with him."

"Why wouldn't he take it with him?" queried Ruso, guessing they had really been hoping Asper had enough money stashed away somewhere to replace what was missing.

Nico looked out the window and around the room, as if he was expecting to find the answer written somewhere on the wall.

"Why wouldn't he take it with him?" Ruso tried again.

"I don't know," Nico confessed.

"Perhaps he was going somewhere else? Did he mention visiting anyone?"

"Oh no, sir, he was definitely going to Londinium."

"I expect it made sense at the time," Ruso suggested, recalling the extremes he and the apprentices had gone to during their desperate hunt for the missing letter. "I'll be checking his office myself. Did he say anything about his security guards?"

Nico's eyes widened in alarm. "I don't know about visits and guards. I only know about money."

"And you're absolutely sure the money went out?"

"Oh, yes! I was there." He seemed relieved to have an easy question at last.

"What time of day was it?"

"In the morning."

"But he didn't leave town until the afternoon."

"Oh dear," muttered Nico. "Oh dear, oh dear . . ."

"That's not your fault," Ruso assured him. "Who would have known that he had it?"

This seemed to be something the quaestor had not considered. "Well—anybody could have seen, I suppose. The Hall's usually busy in the mornings." Unprompted, he continued, "We had the guards put a watch on the gates. They called in reserves and sent all their best men out to look. We made a sacrifice to Jupiter and we offered a raven to Sucellus, and still nothing."

"I heard it was a dog," said Ruso. "But I'm sure he liked it, whatever it was. Is there any way we could identify the money if it's found? Anything distinctive about it?" It was something he might never have thought of had Tilla not been given the stolen money that had somehow drawn her into Metellus's web. When Nico still did not answer he rephrased the question. "Is there any way we can tell your money from anybody else's?"

"Oh no!" The quaestor shook his head, as if "No" were not a clear enough answer. "No, no. It's just ordinary money. Mostly silver." He paused. "You could talk to our money changer. He labels all the bags."

Ruso, who could think of nothing else to ask, thanked him and got up to leave. He was almost out the door when Nico blurted out, "Nothing like this has ever happened before! What will the procurator say?"

Ruso said truthfully, "I can't tell you."

46

APPARENTLY THE COUNCIL clerk had the key to Asper's office on his belt and he was still trapped over in the Council meeting. Ruso decided to check the strong room below the shrine.

The guards stationed at the top of the descending flight of stone steps snapped to attention as he approached. Glancing down at the iron-studded door, Ruso ordered the men to stand easy. They seemed to like being addressed as soldiers. They liked it even more when he showed an interest in their duties, answering all his questions in passable Latin with the eagerness of the underappreciated. They told him there was an eight-man rota for guard duty in the Hall, alternating between the strong room and the entrances. At night everything was locked up and two men remained on patrol while two others slept at the top of the strong room steps. "Four hours on, four hours off, sir."

"Very good," said Ruso, as if he were a visiting dignitary come to inspect them.

He was informed with pride that this was a top job, which he understood to mean that it was under cover and involved very little effort. He restrained an urge to warn them about the dangers of varicose veins and bad feet from standing around all day. "And if I want to get in?"

They seemed genuinely sorry they were not able to oblige. "Nobody allowed in without the quaestor, sir. And him not on his own."

"That applies to everyone? Even the tax collector?"

"Especially him, sir. If we knew what he was doing we would have kept him out."

Ruso said, "You were on duty when he took the money?"

"He was with the quaestor, sir." The tone was defensive, as if they were afraid he was accusing them of negligence.

"Was there anything unusual about him that day?" asked Ruso, noticing Nico emerge from his office and scurry across the hall to the exit. "Anything he said or did?"

The guards thought about it. Finally one of them said, "It is not our job to notice what our betters do, sir."

"So you just saw him take the money out as usual?"

"It's not our fault, sir!" put in the other one, suddenly anxious.

"No," agreed Ruso, "I'm sure it wasn't." It was hard to imagine them being bright enough to steal anything.

The sign said, "Satto, official money exchange," and there were crude paintings of coins, but the money changer's office was chiefly notable for the guards standing on either side of the entrance. They were not as smartly turned out as Dias's men, but the studded clubs and steely stares suggested that they would be happy to respond to any complaints.

Satto was a small wiry man of about forty. He was seated between a hefty oak chest and a counter substantial enough to hold a considerable weight in cash without rocking his weighing-scales. He responded to Ruso's request for a private conversation by gesturing to his guards to wait outside. Ruso ordered his own men to join them.

When they were alone, Satto reached behind him for a folding stool. Ruso opened it, guessing that most of Satto's clients had to stand and wait while he decided what rate he was prepared to offer them. "I'm investigating the theft of the tax money."

"So I hear."

"I'm told you might be able to show me how to identify it."

Satto extended one bony hand across the counter. On his little finger was an oversized bronze ring with a red stone. As he rocked his fist from side to side, the light from the window caught the dip of what looked like a tiny human figure engraved into the stone. "I inspect all the coins that go into the strong room," he said. "If it's still bagged, my tag should be on it with the date and that seal."

Ruso tried to picture the little figure in reverse, stamped into wax. "I'd imagine it's been rebagged by now."

Satto withdrew the hand. "Unless it's been stolen by someone very stupid."

"What do you think a thief would do with it?"

Satto pondered that for a moment. "He could trickle it out slowly, or go somewhere nobody knows him—but arriving with a lot of coins would make him noticed. I would melt it down. It would be worth less, but much easier to hide."

"How would it be worth less? It's still silver."

He caught the surprise on the money changer's face and guessed that a real procurator's man would have known the answer to that. He said, "I've only just been transferred to the procurator's office."

"So I see." Satto leaned back, lifted the lid on the trunk, and groped about inside. "You'll find that money is very rarely what it seems, investigator." He produced a little wooden box, pushed it toward Ruso, and lifted the lid to reveal three small silver coins. "Take a look. They're all the same."

Ruso held one toward the light, peering at the profile of an emperor and the worn inscription around the perimeter.

"You won't see many of these."

"Are they fake?"

"No."

The worn lettering was largely illegible, but something about the fat cheeks and the bouffant hairstyle was familiar. "Nero?"

"The emperor known as Nero," Satto confirmed. "You won't see many of them because coins are not what they once were."

"No?" Ruso flipped it over in his palm. It looked much like any other denarius to him. The sort that arrived in his possession in depressingly small quantities and usually left very shortly afterward.

"Around about the time of the great disaster," explained Satto, presumably referring to Boudica rather than Vesuvius, "the emperor Nero gave orders to have the amount of silver in the coinage reduced. There's more silver in one of these than in anything they're minting today."

Ruso thought about that for a moment. He had never before considered that a denarius might be anything other than—well, than a denarius.

"So," he said, "if I melted down ten of these, and I melted down ten modern ones, what I ended up with from these would be worth more?"

"Exactly. Although not as much as they're worth as coins."

"So if somebody brings you one of these and wants change, do you give them more for it?"

"As I said, I rarely see one. Except perhaps when somebody's turning out some old savings."

It was a neat avoidance of the question. Ruso said, "And do they always know what they've got?"

"Not until I tell them." Lest Ruso should not believe him, he added, "Don't listen to what people say about us, investigator. Most of us are honest men. You may not recall that the emperor Galba once had a false money changer's hands cut off and nailed to his counter, but you'll understand why we find it . . ." He paused as if searching for a word. "An inspiration."

Ruso said, "I'll check my cash more closely in the future."

Satto retrieved his treasure, glancing at it before he lowered the lid as if to make sure that Ruso had not performed some cunning sleight of hand and exchanged his valuable antique for some worthless modern bauble. "Not everything with Nero's head on it is worth more. You have to know which is which."

It was clear that there was more to coin exchange than Ruso had realized. It was not, after all, simply a matter of raking off a percentage of the bronze people used to buy bread as a reward for giving them the silver or gold they needed to pay their taxes. "So would there be any of these coins in the tax money?"

"Only if I was having a bad day when I checked it," said Satto. "It should be all modern."

Ruso returned to the center of the Great Hall deep in thought. There was no doubt that many things weren't what they used to be, but he had always assumed that silver was silver and that a coin was worth what it said, no matter how old it was. Yet now it seemed that silver was not really silver despite bearing the emperor's name and the stamp of the official mint. Passing beneath the plaque over the main entrance, he was reminded that Domitian had really been a murdering bastard despite all the toadying inscriptions that had been erected during his lifetime. You couldn't trust a word you read.

He was beginning to think Tilla's ancestors, obstinately illiterate and coinless, might have had a point.

47

THE COUNCIL SESSION had just broken up when Ruso returned to the chamber. Several toga-clad figures were striding toward the doors. Others were clustered in groups. The urgency of conversation and the way the groups were eyeing one another suggested that the meeting had ended in disagreement. One or two men approached Ruso to thank him, but nobody offered any new information. The clerk gathered up a collection of scrolls and hurried away with his head down, as if he was hoping to escape without being noticed.

Caratius abandoned what appeared to be an argument, raised his hand to acknowledge Ruso's presence, and advanced toward him. Immediately Gallonius broke away from another group on the far side of the hall, gathered up fistfuls of toga, and set off in the same direction. For a moment it looked like a race down the chamber, with Ruso as the finishing post.

Caratius got there first and opened his mouth only to be drowned out by Gallonius with, "Sorry about the lively debate earlier."

"Outrageous!" put in Caratius. "No respect. Can't even let a guest speak without interrupting. This place is a disgrace. I'm sorry, Investigator. You and I are trying to find out why men lie murdered and money is missing, and these people are interested in nothing but petty squabbles about who's allowed to be seen where."

"Since it turns out Asper wasn't the thief my fellow magistrate has been making him out to be," said Gallonius to Ruso, "it's just as well some of us went to pay our respects."

"An action for which you did not have the Council's approval," said Caratius.

Gallonius turned on him. "The quaestor and I went to the funeral as private individuals. It's not at all the same thing as illegally representing the Council to the procurator, as you well know."

Caratius looked as though he was considering punching his fellow magistrate, then managed to get himself under control. "The investigator isn't here to waste his time on this kind of nonsense," he said. "I know what kind of game this is. Ruso, I'm counting on you to find out the truth. If not, I shall appeal to the governor. One way or another, I will have justice!" He turned to Gallonius. "In the meantime I suggest you stop talking nonsense and concentrate on finding something useful to tell him."

Ruso watched the tall, straight-backed figure march out of the chamber, gray hair flowing over the folds of the toga. He had to admit it was an impressive exit.

When his rival was gone, Gallonius took Ruso by the elbow as if he were an old friend. He steered him into an alcove and gestured him toward one elaborately carved chair while squeezing himself into the other. "Sorry about that, investigator. It's been a difficult morning. Do sit down."

Ruso sat. It was almost as uncomfortable as Valens's couch.

"Would you believe the man refused to resign?" continued Gallonius, "even though the brother's body turned up on his land."

"He says he knows nothing about it."

"Of course. But it doesn't look good, does it?" Gallonius's expression suggested it was not especially bad, either.

Ruso wondered if Caratius's enemies on the Council had retained Asper's services out of spite.

"On behalf of the town, I apologize for the way he came bothering the procurator. It's beginning to look as though we should have dealt with this ourselves."

Ruso's insistence that there was no need to apologize was brushed aside with a wave of the hand. "He's always been a difficult man. Doesn't listen. Rushes in without thinking. We've tried to get rid of him before on the grounds that he doesn't live in the town, but until now he's always managed to wriggle round it. This morning we've finally done it."

"But I haven't finished my—"

"Oh, nothing to do with the theft and the murders, even though everyone can see what happened there. No, we've finally nailed him on a technicality." The chair squealed in protest as Gallonius leaned back. "Caratius took money for overseeing drainage repairs outside the meat market eighteen months ago. The work's not finished, I'm still getting flooding into my property, and the money's not accounted for." He lifted a pudgy finger toward one of the brass plaques on the far side of the Hall. "It's clearly laid out in the Constitution. Tablet six, halfway down, The Sending Of Ambassadors. No man who has not accounted for public funds—you know the sort of thing."

Ruso neither knew nor cared, but he was wondering whether Caratius was in the sort of financial trouble that would tempt him to steal the town's money.

'The man's a menace,' continued Gallonius. "No matter how the Council votes, he does as he likes. Things would never have come to this if he'd listened to the rest of us about the Iceni."

"The Iceni?"

"Oh, he was all for some sort of alliance. The Council refused to get involved. Everyone could see the woman would be a disaster, but he went ahead and married her anyway." Gallonius sighed. "And now we have two men murdered and the procurator sending a man to chase our tax payment."

So Verulamium's suspicious alliance with the Iceni had been nothing more than the ambitions of a rogue politician. The procurator would be relieved to hear it. "I just came to help," Ruso said. "I'm not involved in the politics."

"Please thank the procurator for his understanding. We're sorry you've been troubled. You can assure him we'll deal with it from here. Caratius will be paying up."

"He will?"

Gallonius ground his palms together as if he had his rival trapped between them, and intoned, "Any ambassador who knowingly acts contrary to the rules shall be liable to pay the value of the case." It sounded as though it was his favorite quotation. "The value of this case," he added, "is seven thousand five hundred and thirty-two denarii."

Ruso was confused. "But I thought it was the Council who sent him to Londinium in the first place?"

"That was Caratius's argument too, but the Council took the view that he should have reminded us that he was ineligible. Instead he insisted on going."

"I see," said Ruso, appalled at the way in which a double murder had been reduced to an unsavory squabble about Council regulations.

"So it may not have been resolved in the way any of us expected, but you can go back to Londinium with the news that the money will be paid as soon as possible."

Ruso said, "You should know that somebody sent me an anonymous note this morning warning me to get out of town."

It took a moment for the words to puncture Gallonius's self-satisfaction. When they did, his throat wobbled as he swallowed. "You've received a threat?"

"Yes."

"A threat against a senior—oh, dear! This is terrible. Do the guards know?"

"I've told Dias."

Gallonius shook his head in disbelief and repeated, "Terrible. Whatever was he thinking of? This is a civilized, law-abiding town. The governor says we're an example to our neighbors. We're hoping for a visit from the emperor." The squabbling politician had vanished. The man looked genuinely upset. "A guest being threatened. I really can't apologize enough. That a magistrate should stoop so low! Not to mention murder and theft from his own treasury! Shameful!"

"You think it was Caratius?"

"We'll deal with him, don't worry." The magistrate sighed. "If only we had made Asper leave town after the scandal."

"Yes," agreed Ruso, getting to his feet. "If only."

As he came out of the Council chamber he saw that a sizeable crowd had gathered around a cart parked in an open area of the Forum with a hefty wooden frame set up inside. A gangly youth dressed only in a loincloth and blindfold was manhandled up to it by a couple of guards, who stretched out his arms and roped them to the horizontal beam of the frame. One of the men stepped down. The other remained.

There was a pause while Dias's voice made the announcement. This man had been caught with a ewe and a lamb stolen from his neighbor.

Moments later the thin black tail of a whip flashed against the white of the Forum columns. A cry of pain rose above the murmurs of the crowd.

Ruso counted fifteen lashes: plenty of time for the guilty party and his audience to consider the folly of stealing their neighbors' sheep. He wondered what they did to women who stole cockerels. As for magistrates who murdered tax collectors . . .

It dawned on him that as soon as he could prise Tilla away from Camma and the red-haired baby, he could follow the well-wisher's suggestion and get out of this decent law-abiding town. Clearly the locals were embarrassed about the whole fiasco and desperate to clear up as much of the mess as possible for themselves. It was all very well for Caratius to say he was counting on Ruso to "find out the truth," but Ruso had been sent here to serve the Council, and Caratius was no longer a councillor. Those who were wanted no further investigation.

Caratius would be accused and tried before the governor. Camma would have revenge, Metellus would have the name of the man who had murdered his agent, the Council would finally be free of a difficult man, and the procurator would get the cash. Ruso could go back to being a doctor and Tilla would never need to know that her name had been on that list. By the time Hadrian decided to visit, the town would probably have recovered its dignity. And Ruso might have recovered from the uneasy feeling that there was something wrong with all this, and that he had just been used as a weapon in someone else's political war.

He turned away from the crowd, shrugging the tension out of his shoulders. He had not done much to be proud of here. The discovery of the incriminating body had been the result of chance rather than investigation. Still, it was hardly his fault. If they had wanted a real inquiry, they should have hired someone who knew what he was doing. He would just pin down one last piece of information to satisfy himself that he had done as much as he could, and then he would face the challenge of extricating Tilla.

He turned to his guards, who were watching the youth's supporters struggling to untie him and bathe his wounds. "I need to go to Julius Asper's house," he said.

48

To his surprise he did not need to ask where to find the housekeeper. She was already standing over the kitchen table with her hair scraped back from her face and an old tunic flung over her dress, pounding a pungent mix of garlic and coriander with a pestle.

This was not the time to discuss Tilla's behavior at the funeral. Instead he exchanged good news with the women: on his side the fact that the Council would deal with Caratius, and on theirs the return of Grata and the fact that Camma had found forty-seven denarii and some bronze hidden in a box upstairs. Tilla, perhaps trying to make up for her performance earlier, meekly agreed to be ready to leave in the morning. He did not even need to tell her about the anonymous note. For once, everything seemed to be fitting into place.

The way Camma flung her arms around his wife and cried that she had saved her life left him feeling guilty for all his dire predictions about the folly of getting too involved. To his surprise Camma then flung her arms around him as well. Somewhere beyond his embarrassment and his desire to stop her hair from tickling his nose, he felt a warm glow of satisfaction.

"It was nothing," he assured her, disentangling himself after a suitable interval. "Actually, it's not quite over. There's one last thing I need to check before I'm finished. Grata, the Council are bound to ask you to identify the person who brought the message from Caratius."

Grata crushed a clove of garlic into submission against the grits in the surface of the bowl. "One of his slaves," she said, not looking up. "I don't know his name."

"Could you pick him out?"

"Whoever it is will deny it," said Camma. "You will have to beat him to get the truth."

"I don't suppose the message was written down?"

All three women eyed him with varying levels of scorn. "We don't bother with all that here," explained Grata. "We remember things."

It was a speech he had heard before from his wife, when he had assured her that she would have no trouble learning to read. "So what was the wording, exactly?"

She shrugged. "Just asking him to visit later that day to talk."

"Did it say what about?"

The scornful expression returned. "No, but I think he could guess."

When Ruso did not reply, she turned to Tilla. "So, now your man has asked all his questions, when are you leaving?"

Ruso did not listen to Tilla's response. *So, now your man has asked all his questions* . . .

Seen from the outside, his trip had been remarkably successful.

Extraordinarily successful.

Unbelievably successful.

The vague doubts that had been drifting around the edges of his mind had finally reached the front. He had not asked nearly enough questions.

What were the chances of a man stumbling across a body in the woods on the very evening that the investigator was visiting?

Come to that, why had it been possible to stumble across it at all? If it had been buried by the landowner, why had it not been properly hidden? There would have been plenty of time. Moreover, surely a murderer who lived near the scene of his crime would have wanted to dispose of his victim thoroughly lest he rise up and haunt him?

Camma was talking now, holding something out to him and looking as though she was waiting for an answer.

It appeared to be a badly formed burned tile with holes stamped into one side. Camma said, "I thought it might be a doctor's mold for drying out pills in an oven, but Tilla says no."

He took it from her with a sense of foreboding. As the only man in a house full of women, he seemed to be expected to know instinctively what this piece of equipment was. "It looks more like something to do with the kitchen," he offered. He turned it over, exploring the pocked surface with a forefinger that would not fit into the holes. "Some sort of fire brick?" he suggested. "Something to set hot dishes on?"

"It was in the box with the money," explained Tilla.

"If it is of no use to you," said Camma, "I will throw it away."

He turned it over and held it toward the window, squinting along the edges for some sort of clue. Whatever it was, if Asper had hidden it in the box with his savings, it must be significant. He peered again at the side with the holes, then poked at a small green speck with one finger. "Is that copper?"

Camma had lost interest in it. She picked up the baby, wrinkling her nose at the smell. "Another cloth!"

Tilla was silent. He knew she could tell from his expression that something had changed. "The bronzesmiths next door," he said, slapping the clay tile against the palm of his hand. "Can they be trusted?"

Grata shrugged. "As much as any man can be trusted."

"Good," he said, ignoring the insult. "Tilla, come with me. We're going next door for a chat."

49

THE ELDERLY MAN who was sweeping the clay floor of the bronzesmiths' shop put the broom aside as soon as he saw them. He eyed Ruso's Gaulish clothes, assessed the shaggy remains of his foreign haircut, then greeted them in Latin. "Good afternoon, sir and lady! What can we do for you? We have quality lamps, beautiful brooches . . . A nice figure of Venus for the lady? Take a look. We can make anything to order on the premises."

Tilla, as they had agreed, went to distract the guards with a message of thanks to Dias for his help with the funeral.

"I'm working for the procurator's office," explained Ruso, stepping into the workshop so the tile could not be seen from the street. "I've just been given this. I wondered if it was yours."

The man took one look and backed away, clutching at the little bronze phallus hung around his skinny neck as if Ruso had just offered him poison. "Oh, no, sir! Nothing like that. You must be misinformed. This is a respectable workshop."

"I'm not informed at all," said Ruso, taken aback. "I don't know what it is."

The man retreated so fast that he bumped into his display and sent a couple of lamps and a six-inch high miniature of Mercury tinkling to the floor. As he did so a second man of similar vintage emerged from the back of the shop, wiping his hands on a cloth. There was a hurried conversation in British, most of which Ruso could not catch.

The second man stepped forward. "What you have there must be very old, sir. Nobody we know has used one of those since our grandfather's day. Even if we had one, we would never use it. They make all the coins in Rome these days."

Ruso blinked. "It's for making money?"

"In the days of the old kings, sir, yes. To make the blanks for stamping into coins. But nobody alive has ever seen it done, I promise you."

A slack-faced lad with lank hair about his shoulders came forward and grabbed the man by the arm, pointing at Ruso and saying something in British. The man was trying to reassure him.

Ruso backed away, conscious that he was frightening them all. The lad repeated his question. The man said the same thing again, assuring him there was nothing to worry about.

He switched back into Latin. "I am sorry. He doesn't understand. He thinks you are angry with us."

"I'll go," said Ruso, sorry for them.

"Sir, whoever told you to ask about that mold—"

"Oh, it's nothing," Ruso assured him, turning to call across the street to Tilla. "I told you it was rubbish, wife. We've been swindled."

The women were surprised to see him back. They were even more surprised when he laid out all of Asper's coins on the kitchen table Grata had just wiped clean. First he pushed aside the bronze sestertii, which were much too big to fit in the holes of the mold. He sorted the rest into denominations, turned them all face up, and peered at the profiles of various and mostly dead emperors. Some of the emperors, he now saw, were not stamped very clearly. Some of them had worn flat and others had never been quite in the middle in the first place. The designs on the reverse sides were even more confusing. Some of the backs aligned with the fronts while others did not.

He heard Camma whisper to his wife in British, "What is he looking for?"

"You said Asper was trying to find a way out," said Tilla as Ruso tried a juggling motion, weighing one coin against another in his hands. "Perhaps this was it, whatever it is."

He peered at the edges of the coins. He tried stacking like for like on top of one another to check for size: an exercise that proved futile because very few of them were really round. He even attempted a tentative bite on one or two, trying not to recall the screams of a patient whose molar had been cracked by the very same exercise.

After the third or fourth attempt to sort them into piles that shared one particular odd characteristic or another, he concluded that either the official mint was not terribly fussy about the standard of its coins, or that most of these were fakes. Or more likely he didn't know what he was doing. How foolishly overoptimistic he had been when he had walked along that street in Londinium telling himself that you didn't need to know much to be an investigator.

He arranged the coins into a grid and counted them. "You said there were forty-seven denarii?"

"We spent one of them today," said Tilla.

He scooped the grid across the table with one hand and slid it toward the edge. "I'll need to borrow all of this."

Camma shot a look at Tilla.

"It is all right," Tilla assured her. "He is honest."

As he got up to leave, he reflected on the very Britishness of that exchange. At home, he would have needed to offer a written receipt.

"I'll bring it back as soon as I can," he promised.

Tilla said, "I will walk toward the mansio with you. I must say hello to Serena before we go."

"We won't be leaving early," he told her. "I may have one or two things to finish off tomorrow."

Her face brightened. When she said, "So we can stay a little longer?" he knew she was not thinking of the inquiry, but of the baby.

50

As RUSO APPROACHED, the money changer's eyes went straight to the clenched fist that was hiding Asper's bag of cash, then flicked away as if he had noticed nothing. Satto propped his elbows on the counter, clasped both hands together, and rested his chin on them. "Welcome back, investigator. Congratulations. I hear the murderer stands accused and the tax will be paid. So what else can I do for you?"

When they were alone Ruso said, "I'm just weaving in a few loose ends."

"And would that have something to do with what's hidden in your hand?"

Ruso was not sure how far the man could be trusted. On the other hand, if he went to Londinium to consult the procurator's officials, he might not be allowed back. He brought his fist up over the counter and straightened his fingers. The little bag landed on the surface and slumped sideways.

Satto smiled.

Moments later Ruso watched in awe as the trick he had pretended to perform at the Blue Moon was enacted in front of him. Satto was sorting the coins into two piles, muttering, "Yes," and "No," and occasionally, "Hm," as he pondered a coin, peered at it, weighed it against another, and even held it up to his nose and sniffed it. Eventually there were thirty-nine coins in the "Good" pile, seven classed as "No," and one about which he seemed unable to decide. Reaching under the counter, he produced a small hammer and some sort of awl. He flipped the coin over. "Better not make a hole in the emperor," he observed before tapping the awl into the surface.

He handed the result across the counter. Where the damage was done, Ruso could see a glint of something beneath the surface that was not silver. That made eight fakes out of forty-six. He wondered which sort of coin Tilla had spent this afternoon, and how Camma would take the news that a sizeable chunk of Asper's savings had just disappeared.

"You could say," said Satto, dropping the coin on the "No" pile, "That as long as everybody thinks it's worth something, then it is. Only I wouldn't agree with you because I can tell the difference."

"Do you ever get asked to pretend not to notice?"

"I can't pretend not to know what I know."

Ruso was not sure if he had just been given a lesson in coinage or in philosophy.

"Where did you get this money?"

Ruso had anticipated the question. "Londinium."

The man's face betrayed nothing as he raked the "No" pile toward his side of the counter. "I'm sorry to say that someone in Londinium has swindled you. Julius Asper brought me a false coin from the same source a few months ago. If you can trace the forgers, they'll be put before the governor and executed."

"They?"

"It usually takes two men. One to hold the dies in position with tongs, one to bring down the hammer for the stamping. That's always assuming one of them is the engraver, which isn't always the case—it's skilled work."

Ruso watched the "No" pile being placed on a workbench at the back of the office. "Don't I get them back?"

"It's my duty to destroy false coins. I also destroyed the one Asper showed me."

"I'll have to track down these people in Londinium once I've finished here. Tell me how they make the forgeries."

"These? A thin layer of silver stamped over a core of bronze. Sometimes they use iron, but there is the problem of rust."

"And they make the core—how?"

"Usually in a clay mold: not as easy as it sounds. Your next question is, how does he engrave the dies for stamping the coin?"

"Yes."

"And the answer is, not quite well enough. The S on HADRIANUS is damaged: I'd guess the engraver got confused when he was trying to reverse the shape and then had to correct it." Satto picked up something that looked like a chisel. He placed a coin on the bench and aligned the edge of the chisel with its center. "But they are quite good," he said, reaching for the hammer. "I wouldn't like the procurator to think I was keeping them."

The sound of the hammer smacking into the head of the chisel must have been heard outside in the Hall. Ruso wondered what the guards would make of it.

Only when he had finished mangling Ruso's evidence did Satto say, "You should know that if Rome doesn't send enough small change, a man who makes bronze coins is helping the soldiers spend their wages and his neighbors buy their bread."

"Does that happen?"

"Not these days. And I'm talking about bronze, not silver. All I'm saying is, good men have made coins as well as bad."

Ruso got to his feet. "Thank you. You've been very helpful."

Satto handed him half of one of the ruined coins. "Two more things you should know, investigator. The first is that apart from the one Asper showed me, I've never seen denarii like these before in Verulamium."

"And the other?"

"If a forger is caught, he has nothing to lose."

51

THE SOOTY-FINGERED BOY who was mixing ink at the table in the Council clerk's office had a lopsided mustache smeared beneath his nostrils. Ruso saw it just after the lad looked up in alarm and before the chain-mailed bulk of the guards came between them. Moments later the clerk was fiddling with the lock on Asper's office door and muttering that this was all quite irregular: He had been told the investigation was over and he really needed permission from the quaestor.

He need not have worried. The cramped space contained nothing but furniture and disappointment. There was no money stashed away anywhere. No discernable notes about evidence or investigations. No lumps of iron with hammer scars on one end and the emperor's profile engraved in reverse on the other.

Ruso put the last records box back on the shelf. Then he leaned against the wall, folded his arms, and stared around the room. If only he had Albanus here. Even if there were secrets hidden among the lists of names and figures in the records, the only thing Ruso could deduce from them was that neither Asper nor his brother was an overly tidy man.

The desk where Asper must have sat was the larger of the two. Carved legs, polished sheen on the surface, set squarely in the middle of the room facing the door. Designed to impress. The one that must have belonged to Bericus was crammed into the corner and had a chunk of wood wedged under one leg to level it up. Asper had a brass inkstand, Bericus a simple pot. He imagined the brothers had argued over more than Camma.

If only the man had spoken to her about his suspicions. If only he had left some hint of where he had found that coin mold. No one was going to admit to owning it, even if he could track down every metalworker in town to ask, and that would take hours. Camma's neighborhood seemed to be full of them. The elderly bronzesmiths next door, the silversmiths farther down the street . . . then there were the repair shops and the wagon works at the stables, not to mention any number of forges scattered across the local farmsteads where smiths would call for trade or where laborers with some rudimentary skill might bash out repairs to damaged tools. It would be impossible to search them all and even if he did, what were the chances of him finding what the owners would be careful to hide?

Ruso leaned back in the chair and scowled at the door handle. It was possible that he was wasting his time. He was not even sure that the forgery business had anything to do with the murders. Caratius was as likely to be guilty as not. One thing of which he was certain, though, was that if he was going to find out anything else, he needed to do it quickly. He had fulfilled the procurator's orders to look helpful. He should be on the way back to Londinium with a reassuring report about the links with Iceni. Tilla would be packing her bag in the morning and the Britons, to whom he had been seconded, were expecting him to leave.

One of them was desperate for him to leave.

For your own safety, get out of town.

If only he could track down the person who sent that message, he might find out what was really going on here. Whatever it was, he was convinced that Dias was involved in it.

52

THERE WAS STILL plenty of daylight, but the bustle of the day was over. Workshops had fallen silent, children had been called indoors, and there was hardly anyone about as Tilla hurried across the Forum on the way back to Camma's house. She had hoped the scribe's office might still be open, but the shutters were already in place. There was no reason to linger. Ahead, she noticed one of Dias's men staring at her from the doorway of the rooms the guards used as their headquarters. How long had he been watching her?

She quickened her pace, telling herself he was probably just an ill-mannered man who was bored. Even though Dias could not be trusted, that did not mean all the other guards were corrupt too. She passed him and walked out under the arch to the street without glancing back.

Back at the house, Grata would be preparing the evening meal. Tilla had turned down the Medicus's invitation to dine with him in his grand suite of rooms tonight, preferring one last evening with Camma and the lovely baby. Ruso had accompanied her across to the mansio and then left her to talk to Serena while he rushed off somewhere like a dog on a fresh scent. She had no idea where he was going, nor what time he would be back.

In the morning she would go with Camma to bury the ashes, and then talk to her about a name for the baby. Perhaps a name would mark a new start. After that she would go and visit the scribe again, and then she would be ready to leave for Londinium whenever her husband had finished his investigations.

Just now she had tried to persuade Serena to come back to Londinium with them, but Serena had refused to budge. It was obvious the girl was lonely: Her husband and friends were twenty miles away and her cousin was too busy to spend much time with her. Perhaps that was why she was unusually friendly. As a rule, even though nothing was ever said, she was sure Serena still saw her as the housekeeper.

Today, however, she had seemed delighted to welcome Tilla into the mansio garden, where a maid was supervising the twins at play, and congratulated her on her marriage. "I suppose you're pregnant," she said. "It's very decent of Ruso to marry you."

Tilla said, "It is very decent of me to marry him too."

Serena looked taken aback, then the broad face broke into a handsome grin. "Perhaps all men are a trial when you have to live with them," she said. "I've done my best, but Valens just makes no effort. I've told him what he needs to do to shape up. He agrees with everything I say and then carries on the same as before." She paused. "He might listen to Ruso. I don't suppose you could get him to—"

"No. But I think Valens is hoping you will be back soon."

"Hah!" Serena had managed to look both outraged and smug at the same time. "He thinks I don't know what he got up to after I left. One of Pa's old friends from the garrison went over when they had a burglary. He said people heard women in there in the middle of the night!"

Tilla paused. "A burglary?"

"It's all right. They didn't steal anything."

"That was me," said Tilla. "The woman in the night. We were staying there."

"You?"

"And my patient, and her baby. Your father's friend should find out the truth before he gossips."

For once, Serena was silent.

Tilla said, "Valens asked me to talk to you. I said no. He must talk to you himself."

Serena paused to watch one of her sons trying to throw a ball at the other. It looked more like war than sport. "But he hasn't," she said.

"Not yet," agreed Tilla. "I can take a message if you like."

"It's not my fault!"

Tilla sighed, gathered up her skirts, and got to her feet. "Many things happen that are not our fault," she said. "At least, that is what we tell ourselves. But if you will not talk to each other, how can anyone help you?"

"What am I supposed to have done wrong?"

"I do not know," said Tilla, fighting an urge to tell this pampered girl how lucky she was to have a husband and two healthy children, "But my mother used to say that if you cannot bang your head through the wall, you will have to turn to the left or right."

Serena pondered that for a moment. "Maybe that sounds better in British."

"No," Tilla conceded. "It sounds annoying in British too."

In the end she had left with a message for Valens that his wife was not missing him one little bit. It had not been a successful meeting.

A ginger cat stopped lapping at the puddle under the water trough as she approached. Out of habit, she paused before crossing the road, but there was no traffic. There was only the fleeing cat and an old woman limping away in the distance. She glanced behind her and was surprised to see the guard she had noticed earlier. He dropped hastily into a crouch and began to fiddle with his bootlace, but she had already recognized him. He must have followed her all the way from the Forum.

Tilla told herself to be sensible. She was in a public street and there was still plenty of light. The man might just happen to live in the same area as Camma, but the business with the bootlace was very suspicious. Still, if he were going to accost her he must have had plenty of chances to do it before now. She paused to scoop up a handful of cool water from the trough. She wiped her mouth with the back of her hand, dried her hand on her tunic, and waited. The guard looked up and stopped pretending to tie the lace.

As he approached she folded her arms and stood defiantly, at the same time mentally pacing out the distance behind her to Camma's door and wondering whether she could outrun him.

She said in British, "Are you following me?"

The guard's grin faltered when she did not return it. He said, "Cheer up a bit, love. You won't get much business with a face like that."

"I am not looking for business!" Was he lying, or had he made an honest mistake? "I am a respectable married lady on the way home!"

He backed away, both hands held up in surrender. "Sorry, missus. No offense. I saw you in the Forum on your own, and at this hour—"

"Can a woman not walk across the Forum without being ogled?"

The grin returned. "Fair enough. I'll see you safe home if you like."

"No! Go away."

To her relief, he did not argue. She watched him head off down a side street before turning back toward the protection of Camma's house. Were it not for her friend, she would be glad to get out of this place.

She glanced back along the street before crossing the next junction by the silent meat market. To her relief there was no sign of the guard.

She wondered why the Medicus had rushed off and whether he was back at the mansio yet. He had looked disappointed when she refused to join him, but this evening she wanted to say good-bye to Camma and the baby.

She must be strong. There would be other babies. Perhaps—

She did not see the stranger until his arm was around her throat.

She managed a stifled scream as he dragged her backward into the alleyway. She was off balance, gasping for air, struggling to pull his arm away, and trying get back onto her feet as something jabbed into her back and a voice growled in British, "Shut up, keep still, and you won't get hurt."

Her heart was thudding. Her body was desperate for air. She could not think. He was saying something. She heard only, "Got that?"

She shook her head, unable to speak. What a fool she was. If only she had not been so rude to that harmless guard . . .

The grip around her neck tightened. "I said, this is a message for your man. Tell him to clear off and keep his nose out of other people's business. And you, keep your mouth shut from now on. If you don't, me and my mates will get ahold of one of your friends and show you what happens to blabbermouths."

The release was so sudden, and the shove in the back so forceful, that by the time she had picked herself up, he had gone. She stumbled back toward the empty street, filthy and trembling and short of breath. Pain radiated from her elbow and her knees where she had fallen in the mud. She could still feel the roughness of his arm around her bruised throat.

This is a message for your man. And you, keep your mouth shut.

53

B Y T H E T I M E Ruso had finished searching Asper's office, the guards who had been waiting outside for him were looking exceedingly bored. The Forum was empty. The working day's clamor had fallen silent. There was hardly any traffic: Vehicles had been unhitched and drawn into secure yards for the night. The guards escorted him to the mansio and did not look sorry when he dismissed them.

Publius greeted him at reception with the news that Tilla had left some time ago, and he was sorry but there was still no news of who might have delivered an unsigned note yesterday. Ruso made a quick tour of the building, annoying any staff he could catch by asking them the same questions Publius had obviously asked already. Finally convinced that nothing more could be done to trace the well-wisher tonight, he locked the door behind him, shut out the world, and stepped into the tasteful privacy of Suite Three. A couple of blank writing tablets had been thoughtfully provided on the side table and someone had filled the brazier with hot coals, anticipating a chilly night.

Further in, he realized that the cloak he had flung over the end of the bed had disappeared. He found it hanging behind the door. The cupboard where he had unloaded his few belongings had surely not been that well arranged last time he looked.

It was like having an invisible wife.

He pushed open the shutters and surveyed the garden. A slave hurried past the window clutching a tray and he heard a burst of male laughter from other guests somewhere farther along the walkway. He swung the shutters almost closed again. His wife had spurned his invitation, preferring to spend the night with a couple of women and a squalling baby. He did not want a jovial bachelor evening with a bunch of traveling officials.

As he bent to unlace his boots, the bag of Asper's savings slung around his neck swung forward, reminding him that he should have returned it tonight. He wondered about walking across to Camma's house, but there was nowhere to spend it at this hour. The women could wait until morning.

Someone was knocking at the door of the reception room. He braced himself for another encounter with Serena, but it was only a slave come to ask whether he wished dinner to be served in his dining room or in here. Being offered the choice was such a luxury that he was reluctant to surrender it straightaway. Instead he asked what was on tonight's menu.

The slave took an ominously deep breath. It seemed tonight's meal started with Finest Gaulish Honeyed Wine and ended with some sort of cakes in Smoothest Syrup of Baetican Grape Must. In between came Numidian-style Chicken, Parthian-style Lamb, and oysters with piquant relish from Baiae. The origins of "Tenderest leaves of winter vegetables" were not stated. Presumably that was local cabbage. He pretended to ponder this for a moment, imagining how ludicrous and lonely he would feel tackling all these complicated courses in the tiled expanse of the dining room across the corridor and then declared his preference for staying where he was. The slave bowed and left, his face impassive.

Ruso lay on the bed and stared at the ceiling. He would much rather be in a simple lodging room with his medical books and something from the local snack bar. This wretched business grew more complicated by the minute, and now he was supposed to be leaving in the morning with more questions raised than answered.

When the ceiling proved no inspiration at all, he tried closing his eyes. The facts writhed around in his brain like a nest of snakes. Finally he got up and opened one of the writing tablets. He was supposed to be keeping the procurator informed, but they had not arranged a code. Perhaps it was just as well. If the forgers had suspected that Asper was onto them, the fact that he was sending mysterious coded letters to Londinium might have been his death sentence. Accordingly, Ruso scrawled the bland, "Further information discovered, Council feel they can investigate from here. Back shortly." He contemplated sending a note saying "Bastard! You might have warned me!" to Valens, but decided the satisfaction was not worth the money.

He was sealing the first tablet when two slaves arrived bearing trays. They proceeded to unload far too much food for one person onto the tables by the brazier. As more and more dishes were placed in front of him, Ruso wondered if he had misunderstood the arrangements. Perhaps he had been supposed to select some dishes from the list and refuse others. Were they cursing him over in the kitchen? Complaining about the waste of taxpayers' money? Or were they laughing at his naïveté? Perhaps this was how officials on tour normally ate. He thought of Tilla and the women over in the house with the mended door. He should have invited all of them. Perhaps he could save them some of this.

To his alarm there were more footsteps in the corridor. Another slave backed in through the doorway. He was only mildly relieved when the tray turned out to hold several jugs of drink. Once these were in place, two of the men disappeared, but not before assuring him that they had no idea who might have put an unsigned note under his door and that the manager had asked them the same question. The third stayed to pour his wine. Ruso tried a jovial, "Is this all for me?"

The slave offered a polite smile and said, "Enjoy your dinner, sir!" before retreating to stand in the corner.

Ruso considered asking him if he was hungry, then decided he would be insulted. He took a deep breath and reached for a spoon. Holding it in midair, he turned to the slave. "You don't have to stand there," he said. "Don't you have something more important to do?"

"No, sir."

"Then go and do something unimportant, will you? I really can't eat with you watching me."

"If you're sure you don't need any help, sir."

"It's just eating," Ruso told him. "I'll manage."

"I'll be just outside, sir."

He supposed that would have to do. Alone at last, he was just reaching for the honeyed wine when there was a tap on the door and the slave reappeared clutching a thin sliver of wood tied with twine.

"Yes?"

"This has arrived for you, sir. It was in the corridor, slipped under your street door."

Ruso took the tablet and read "To the Procurator's Man" as the slave glided out of the room again. Slicing the twine with his knife, he flipped the note open and took a gulp of wine before he read, *Get away now. They will do to you what they did to Asper and Bericus. From your well-wisher.*

The wine went the wrong way. Coughing and struggling not to inhale, he flailed at the air with the letter as he tried to cough up the liquid blocking his windpipe. When he regained his composure the slave was back in the room.

"Is everything all right, sir?"

"Fine!" he gasped. The one word brought on another fit of coughing.

The slave was crouched in front of him, holding out a cup of water. He sipped gratefully, feeling it run cool and soothing down his throat. "Went down the wrong way," he explained, pointing at the jug. The note was open facedown on the floor. He retrieved it, just in case the man could read, and hurried out past him.

The only thing moving in the alley was a cat slinking away along the foot of the stable wall. From somewhere nearby he could hear the evening warble of a blackbird. Whoever had delivered that letter was long gone.

Get away now. Tonight? He could hardly go to the stables and demand horses at this hour. By the time he and Tilla were halfway to Londinium it would be dark.

Ruso hung the key back on the hook and returned to try and settle in front of his dinner.

They will do to you what they did to Asper and Bericus.

There was no mention of Tilla, thank the gods. That might mean something. It might not. He didn't know. Dealing with this business was like punching fog.

The slave said, "Is there something wrong, sir?"

"You didn't see who delivered that note?"

"No, sir." The man hesitated by the door. "Would you like me to stay, sir?"

"Perhaps you'd better." Ruso took a spoonful of cabbage and paused with it halfway to his mouth.

. . . They will do to you . . .

He lifted the spoon and held the contents up toward the lamp. It looked like normal cabbage. He licked the spoon. It tasted like normal cabbage. Besides, Asper and Bericus had been bludgeoned, not poisoned.

Still . . . He glanced up at the slave, who was doubtless wondering whether this oddly behaved guest was about to complain.

"Is there anything I can to do help, sir?"

Get away now . . .

Ruso eyed the challenge contained in the dishes laid out around him, and considered asking the slave to taste them all first. The best that could happen was that the man would tell the kitchen staff and everyone would be insulted. The worst was that he would drop dead. That would be very bad for both of them. Although worse for the slave, obviously.

If only the well-wisher had been bold enough to put his name to the note. Ruso put down the spoon and held the tablet up so the slave could see the writing on the outside. "Do you have any idea at all who this might have come from? Someone who might want to help me?"

The man looked nonplussed. "No, sir."

Ruso reread the message. His instinctive reaction had been alarm. Now he must think logically. If the unknown correspondent had intended to poison his dinner, he would not have bothered writing to him first.

He swallowed the cabbage, tried a spoonful of the sauce around the chicken, and savored it before glancing up at the slave. "This is very good," he said. And then, because he did not want to be alone after all, "Want some?"

Later, after the staff had cleared away the dishes and removed the brazier, he checked the locks on the doors and shutters twice, then rammed a chair under each door latch. He reread the note, trying and failing to pick up some hint of who might be warning him and what that person might know that he didn't. Then he snuffed out all but one of the lamps and settled down to an uneasy sleep.

54

THE BREAKFAST WAS not poisoned, either. Ruso had finished eating and plunged his head into a bowl of cold water when he was conscious of a tapping noise. He lifted his head, toweled his ears, and listened again. Someone was rapping on the shutters. An apologetic slave announced that there was a visitor waiting in reception.

"I'll be there in a minute. I'm in the middle of washing."

"He says to tell you he's called Albanus, sir."

"It's all right," Ruso assured his guest, who was perched uneasily on the edge of the spare chair in the reception room of Suite Three. "You don't have to be frightened of the furniture."

Albanus sat back. His gaze kept shifting between Ruso, still toweling his hair, and their surroundings, as if he was waiting for the rightful occupant to come and throw them both out.

"They were very keen for me to find their money," Ruso explained. "And they want to keep on the right side of the procurator."

"And is your wife here too, sir?"

"No, I've got this all to myself. Ridiculous, isn't it? There's a whole dining room across the passage that I've never even used." He waved the towel toward the table. "Help yourself. The cheese is quite good. I'm not sure about that pastry thing with the raisins."

"Can I ask how the inquiry's going, sir?"

"It's finished," Ruso said. "They're going to accuse the chief magistrate." He put his finger to his lips and added very quietly, "It's not finished, but I don't trust the guards. What the hell are you doing here?"

Albanus glanced around the room again before murmuring, "I've come to warn you about something, sir. I don't think you're going to like it very much."

Albanus was right. He did not like it very much. Albanus had done some more ferreting around in Londinium and worked out for himself that Julius Asper was in the pay of Metellus. "I thought you'd want to know straightaway, sir."

"Thank you."

"And that's not all, sir."

"It's not?"

"No, sir. I made some inquiries about what Caratius was up to while he was in town. According to his friend's cook, he arrived at the friend's house and stayed there all night."

"I see," said Ruso, who had never thought Caratius was the mysterious hooded burglar anyway.

"You might like to know that his friend is a man, sir."

Ruso frowned. "Well, of course he's a man. He's a priest of Jupiter."

Albanus shook his head. "I don't think you quite grasped my meaning, sir. His friend, where he stays all night whenever he goes to Londinium, is—"

"Ah!" So Caratius had a male lover. He wondered if Camma had known.

"Anyway," continued Albanus, "the point is, he definitely didn't go anywhere all night. But his guard went out." Albanus paused to scratch his head. "I'm not sure this helps us much, sir. I don't think the guard could have done any burgling in the small hours. Not unless he was acting earlier in the evening. The cook said he was back on the doorstep before long, so drunk he could hardly stand up."

Ruso reached for his knife without thinking and cut a slice of cheese he didn't want to eat. The only part of Albanus's information that was new was the business of Caratius's lover. It was unlikely to be relevant, but the man had traveled a long way to bring it and the sight of a friendly face was more of a relief than he cared to admit. He thanked him. Then he began the difficult task of persuading him to go away.

"It's good of you to take the day off to come and see me," he said, leaning back in his chair and speaking normally again. "I'll see if I can get the procurator to cover your expenses."

"Oh, I haven't just taken the day," explained Albanus brightly. "I've given the boys a week's holiday."

"Ah."

"And the expenses are already dealt with, sir." On any other face, that expression would be called "smug." On Albanus it still retained vestiges of innocent delight as he announced, "I've never been on the fast coach before. It's rather exciting, isn't it? A bit bumpy, though."

Ruso felt a deep sense of foreboding. "Your expenses are dealt with?"

"Oh yes. Young Firmus gave me a travel warrant."

Ruso glanced at the window before mouthing, *Why?*

Albanus whispered, "The procurator thought you ought to be warned about Metellus, sir."

The procurator knew about Metellus too?

The procurator knew about Metellus. Ruso closed his eyes and wished he believed in Tilla's Christos, the god who answered prayers anywhere and did not demand cash in return. How long would it be before Metellus found out and assumed Ruso had betrayed him?

When he opened his eyes again, Albanus was looking uncertain.

"I asked young Firmus to tell the procurator what I'd found out, sir. I hope I haven't done the wrong thing?"

"No," Ruso assured him, feeling something curl up inside his stomach. "No, you've behaved absolutely correctly. Although I do recall telling you both not to get further involved."

"I know, sir," Albanus confessed. "But frankly I wasn't sure that you'd followed every possible line of inquiry before you left. And you've been very good to me in the past, so I thought I'd give you a bit of help."

"Thank you."

"The procurator didn't seem very happy, sir. I think his ribs are rather painful."

"You've actually spoken to him?"

"Yes, sir. And he said to tell you to wrap up the investigation and get straight back to Londinium."

First the well-wisher, then the Council, and now the procurator. It seemed everybody wanted him out of this place. "It may take me a while to finish here."

"I'm happy to help in any way I can, sir."

"I'd like you to escort Tilla back to Londinium this afternoon."

The disappointment showed on Albanus's face, but his voice remained neutral. "There are a couple of other things, sir. They might be a bit embarrassing."

"Don't worry," Ruso assured him. He was beyond embarrassment now.

"Well, I think I might have upset the local doctor. I stopped at the gates and asked for Doctor Ruso and somebody fetched him instead and he was rather cross when I wasn't ill."

"Never mind," said Ruso. "I'm not his favorite person, anyway. What's the other thing?"

Albanus cleared his throat. "Sir, is there something going on that I don't know about?"

"Yes." At least he could reveal that much. "But it's complicated."

"I know it's none of my business, sir, but it would help if I just know what to say to whom."

Ruso said, "I don't want you getting involved in it."

"No sir," said Albanus in a tone that signified disapproval. "And, frankly, it's all very awkward, but I need to know what to say to Doctor Valens."

Ruso frowned. "Valens? What's he got to do with it?"

"Well, sir, how much does he know? Have you told him your own wife is somewhere else but his wife is staying here with you? Or am I supposed to pretend I didn't just see her in reception?"

55

RUSO HAD JUST finished installing Albanus in Julius Asper's office with an abacus and instructions to check what pay was owed to the guards—a task that should keep him out of trouble until it was time to leave—when he opened the door to see three women hurrying toward him across the noisy expanse of the Great Hall.

Tilla was wearing a blue plaid overtunic he had never seen before, hitched up over a belt because it was too long. Camma was carrying the baby, Grata clutching the wooden box that had contained Asper's money and the coin mold.

"What's wrong?"

"Your wife has been attacked!" declared Grata.

With three of them trying to explain at once it was a while before he grasped that the attack had taken place last night. He had not been told earlier because Tilla had insisted she was not hurt and she did not want everyone to make a fuss.

"That's ridiculous!" He put a protective arm around her, thankful for once that this morning's guard included Dias. "My wife's been attacked in the street!" he declared, formally inviting Dias to intervene, as if he might not have overheard while standing three feet away.

The guard captain asked for details. Tilla repeated that she was not hurt, she did not want a fuss, nothing was stolen, and no, she had no idea who had done it. Meanwhile Grata was insisting that the man had tried to strangle her and Camma was tugging at the elbow of Tilla's under-tunic to show where it had been freshly darned in wool that did not match. "He threw her on the ground. Look! Her other dress is covered in mud and ruined!"

Ruso felt his wife shrinking against him, as if all the well-intentioned outrage were a further assault. "Come with me," he insisted, drawing her back toward Asper's office. "We'll clear Albanus out and you can tell me exactly what happened."

"Albanus?"

"He's going to take you back to Londinium this afternoon," said Ruso, letting Albanus tactfully scuttle out before closing the door and holding her close. Finally he settled her into Julius Asper's chair. "You're very pale. Are you really all right? What did he do to you?"

He examined the movement of her neck, checked the bruised knees and the grazed elbow, and conceded that the damage could have been worse. "Did he try to—"

"No," she said, guessing the question. "He said it was a message."

As she explained, he felt himself begin to tremble with rage. He wanted to throttle the unknown bully who had terrified his wife. He was angry with himself too. He should have warned her about that first anonymous letter. He should have arranged for someone to walk her home from the mansio.

"And you really didn't see anything?" he persisted. "What about his voice? Was he a local?"

"Please stop walking up and down."

"Could you guess his height? What was he wearing?"

"I don't know! Stop. You are giving me a headache."

"I should never have let you come here. I'll get you back to Valens. I don't care how it looks, at least you'll be safe there."

Tilla looked up. "I forgot. There is something to tell you. When we went to the mansio to find you this morning we saw Serena. She said there was a man who asked the boys' nursemaid which room the investigator was using."

"What?" He stopped pacing. "When? Why didn't she say so before? Can she describe him?"

"Two days ago. They asked all the mansio staff, but nobody thought to ask Serena's people." When she had finished passing on the description she said, "I think I have seen this man before."

He frowned. "So have I, but I don't believe it. I can't imagine him attacking you in the street."

She managed a smile. "Perhaps he has a big strong friend."

"He'll be needing one when I get ahold of him." He bent to kiss her on the forehead. "I'll be back as soon as I can. Stay with the other women and don't—"

His warning was interrupted by a sharp rap on the door. He was about to turn the visitor away when Tilla said, "It is all right." She squeezed his hand. "I am feeling better now."

The caller was an out-of-breath Gallonius, red in the face and full of apologies for the dreadful outrage that had taken place last night. He had only just heard the news. He had come right away to offer condolences to the lady and the services of the local doctor. He did not know what was happening. The whole town was appalled. Verulamium was usually such a law-abiding place, priding itself on welcoming its visitors . . . He could not believe it. Really, he could not. It had brought shame on them all. He could not apologize enough. When they caught the man, he would be made to pay for this appalling attack on an innocent and respectable married woman.

Concerned that Gallonius would soon be in need of a doctor himself, Ruso tried to calm him down.

Finally reassured that Tilla had suffered little more than a serious fright, Gallonius promised to have stern words with the guard captain about street patrols and said he would arrange a personal armed escort for the rest of her stay.

"My wife's leaving for Londinium at midday," Ruso explained.

Gallonius looked disappointed, as if this confirmed his worst fears. "And I had hoped you would both come to dinner at my town house tonight. As a small compensation, on behalf of my people. Investigator, perhaps you might . . . ?"

While Ruso was trying to excuse himself from an evening of more apology and outrage, Tilla took his hand and looked up at him with an air of innocence that he recognized as the prelude to insubordination. "I would like to stay for dinner," she said. "I would feel so much safer traveling back tomorrow with you, husband."

"That would be marvelous!" exclaimed Gallonius. "My wife will be delighted to meet you both. I'll go at once and tell cook."

Having refused to leave as ordered, Tilla then insisted that she did not need a guard escort to go and help bury Asper's ashes, which were in the treasure box. She also refused the suggestion that Albanus go with them. "It is the middle of the day, husband, there are lots of people about and there are three of us."

"I know, but—"

"I am not going to hide forever because of one man."

"I'm not saying you have to hide forever. I just want you to be careful."

"I am careful!"

"Last night—"

"This is not last night! Do not treat me like a child."

"I'm not! I'm treating you like the woman who may be carrying my child."

She looked at him for a moment, then squared her shoulders. "That is not fair."

"I don't care," he said. "I don't want you getting hurt. And by the sound of it, the others will be safer with you out of the way."

She took him by both hands. "You are a good man," she said. "And a kind husband. But I am a grown woman and I will be safe with my friends."

"Promise me you'll stay close to them."

"All the time," she promised. "Believe me, I do not want to meet that man again."

Albanus looked relieved at being allowed back into Asper's office. "I couldn't quite think what to say to that very tall woman out there, sir. The other one left to go off and argue with your guard chap so she was just standing there with her baby. I wasn't sure whether I was supposed to be making conversation with her or not, so I didn't say anything. It was all rather embarrassing. Is it true she's a descendant of Boudica?"

"So she says."

"Dear me." said Albanus. "I hope I haven't offended her."

56

THE QUAESTOR'S OFFICE was closed. There was no response to Ruso's knocking. His impatient rattling of the handle only brought out the clerk from two doors down, who told him Nico was ill. The doctor had given orders that he was not to be disturbed.

As they left the Great Hall by the street doors, Dias looked to right and left. "Where to now, sir?"

"The quaestor's house. I need to check some final details for my report to the procurator." He hoped the excuse did not sound as lame as it felt.

"The quaestor's ill, sir."

"I know."

Dias said nothing as they tromped through a series of right angles from the forum to the narrow and quiet street where Nico lived. On arrival he looked disgruntled at being left to guard the dandelions sprouting in the gutter, but he had to agree that a sickly and mouse-sized quaestor was unlikely to present any danger. Inside, Ruso was in luck. The buxom landlady in charge of the building in which Nico rented rooms was more impressed by the arrival of an investigator than by the faint voice reminding her from somewhere above them that the doctor had said he was not allowed visitors.

"What's the matter with him?" Ruso asked as he followed her up the creaking stairs of lodgings that were surprisingly modest for a man who controlled the town's money.

"He's come out in a terrible rash, sir. You can ask him." The woman flung open a door and announced, "The man from Londinium to see you."

Nico was huddled in a narrow bed in the gloom, enveloped in a blanket and an atmosphere that smelled of unwashed man, unemptied chamber pot, and linseed oil. At the sight of his visitor, he shrank away and looked as though he was hoping to slide off his pillows and scuttle away down a gap between the floorboards.

"I can't talk to you," he said. "I'm ill."

Ruso waited until the woman had gone, then opened the door again to make sure she wasn't listening on the stairs. Somewhere outside a dog erupted into frantic barking.

He said, "What's this about a rash?"

Nico's eyes widened.

"I used to work in an army hospital," Ruso explained, clapping back the shutters to let in some light and reveal the source of the barking. A terrier was chained to a stake in the middle of an untidy yard. It was leaping up and rattling the chain, straining to escape toward a rubbish heap piled against a tumbledown fence. Beyond the fence was the stolid form of Gavo, evidently under orders to watch the back of the house no matter what the dog had to say about it. Ruso was satisfied that none of the conversation inside the room would be overheard.

Nico had pushed his bedding down to his waist. He lifted his pale linen tunic to reveal a bony chest that was indeed covered in an angry rash. A greasy brown substance had been plastered over it.

"Is it on your back as well?"

Nico leaned forward to demonstrate that it went across the top of his shoulders and around his waist, but the center of his back was normal.

Ruso gestured to him to replace the tunic. "Any back pain, headaches?"

"Terrible pain in my back and legs," said Nico. "My head hurts and my tongue is hawble." It was halfway out of his mouth before he finished the sentence.

"So it is," agreed Ruso, cocking his head sideways to get a better view of the ugly white coating Nico was demonstrating.

"The doctor says I mustn't be disturbed." Nico waved one hand weakly toward a bottle on the shelf. "He's given me a powerful new medicine to try, but it's doing no good."

Ruso took out the stopper, sniffed, and wished he hadn't. "Very powerful," he agreed.

"He's read the signs. He said I mustn't speak to anybody about the missing money."

There was no point in asking which signs: It would be some conjunction of the stars, or an arrangement of freshly spilled animal guts, or whatever local equivalent was peddled to the gullible.

Ruso crouched to peer under the bed and reached for an old scrubbing brush that lay beyond the chamber pot. He ran his forefinger over the bristles, and then put it back and wiped his hand on his tunic. "How are you sleeping?"

"Terrible. I just lie awake for hours."

"Well, you wouldn't be the only one last night. What did you think of the thunderstorm?"

"Dreadful," said Nico. "I hate thunderstorms."

"Right then," said Ruso, straightening up. "I wouldn't worry too much. I've seen this before. It gets better by itself."

"It does?"

"Usually when the patient stops scrubbing his chest with a stiff brush and putting chalk on his tongue. I was an army medic, Nico. I've seen some of the best malingering there is and yours doesn't come close. There wasn't a thunderstorm. Now sit up and tell me who attacked my wife last night."

Nico positively jolted with shock. "Your wife? Attacked? Oh, this is terrible! Was she hurt?"

"Didn't he tell you?"

"Who? I know nothing about it! What's happening to us all?"

"I don't know," said Ruso. "Maybe I'll work it out if you tell me why the hell you're sending me anonymous death threats."

"Me?" Nico drew up his knees under the blanket and wrapped his thin arms around them, but it did not disguise the trembling. "Death threats?"

Ruso gestured toward the stairs. "I'll ask the landlady whether you went out of the house last night, shall I?"

"No! Please, I'm . . ." He stopped.

"You're not ill," said Ruso. "We've just established that." He leaned back against the wall and folded his arms. "I'm willing to accept that it wasn't you who attacked my wife. So are you planning to sneak out and murder one of us, or do you think somebody else is?"

"Oh, no! I would never hurt anybody."

That much at least was credible.

Nico clamped one hand against his forehead in a gesture that would get him a job in the new theater if it were ever built. "You will think I am deranged."

"Try me."

"I was trying to warn you," he said. "I have dreams. Terrible dreams, always the same. A man is being stabbed in the back, and I am supposed to save him but I can't move. I never knew what it meant until you arrived. Then I realized. You are the man in the dream!"

"Rubbish," said Ruso, hoping he was right. He had heard plenty of stories of premonitions in dreams. Some were true and others were nonsense, but he had never heard of one quite so specific.

"And now your wife has been attacked!" Nico shuddered. "I don't believe in these things, either, but how would I feel if it came true?"

"Not as bad as I would," said Ruso. "So in your dream, who's doing the stabbing?"

"I don't know. I never see his face."

"Let me help you," suggested Ruso. "There isn't a dream, any more than there's an illness. You and I both know there's something illegal going on here, and whoever's doing it is desperate to cover it up. Dias is involved in it, and probably another man too, and it's something to do with forged denarii."

Nico gave an anguished howl. As he was saying, "I don't know anything! Help!" the landlady's voice sounded up the stairs. "Are you all right in there, gents?"

Ruso grabbed the undersides of Nico's bent knees through the blanket and jerked them upward, tipping him flat before clamping a hand over his mouth. "Shut up," he hissed. Nico's arms flailed helplessly as Ruso called down the stairs, "We're fine, thank you." He removed the hand. "Talk."

Nico took a deep breath, as if he had been starved of air. "Go away. Please, go away before they come after you too. I can't tell you anything."

Ruso closed the shutters and checked the door again. Returning to stand over the bed, he said softly, "If you really want to help me, tell me what's going on."

"I can't. Just go away."

"Do you want me to go to the procurator and tell him you're part of it? They'll put you in chains and have you tortured."

Nico snatched at the blanket and pulled it up over his chin. "They made me do it," he whispered. "I didn't want to."

"Do what?"

His head jolted from side to side as if he was trying to burrow down backward into the pillow. "I can't! I can't tell you!" He seemed to be having trouble breathing.

The man was reaching a state of panic in which there would be no chance of getting any sense out of him. Ruso seated himself on the floor, leaning back against the bed so he could not see Nico's face. "This is very difficult, isn't it?" he observed to the flaking paint on the wall. "I need to know some things in order to protect my wife and find the money you're supposed to be responsible for, but you don't want to tell me them."

"It isn't that I don't want to!" exclaimed Nico. "I can't. You saw what happened to Asper and Bericus."

"It's all a bit of a mystery, really," Ruso continued, as if he was thinking aloud. "And you know one of the things I can't understand? It's why an obviously decent man like yourself got involved in it. I mean, you don't look the type."

"I'm not! They made me."

Ruso waited. He could hear the landlady moving about downstairs. He had hoped Nico would feel the need to fill the silence, but as the moments drifted by he began to wonder if the man had fallen asleep. Outside, a distant blast on a horn signaled midday. He was about to try again when he heard, "It was when I went to Londinium."

Ruso held his breath.

"The Council sent me to hire the architect for the theater plans. I had quite a lot of money for the deposit."

There was another long pause during which Ruso wondered if he was supposed to guess the rest.

"I couldn't see him till the next morning," Nico continued. "There was what seemed like a nice bar down the road from where I was staying, and there was this very friendly girl . . ."

Ruso had a feeling he knew what was coming.

"And when I woke up," said Nico, leaving events with the girl to Ruso's imagination, "she was gone and so was the money. The people at the bar said they'd never seen her before. I didn't know what to do. I couldn't come home and say I'd lost it. I'd have been shamed. So . . . somebody said he would help me."

"Dias?"

"I didn't say the name!"

"No," agreed Ruso. "So Dias helped you—how?"

"He knew somebody who could lend me the money."

"And in return?"

"I can't talk about that. They'll kill me!"

Ruso turned to crouch beside the bed. "We can protect you," he promised, hoping it was true. "We'll get you sent somewhere out of their reach."

"I shouldn't have told you anything."

"You won't be safe until these men are caught."

"You don't understand."

Ruso's patience snapped. Grabbing the scrawny throat, he hissed, "What I understand, Nico, is that my wife's been dragged into an alleyway and threatened with heaven knows what if I don't keep out of this investigation and she doesn't keep her mouth shut. If I can carry on, so can you. What did they make you do?"

"Let me go!" Nico seemed to be shriveling in terror.

"It's something to do with forging money, isn't it?"

"Please!"

"It must be someone who knows about metalwork. Someone whose family used to make coins in the old days?"

"You can't hurt me! You're a doctor!"

"Someone with access to a forge. Are we talking about someone in town, or outside? Is it somebody on the Council?"

"Help!" Whatever else Nico would have said came out as a strangled gurgle.

Ruso looked down into the bulging eyes for a moment, then sighed and relaxed his grip.

Nico took a gulp of air, grabbed the blanket, and pulled it up over his head. From underneath came a muffled, "I can't tell you anything. Please, go away!"

"Caratius's grandfather worked in silver. Is it Caratius?"

"Go away!"

"Why did he invite Asper to visit him?"

"I don't know."

"Did Caratius know about the plot to murder Asper and his brother?"

"I don't know! I don't think so. No."

"Did you?"

"I had nothing to do with it! They just told me to take Asper into the strong room in the morning."

"And do what?"

"Nothing! I've done nothing!" Nico was still hiding under the blankets. "I didn't know they were going to kill anybody. I just did what I was told. Please, I beg you. Go away."

"Where's the money now?"

"I don't know!"

"Where do the false coins go after they've been minted?"

There were footsteps on the stairs. Nico gave a muffled squeal. "They're coming!"

Ruso, hand on the hilt of his knife, moved to shield the bed from whoever was opening the door.

"You! What are you doing here?"

Ruso let his hand fall to his side.

The doctor's pot belly was still bulging under the same blood spatters as yesterday. "I gave specific orders that my patient was not to be disturbed. I can't have this constant interference. If it goes on I shall complain to the Council. This man is seriously ill."

"Seriously ill with what?" inquired Ruso, interested.

"None of your business," replied the doctor, just as Ruso would have done.

"I only ask," said Ruso, "because it looks like something a lot of men go down with in the army."

"Yes. I hear you've been passing yourself off as a doctor."

"I just thought you might be able to help," he said to Nico, "but never mind. And don't worry, I'm sure that medicine will have you back on your feet very soon." He smiled. "And then we can talk again."

After this thinly veiled threat, he paused for a word with the landlady, who was lurking in the hall and jabbing at invisible cobwebs with a feather duster. In response to his request, she assured him that no other visitors would be allowed upstairs no matter how they tried to get in. This was a properly run house and when she and her husband were asleep, the dog was loose downstairs.

Reassured that his witness was being safeguarded, he gathered up Dias and Gavo. "Well," he said, as casually as he could manage, "That was a waste of time. Anybody mind if we go and hunt down some lunch?"

Was that suspicion on Dias's face, or the reflection of his own tension? He was fairly confident that whatever the man might be thinking, he would not act on it in broad daylight—certainly not while the innocent Gavo was with them to witness it. All the same, he was relieved when they left the quiet street in which Nico lived for the bustle of the main thoroughfare, where to his guards' evident amusement, he paused to buy a bunch of bluebells from a street vendor.

57

"WHAT WE NEED, sir," murmured Albanus, scooping crumbs off Julius Asper's desk and into his cupped hand, "is a way to make this Nico more frightened of us than he is of Dias."

"He thinks Dias is going to kill him," said Ruso. "It's hard to be more frightened than that." He glanced at the bluebells, temporarily stationed in a cup of water, and wondered whether the women were back from the cemetery yet. Perhaps he should go and see.

"Has he got a family he cares about?"

"Not as far as I know."

"That's a shame." Albanus walked across to the high window, stood on tiptoe to check that nobody was outside, and then tossed the crumbs away. "Perhaps we could threaten to kill him more slowly than Dias will."

"Albanus, that isn't funny."

The clerk sighed. "I don't think he'd believe us anyway, sir."

"I offered to rescue him," said Ruso, "but I don't think he believed that, either."

Albanus, to whom Ruso had now explained everything it was safe for him to know and much that wasn't, shifted the box of records he had just finished checking and perched himself on the desk in an informal pose that he would never have dared to adopt during his official years as Ruso's clerk. "I've had a good look through but I can't find any details about the wages Asper owed to the guards, sir."

Ruso had forgotten about the unimportant task to which he had assigned his clerk before deciding to tell him the truth.

"In fact, I can't find any sign that Asper ever paid them anything at all."

"Really?"

"Nothing. I'd imagine the Council considered escorting the tax money to be part of their normal duties."

Ruso scratched one ear. "So when Dias said he was looting Asper's house to make up the wages, he was lying."

"He's the chap with the flashy hairstyle, sir? The one you think was your burglar?"

"And the one who's been blackmailing Nico. I suppose he was searching for anything Asper had stashed away that might incriminate him."

"If Dias is really forging money, where does he spend it?"

"He's up and down to Londinium all the time. Perhaps he's distributing it there." Ruso paused. "You don't look convinced."

"Sir, if I were making false money, the last place I would pass it round is the town where all the treasury officials live."

"Good point." Ruso checked again that there was nobody listening outside the window before settling himself into Bericus's chair and tipping it back so it was balancing on two legs. "Nico doesn't think Caratius had anything to do with the murders," he said. "If that's true, then he hasn't got the money. I think the brothers were killed because Asper was on the trail of the forgery. But I can't tie the forgery or the murder to Dias, and I can't find the money if I can't work out the sequence of events, and I can't hang around here much longer with somebody threatening Tilla and the Council and the procurator both telling me to get out of—aargh!"

He grabbed the edge of the desk to steady himself and rocked the chair forward to a safer angle. "Out of town," he concluded. "Nico was coerced into taking Asper to the strong room, presumably to make it look as though Asper was taking the money. But Camma's certain he never took it. Now Nico says he doesn't know where it is." Ruso looked up. "You don't suppose it's still in the strong room after all?"

Albanus stared at him. "Well, if it is, sir, why would the Council say it's missing?"

"Because Nico told them it is. It's his job to keep track of what's in there." He paused. "You don't think they're all lying because they don't want to pay up, do you?"

"But they always pay up."

"Exactly. Verulamium always pays on time. So when Hadrian canceled everybody else's tax arrears, they must have been mightily annoyed."

"There's only one thing for it, sir." Albanus's tone was resigned, but Ruso recognized the light of battle in his eyes. "I'm going to have to do a complete audit."

"Can you do that?"

"I don't know, sir. But I can add and subtract, and it can't be that difficult, can it?"

Having listened to Nico's explanation of how the Council ran its finances, Ruso decided not to answer. Albanus reached for a records box and began to riffle through it, muttering about confirming the balance due.

"I'd imagine Dias found out that Asper was sending coded letters to Londinium," said Ruso. "A forger would have no problem opening somebody's correspondence and resealing it. Anybody who can make a fake coin can make a fake seal, but if he couldn't read the code he wouldn't know whether Asper was writing about him or not. No wonder he was prowling around Londinium trying to find out."

Albanus reached up onto a shelf. "It's especially easy to intercept a man's letters if he leaves his seal lying around instead of wearing it, sir."

Ruso peered at the ring Albanus was holding out to him and wondered how he could have missed it during his search yesterday. He carried it across to the window and looked at it again. Then he slid it onto his little finger and twisted it around so the stone was hidden in his palm. "Wait here a minute," he said.

Satto the money changer halted his queue when he saw Ruso approach.

"Take a look outside," Ruso urged, stepping past the counter to the window at the back of the office and glancing over his shoulder to where Dias was watching from the doorway.

"What for?"

"Quick," Ruso urged, placing his own hands up on the high sill and leaning out. As he had hoped, Satto did the same. "Over to your left," said Ruso, pointing. "See?"

"What?" demanded Satto, craning for a better view of the unrelenting British clouds.

"Damn," Ruso muttered. "It's gone now."

"What's gone?"

"I thought I saw an eagle," said Ruso. "It's a good omen. But I might have been mistaken." He apologized to the queue on the way out, ignored Satto's confused shout of "Which way was it flying?" and nodded to Dias, who was hopefully none the wiser despite having witnessed the whole exchange. Then he hurried back to tell Albanus that the seal he had found in Asper's office was not Asper's seal. It was a replica of the one on the hand of Satto, the man who authenticated the bags of money stored in the strong room.

"Oh, no," groaned Albanus, uncharacteristically despairing. "Sir, every time I start to get a grip on what's going on here, it changes shape. So was Asper up to something himself? Authenticating fake money, perhaps?"

"Possibly. Or somebody wants us to think he was. I'm sure that ring wasn't in here when I looked before."

"Perhaps Asper and his brother were working with Dias and they fell out."

Ruso shook his head. "I don't know. I'll try and have another go at Nico but we need to find out what's in that strong room. Preferably not when Dias is around."

"This evening?"

Ruso shook his head. "I'm supposed to be dining with one of the magistrates tonight," he said. "Which reminds me, I've got another job for you while I'm there."

"Sir, I may not have finished the audit by this evening."

"Oh, you can take some records with you. This is guard duty. I want you to look after the two witnesses you saw earlier in the hall."

"Me, sir? The ladies? Are you quite sure?"

"You're an intelligent man with military training. I can't think of a better man for the job."

It was so easy to make Albanus happy. In truth Ruso could not think of any other men at all for the job, but he was not going to say so.

58

RUSO HAD NOTED before how the arrival of an infant released a deluge of washing. Rows of it were dripping into the vegetable patch behind Asper's house, and when he queried Grata's absence, he was told she had gone to take bedding to the laundry.

"I was hoping the three of you would stay together."

"I asked her to stay," replied Tilla, holding up a bone-dry linen towel and pulling it to tug out the creases before folding it and adding it to the pile beside her. "She is nothing but bad temper. I offered to help her turn out Bericus's room this afternoon, but she says I will only get in the way."

"She is upset," put in Camma from beside the hearth. She had removed the baby's swaddling to massage his limbs, just as Ruso had read in the textbook. "She has a kind heart underneath."

Tilla reached into the basket for another towel. "I hope so. Did you find the man who sent you the strange letters, husband?"

Ruso helped himself to a stool. "Yes, but he doesn't know who attacked you." Their eyes met and he knew she understood that there were things he could not tell her in Camma's presence.

Tilla grasped a crumpled linen undertunic in both hands and snapped it out flat. The sound startled the baby, who flung his arms into the air. Ruso suspected that Grata was not the only woman here who was in a bad temper. The bluebells had been received politely, but without the gratitude a man deserved for being seen carrying a bunch of flowers through the streets. He wondered if his wife was jealous. She would be returning to Londinium tomorrow, leaving Grata here with the baby and the woman who had become her friend.

He felt partly responsible for Grata's bad temper. Her upset state was his own fault. The sight of Bericus's body would have shaken anyone, let alone somebody who had shared a home with him. Even Dias had seized her by the wrist to try and keep her away. Later he had rebuked Ruso for allowing her forward.

Something whispered at the back of Ruso's mind. For a moment he could not think what it was. He ran over his thoughts again, trying to catch it. It was something Albanus had said this morning. Albanus was alone in the hall with Camma because *the other one left to go off and argue with your guard chap.*

He looked up. "Camma, what's the connection between Grata and Dias?"

"Who knows?" she said lightly. "One minute they are friends, the next not. He is not the sort of man to settle with one woman. Why do you ask?"

Tilla said, "That is another reason for her bad temper. Camma, where do you want me to put these clothes?"

The two women carried on discussing the domestic arrangements as if nothing had happened. Meanwhile Ruso was considering the sudden collapse of the case against Caratius. Nico had already suggested that Caratius knew nothing about the murders. Anyone could have put the body on his land. The only real evidence against him was the message luring Asper and Bericus out of town. The message that only Grata had heard. Now it seemed that same Grata was close to Dias. What if Dias had persuaded her to lie?

A further thought struck him. Grata had been in the room when they had been discussing the coin mold. If she had told Dias, then he would know they had found the evidence of forgery.

Ruso would say nothing to Camma. He might be wrong. Even so, he would warn Albanus before leaving him in charge here this evening. Grata could not be trusted.

On the way out he beckoned Tilla into the garden. Gavo's large form stood awkwardly amid the washing as he kept guard over the back of the house. When Ruso explained that he would like a moment alone with his wife, Gavo nodded and made his way back through the alleyway toward the street. Ruso noticed he did not look at Tilla. After the way she had stalked them through the woods on the way to dinner with Caratius, he probably thought she was dangerously unstable.

When they were alone together beside the bean patch, he gathered her into his arms. He kissed her for the benefit of anyone who might be snooping before murmuring his suspicions about Grata.

"Dias is definitely involved in forging money," he said, "but I can't get any more names out of Nico."

She nibbled his ear and breathed, "It must be a man. A woman working in a forge would be noticed."

He let her think he had already considered that possibility and dismissed it.

"What about the other man Dias was with when I found them stealing the furniture?"

"What other man?"

She broke away from him. "Wait here."

She ran back into the house, and returned to whisper, "Camma says his name is Rogatus."

"The overseer at the stables?" Ruso stared at her. Several things fell into place. Rogatus could intercept the post. He had access to a forge at the vehicle repair workshop. It was Rogatus who had sworn that Asper said he was going to Londinium and had sent him out in a carriage without even the basic protection of a driver. At last this wretched business was starting to make some sense.

He grasped both her hands. "Promise me you'll stay in the house till I come and collect you," he said. "And dress for dinner."

59

THERE WERE MANY reasons why Ruso was glad he was not the emperor, but one that he had never considered until this evening was that the more power you appeared to wield, the more determined people were to impress you in inappropriate ways. The conversation in the dining room of Gallonius's town house was conducted across a fleet of little tables while the staff appeared to be carrying out an experiment to see how much could be loaded onto each one before its expensively spindly legs gave way.

It was hard not to conclude that the food and wine had been arranged by Gallonius while the delicate furnishings and the tasteful red and marble effect walls had been the choices of his wife, a small pale creature whose skin seemed barely able to stretch over her bones and whose conversation consisted mostly of, "Yes, dear." She did manage to ask Ruso whether he was finding Britannia rather cold and should she ask for more coals on the brazier, but when he assured her that he was quite warm enough, her husband said, "Our guest's been here before, woman. Right up on the border. He knows what cold is."

The wife retreated back into, "Yes, dear."

"Boy? Go and see if the piglet's done!" Gallonius gave a sonorous belch, sighed, and explained that he was a slave to his digestion.

"My poor husband has been to all sorts of doctors," ventured the wife, perhaps feeling this was a safe subject on which to expand, "but they can't do anything for him."

Gallonius said, "My father was just the same," as if eating too much and too fast were passed from father to son like a family heirloom.

Tilla reached up to check that the bluebells were still tucked into her hair and said innocently, "Have they recommended any special diets?"

As the staff began to clear the tables, Gallonius and his wife began to describe the various regimes he had followed in the hope of relief.

Ruso was not listening. Now that Tilla had given him the final name, it was all beginning to make sense. Realizing—perhaps with Grata's help—that the tax man was on their trail, the forgers had arranged to murder Asper in such a way as to make it look as if he had run off with the tax money. Asper would be lured out of town by a false message to visit Caratius. Rogatus would tell everyone that he had gone to Londinium, but in fact he and Dias would have intercepted him just outside of town.

Things had gone wrong. Perhaps they had not been expecting Bericus to go too. Somehow Asper had escaped. The killers had also underestimated Camma. Instead of going to the local guards, where her testimony would have sunk without a trace, she had traveled twenty miles to appeal to the procurator.

The trouble was, if everybody stuck to their lies, he could not prove any of it.

Ruso was wondering what Dias was up to this evening—the guards currently waiting to escort them home were strangers—when a roasted piglet appeared on the table in front of him, accompanied by the sort of silence that told him his host was waiting for a reply.

The tentative "Er—" was a mistake. It implied that he had heard the question and was considering the answer.

"Have a try," urged Gallonius, failing to stifle another belch.

It was Tilla who saved him. "It is no good asking my husband to guess what is in there," she said. "He is from Gaul, where the food is very strange and has different names."

It was their host's turn to say, "Really?"

"Oh, yes," Tilla assured him. "When I cook for him, I have to tell him what he is eating."

Gallonius threw his head back and guffawed. His wife smiled wistfully, as if she wished she understood the joke. Tilla adjusted the bluebells again and grinned at her husband. Gallonius answered his own question with obvious pride and a servant stepped forward with a carving knife.

Musing while he ate, Ruso wondered how anyone could think that the best way to astonish and delight a visiting official was to see how many items of unrelated food could be crammed inside a deceased piglet before it exploded under the strain.

"Well!" exclaimed Gallonius as the debris of honey cakes dipped in wine was cleared away and Ruso was congratulating himself on having politely managed a taste of everything, "I'd imagine that's better than you got from old Caratius."

"Much better," said Tilla, dabbling her fingers in the bowl of water the servant was holding in front of her. "More food and no bodies."

Ruso wondered how much wine she had drunk.

"Our guards frightened Caratius's mother," she added.

"A very sad case," put in the wife, seizing on another safe subject. He never brings her into town these days, does he, dear? She wanders off looking for the family silver."

"She's been dotty for years," said Gallonius. "His father only married her because she convinced him the silver was really there. Of course, they never found it. I expect the Iceni had it. If it ever existed." He turned to Tilla. "Which reminds me, my dear. It's very good of you to look after that girl, but you should be careful. The Iceni can't be relied upon."

The awkward silence that followed was broken by the slaves carrying out the last of the empty tables and Gallonius announcing, "And now . . ." in a tone that sounded alarmingly as if they were about to reappear with more food on them. To Ruso's relief he was only announcing that the ladies could withdraw next door while the men talked about things that would not interest them.

Tilla said, "What things?"

"Off you go, wife," Ruso urged her. "Perhaps you could ask the cook for the piglet recipe."

Gallonius's wife dipped her thin fingers in the water bowl, rose from her chair, and began to drift toward the door. Tilla followed, but not before giving her husband a look that said he would be hearing about this later.

As soon as the door had closed behind them, Gallonius sat up straight and said, "I hear you've brought in an assistant."

"He's taking a look at the finance records," said Ruso, adding, "I've spoken to Nico," as if the two facts were related and Nico had given his blessing to the audit.

"Is that really necessary?"

"Yes. You need to be careful what you say about Caratius. Some new information has come up."

Gallonius's eyes widened. "What sort of information?"

Ruso decided not to name his suspects in case Gallonius tried to interfere. "I can't explain until I'm certain," he said, "but Asper's death may have been nothing to do with Caratius. I think there was something illegal going on and Asper got mixed up in it. As Nico's off sick I'll need your permission to go into the strong room."

Was that a brief hesitation before Gallonius stifled a belch and reached for his wine? "We've nothing to hide," he said. "I'll take you in there myself tomorrow morning. But don't be fooled by the amount you find down there. Everything we have is set aside for some purpose or other. Did Nico tell you we have a generous fund to provide bread and schooling for orphans?"

"I did hear you have a fund for the theater."

"A lot of the money for the theater is still just promises, I'm sorry to say." The magistrate called for one of his servants to come and adjust his cushions before leaning back and removing his belt. "If you're right, and Caratius doesn't have the money, where is it?"

"I'm working on that."

"We shall struggle if the procurator expects us to make up the missing payment. There will be a lot of dissatisfaction."

"Yes," said Ruso, "that's more or less what Caratius said right back at the start of this."

Gallonius looked up. "I hope you don't think, Investigator, that this is some sort of elaborate ruse to defraud the procurator."

"Oh, no," said Ruso. "Because if it were, and you were caught, it would be catastrophic for everyone involved, wouldn't it?"

60

AFTER THE WARMTH of the heated dining room, Tilla was shivering inside her shawl as they walked down the moonlit street past the deserted meat market. Ruso put his arm around her shoulders. There was almost nobody around to see them apart from a slinking cat and the two guards behind them, who could think what they liked.

Albanus answered their knock at Camma's house, explaining that the ladies had gone to bed. He had two lamps and a short stump of candle burning on the kitchen table, perilously close to the piles of records he seemed to have spent all evening examining.

"Anything interesting?" said Ruso, more out of politeness than hope.

"Just a moment, sir." Albanus flicked the beads of the abacus with his left hand and scratched a figure on the wax tablet with his right. Then he frowned at the figure and flicked the beads again but made no alterations to what he had just written. "I do have some questions, sir. Probably very foolish ones but I'm only a schoolteacher, I'm afraid. They seem to have an awful lot of different funds and it's rather hard to tell what's where, especially when they seem to keep moving money from one to another."

Ruso squinted at the tablet. "I don't know how you can work in this light. Have you found the orphans' bread and education fund?"

"Oh, yes, sir. And the maintenance of streets fund and the extension to the mansio fund and the fund to pay the municipal slaves and the cost of keeping the guards going. I have to say I didn't realize how complicated this would be."

Ruso pointed to the largest figure. "What's that one?"

Albanus peered at his list, referred to a second list, and said, "That's the running total for the theater fund, sir, as of last January. I'm sorry I haven't finished, but Dias came to call and there was a bit of a fuss over getting rid of him."

Tilla said, "Dias? Here?"

Ruso frowned. "I should have known he wasn't taking the evening off."

"He wanted to talk to Grata, sir. She told me to tell him to go away."

Tilla said, "I knew I should never have left them!"

Albanus visibly bristled. "I got rid of him, sir. The ladies were quite safe."

Ruso said, "Well done," just as Tilla said, "How did you do that?"

"Grata ran back into the kitchen, sir, and I stood in his path and told him that if he tried to come past I would be forced to use violence. And then he tried to insult me, and I told him I was a trained legionary acting under the orders of the procurator, and if he didn't leave straightaway I would report him to you."

"Excellent," said Ruso, picturing the scene. "I knew I could rely on you."

"I think it may have helped when Camma pulled the poker out of the fire and waved it at him," admitted Albanus. He spread one arm to indicate the piles of documents on the table. "So I'm afraid with all that I haven't got as far as I would have liked. I was wondering whether you'd mind if I stayed here to finish, sir? Grata's kindly left me some blankets on the couch."

Ruso recalled the splendor of Suite Three, where the sheets still retained a faint memory of lavender. "Well," he said, "if you're sure you don't mind staying, Tilla can come back with me."

Albanus squared his shoulders. "Absolutely not, sir. I think one of us should stay here to look after the ladies."

Ruso nodded. "Make sure everything's properly locked up," he said. "I don't think he'll be back, but if he is, don't tackle him on your own. Shout 'Fire' and rouse the neighbors."

"Fire, sir?"

"Yes. They may not get out of bed for anything else."

The route Ruso chose toward the mansio took them past Nico's lodgings. There were no lights visible. He stepped up to the entrance to check that it was secure. There was a thud and a rattle of ironwork. The dog that had hurled itself at the door began to bark.

As they fled down the street with the guards clattering along behind them, Tilla gasped, "Nobody in that house will thank you for making sure he is safe."

Once his guards had checked the mansio rooms and declared them free of lurking assassins, Ruso dismissed them for the night. "You'll be safe in here," he said to Tilla, locking the outside door and picking up the lantern that had thoughtfully been left burning in the hallway. Once inside Suite Three, she stood in silence as he lit more lamps and the simple elegance of his accommodation sprang into view. "You have to admit," he said, "we've come a long way since the damp rooms in Deva."

"All this is for one man?"

In the confined space he was conscious again of the clear scent of the bluebells. "There's a dining room and private kitchen as well," he told her. "But I told them I hadn't brought my cook."

"I will go into your kitchen in the morning and start stuffing piglets."

"Tomorrow," murmured Ruso, sliding one arm around her waist and plucking the bluebells from her hair, "you can do whatever you like. Tonight, I want you here."

61

THE BATHHOUSE WAS full of stuffed animals and slaves to digestion, and the masseur was tightening an iron band around Ruso's forehead. He lifted one arm to push the man away, but the stone weighing down his stomach was too heavy. It hurt to move his head. He was too tired to complain.

Beside him, something stirred and muttered. A voice somewhere at the back of his mind said that this was not right. There was no masseur, just the aching head. This was not the bathhouse. He was lying in his bed at the mansio. He had eaten and drunk too much, too late at night, and the body beside him was his wife.

His skin prickled with sweat. The sheets were sticking to him. He was short of breath. He kicked off the covers, flinging them over onto Tilla, who hated to be woken by a cold draft. He lay on his back in the darkness with one arm and one leg trailing over the edge of the bed, trying to cool off.

There was no light around the shutters. It must still be the middle of the night. Wincing as the pain throbbed behind his temples, he rolled over to grope for the cup of water he had left beside the bed. As he drank he noticed a faint red glow in the corner. It must be the reflection of . . .

It couldn't be. There were no reflections in the dark.

He rubbed his eyes and opened them again. The red glow was still there. He could pick out a black curve beneath it. The lip of the brazier. That was why he was so hot. He closed his eyes, wishing someone would come and move it. Or open the window.

He swung his feet down onto the floor and stumbled across to where the window should be, but he must be still dreaming. Instead of a window he found himself fighting with a tangle of blanket that seemed to have draped itself between him and the latch. Finally lifting it out of the way, he managed to unfasten the shutters. Cool air wafted across his face and down over his bare feet. He took a couple of deep breaths. He could see the shape of the flowerbeds and the outline of the roof opposite. There was a lantern burning over by the door to the reception area. He was not dreaming.

A brazier? In the bedroom?

"Tilla!" He ran to the bed, colliding with some piece of furniture and kicking it out of the way. "Wake up!" He flung back the covers and hauled her out of bed. His head was thumping. She was muttering in protest. Struggling. That was good. That was definitely good.

"Wake up," he urged, dragging her across to the window.

She was mumbling something in British.

"Breathe," he urged, holding her up to the fresh air. "Deep breaths."

"Leave me alone!"

"Breathe." He was shaking her now. "Breathe in!"

"I *am* breathing! Get off!"

He loosened his grip. "Did you order some heating?"

"What?"

"Stay by the window." He filled his lungs with fresh air before searching for a taper, and again before leaving the window to light the lamp. When he had satisfied himself that they were alone in the rooms, he said, "Did you ask the staff to put coals in the brazier?"

She shuddered. "Someone has been in here while we were sleeping?"

Would fumes work faster in a smaller body? "Keep taking deep breaths." He put his hands on her shoulders and turned her back toward the open window. "Do you feel sick?"

"A little. But I felt sick anyway after all that food."

She was answering questions sensibly. That was good too.

He opened the doors wide, then wrapped his hands in the blanket and carried the brazier out to discharge its poison harmlessly into the night air.

Yellow light spilled onto the walkway from the reception door. The shape of the night porter appeared. "Everything all right, sir?"

"No," said Ruso. "No, it's not. Somebody's just snuck in and tried to kill us."

62

SUMMONED EARLY, DIAS arrived with six other guards just after dawn. By then a frantic Publius had already threatened the night staff with flogging, arranged to have the locks changed, settled Tilla in with his own family and four yawning slaves to watch over them, and apologized profusely while assuring Ruso that nothing like this had ever happened here before in the whole time he had been in charge. Ruso had to restrain him from sending for both chief magistrates and the doctor.

Dias did all the right things. He declared that no one was to leave. He searched the rooms. He announced that his men would be questioning everyone.

The night staff, still lined up in the chilly reception area, looked terrified.

"Everyone," repeated Dias, looking at Publius, who said, "But my wife isn't—"

"Everyone."

Publius's "Of course" sounded faintly strangled.

Dias commandeered one of the guest rooms for the interrogations. Publius's request to listen in was denied. So was Ruso's, and his, "I think this was done by somebody from outside," was dismissed with, "We'll see, sir."

While Ruso had Dias's attention, he murmured, "I hear you went to visit Grata last night."

Dias looked him in the eye. "She's upset," he said. "That body was no sight for a woman."

"It was her decision."

"And this is mine," said Dias. He turned to his men, giving orders for the staff to be taken into the questioning room one by one. When he saw that Ruso had not moved, he said, "I'll assign you two good men, sir. You can get on with your inquiries, but don't leave town. I'll need to talk to you again."

"You go, sir," urged Publius, looking haggard. "There's nothing you can do here."

It was true. He left Publius to defend his staff as best he could, slipped across to make sure Tilla was still making a good recovery, then left.

The Albanus who lifted his head from the tax office desk at the sound of Ruso's arrival was not looking his best. His eyes were bloodshot and his hair was awry. He had not shaved and he had a red V shape across one cheek where it had been resting on the corner of a writing tablet.

"Long night?" said Ruso, fixing the latch behind him so they would not be interrupted.

Albanus struggled to his feet. Instead of the salute he would have once given, the hand was raised to stifle a yawn. Ruso found himself yawning in sympathy. He still felt too shaken by the events at the mansio to want to talk about them. Instead he grabbed a stool and they both slumped back down with their elbows on the desk. Standards had definitely dropped since they had left the army.

Ruso put a finger to his lips and pointed to the window, outside of which Gavo had stationed himself, and quietly explained his suspicions about Rogatus, the stable overseer. Instead of admiration the clerk's face was one of concern. "Are you all right, sir?"

"No," admitted Ruso, realizing he would have to explain that too.

When Albanus had finished expressing sympathy and outrage, he reached for the wooden tablet he had been sleeping on. "There is some good news though, sir. I think I've found something." He unfolded the thin wooden leaves for Ruso's inspection. One ink-stained finger pointed to a set of figures in spidery black writing with illegible scribbles against them.

"More shorthand?"

As Albanus leaned very close to whisper his response, Ruso was aware that it was some time since his clerk had washed. "No, sir, Asper had terrible handwriting at the best of times. That's his note of taking the money out of the strong room to deliver to the procurator's office."

"So he did have it after all?"

Albanus reached for another record on a much longer, narrower sliver of wood. "This is the Council record, where the quaestor signed it out to him."

Ruso recognized the record Nico had shown him two days ago.

Albanus glanced up at the window, then put both sheets side by side for inspection. "What do you notice, sir?"

Ruso looked from one to the other without enlightenment. "Nothing."

"Not the writing, sir. The ink."

"Nothing."

"It's the same, sir," Albanus whispered. "Different batches of ink come out slightly different, depending on the proportions of the soot and the glue, but I'd say they're the same color."

Ruso angled them both to catch the light. "You noticed this last night by lamplight?"

"No, sir. Not till the sun came up this morning. It shines directly into Asper's kitchen."

"You haven't been up all night doing this?"

"I thought I ought to work fast, sir. Before the procurator starts to wonder where we are. And to be honest I was a bit worried about that Dias coming back."

"I think he was busy elsewhere," said Ruso grimly. He arched his back, stretched his arms to the ceiling, and yawned. "This business will drive us all mad. I hope the women appreciated what you'd done."

"They tried to feed me a huge breakfast, sir."

"Yes," said Ruso, who had barely been able to face his own. "That seems to be the way they show their appreciation around here." He picked up the records again. He was still not sure what he was supposed to be seeing. He whispered, "So they borrowed each other's ink?"

Albanus shook his head. "The boy who looks after the stationery in the Council office isn't allowed to give it to anybody else. Asper would have had to supply his own." He ran his forefinger down three lines of the Council record. "All these are in the darker color, so it must have been their ink, but it only appears once here in Asper's." He pointed to the final entry. "The writing isn't quite the same as the rest. See the way the line crosses on the ten, sir?"

Ruso could not see it, but he was not going to argue with a man who had been examining these records almost nonstop for the last eighteen hours. "So?"

"So someone working for the Council came in here after Asper was gone and added a note to his records."

"The lock had been changed when I got here. I queried it and Nico said he'd been in to search for some clue about where Asper had gotten to."

"I think he already knew, sir," said Albanus. "I think he wanted to get in here and change the records to cover his own tracks. I think this proves Asper never had the money."

Unfortunately it did not prove who did. "If the money were still here, could you tell?"

"I don't know, sir. I know how much I think ought to be there, but it's all very complicated and the Council clerk isn't very keen to tell me anything without the quaestor there. I think he thinks I'm trying to catch him out and steal his job."

Ruso got to his feet. "I doubt the quaestor will be turning up for work. Let's go and see if I can frighten some sense out of the clerk. Then with luck Gallonius will be here and we can check what's actually in the strong room."

63

Verulamium's treasure was stored beneath the Great Hall in a dank underground cell that was barely seven feet square and not high enough to stand up in. Ruso caught a glimpse of boxes and bags piled onto rough shelving against the far wall before Albanus's arrival at the foot of the stone steps blocked much of the light. Then the view faded completely with the shriek of rusty hinges, leaving only the feeble yellow glow of the lamp.

"I didn't mean shut it completely!" Ruso hissed.

The hinges squealed a new note and the shadowy walls reappeared around him.

"Pass me the candle," he said, more nervous than he cared to admit. "Then put something in to jam the door open. We don't want to be locked in here."

"I can't see, sir. I'll put my foot—oh, sorry, sir!" Albanus had just collided with him. "There's not much room in here, is there?"

Ruso closed one eye while he lit the candle. "At least there's no chance of Gallonius wanting to come in and see what we're doing." He put both lights on the floor out of his line of vision. His sight was beginning to adjust now: He could make out the shelving again. He reached for the smallest of the boxes, a crude effort about six inches square and surprisingly heavy. "Try this," he said.

Albanus lifted the box from his hand. "It says 'Orphans,'" he announced. "One bag tied shut with the money changer's seal on the cord, and some loose coins, mostly bronze." Ruso heard the lid clap back into place and the scrape of the box being slid into position on the floor.

"Was that what you were expecting?"

There was a pause while Albanus retrieved the list that was tucked into his belt. "Orphans. One hundred and twenty-three. That's probably about right."

"Is Gallonius still watching?"

The light altered again as Albanus peered around the door. "I can't see him, sir. I can just about make out one of the guards. But I can't see much at all from down here."

"We'll just have to do this as quickly as we can," said Ruso, handing him the next box. "It doesn't matter if he sees us checking the totals: That's what we're here for. What's that one?"

"Wages, sir. Three bags, all sealed, some loose coins . . . I'm looking for three hundred and . . . that's right. This is all very reassuring, sir."

"Good," said Ruso, not feeling in the least reassured. He was trapped in a cold dark hole whose door could only be opened from the outside, and he was looking for something to incriminate the commander of the man who was standing at the top of the steps with the key. He put the wages box back at the right-hand end of the shelf and went on to the next one.

As they progressed along the shelf, Ruso tried not think about what he was handling. There was more money in here than he had ever seen in his life. What a man could do with this! He would have power. He would have choices. He would no longer be compelled to go anywhere to earn a living.

Albanus caught him musing over a bag from the theater fund, a deposit that spread to three heavy boxes. "Tempting, isn't it, sir?"

"Let's not think about it," said Ruso hastily. "The sooner we get out of here, the happier I shall be."

Before long all the boxes and bags had been moved from left to right and had proved to contain more or less what Albanus had been expecting. "That's rather pleasing, isn't it, sir?"

"I'm glad you think so," said Ruso. "I was hoping for an extra seven thousand."

"You think Nico signed the tax money out and then brought it back?"

"Put that way," admitted Ruso, "it doesn't seem very likely."

Albanus was leaning around the door again. "I can see Gavo up there, sir. He's talking to the other guard."

"Right. We need to do this quickly." Ruso chose the position where the light was best, crouched to check that he could not be seen from outside, and sat with his legs stretched out on the cold floor and his back against the shelving. He unsheathed his knife. "Throw me over a bag from the 'Orphans.'"

The heavy little bag landed in his palm with a chink. "Sir, are you sure you can see what you're doing?"

"No," said Ruso, prizing open the lid of the seal box, "but I'm going to give it a try." The coins that cascaded into his lap glistened like a shoal of silver fish.

"It's true what they say about metal, sir, isn't it?"

"What?"

"That it reflects its own color. Whereas everything else shiny just looks white. If we got some gold out—"

"I'm not checking the bloody gold as well." Ruso grunted, placing a coin on his palm and rocking it from side to side so the light caught the edges of the design. After the tenth coin he scooped them all up in his hand, tipped them back into the bag, and retied the cord. "I haven't got time to do them all. That one can go back."

Albanus picked up the wax candle. Meanwhile Ruso removed his left boot and took the seal ring from his middle toe.

Albanus glanced out the door before whispering, "It's as well the guards didn't search us properly, sir."

"They're worried about us taking things out," said Ruso, reaching for the candle. "Not bringing them in. I just hope I'll know what I'm looking for when I see it."

Albanus cleared his throat. "Do you mind me asking exactly what you are looking for, sir? I mean, there wouldn't be much point in them hiding the forged money down here, would there? They'd want to take it somewhere they could spend it."

Ruso, busy resealing the bag, did not reply.

Albanus reached behind him and lifted the lid of the box labeled, "Road and Building Maintenance." He was working the knot open from beneath the seal on the first bag when Albanus observed, "You know, sir, this is very odd."

Another shower of silver fell into Ruso's lap. "I'll say."

Albanus squinted at the holes in the seal box of the first bag and threaded one end of the cord through. "I don't mean the being down here, sir. I mean keeping the money separate like this."

"Really? It seems quite sensible to me."

"But it's completely unnecessary. It's just a lot of extra work. If you know how much is in here, you just leave it all together and keep some working cash and separate records upstairs in the warm. That way you don't have to come trotting down here in the dark every time the Council decides to give two sesterces to the orphans."

Ruso stared at him. Then he abandoned the knot and tossed the bag across. "Seal that one up, Albanus. We've been looking in the wrong place."

He found it in the theater fund: the oldest bags, faintly damp and dated from before Asper had even arrived in town. At least half the coins in the first bag he checked seemed to have blurring around the *s* of "Hadrianus." The second seemed so full of forgeries that he began to wonder if his eyesight was failing in the poor light. "That'll do," he said, handing the bag across to Albanus for resealing. "Let's get out of here. I'm—" He stopped. Someone was coming down the steps.

Albanus gave a squeak of panic and dropped the candle, which went out. The door hinges shrieked and Albanus cried out as the heavy oak door crashed into his arm.

A hefty figure in chain mail filled the doorway. "Sorry, sirs," it said. "But I've been told to come and get you. Something's happened."

64

RUSO RECOGNIZED GALLONIUS'S slaves among the men gathered outside Nico's lodgings. Inside, the landlady looked at him and Albanus through eyes that were red and swollen. Ruso said, "What happened?"

She shook her head as if she could not bear to speak and blew her nose on a scrap of soggy linen.

"Are you all right? You're not hurt?"

Another shake of the head. She pointed to the stairs. "Everyone's up there, sir."

It was not a big room and Gallonius and the doctor had already occupied what space there was beside the bed. Between them, Ruso glimpsed Nico looking more peaceful than he had ever known him to look. The doctor was busy explaining Nico's mysterious illness to Gallonius, concluding, "So I gave him something to help him sleep."

Gallonius's deep voice lent just the right tone of gloom to, "A tragedy."

Ruso stepped across to the empty brazier in the corner. The metal was still warm. He said, "He's been murdered."

The doctor groaned. "You again."

"We've had a tragedy, Investigator," Gallonius explained. "The quaestor was ill, took a sleeping potion, and was overcome by fumes from the brazier."

Ruso squeezed past him to get to the window. "He must have come in this way," he said, examining the edge of the shutters. The dog that had been indoors last night was back on its chain in the yard. It gave a hoarse bark, as if it had worn itself out already. The ground was too hard to betray any footprint of a ladder, but, "You can see where he's forced the latch."

The doctor said, "Magistrate, please have this man removed. He does nothing but interfere."

Ruso said, "He wouldn't have gotten past the dog if he'd come through the house."

The doctor said, "As I was saying, sir—"

"Somebody tried to kill me the same way last night."

"What?" Gallonius turned around as fast as a man his size could manage.

Ruso explained. "The guards are over there now questioning the staff."

Gallonius looked shaken. The doctor looked sorry that the attempt had not succeeded. "You're suggesting somebody climbed in through the window here carrying a brazier full of hot coals? You don't think the dog and half the neighbors would have noticed?"

"The brazier was already in here. All the killer had to do was bring up a few lit coals and arrange the others round them. Nico was doped, so he wouldn't have woken up."

The doctor squared his shoulders. "Are you saying this was my fault?"

"No," said Ruso. "He wasn't ill, but he was very anxious. I'd have prescribed some light reading and given him a sleeping potion myself."

The doctor gave a sigh of exasperation. "If you hadn't interfered, he would have been less anxious."

"Yes," said Ruso. "I know."

"The investigator was just doing his job," insisted Albanus.

"Quite," put in Gallonius. "I have no words left to express how appalled I am by this latest news, Investigator. But there's no need to jump to conclusions here." He moved a little sideways to allow Ruso a better view of the bed. "Look underneath."

Anticipating nothing more than a brush and a chamber pot, Ruso crouched. Brush and chamber pot were still in place, but in front of them was a familiar-looking linen bag filled with something that made it bulge in odd places. He dragged it out, blowing off the dust that had accumulated under the bed. The seal had been broken but a small bone tag was still threaded on the cord. It bore the message: "Satto, the kalends of July."

"If those bags inside are correctly labeled," said Gallonius, "we're looking at over seven thousand denarii."

Ruso whistled softly. "The missing money."

"So he did have it!" exclaimed Albanus. "Well done, sir!"

"He didn't find it," pointed out the doctor. "I did."

Ruso tightened the drawstring on the bag. "Who opened it?"

The doctor said, "It was already open."

Gallonius said, "The doctor was just explaining his findings. Perhaps you'd like to finish?"

"Certainly," agreed the doctor, addressing the magistrate and pointedly ignoring Ruso. "As I said, my patient had become more and more anxious over the business of the stolen money. I had already prescribed treatment for a range of symptoms and yesterday I found the investigator here harassing him, pretending a knowledge of medicine and insisting he was not ill at all. Afterward my patient begged me for some potion to allow him to sleep. I left him with a harmless amount of poppy juice. Later that night it seems he closed the shutters and lit the brazier that the investigator admits was already in the room. Then he took the medicine and deliberately lay down to die."

"Tragic," declared Gallonius, looking down at the figure on the bed. "Thank you, Doctor. The investigator and I will carry on from here." He glanced at Ruso. "A word in private, if you will."

The doctor snapped his case shut. Albanus shot an anxious glance at Ruso, who murmured, "It'll be all right. I'll be down in a moment."

After a confusion of footsteps had retreated down the stairs, Gallonius said, "Well, at least we've found the money, Investigator. It's very embarrassing to find it was our own quaestor. As I've already said, I'm sorry we had to trouble the procurator's office."

"You think Nico stole it?"

Gallonius glanced around the room. "A man living in these shabby lodgings, handling large sums of money every day . . . when Nico realised Asper and his brother had left with no guards, the temptation was too much. He must have paid some ruffians to attack them on the road, stolen the money, and hidden it in his room. Then after you began to close in on him, he realized there was no escape." He glanced from brazier to window. "There was nobody climbing in with lit coals, Investigator. This was a suicide."

It was all more or less plausible, but none of it fit either with Ruso's impression of Nico or with what he had said yesterday.

"Nico was in a position of trust," Gallonius continued. "He couldn't live with the shame of having betrayed his people. He left the money where it could be found and did the honorable thing."

Ruso said, "I want that coin tested by the money changer."

Gallonius frowned. "It's already been tested: You can see the tags."

"Even so."

"I'll call the guards and have it taken over."

"No," said Ruso. "We both need to keep it in sight until Satto gets it."

Gallonius raised his eyebrows.

"This way," said Ruso, not wanting to raise the subject of forgery, "nobody can tamper with it."

"Very well." Gallonius grunted as he pushed the heavy bag of coins across the floor with his foot. "While it's being checked, I'll call an emergency meeting of the Council and announce the news. I'm sure they will want to thank you for your efforts. And Caratius certainly should."

"I still haven't finished."

"But what is there left to do? You helped us flush out the real thief and we have our money back."

"Somebody tried to murder me."

"Obviously some madman who feels he has a grudge. Our men will look into it. But for your own safety, you and your wife should go straight back to Londinium as soon as you've reported to the Council."

"But . . ."

Gallonius took him by the arm. "I insist, Investigator. You've done an excellent job for us, we have our money back, and we don't want anything to happen to you."

65

"SIR," WHISPERED ALBANUS as they followed Gallonius and his entourage of slaves and guards along the street toward the Forum, "if that man killed himself, I'm the emperor Augustus."

Ruso glanced around to make sure Gavo was still following at a distance where their conversation would be covered by the bustle in the street. "I don't trust any of these people," he said. "I've just been given another order to shut up and go away, and I want Tilla safely out of here. Would you go to the mansio and make sure she's ready to leave?"

"What about the other women, sir?"

"You can't go around defending every woman you meet, Albanus." Before the clerk could object he said, "Slow down and let the guards catch up."

As Gavo drew closer Ruso turned and explained that Albanus was going somewhere else and would not need protection.

Moments later Ruso watched the guards mark his clerk's departure down a crowded street. Even though he knew that nobody would murder either of them in the middle of town in daylight, the loss of his only ally made Ruso feel curiously vulnerable.

★ ★ ★

As they entered the Great Hall, Ruso was conscious of the babble of noise fading away. People turned to watch as magistrate and investigator made their way first down into the strong room, and then across the hall to Satto's office carrying yet more bags of cash. Ruso was briefly grateful for the protection of his guards. Anyone bold enough to approach was blocked by a large man in chain mail. Anyone daring to call out a question—"Have you found our money?" or, "Is it true about the quaestor, sir?"—was fended off by Gallonius's "We'll be making an announcement later."

Satto looked up in horror as several guards marched into his office, turned his own men out, and announced to the annoyed patrons in the queue that the money changer was closed until further notice. He was even more outraged by the demand that he perform an instant examination of numerous bags of coins, most still sealed and some old and faintly damp, that already bore his own tag. "Whose idea is this?"

"The investigator's," said Gallonius.

"What for?"

"We'll be making an announcement later," Ruso told him. "Make sure you keep the two sets of bags separate, will you? Otherwise you'll wreck the system."

While Satto got to work, Gallonius went off to organize his emergency Council meeting. Ruso unlocked Asper's office. He sat in the chair that Julius Asper would have sat in, leaned his elbows on the desk where Julius Asper would have leaned them, and wondered if this was how Julius Asper had felt when he realized what was going on.

When the knock on the door finally came, he was tempted not to respond. To spin out these last few moments of peace for as long as possible. Then the rapping grew louder and he heard Dias announce, "Visitor for you, sir," and in response to his, "Who is it?" one of the last voices he had expected to hear replied, "It's me, Ruso. Can somebody tell me what on earth is going on?"

Ruso almost fell over the desk in his hurry to open the door. "Valens! What the hell are you doing here?"

"Frankly," said Valens, seating himself on Asper's desk as Ruso shut the door behind him, "I have no idea. There's nothing wrong with Marcus. Did Tilla put you up to this?"

"Up to what?"

"Writing to say my son was ill. I've just ridden up here like the wind only to find that nobody's expecting me, the place is in chaos, half the staff are in tears, and my wife's too busy fussing about Tilla to bother thanking me. So the guard fellow with the dangly bits in his hair brought me over to ask you what the hell's going on."

"What's the matter with Tilla?"

"I don't know. Albanus caused some panic because he came to find her, but she'd already gone off somewhere to meet you."

"I told her to stay with Serena!"

"Yes, but then you sent a couple of chaps in chain mail to fetch her."

"No I didn't."

"No? And you didn't send me an urgent letter, either? Well, obviously somebody's got it all arse about face." He stopped. "Is there something the matter? Where are you rushing off to?"

Dias wasn't expecting to be grabbed by the throat. He wasn't expecting to have his fancy hairstyle slammed back against the wall and Ruso yelling in his face, "Where's my wife?"

Dias's spear clattered to the floor. He looked stunned. Ruso heard his own voice echoing around the hall. There were hands grabbing him, hauling him backward. People were clustering around. Dias was stepping away from the wall and rubbing the back of his head.

"Where is she?" Ruso yelled, struggling to free his arms and stay on his feet. "What have you done with my wife?"

Dias looked up. "I don't know anything about your wife."

"Yes you do, two of your men took her!"

Valens was there now, approaching with his hands held up in a gesture that was supposed to be calming. "Steady on, now, old chap. There's no need to go attacking people."

"He's taken Tilla," said Ruso flatly.

"Gentlemen, I'm sure if you let him stand up . . ."

Dias gave the order. Instantly, they let him drop. Ruso staggered, then regained his balance. Both chief magistrates were hurrying across the hall toward him. He looked at Dias. "Where is she?"

Dias said, "He's out of his mind. I don't know what he's talking about."

Valens was saying something soothing and trying to steer him back toward the privacy of the office. Ruso shook the hand off his arm. "I'm not one of your bloody patients!"

"Then try and behave like a sane man!" hissed Valens. "What's the matter with you?"

Ruso reminded himself to breathe. The shaking would stop if only he could breathe properly. "They tried to kill us last night," he said.

"Oh, come on. I'm sure nobody—"

Ruso spun around and seized his friend by the shoulders. "Make sure Serena's safe with her cousin," he said. "Tell her not to leave the mansio. Then get some of your own slaves and find Albanus and Tilla. Try the guard headquarters in the Forum. Try the stables. Try Asper's house. Try anywhere you can think of. If I don't meet you at the mansio, take everyone back to Londinium and say . . ." He paused, realizing he could be overheard. "Just take them home," he said. "I'll be along as soon as I can."

Valens frowned. "Are you quite sure you're all right on your own?"

Ruso took a deep breath. He wasn't going to be all right until he found her, but he had to stay in control. It might be the only thing that was keeping her safe.

66

Ruso stood on the podium. One or two of the councillors crammed onto the benches had taken the time to dress in their togas but most were in their everyday clothes. He looked over their heads to the ordinary men and women crowding all the way to the back of the chamber. He recognized the bronzesmiths who lived next to Camma. Nico's landlady. The masseur with the mole on his nose. These Britons with their shaggy hair, their bright stripes and checks and their legs encased in workaday trousers, were once more waiting for him to make a speech.

The chief magistrates were watching him from one side, seated in their metal-framed chairs. At the far end of the chamber, Dias was standing in the open doorway, well placed both to hear what was being said and to issue orders to his men outside.

Those were the listeners he could see, but whatever he said here would have wider consequences. Other people had expectations of him. Metellus. Firmus. The procurator. Camma. *Tilla.*

Ruso cleared his throat and glanced at the magistrates. They knew what he was about to say. They had called him into a side room to discuss it as the chamber was beginning to fill.

Gallonius had been the more apologetic of the two, saying, "We had hoped it would not come to this."

Caratius had insisted that if he had known what was going on, he would have put a stop to it. But both were agreed that there was only one way forward.

"Nico had threatened suicide before, you know," explained Gallonius.

"Really?"

"On the day he confessed to me about all the false coins he had slipped into the theater fund to replace the money he took out."

Ruso stared at him. "You knew?"

"He came and told me all about it after we heard that Asper was dead. Nico was planning to slip the stolen tax money back in to replace the false coins, but when your investigations began, I think he realized there was no way out."

"I knew none of this when I came to Londinium," put in Caratius.

Ruso said, "But all the time I was here, you knew—"

"*He* knew," said Caratius, glaring at Gallonius. "I was only told the whole sorry tale this morning. It's an utter disgrace."

"And have they told you where my wife is?"

"Your wife is in good hands, Investigator," Gallonius assured him. "All you have to do is make your final report to the Council as we've agreed, explain that the money has been found and the investigation is over, and I'm sure our guards will bring her back safely to you."

"I'm representing the procurator. I can't lie."

Caratius said, "Nobody is asking you to lie."

Gallonius's face softened into a smile. "We are simply asking you not to announce wild conclusions that will do nothing but stir up trouble. We asked the procurator for help, we have received it, the money is found, and we are satisfied that the investigation is over."

Ruso turned to Caratius. "I think Dias and Rogatus murdered Asper and his brother and tried to put the blame on you. I'm sure Dias killed Nico and he nearly killed me. If you don't get him under control, you could be next. Why the hell are you covering this up?"

Gallonius said, "If I were you, Investigator, I wouldn't be making wild accusations about our guards while they are looking after your wife."

Caratius held up a hand to silence him. "Your complaints have been noted," he said. "And we're grateful to you for pointing out the problem. But this town paid a very large price for its independence and we don't intend to lose it by calling in Rome's help for an internal problem."

"We don't want anyone saying we can't control our own affairs," said Gallonius.

Caratius said, "We'll deal with our own people in our own way after you've gone. Please make your report and leave."

"Exactly," said Gallonius.

Shut away in the side room, listening to the babble of natives gathering outside, Ruso realized he had achieved a small and unwelcome miracle. The quarreling Britons had finally managed to unite in the face of a common enemy.

The hubbub in the Council chamber had fallen silent now. Ruso cleared his throat again and wished there were something in front of him to hold on to. He should have made notes. He should have done many things. Now that it was too late, he was beginning to see what they were.

Someone coughed.

A voice shouted, "Get on with it!"

Ruso glanced across to make sure Satto was still in the side room, where he had been advised to keep out of the way. He took a deep breath and set out across the tightrope. "My name is Gaius Petreius Ruso," he announced. "I was sent here by the procurator at the request of Chief Magistrate Caratius to help your Council find out what had happened to a missing consignment of tax money. As you know, the money has turned up."

There was a general cheer, prolonged by the catching-up of people who needed his words translated by their neighbors or repeated into deaf ears.

"As you also know, both of the men who were supposed to deliver it were found murdered, and this morning we've all been told about the sad death of your quaestor, Nico. He was suffocated by the fumes from a brazier during the night."

The low volume of the murmur that followed suggested most of his audience had already heard this. Someone shouted, "Tell us something we don't know!" The ripple of laughter around the hall did not disguise the sound of the scuffle at the back. Ruso waited until the guard had hauled the heckler out past Dias, and began again.

"The missing money was found in the quaestor's room by his doctor." Ruso glanced at Gallonius. "The circumstances of his death were consistent with suicide. We know he went into the strong room with Julius Asper on the day the tax money was taken out, but we'll probably never know how it ended up under his bed."

Undeterred by the fate of the previous heckler, someone called out something in British, and there were cries of agreement. Someone helpfully translated, "He pinched it!"

"Anyway, the point is, you've got it back," said Ruso. "But I'm afraid there's more bad news." He beckoned to the Council clerk, who stepped forward and handed him the clay mold. He held it up for everyone to see, glanced down the hall in the hope of catching the expression on Dias's face, and stopped. Camma and Grata had just appeared in the doorway with Albanus. Camma had the baby tied in a shawl against her chest. Dias was letting them in but Albanus remained outside, shaking his head from side to side, his hands raised in a gesture of hopeless confusion that said he had not yet found Tilla. Ruso gave a nod of acknowledgment. Albanus stepped back and disappeared from view.

Camma's height and her bright hair made her easy to follow in the crowd, and he watched as the women edged along the back wall to find a space. Albanus had probably brought them here to keep them safe, but he had done it at the worst possible moment.

"Get on with it, man!"

There was no time to explain.

"Some of you will know what this is," he said, returning his attention to the mold. "If you don't, it's a mold for making coin blanks. But of course coins can only be made with the approval of the emperor." He held up something else. "This looks like a denarius. It isn't. Your money changer has confirmed that it's a fake. The silver is just a coating."

There was a murmur of unrest around the room.

"I'm sorry to say that a proportion of the money in your theater fund is made up of this sort of thing," said Ruso.

The unrest swelled to outrage and disbelief. The words *money changer* and *fraud* rose from the general hubbub.

"It isn't—" Ruso stopped, waiting for quiet. "It isn't your money changer's fault," he said. "The coins were switched after they had been counted and checked and stored in the strong room."

The uproar he had been expecting erupted. Everyone was either talking to his neighbor or shouting at Ruso. One voice was demanding, "Why the theater fund?" That was when Satto appeared and shouted, "Because you idiots will never get round to spending it!" and was engulfed in a storm of accusations and demands to know why he hadn't spotted it before. "Because it was stashed away in the theater fund!" did not seem to satisfy anyone. Dias's hand rose in a signal to a group of guards. They pushed their way forward to drag Satto and a couple of councillors apart before a fight started.

Gallonius lumbered onto the podium and raised both hands in the air, shouting, "Order!" to little avail. The clerk appeared with the horn and blew an off-key blast that had to be repeated three times before anyone took any notice.

When Ruso could finally make himself heard, he said, "The unfortunate death of the quaestor means he can't shed any light on how this was done."

"He was the one doing it," prompted Gallonius, squeezing back into his seat.

"Not alone," Ruso said. "He wouldn't have enough hands. Forging money is at least a two-man job. And if he was putting false coins into the theater fund so he could steal the real money, what was he doing with it? Did anyone see any evidence of him being wealthy?"

For once, nobody had anything to say. Gallonius glared at him. This was a departure from the script.

"I think Nico was forced to help," Ruso said, "by someone who had some power over him. Someone who had caught him out in some way, or threatened him."

Both magistrates were listening intently now. Ruso tried to look over the heads of the crowd, to catch Camma's attention. Their eyes met. He was about to say more or less what he had been told to say, and he willed her to understand that he had no choice. He hoped Albanus had warned her that Tilla was being held hostage. He hoped the guards here would have the decency to protect her when he had finished speaking. Lifting up the evidence again, he hoped he wasn't about to make things worse for everybody. "I found these things," he said, "including this copy of the money changer's seal, in with the possessions of Julius Asper and his brother."

Camma's scream of "No!" penetrated the uproar. Someone yelled, "Where's our money, bitch?" Caratius was shouting, "I warned you about him! Didn't I warn you?"

People were crowding toward the back of the room. He could not see her now. He felt a sudden lurch of panic. What if the Dias's men stood back and refused to intervene?

He leapt down from the platform shouting, "Keep away from her!" and was instantly surrounded by a gang of councillors. As he struggled to push past them, an elbow landed in his ribs, a boot on his toes, and he had to grab at someone's arm to avoid being knocked over. By the time the guards reached him, he had barely made it as far as the second bench. Shouting, "Keep them away from her!" and "Where's my wife?" he was hauled back toward the platform. Breathless, unable to yell above the din, he gazed out over the chaos and saw a commotion going on at the far end of the hall. Dias and a couple of his men were blocking the doorway with their shields, sticks raised to beat anyone who dared to approach. Ruso scanned the crowd but could not see Camma or Grata anywhere.

"It's all right, Investigator." Gallonius's voice in his ear made him jump. He had not noticed the magistrate joining him on the platform. "We're not barbarians. Our guards allowed the women to leave safely."

"Where's my wife?"

"I'm sure she can't be far away. Finish your speech and we'll send someone to look for her."

"I've got no more to say."

"That was a good speech, but you left out who murdered Julius Asper."

He had left out a great number of things. It was just as well that logic was not the Britons' strong point. His listeners had leapt to the conclusions they were supposed to reach, despite the fact that much of his statement was equivocal and there were wide enough gaps in it to drive one of Boudica's chariots through. Ruso looked Gallonius in the eye. "I'm not going to tell anybody Nico killed Asper," he said. "You might have got them believing Asper was a forger, but they'd never fall for that. Just remember that Camma's got the procurator's protection, so if anything happens to her, you'll be getting more visits from investigators. Where's my wife, Gallonius?"

Gallonius beckoned to the clerk. "Have the guards escort the investigator back to the mansio, will you?" He turned to Ruso and smiled. "Thank you, Investigator. I think you'll find that, as I said, we are not barbarians."

67

SOMEONE HAD BEEN in Suite Three again. It had happened while she was out, this time, and for the best of reasons. After the guards had finished their searching, the floor had been swept, the lamps filled, and the unmade bed straightened. Still, it made Tilla uneasy. She hoped the Medicus would finish his speech soon. Once he had explained what he had found out, they could leave.

She moved one of the chairs close to the open window, sat back, kicked off her boots, and yawned. She did not want to be in this room, but she was tired of all the questions and the sympathy. Besides, she wanted to leave Valens and Serena on their own.

So far, her plans had not gone well. It seemed the weedy clerk Albanus had arrived with a message for her from the Medicus just after she had been called away by the soldiers, and the clerk had created a terrible fuss because she was not there to receive it. Then minutes after Albanus had hurried away to hunt for her, Valens had arrived on the fast carriage to find that neither of his children were ill, but instead everyone was in a panic looking for Tilla. So he had left Serena alone with the children yet again while he rushed off to track down the Medicus and find out what was going on.

Now she finally had Valens and Serena in the same building, she had retreated and left them to find ways of talking to each other.

There were plenty of women who envied Serena her charming and handsome husband, but Tilla was not one of them. Valens was like a polished surface: Everything slid off him. As she retreated from their company, she had whispered, "You must pay some attention to her!" and Valens had beamed and said, "Of course!" as if it was what he had intended all along.

She yawned again, and gazed around the room. Apart from the dreadful business with the brazier last night—the guards had gone now, but some of the staff were still in tears—these were elegant lodgings. They were much better than most of the places she had stayed at with the Medicus on his travels. She would like to have shown this suite to some of the innkeepers they had met in Gaul who thought they were so superior. The only trouble was, with all those servants around there was nothing left for a normal person to do to occupy her time.

She had left Londinium in a rush and she had not thought to bring any work with her. Besides, she was tired of spinning to no purpose. Already there were three big bags of skeins stored in sacks down at Valens's house, ready to be given to a reliable weaver as soon as they were settled somewhere. Perhaps that workshop around the corner from Camma's house—

A shadow fell across the window.

"Tilla!"

The Medicus was reaching for her. His grip was feverish, as if he was afraid to let go.

"It is all right," she assured him. His eyes were bleary and the lines around his mouth deeper than usual. After finding that brazier he must have been awake for the rest of the night. She leaned forward to plant a kiss on his nose. "I am feeling better, and I have a surprise for you."

"But Valens said—"

"It was all a muddle." She pulled her hands out of his. "Come in quick, before he sees you and wants to talk."

Inside the room he still clung to her. "I told you to wait here for me!"

"The guards said your work was all finished," she said, "and that you were giving a report to the magistrates. They said they would tell you where I was."

"They didn't."

"Sit down and listen. You are worn out." She rang the bell for the servant. While they were waiting she explained what the guards had told her—that after questioning people all morning, it turned out the brazier had been put in their room by the man who had been slipping the frightening notes under the door. "It was that Nico all along," she said. "The one who was supposed to look after the money. It was him who paid somebody to attack me. After he thought he'd killed us, he went home and killed himself. Did you know?"

Instead of saying yes or no, he just looked at her with dull eyes. She was reminded of the times when the fighting had been at its worst in the North: He had come home from dealing with the never-ending queues of wounded men, too tired to wash or change, saying he could not sleep and then dozing while his food went cold in front of him. She was surprised: it should have gone well over at the Council. Still, he was tired. He was not a man who liked making speeches. And he must be upset that Nico had nearly managed to kill them both.

The servant arrived. Tilla ordered wine and began to tell him about the misunderstanding with the guards. At first she had been worried about going with them, especially since he had told her to stay here, but as soon as she looked across the street and saw that Gallonius's wife really was there waiting for her, she had realized they were telling the truth. It was to be a surprise. "The Council are so pleased that you helped them find their money!"

"Is that what she said?"

"She wanted me to look at the house before they spoke to you." She caught his eye. "We do not have to stay if you don't want to. But it is a good house. And there would be plenty of patients coming through the mansio and Valens could come and visit and I could keep company with Camma and the baby until her family—" She stopped. She had not told him about the letters. No wonder he was looking blank.

"When you are not so tired," she said, "you will think this is funny. I have started sending letters."

"You?"

"I have come to see that there is a use for reading and writing. When someone is a long way away." She smiled. "And you can pretend to be anybody in a letter." She had gone to the scribe in the Great Hall and paid him to write two letters for her: one from herself, the midwife, to Camma's family, telling them their sister was left on her own with a healthy and beautiful son, and one from somebody called Ruso to Valens, telling him to get here fast as young Marcus was seriously ill but he had not wanted to frighten Serena by telling her. "So here he is," she said. "I knew you would not mind. It is not going well between them, but I think they are both even more unhappy apart than they are together."

He said, "You were out looking at a house with Gallonius's wife?"

"Just around the corner. With a garden. We could have hens." She wrinkled her nose. "But not a cockerel."

He ran a hand through his hair and made it stick up. "I came here to do a job for Firmus."

"And you have," she said. "Never mind if the speech was no good. If you are doctor to the mansio you will not have to make any more speeches."

"Is that what you want? To live in a place like this with these people?"

She had chosen the wrong time to tell him: She could see that now. He was tired and bad tempered. "It is not home," she agreed. "And it is the Catuvellauni. But we have to go somewhere."

"The magistrates say they're going to deal with Dias," he said, not sounding as though he believed it.

"Dias cannot be trusted," she agreed. "But Camma will curse him and perhaps the gods will bring justice."

"I think he flattered one of the housemaids into lending him the key to our room. No wonder he wanted to question them all in private. And I'm sure he was Valens's burglar. There's nothing wrong with his back that I can see. If I had longer I'd—"

"But you are not an investigator now! It is finished. Let the Council deal with it. You are a Medicus."

"I know it was him. And Rogatus over at the stables was helping him."

She was not going to argue about that now. "When you are feeling better, you need to go to the baths," she said, smoothing his hair down. "Serena's cousin wants us all to have dinner together and I said they could use our dining room."

Sometimes there was no pleasing him. A few moments ago he had been worried about her. Now it seemed he could not even bring himself to speak to her. When the servant arrived with the wine, he seized on it like a drowning man grasping for a rope.

68

ALBANUS HAD DEVISED himself a program of searching for Tilla for an hour and then returning to the mansio to see if there was news. He was lurching up the steps to make his second check when he met Ruso and the object of his quest leaving him a message in the reception area.

Tilla's, "There you are! You look even worse than the Medicus!" did not go down well.

"What my wife means," explained Ruso, "is that she's sorry everyone's been put to all this trouble because she failed to tell anyone that the guards who took her away from here were in fact taking her for a pleasant tour of the town."

Albanus blinked. "But sir, I thought—"

"I know," said Ruso. "I'm on the way to try and explain to Camma."

Tilla said, "Explain what?"

Albanus shook his head. "I've just come from there, sir. She isn't at home. Grata can't find her." He paused. "So now do you want me to look for her instead?"

Ruso looked him up and down. "I think you've done enough running around today," he said. "Go and take yourself off to the baths for a cleanup. Apparently we're all dining here tonight. I'll see if I can find her."

Tilla said, "Did she take the baby with her?"

"No." Albanus covered a yawn with one hand. "Grata is coping on her own."

"Then she cannot be far."

There was no sign of Camma in any of the shops around the Forum, and the women Tilla approached on the way out of the Great Hall had not seen her. Ruso left her to ask around while he went to the guards' office. A man he did not recognize looked up from the desk and said, "Did you find your wife, sir?"

"Yes, thank you." He wondered how many of the guards knew what had been going on this afternoon. Doubtless all of them would have heard that he had attacked Dias in front of everyone in the Hall. "I'm looking for somebody else now. A different woman."

The man grinned. "Really, sir?"

Ruso put his hands on the desk and leaned across. The man's breath smelled of onions. "Really."

The grin faded. The man promised to put out a Missing Person Report immediately.

A *Missing Person Report*. They even had a name for it. Whatever else Dias was, he was a good organizer.

"Now where do we look?" asked Tilla, rejoining him in the middle of the Forum just as a rich voice bellowed, "Investigator!" He spun around to see Gallonius emerge from the Council chamber and head toward them with his arms spread wide as if he was trying to stop them escaping.

"Investigator," he repeated, clapping Ruso on the arm, "good to see you. I think it went rather well at the meeting, don't you?"

Ruso said, "Were you behind that game with my wife, or was it Dias's idea?"

"You mean our little offer of thanks, Investigator?" Gallonius gave him a conspiratorial wink. "Or should I call you Doctor?"

"Someone deliberately arranged it to look as though she was being arrested."

The smile faded. "Why didn't you say something? Did anyone tell you that your wife was being threatened?"

"Not exactly, but—"

"I think you've been jumping to conclusions again." He looked from one to the other of them. "I'm sorry if you felt misled, but I hear the lady approves of the house and we have to keep the ladies happy, don't we? She's welcome to stay here while you go down to report to the procurator. That reminds me. If you would kindly explain to him that the forgers are dead, he's welcome to send as many men as he likes to witness the destruction of the false coins."

Tilla began to say, "But they aren't—"

"Obviously," said Ruso, talking over her, "you won't be asking him to write off the tax."

"No, no. We'll find the money from other funds and send it down in a day or two. It will be a shame for the orphans, of course. Most of the maintenance work will have to wait and it will be disappointing not to have the theater under way by the time the emperor gets here, but don't worry. We will pay our dues."

"Never mind about the orphans and the emperor," put in Tilla, who perhaps now understood the real reason for her escorted trip around town. "Where is Camma?"

Gallonius scratched his head. "I'm sorry, my dear," he said, "I have no idea where your friend is. There's no reason why I should know, is there?"

Ruso sighed. "No," he said. "There isn't. You don't even need to shut her up now, do you?"

Tilla watched the magistrate walk away toward the Great Hall with his trail of slaves. "That man," she said, "is a liar."

"He's a survivor," said Ruso. "We'll try the house. Perhaps she's come home."

They could tell before the door was open that Camma was not at home. Her son's screeching complaints almost drowned out Grata's shout of, "If you've come wanting money, piss off!"

"It is me!" called Tilla. "Let us in!"

Grata wrenched open the door and thrust the baby into Tilla's arms. "You try," she said, handing her the feeding pot with the spout. "These things are useless." She dabbed at the wet patches on her tunic with a cloth. "I'm not paid to do this, you know."

As she turned to lead them through the house, Ruso saw that the skin over her left cheekbone was flushed and swollen, as if someone had struck it.

The kitchen air was thick with the smell of stew and soiled baby cloths. Tilla seated herself by the fire. Preoccupied with trying to calm the infant, she did not seem to have noticed the bruising on Grata's cheek.

Ruso said, "How long has she been gone?"

Grata gave whatever was in the pot a stir and banged the spoon on the side of the cauldron. "I don't know." She had been working in the kitchen, trying to prepare a meal, while Camma sat nursing the baby and weeping and saying she was all alone and nobody understood her.

"Then the baby fell asleep," said Grata, "and I told her to go and get some rest." She glanced from Ruso to Tilla. "I need a rest too. This house is full of nothing but trouble and crying."

Tilla reached across to the table and balanced the pot so nothing would tip out of the spout. "He is not hungry," she said.

"Then what's he got to cry about?"

Tilla shrugged. "Perhaps he wants his mother."

Ruso said, "I've alerted the guards to look for her."

Grata snorted. "You are asking Dias for help?"

"I don't trust him," said Ruso, "but his men are our best bet. I'll carry on looking, but if she comes back in the meantime, tell her I'm truly sorry about what happened at the meeting. You both turned up at the wrong moment."

Tilla looked up from rocking the baby. "Camma heard what you said to the Council?"

"He let the Council think everything was the fault of Asper and Nico," said Grata. "Nobody spoke the name of Dias, still there throwing his weight about."

He said, "I can explain."

"No need," said Grata. "I know how it happens. They have frightened you like they frightened me. And this is not all your fault." She scraped a stool across the floor and seated herself on the other side of the fire. "This afternoon I told Camma something I should have said a long time ago," she said. "But I thought . . ." Her voice drifted into silence. Then she shook her head. "Anyway, I have been first a fool and then a coward. And now perhaps more of a fool for telling it, but I am weary of all the lies. And I keep thinking about what happened to Bericus."

Ruso and Tilla exchanged a glance. Tilla said, "What is this thing, sister?"

"There was no message to meet Caratius at his house," said Grata. "Dias asked me to say it."

Ruso felt a lurch of disappointment. He had been hoping for something new: some unexpected revelation that would point the way out of this mess. "Don't worry," he said. "I'd already guessed that."

"But Camma had not," said Tilla.

Ruso said, "Does Dias know that you told her?"

Grata lowered her head. "He was here just now," she said, "pretending he wanted to make sure we were all right after the trouble at the meeting."

"And did he know you had told her the truth?"

Grata sniffed. "I told him I was sick of him and I never wanted to see him again. And he said I had better keep my mouth shut because I would be in trouble if I didn't, and I told him it was too late." She cupped one hand over the bruising. "That was when he hit me."

"I think she has gone to the cemetery," said Tilla. "She has gone to lift the curse on Caratius in the place where it was spoken."

Ruso said, "Dias's men will have seen her go through the gate. If she's there, he'll know where to find her."

Tilla laid the baby back in his box and pulled the blanket up to his chin. "If he wakes again, try warming the water and putting a little honey in it."

"What if Dias comes back?"

"Dias will be too busy chasing Camma," said Tilla.

"Because of me? Because I told her there was no message?"

"Because she might tell everyone who is behind all this," said Ruso, wishing he had done so himself. "I'll go after her."

"We need horses," put in Tilla, plainly not intending to be left behind. "We can take Grata to the mansio on the way to the stables. She will be safe there."

"You are a sensible woman with a good heart," she assured Grata breathlessly as Ruso unlocked the street door to let her into the safety of Suite Three. "Keep this door blocked, because Dias may still have a key. If you have any trouble, run into the garden and shout for Doctor Valens and Serena. I will be back as soon as I can, and when we find Camma, I will tell her to give you extra pay."

69

AFTERWARD, ON BAD days, Tilla would blame herself for the delay she had caused by insisting on taking Grata and the baby to safety. On those days, she would blame herself for everything. Sometimes the Medicus would tell her that they were both at fault, and at other times they would agree that Dias had been the cause of it all. The truth was that they would never know. All they could say with certainty was that if they had been a few minutes earlier, it might not have happened.

If only Tilla had demanded a proper horse, instead of the fat little pony that the stable boy had insisted on leading across to the mounting block because he seemed to think a woman would not know how to get on without help. If only she had not distracted him by asking if he had never seen a woman in skirts hitch them up and ride astride before. If only it had not begun to rain in thick cold drops as they trotted through the town toward the south gates, and if only they had not had to shout for the men to come out of the guardhouse and confirm that, yes, they had seen Camma hurrying past less than an hour ago.

If only they had not wasted time riding through the cemetery and calling her name into the woods, with Tilla pushing windswept hair out of her eyes and shivering, wishing she had brought a cloak, while the horses' hooves churned up the wet grass between the graves. If only there had been a funeral that afternoon, the cemetery slaves might not have smelled of beer as they wandered out of their hut to see what was going on. They might have remembered which way the wild-haired woman had gone after she had left.

If only she had not paused to cut a switch to wake the fat pony because it refused to speed up even when the Medicus tried to lead it with his own horse, and if only he had not slowed so that he could keep her in sight . . .

If none of these things had happened, then Dias might not have already been on his way back from Caratius's farm by the time they arrived, galloping headlong toward them on the track through the woods and reining his horse in as he saw the Medicus waving at him. Tilla was too far away to hear what they were saying to each other before Dias yanked the horse's head around and both men raced back toward the house. Even the fat pony seemed to understand, too late, that she needed to hurry.

Through the rain Tilla could see servants clustered around something at the foot of the house steps. The Medicus slid down off his horse and ran toward them. As they parted to let him through, she could see a splash of bright hair on the ground, golden against the scarlet of blood. The fat pony's hoofbeats slowed and she heard the thin, terrified screams of the old woman.

The Medicus was bending over Camma, talking to her, but he was asking the same questions again and again. *Can you hear me? Camma, can you hear me?* He was trying to wipe the blood from the side of her head and shelter her from the rain with a borrowed cloak and organize the servants to bring something to lay her on and get her up to the house.

All the time the old woman was clinging on to the door frame wailing and crying and the maid was trying to reassure her and coax her back inside. Dias was saying, "I couldn't stop her. I saw it happening and I couldn't get there in time to stop her." Caratius was there, kneeling in the mud beside his former wife, his gray hair lank and dark with the wet. When he looked up and roared, "Silence!" to Dias, was that rain on his face, or tears?

According to the maid, Caratius had been up in the top paddock assessing a lame foal when Camma had appeared out of the rain, running toward the house with dripping hair, her skirts gathered in her fists and mud splashed up her legs and a warrior chasing after her on horseback. The maid had opened the door, then rushed to the kitchen to fetch the cook and tell the kitchen boy to find the master. In that brief moment it seemed nobody except Dias had seen the old woman shuffle out onto the porch with a bag clutched in one hand and her walking stick in the other, and lunge with the stick. Camma had fallen back down the steps while the old woman cried out something about Boudica and a little boy.

Dias told them he had been trying to catch up with Camma to offer her protection. Tilla said, "Like you did with Grata?" and he said nothing. When he left, saying he would take the news back to town, the Medicus followed him out into the rain.

She could hear the maid in the old woman's room, singing softly to calm her. Caratius was bending over his beautiful dead wife, stroking her hair. He looked up. His voice was strained, almost pleading, as he formed the words, "I never meant her any harm." For once he was speaking in the tongue of his ancestors.

"She knew that," said Tilla, crouching beside the old man she had once thought dangerous, and then merely foolish and pompous, and putting a hand over his. "She was coming here to make her peace with you."

70

I T OCCURRED TO Ruso that anyone watching the farewell on the sunny steps of the mansio the next morning would have thought they were witnessing the end of a happy and successful visit. It was not obvious that the redheaded baby in Tilla's arms was there because nobody else wanted it. Gallonius and Dias might have been there to honor Ruso rather than to make sure he was off their territory.

While Gallonius was assuring him yet again that the job of mansio doctor and the house that went with it were his whenever he wanted them, the cousin was begging Serena to "come back and see us soon," as if she and her husband had not subtly thrown her out over dinner last night.

Ruso envied Valens his ability to ignore what he did not want to hear. Serena was busy supervising the loading of her voluminous luggage onto the second carriage. Valens was bouncing up and down the steps with one or other twin on his shoulders. He seemed to have decided that his wife was returning home because she had succumbed to his charms. As their hosts had remarked over dinner several times before the first course was cleared away, it was *so* considerate of him to come and fetch her.

The baby really was very red haired. Ruso waited until his wife had climbed into the carriage and then handed him up to her, careful to support the wobbly head with a hand that looked huge against the size of the creature that might be about to change both their lives. Tilla took the baby without a word. Last night they had agreed not to talk about it, both afraid of saying things that could not be unsaid later. This agreement seemed to have carried on through breakfast, and now he was wondering if they would ever talk about it, or if Tilla was hoping that one day he would forget that the child belonged to neither of them.

She settled down in the corner and brought out the clumsy feeding cup. He swung up to sit beside her. He supposed she would find a wet nurse when they got to Londinium. He supposed he would be expected to pay. He wanted to say, "It's not the baby I object to, it's the not being consulted," but he was not sure it was true.

The carriage shifted and creaked as the driver climbed on board. To Ruso's surprise Valens appeared in the doorway. "Mind if I ride with you? It's a bit crowded back there. Our driver says we'll never make it up the hills with the weight."

"Give us some luggage instead," suggested Tilla. "Then you can talk to your wife."

"Oh, I can talk to her anytime," said Valens breezily, settling himself on the seat opposite. "Whereas you two are likely to push off at any moment. Actually, that's what I wanted to chat with you about. Ruso, are you taking that job offer?"

Ruso said, "I'd rather starve."

Valens's eyes widened. They widened even farther when Tilla said, "We are wiping this place off our shoes and never coming back."

Valens shook his head sadly. "The business with Camma was always going to end badly, you know. You could see that from the start. And now you're left holding the baby." He peered across the carriage. "It is awfully red, isn't it?"

"Like fire and the sun," said Tilla.

"If you say so."

"And beautiful."

"Oh, absolutely. Anyway, those chaps back there obviously took to you both, even though you did try to strangle the one with the things in his hair. And the place can't be that bad. Albanus says he's staying on for a few days after the funeral."

"Albanus is staying because Grata is there," said Tilla, setting the pot aside to wipe up the milk the baby had just dribbled all over her lap, "and because Londinium is full of small boys who do not want to learn Greek."

Ruso did not want to think about Albanus and the disappointment on his face last night. Ruso had broken the news of Camma's death to both clerk and housekeeper in Camma's kitchen. Through the tears Grata had said, "Dias did it."

"I think so too," he agreed, "but he's clever. If Caratius's workers saw anything, they were too frightened to say. The only thing we can prove about Dias was that he was in Londinium. And that's using a witness who was drunk at the time and may be too loyal to testify."

"And me," put in Grata.

"I've been talking to this young lady, sir," said Albanus, placing one hand on Grata's shoulder with surprising boldness. "She is prepared to testify that Dias sent a false message to lure Asper and his brother to their deaths."

Ruso had promised them both that he would see what the procurator said. The Albanus he had known back in the army would have been satisfied with that. These days he was confident enough to argue.

"Grata is being very brave, sir. She's prepared to give evidence despite being threatened."

"I know," Ruso had said, "and I appreciate it." The trouble was, he suspected nobody would want to listen.

The carriage lurched as the driver urged the horses forward. Valens gave the group on the mansio steps a cheery wave. Ruso raised a hand in farewell to Publius and his wife, and if Gallonius and Dias thought he was acknowledging them, they were wrong.

"What I was thinking," said Valens, settling back into his seat, "was that if you aren't taking that job, I might pop back while you're all at the cemetery and have a chat with them about it myself. To be honest, things are a bit tricky with Serena at the moment, and a move might—"

"It's not a job," said Ruso. "It's a bribe."

Valens frowned. "Are you sure?"

Tilla said, "The handsome one you just waved to was your burglar. He has killed four people and we think the man who is in charge of these carriages was helping him. The fat one made my husband cover everything up because they do not want Rome saying they cannot govern themselves."

Valens leapt up and hung out of the open doorway, narrowly missing a collision with a stack of wood as they overtook a lumbering ox wagon. "That chap back there was in my house?"

"He and the stable overseer killed Asper and his brother. Then he did away with the town finance officer and probably Camma as well," said Ruso. "Not to mention having a crack at us too."

"Jupiter almighty! So what are we going to do about it?" Valens looked as though he was ready to jump out of the carriage and confront him.

Ruso remembered when he had been that naive too. It seemed a very long time ago. "The plump one is a local bigwig," he said, "and your burglar's in charge of the town militia. The procurator won't care as long as the money's straight, so . . ." He stopped.

"But surely we should be able to do something?"

Ruso ran both hands through his hair. "Wait a minute."

"This is outrageous!" exclaimed Valens, slumping back into his seat. "These people can't go around murdering Roman citizens!"

"Or the rest of us," put in Tilla. "What are you thinking, husband?"

Ruso was not ready to put it into words. He needed to go back over what had happened, seeing events through the new window that had just opened in his mind. He got up. "I need to talk to the money changer. Satto saw the money."

"What are you—"

"Satto saw that money! That was what he showed me!"

"What money? Be careful!"

He had already leapt. He landed unsteadily on the side of the road, calling, "I'll see you at the cemetery."

"Where are you going?"

"I think I may have gotten it all wrong!"

71

WHEN TILLA LOOKED back on their time in Verulamium, the things she would remember most were not the grand buildings or the busy markets, the sight of Camma nursing the baby beside the kitchen fire, or even the terror of waking in Suite Three to find that someone had tried to suffocate her. What she would remember was the funerals.

This was the last of them: a farewell to the woman who had drawn her into this and become a friend. Now Camma was following her lover to the next world: being sent off by a man who had married her, perhaps out of vanity, but certainly with no malice and perhaps even some hope of good.

A surprising crowd had turned out to watch the baby that still had no name see the flames lit for a second time. She supposed it had to be expected: Camma's life had ended in scandal, and the number of onlookers, the sound of wailing, and the sight of the official carriages drawn up on the roadside was causing other travelers to stop and see who was being cremated.

There was another, more modest pyre already burning on the other side of the clearing. A little knot of mourners clustered around it defensively as the crowd and the noise swelled. Tilla approached one of them. "This was your child?"

"Six years old," said the woman. "She had a fever."

"I am sorry."

The woman looked at the baby. Tilla was glad she did not try to touch him. You could never tell how bad luck might spread. The woman said, "Treasure that one while you can, sister."

Six years old. Six years of caring for a child, only to lose her as so many were lost to illness and accidents against which neither midwife nor the Medicus had any power.

She had not yet found the right time to tell him that she had woken late in Serena's room with a familiar dragging sensation in her lower belly and risen to confirm that the medicine had failed. She would wait until they were well away from this place to break the news that the child who lived only in their hopes was as far away as ever.

Tilla moved back toward the fresh pyre on which the slaves were laying the shrouded form of Camma. On the far side of the clearing, a squad of guards was forcing its way to the front of the crowd, making way for Gallonius, here to be seen yet again paying his respects. As if anyone was likely to care. She recognized Gavo and, behind him, lurking in the third row, Dias. *Even here,* she thought, *he cannot leave us alone.* She wanted to march up to him, wrench the spear from his hand, and shout, "That child over there was six years old! Is there not enough death and misery without men like you dealing out more?"

When the slaves had done their work, Caratius stepped forward and unwrapped the shroud to reveal Camma's face. Dias was looking across the pyre with a smug expression. Tilla followed his gaze and realized it was aimed at Grata. Grata's expression was sullen, but what could one woman do? As if he had asked and answered that question himself, Dias gave her a half smile and turned to say something to the man next to him.

The Medicus appeared on the far side of the circle, out of breath and seemingly lost in his thoughts. If he did not do something soon, their final duty in this place would be over. They would be on their way back to Londinium with a shameful tale of fear and deceit, but also with the news that the tax would be paid, which was very likely all anyone would care about. The procurator would accept the tax and then send the money north to pay the army, who were there to keep her own people under the emperor's thumb.

If there was any honor in this place, it was very well hidden. She would be glad when the Medicus went back to treating the sick.

He was moving now. Striding across the grass to say something to Caratius, who looked surprised and annoyed, and who finally said something brief in return. Then the Medicus stepped aside and Caratius moved forward to stand at Camma's feet, facing the pyre. The onlookers fell silent. Everyone wanted to know what a man could say to honor a wife who had abandoned him for a tax collector.

"You are Camma of the Iceni," he announced, "and you were my wife."

Someone close to Tilla put in, "Till she ran off with a thief!" and several people sniggered. The comedian, a short man with buck teeth, grinned and took a swig from a flagon. Caratius said, "You are beautiful in death as in life." The comedian surfaced from the flagon and managed to get out, "And you stole our money!" before Tilla snatched the flagon and hurled it onto his foot. His howl mingled with the sounds of mourning from the other pyre.

Caratius was still speaking but nobody seemed to be listening. There was some sort of disturbance behind them. A dozen horses and riders had broken out of the woods and were thundering across the grass toward them. Someone shouted, "The Iceni!" There were screams of "The Iceni! The Iceni have come!" as the crowd scattered, mothers grabbing children and dragging them away in search of safety. Some headed for the slaves' hut, some tried to hide among the graves, and others rushed back toward the road and the town gates. Valens and Serena had snatched up the twins and were running for the carriage. Dias was yelling orders to the guards, who gathered around Gallonius.

Suddenly Grata was standing beside Tilla, with Albanus firmly in front of them both as if he stood some chance of defending them. Caratius was left unprotected beside the pyre as the riders circled around it. Their eyes were fierce. Their scars spoke of old battles and their long swords of readiness for new ones. All wore rough clothes topped with thick leather jerkins to protect them against weapons, and it was a moment before Tilla realized that a couple of them were women. She stood her ground, trying not to be afraid. These were her friend's people: the family she had summoned. One of the women had hair like Camma's, and also like the baby she was clutching against herself in case the Iceni chose to seek revenge on the nearest people they could reach.

The Medicus had not run, either. He was walking around the pyre toward her when a rider with thick fair hair roared in British, "Who is responsible for this?"

Dias gave an order and the town guards raised their spears. They were probably wishing they too had armed themselves with their swords. Well, that was what happened when you groveled to Rome.

"You!" the leader shouted at Caratius. "We trusted her to you, old man."

Caratius was looking stunned, as if he could not understand what was happening.

Tilla called, "This is not his doing!"

The leader turned to glare at her and gestured with a tattooed hand to Albanus to get out of the way.

Albanus visibly jumped with fright, but he stayed where he was. Tilla put a hand on his shoulder and stepped around him to stand beside the horse. "I am Darlughdacha of the Corionotatae among the Brigantes," she told the man, using the name he would understand. "Sometimes called Tilla. I am the midwife." She held up the baby. "And this is your kin."

He did not bother to look at the baby. "You sent the letter."

She said, "I had hoped to give you a happier welcome."

The Medicus was almost beside her now.

"Who is responsible for the death of my sister?" He glanced at the Medicus, swung around, and jabbed the point of the spear against his chest. "You," he said in Latin. "Keep still. Tell us why my sister is dead."

From behind the safety of other men's spears, Gallonius shouted, "Your sister brought shame on you. She deserted her husband and ran off with a thief."

The Iceni had stopped moving about now. Everyone was listening.

"You're the thief," called the Medicus.

Gallonius's body jolted in sudden outrage, or perhaps fear. "I am the one trying to keep order here!"

Ruso turned to Caratius. "He told me both your grandfathers were craftsmen, sir—they were metalworkers, weren't they?"

Caratius nodded. "What of it?"

"His meat market is on the site of your grandfather's workshop, and everyone knew about the buried silver. I think he found it after your own men's digging disrupted the drainage."

"Nonsense!" put in Gallonius. "I've never seen any silver."

"You showed some of it to Satto and said it was your savings." The Medicus turned to Caratius, talking faster and faster, trying to get his story out before he was stopped. "That's how he knew the old money could be identified, so he started melting it down and making his own, but the forgeries weren't good enough, so he forced Nico to switch them with the theater fund money—"

"Enough!" roared the Iceni leader, giving the Medicus a poke with the spear that sent him staggering backward.

Dias's voice was calm as he said, "Your sister was killed by a mad-woman. I saw what happened. It was an accident." He pointed at Tilla. "The Brigante woman is not to be trusted. She's married to that rambling foreigner and he's one of the procurator's men."

The leader turned to Gallonius. "You! We are not interested in coins and silver. Explain why my sister is dead."

"It was an accident," repeated Gallonius.

The Medicus said, "No wonder he wanted all this covered up. He's been systematically robbing his people and getting the captain of the guard and the stable overseer to do his dirty work. The baby's father found out what was going on and they killed him. Yesterday they silenced Camma too."

Now that Valens had stowed his family safely in the carriage, Tilla could see him hurrying toward them across the grass. The mother of the six year old had crept back to keep vigil beside her pyre.

Gallonius began to speak in rapid British, explaining to the Iceni that the procurator's man had been interfering in local business, jumping to all sorts of conclusions, and demanding money. "You know how men from Rome like to throw their weight about," he said. "Take no notice of him."

"We will speak in Latin," the leader commanded. "Did you order my sister killed?"

"Of course not!"

Dias said, "It was an accident. The old woman pushed her and she fell and hit her head."

Tilla shouted, "You killed her!"

"I tried to save her," said Dias.

The Medicus said, "You were the only one who saw what happened. You and an old woman whose mind is gone."

The Iceni were looking toward their leader, waiting for him to make a decision. It was plain that he did not know whom to believe. That was when Grata saw her chance. "That guard is a liar," she said, pointing at Dias. "He made me give a false message to lure two men to their deaths. Do not believe him."

Dias's handsome face was twisted with anger. "She's a jealous bitch. Take no notice of her."

Why was Serena standing in the doorway of the carriage, waving and pointing toward the road south? Why was Valens hurrying back toward her?

Tilla stood on tiptoe to crane past the riders and around the slaves' hut, but she heard them before she saw them. Everyone did. The rumble of horses at full gallop. Before anyone could move, streams of cavalrymen in glittering armor swept through the cemetery and surrounded the graves, the hut, the mourners, the pyres, and the startled Iceni.

72

DIAS'S GUARDS LOWERED their weapons. The Iceni had bunched together around the unlit pyre, spears raised. Ruso was appalled to see Tilla among them, clutching the baby.

"Nobody move!" yelled the decurion in charge of the cavalry, surveying the scene and evidently trying to make some sense of the disparate groups of natives. His men circled their horses, their own spears ready to impale anyone foolish enough to argue.

"Who's in charge here?"

A bass voice sounded from somewhere among the guards. "I am, sir. Verulamium's guards are at your service." Gallonius stepped out into the clearing and gestured toward the Iceni. "These people came to disrupt a peaceful funeral. They should be arrested for carrying illegal weapons."

"And who are you?" demanded a familiar voice. Ruso looked up to see a shortsighted squint almost hidden beneath the peak of the cavalry helmet.

"Sir, that's young Firmus! Firmus, sir!" Albanus waved one hand high in the air before the nearest cavalryman made a jab with his spear to remind him not to move. "We're over here, sir!"

The squint was turned toward Albanus. "Let them approach."

Glancing at Tilla, Ruso made his way across to where a very cheerful-looking Firmus was stationed next to the decurion. "I've always wanted to do something like this," he whispered to Ruso. "We heard there was an Iceni war band on the move. And since you hadn't come back when you were supposed to, I persuaded Uncle to let me come and look for you. Why are we at a funeral?"

"You by the pyre!" bellowed the decurion to the Iceni. "Drop your weapons."

One of his men repeated the order in British just in case they had not understood.

The Iceni glanced at their leader, who remained motionless.

The decurion repeated the order. Still the Iceni refused to move. They were vastly outnumbered and had only their padded jerkins for protection. Tilla, crouched by the pyre trying to cover the baby, had no protection at all.

"Sir," murmured Ruso, "their sister's been murdered. They came to her funeral looking for justice."

Firmus craned to see the pyre between the Iceni riders. "I can make out red—that's not Camma, is it?"

"Drop your weapons!" repeated the decurion.

Across the clearing, Ruso could see Dias gesturing to his men to take up position behind the unsuspecting Iceni. Gallonius was sidling away, keeping himself out of range.

"Stop!" Caratius was still standing by his dead wife. "Stop, everyone! This is not what any of us wanted!"

"Drop your weapons and you won't be hurt."

Ruso noticed that one or two of the cavalrymen seemed to be having trouble carrying their shields in the same hand as their reins. He spotted another familiar face beneath a cavalry helmet. Then another. Gods above: That was the clerk who had issued his travel warrant. This was not a proper cavalry unit. This was a handful of professionals bulked out by a hastily assembled crew of office workers dragged into active service. They might once have been highly trained military men but they were out of practice and out of condition. The Iceni, on the other hand, looked as though they would put up a good fight. They would inflict a lot of damage before they were overpowered by cavalry on one side and Dias's men on the other. Tilla, caught in the middle, would not stand a chance.

"Sir," he murmured to Firmus, "the leader of the local guards can't be trusted. Let me talk to the Iceni."

Was that relief on the decurion's face? He must have known even better than Ruso that his men were not fit to fight.

Ruso raised his empty hands into the air and stepped forward across the grass to address the leader of the Iceni, deliberately keeping his voice low so he would not be overheard.

"He is a friend," Tilla assured them from her position on the ground. "Listen to him."

The Iceni put on a good show of being reluctant to abandon a skirmish, but finally they agreed to put down their weapons in exchange for a place at the funeral and a cavalry escort back through Catuvellauni territory in the morning.

There was disappointment in Dias's voice as he ordered his men to stand down. Gallonius, suddenly brave again now that trouble had been averted, repeated that the Iceni should be arrested for carrying illegal weapons.

"I haven't seen any illegal weapons," declared Firmus, a statement which was truer than most of his audience knew. "You can send your guards back to town: We'll keep order here. Now is somebody going to light that pyre, or not?"

The wails of the Iceni rose with the crackling of the flames as the fire blazed once more, sending Camma on the way to whatever kind of next world awaited her. Ruso adopted a respectful silence. He itched to explain to Firmus that Dias and Gallonius were the ones who should be arrested, but the attempt would stir up the trouble they had just managed to avert. Yet again, Dias had slithered out of his grasp.

Dias knew it too. He directed a practiced salute at Firmus and the decurion, then smirked at Ruso before turning his men to march them back toward the road. Gallonius went with them. Ruso was still wondering how he was going to explain any of this to the procurator—let alone to Metellus—when Valens appeared and announced that he and his wife wanted to get the boys home by nightfall. Firmus decided the cavalry could escort the Iceni tomorrow without his help, and turned to Ruso. "I'll ride back with you," he said, adding ominously, "You can explain everything to me on the way. I can inspect the milestones at the same time."

Tilla had not been included in any of these conversations. She had produced the feeding bottle from somewhere and was sitting on the grass, wailing with the Iceni women. After several attempts Ruso managed to catch her eye and point toward the carriage that was still waiting over by the road. She said something to the redhaired woman next to her, and got up to leave. The woman stood too, and Ruso realized there was some sort of argument going on. Tilla began to walk away. The woman went after her.

Firmus was still talking, but Ruso was not listening.

There was some sort of struggle. The feeding bottle fell and landed in the grass.

He ran across the middle of the clearing, crouching to shield his face from the heat as he ran.

"Stop!"

The Iceni woman was tugging at the baby. Tilla was trying to kick her away. The baby was crying. The funeral wailing ceased as the other Iceni tried to intervene.

"Leave her alone!" he shouted. The struggle paused, but neither woman let go. The baby was still crying. He had never seen Tilla look so desperate.

"My wife has looked after this baby since he is born," he explained in awkward British over the noise to anyone who would listen. "He knows her. She likes him very much." He looked around. The Iceni were grim-faced. "We can give him a good home," he promised. "We will teach him and look after him and—" What else could he promise?

"He will never go hungry," put in Tilla.

"What will you teach him?" demanded the redhaired woman.

Tilla's chin rose. "I will tell him the story of his beautiful mother," she said, wresting him out of the grasp of the woman and patting his back to console him. She leaned her cheek against his swollen red face and his cries began to die away. "Little one, I will tell you about your father from the Dobunni and your mother from the Iceni and your ancestors who were wronged by Rome and how they took a terrible revenge. And when you grow up, I will tell you about an old woman who was still afraid of them sixty years later and about her son who tried to make things better by a marriage, and how it did not work, and how your family came to this place afterward to make sure you were safe."

"We will bring him to visit his people," added Ruso, putting an arm around Tilla and gazing around at the fierce faces of the family who had come here to rescue a sister and did not look as though they were inclined to leave empty handed.

"What will you teach him, Roman?" demanded their leader.

"Medicine," said Ruso. "Healing." What the hell was the word in British? He switched to Latin for "Surgery."

"In Latin?"

"He will speak Latin and British, like you."

"How to give orders and demand tribute?"

"My wife was a friend to your sister," Ruso tried. "She delivered this baby. Camma trusted her."

"She trusted both of them," put in another voice. Ruso had forgotten that Grata was there. "They are good people."

"Another foreigner!" declared the redhaired woman. "What does she know?"

"More than you," retorted Grata. "And I'm not foreign."

"Don't argue with them!" pleaded Tilla. She turned to the leader. "I am begging you, sir, let me look after this child. Do not take him away from us."

"We want to—" Ruso stopped. How did the Britons say *adopt*? He didn't even know if they had a word for it. "We will make him our son."

He knew from the man's eyes what the answer was going to be. He barely heard the words: just Tilla's anguished cry and a brief and rapid exchange in British. The leader seemed to be asking Tilla something. When she did not answer, the woman stepped forward and took the baby out of her arms.

73

MEDICINE, LIKE INVESTIGATING, was an occupation fraught with failure. Still, back in Londinium, it was a relief to retreat into the relative simplicity of covering out-of-hours calls so that an unusually hesitant Valens could spend more time with his family. In quiet moments, Ruso carried on working his way through a stack of writing tablets, contacting everyone he could think of who might care to recommend him for a job.

There was no shortage of quiet moments. Tilla seemed to have very little to say to him or to anyone else. He had said he was sorry about the baby, but the only response was, "Yes." He had asked what the Iceni man had said to her, but she refused to tell him. Since Serena had now reinstalled a full complement of servants, there was little for her to do. Instead she spent long hours sitting in the bedroom by herself. Asked what she was doing up there, she said, "Thinking."

"About what?"

"Things."

Not sure he was welcome upstairs, Ruso took to spending his evenings helping the apprentices practice their stitching on ox tongues and testing them on the medicinal properties of flavored wines. When the short one offered to take his teetering stack of letters, he realized with a jolt that he had no desire to send them. A new job would mean leaving Londinium. It would mean being on his own with Tilla. He was not sure either of them wanted that. "I'll sort them all out when I've finished," he told the apprentice, doggedly carrying on writing requests and leaving them to accumulate on the new table in Valens's hall.

At night he lay awake regretting the demise of the cockerel. It would have been some sort of company as he waited for the trumpet from the fort to sound the change of watch and hoped for an emergency to give him something to do. In the mornings he slept late.

Tilla's was not the only frustrating silence.

It was three days since he had delivered his report to the procurator's office along with a claim for his expenses. Neither the procurator nor Firmus had been available to speak to him at the time, and there had been no message since. He had used the excuse of his expenses to visit the Residence, but again no one was around. The gap-toothed expenditure clerk told him his claim was being processed and that he would be contacted. The travel warrant clerk—last seen on horseback in the cemetery at Verulamium—had refused to discuss his emergency reinstatement into the cavalry. It was, apparently, "a military matter."

Was his report so comprehensive that the procurator didn't need to question him? Did nobody here care what went on up the road as long as the tax was paid? Maybe it had been a mistake to admit the truth about his coerced speech to the Council. Being honest about one's failures was not a trait much prized among the powerful.

Ruso was even beginning to wish Metellus would get in touch. He had left a note in the Room Twenty-seven pigeonhole, but there had been no response. It had begun to dawn on him that he might never find out the end of the story. He was not important enough to be told. Nor, it seemed, was he competent enough to be given any more work as an investigator. For that, at least, he was grateful.

Thus it was with mixed feelings that he finally received a message ordering him to report to Firmus.

"Ruso!"

Was it his imagination or had the youth grown in the few days since they had last seen each other? His surroundings had certainly improved: no longer a dingy back room but a bright office with sun streaming through the window. Pyramus was perched on a stool just behind his master and a couple of scribes were hovering, waiting for instructions.

Verulamium, Firmus explained with obvious pride, had just delivered its tax along with a large consignment of forged coins for destruction.

Ruso offered congratulations and waited to find out why he was really here.

"And the procurator's read your report and wants to see you. You weren't entirely straight with us about Metellus, were you?"

"I'm sorry, sir," said Ruso, wondering how much they knew.

"We've been in touch with the governor," said Firmus. "My uncle will explain."

On this ominous note Ruso was ushered out by one of the scribes and escorted to the procurator's office.

The great man was sufficiently recovered to be seated at his desk in another crisp white linen tunic, but Ruso barely noticed him. What drew his attention was the very ordinary-looking man silhouetted in front of the window. It looked like . . . Surely it couldn't be?

"Come in, Ruso," said the procurator. "Metellus and I have some things to say to you."

74

THE GOVERNOR AND the procurator's departments are cooperating," explained Metellus, perhaps sensing Ruso's bewilderment.

Was that a faint expression of distaste on the procurator's face, or just the discomfort of breathing inside cracked ribs? He said, "The governor has kindly offered Metellus's help with some of the tidying up after this Verulamium business."

Ruso swallowed.

"Metellus and I have both read your report," the procurator continued, "which leaves us reassured about relations between the Catuvellauni and the Iceni, but unfortunately since you let the presence of your wife compromise your inquiry, we're now in a rather delicate position."

Ruso said, "She happened to be working there as a midwife, sir," but neither man seemed interested.

"The Catuvellauni are trusted allies," said Metellus.

"They demonstrate to the other tribes the rewards of cooperation with Rome," added the procurator.

As if they had rehearsed their parts, Metellus said, "The governor wouldn't like to take any action that might upset them, or look as though we're threatening the independence of Verulamium."

"However," continued the procurator, "since you've brought this forgery business to our attention, we can hardly ignore it."

It seemed that Ruso's uncovering of a capital crime had caused them a major inconvenience. He said, "The men called Dias and Rogatus have murdered four people between them, sir. And I'm willing to bet that the magistrate Gallonius knew all along. He was definitely providing the silver for the false coins."

"As I said, we have read the report."

"The murders aren't anything to worry about," said Metellus. "Just the natives quarreling among themselves. I know they tried to suffocate you with a brazier, Ruso, but there's not enough credible evidence to make a case."

"But if you interview the mansio staff—"

"We don't want to be accused of interfering." The procurator winced as he reached for the notes on his desk. "We might have executed the three of them for forgery, but according to your report, you've already informed the locals on my behalf that the forgers were"—he ran one finger down the notes—"two men called Asper and Nico, who are already dead."

"I didn't tell them that directly, sir, I only said—"

"It doesn't matter what you said," put in Metellus. "What matters is what they think they heard."

"If we start arresting other people now," said the procurator, "it's going to look as though we don't know what we're doing."

"And if you don't deal with them, sir," put in Ruso, "they're going to think they can get away with anything they like."

"Apparently they can," said Metellus. "All they have to do is appear to threaten our investigator's wife, and he'll do whatever they want."

Ruso felt his fists clench. He addressed the procurator. "I did my best under the circumstances, sir."

The procurator sighed. "I'm disappointed in you, Ruso. When you had the sense to tell me you weren't an investigator, I assumed you were an intelligent man."

Metellus glanced up. "Why did you say you weren't an investigator, Ruso?"

"Because I wasn't!" snapped Ruso. "And I'm never doing it again, either. It's nothing but lies and deceit and making people even more miserable than they are already. Now if you'll excuse me, sirs, I have patients to attend to."

It was rude and disrespectful and probably pompous as well, but he managed to get out of the door with his head held high. Somehow that was all that mattered.

He was through the building site that was supposed to be a garden and halfway across the courtyard before he heard someone calling his name. The chain-mailed form of Dias was looking at him across the back of a familiar-looking horse.

Ruso said, "What the hell are you doing here?"

"Escorting the tax money," said Dias. "Like I usually do. Haven't you heard? We're the town that always pays up."

"I could say a few other things about your town."

"Ah," said the guard, slackening the horse's girth, "but who'd listen? Have you thought any more about that job offer?"

Ruso glanced around, then took hold of one side of the bridle. "Since nobody's listening," he said, "tell me something. I can see what Gallonius got out of it, with his town house and his country estate and all his jewelry. But you're no fool, and you're not all that rich, either. Where did your share go?"

Dias grinned. "You think I'm no fool, but you're asking me to incriminate myself?"

"What can I do about it?" asked Ruso. "Asper and Nico are getting the blame for everything. The procurator won't go after you now."

Dias considered that for a moment, then lowered his voice. "You won't believe me if I tell you."

"Right now, I'd believe almost anything."

"Gallonius paid the engraver. But I had to pay Rogatus for the metalwork and a bit of occasional help."

"Like attacking my wife?"

"I'm not proud of that," said Dias. "But it was for a good cause. Most of the money went toward the lads."

"You did it for the guards?" Ruso was taken aback.

Dias sighed. "You've got no idea, have you?"

"No."

"Decent uniforms. Good kit. Proper pay. A man doesn't have to be a Roman citizen to appreciate things like that."

"They could join the army."

Dias snorted. "And be treated like dirt? My people have been allies of Rome for generations, and you know how much our lads get paid if we join up to fight for you?"

"Auxiliaries' wages," conceded Ruso, knowing they were nowhere near what a legionary would receive.

"Meantime we're paying tax to keep your men over here, and what do we see for it?"

"The army keeps the peace," said Ruso, repeating the official line.

"In the North, maybe," conceded Dias. "But when Verulamium needs to show a sharp edge to the neighbors, they send a bunch of old men with a blind fourteen year old in charge."

"Our men came to help. You didn't even know the Iceni were on the way."

Dias was not listening. "You lot haven't changed since you ran and left a bunch of civilians to face Boudica. Well, we learned something from her, even if you didn't. We learned that we can't rely on you. If the other tribes come looking for trouble, we've got to be able stand and fight for ourselves." Dias vaulted up onto the horse and turned its head toward the gateway. "We could've taken those Iceni."

Ruso did not doubt it. The man was a good leader, and shrewd enough to know that Rome would always put its own interests above those of its allies. He had cast himself in the role of a warrior, and he was doing what tribal warriors had always done: defending his people. Dias was almost a hero. What was a little stolen money here or there? Nobody really needed a theater, did they?

It sounded so reasonable. So honorable . . . until he watched the scarlet braids disappear among the rest of the traffic in the street and thought of Camma lying in the rain, and Julius Asper, and the ravaged body of Bericus, and the sleep from which Nico—and so nearly he and Tilla— had never woken.

Ruso strode back across the ruined garden and under the walkway. Swinging into the corridor, he almost collided with the expenditure clerk and barely stopped to wait for "Come in!" before bursting into Firmus's office.

"You can't arrest those three for forgery or murder," he said, "but you're responsible for inspecting milestones and tightening up on travel and transport, right?"

Firmus blinked. "Yes."

"Does that include the Imperial post?"

"I suppose so."

"And interfering with the Imperial post is a serious offense, yes?"

"Of course."

"That's how we nail Rogatus. Talk to Publius up at the mansio. Say you had an anonymous tip-off about people abusing the system and you want to help him clean it up. Dias is probably involved too, but if you can't get him that way, have somebody check all the records of the Third Brittones. You may be able to get him for faking a medical discharge."

Firmus's eyes were bright. "And the magistrate—Gallonius?"

"I don't know," confessed Ruso. "He's overcharging the mansio for supplies, but that's not illegal. Maybe Metellus can come up with something."

"It's worth a try." Firmus got to his feet. "Stay around in case my uncle wants to talk to you."

Ruso doubted that the procurator would want to talk to him ever again, but he supposed he should comply. Thus he was standing on the edge of the governor's landing stage and wondering whether any of the ships moored farther down the glistening Tamesis would take him back to Gaul when a figure materialized beside him. Metellus wanted a quiet word.

There was only one word Ruso wanted to hear from Metellus. "Is my wife's name off that list?"

"I can't forget what I know, Ruso."

"Then I'm not interested in anything else you have to say."

"I'm sorry you see it that way," said Metellus. "I wanted to thank you. And to explain one or two things."

75

ON THE WAY back to Valens's house, Ruso passed the chamber where he had promised Mithras a lamb in exchange for a baby. Had that brief guardianship of another man's child been a cruel joke? Some kind of retaliation for his neglect of the correct rituals? He didn't know. Perhaps he should have prayed to a god who was more interested in women. And if Tilla was praying to Christos and he was praying to somebody else, would the great ones work together, or cancel each other out in a fit of jealousy? He didn't know that, either.

What he did know now, but was still finding hard to believe, was that Metellus had been involved with the whole Asper/Camma mess from the beginning. Metellus had tried to excuse himself, of course. It had been "only prudent" to install an agent in Verulamium with orders to investigate the alarming rumor of some agreement between the Iceni and the Catuvellauni. It was not Metellus's fault that Asper had chosen to flirt with Camma on the pretext of seeking information. It was certainly not Metellus's fault that Asper had lost sight of his orders and instigated a full-blown affair.

"I broke off all contact with him as soon as I found out," Metellus explained. "It was clear that the man had no idea where his loyalties lay. So when he sent the first message saying he was investigating something of interest, I didn't reply."

"You told me you didn't know anything about an investigation."

"I lied," said Metellus smoothly. "I was hoping you would find out what it was, and you have. I suppose he was planning to expose the forgery in an attempt to redeem himself. It's a pity we can't execute the forgers, but it would be politically inconvenient."

"So why are you telling me this?"

Metellus's sigh sounded genuinely regretful. "Because you seem to think I'm some kind of magician, Ruso. You seem to think that I know everything and I'm in control of everything. And I want you to understand that I'm not. Frankly, sending in Asper was a bad decision, and I'm grateful to you for sorting out what was going on up there. So I promise to do my best to have your wife's name taken off the lists, but you must realize these things are widely circulated and copied and to be honest, I can't guarantee to catch every—what are you—*Ruso!*"

It was too late: Neither the arms milling in the air nor the shriek of "No!" could halt his fall from the edge of the landing stage. Ruso was only sorry the tide was in.

Back at the house, Valens was working his way through a queue of patients while Serena was scolding the nursemaid and the cook for letting a sticky twin hide under the couch with the honey jar. He found Tilla upstairs clearing out the box of baby clothes. Leaning casually against the doorpost, he said, "I've just thrown Metellus in the river."

For a moment there was no reaction. Then she put the little pair of sheepskin boots down on the bed and stared at him. "What did you say?"

"I'm sure I'll regret it, but not yet. How did he know you'd been given stolen money last autumn?"

He was not fooled by the blank look.

"I told you to get rid of it," he said. "What did you do with it?"

She picked up one of the boots and slid a couple of fingers inside. "We needed food for the journey."

"But I specifically told you—"

"Yes. But we were leaving, and it was a waste to throw money away."

He bent and snatched the boot away from her. "Listen to me! This is important. Somebody must have reported you. Now he's put your name on one of his bloody security lists and he doesn't seem to know how to take you off it."

There were tears welling up in her eyes.

"I'm sorry," he said, thrusting the boot clumsily back into her hand. "I didn't mean—it's just that if I don't frighten you, you don't take me seriously."

She picked up both boots and a soft woolen tunic and placed them back in the box. "I have let you down."

He pushed the door shut behind him. "I asked you to do something, Tilla, and as usual you did the opposite."

She did not answer.

"I've been trying to buy off Metellus by sorting out this mess in Verulamium, only that didn't work, either, because when I asked you to stay at the mansio, you went off with the guards. Why do you do this to me?"

"Did he drown?"

"I doubt it. It wasn't deep enough, unfortunately." He slumped down on the bed beside her. "I can't go on like this."

She said, "There is something else I must tell you. Then we will decide about going on."

He closed his eyes and lay back on the bed. He was not sure he wanted to hear anything else, but she began to speak anyway.

"After my family died and I went to live with the Northerners," she said, "there was a man who would not leave me alone even though he had a wife already."

"I know."

"You do not know all of it. I found out I was with child. I told his wife. She brought a woman to help me."

Help. A small word with a world of meanings.

"Afterward I was very ill. I think this is why you and I have no baby, and perhaps we never will, and I should have told you this before."

He was conscious of his own breathing. It was almost hesitant, as if any sudden movement would shatter the fragile bond between them. He knew what she must be hoping to hear: something like, *It doesn't matter,* or *I don't mind,* or *You are still a good wife to me.* But it did matter, and he did mind, and he wished she had not told him. Metellus's words came back to him: *I can't forget what I know.*

"The Iceni said if I want to look after the baby I must go to live with them," she said. "So now I am asking what you want. Because if you want a child of your own, and somebody who does what she is told, you must find a new wife."

"Is that what you want?" he asked, his eyes still closed. "To go and live with the Iceni and bring up Camma's baby?"

When she did not answer, he opened his eyes and sat up. "Is that what you want to do?" he repeated.

"I am asking what you want," she said.

"I don't think I can live with the Iceni, Tilla."

"You were not invited."

He shook his head. "I've never really . . . I always just assumed that somewhere in the valley of the unborn there was a son or a daughter waiting . . ." He stopped. "I need to think about it."

"Yes." She got to her feet. "I shall give the clothes to Serena. I expect she will be needing them before long."

"I didn't mind him, you know." He scratched one ear. "He was a fine little chap."

"Yes."

"He would have done quite nicely, really. I'd have gotten used to the hair."

"Yes."

From somewhere in the garden came a burble of childish laughter. He reached forward, put his arms around her waist, and rested his head against the belly that was not holding his baby, and perhaps never would. "Everyone else," he said. "Why not us?"

76

R USO'S GUESS ABOUT Dias was more accurate than he had expected. Not only had Dias not received a medical discharge from
the Third Brittones: His description along with his real name was found
on a list of deserters stored among the records at the Residence. In the
meantime Firmus had unearthed evidence that Rogatus was guilty of
taking bribes and interfering with the Imperial post. The procurator was
recommending that the governor condemn the pair to work in the West-
ern mines, where lead and silver were extracted in conditions so poisonous
that it was tantamount to a death sentence.

Firmus delivered this information to Ruso in person, looking very
pleased with himself. "It was my idea," he said, shifting sideways in an
attempt to get comfortable on Valens's couch. "And Uncle agrees that it's
very appropriate. He's going to clamp down on traveling officials demanding things they aren't entitled to, as well. He says he's glad I
brought it to his attention. In fact, he's written home to tell Mother I've
made a good start."

"What about Gallonius?"

"Oh, he's more useful left where he is."

"But—"

"He'll tell the Council to offer Albanus the job of quaestor."

"But—"

"Gallonius will do exactly what he's told from now on, Ruso. Metellus has put his name on some sort of list."

"I see."

"He knows if he doesn't behave, we'll dig up your report and execute him for forgery."

We. Firmus might have meant *Rome*, but more likely the word was shorthand for *the procurator, the governor, Metellus—and me.* The men who had agreed to leave a corrupt and murderous Briton in place because he was useful to them. Ruso hoped Albanus would think long and hard about that job offer.

"So as you see," continued Firmus as he was leaving, "it's all worked out rather well. Even though you really weren't an investigator, were you?" He bent to squint at the pile of letters on the hall table. "Have you taken up clerking now?"

"Just writing to a few acquaintances," explained Ruso. "Don't worry, I won't be using the official post."

He stood in Valens's doorway and watched the youth and his escort of guards strut off in the direction of the footbridge that led across the stream to the Residence. Pyramus was hobbling along behind. At this rate, Firmus would go back to Rome a success.

As for Ruso—he was living in a backward province with a barbarian wife whose name was probably on several security lists. They were both mourning the loss of a baby who belonged to neither of them, and of the other children who had existed only in their own imaginations. Instead of using his training and his ingenuity to help live patients, he had been wasting inordinate amounts of time investigating suspicious deaths and disappearances for the benefit of men who didn't deserve it, and his career was no further forward than it had been when he first joined the army. He glanced down at his stack of requests for jobs in Britannia. He could not impose on Valens for much longer. He needed either to send them, or to burn them and go back to Gaul.

Valens had taken the apprentices out on a house call. Serena and the twins were visiting a friend for the afternoon. He found Tilla kneeling beside a freshly dug patch of earth in the garden. Her hands were smeared with wet mud. He crouched beside her, watching as she gently teased apart a web of delicate roots. The seedlings they belonged to looked as though they were clinging together in the last stages of exhaustion.

Finally she had several safely detached and lying limp and pale on the soil. "Lettuce," she explained, stabbing a grimy finger twice into the earth before reaching for the jug behind her and filling the holes with water. Lifting a seedling by its undersized leaves, she lowered it into position and carefully firmed the mud around the wilting stem.

"They don't look too happy," he observed.

"Serena's neighbor gave her a pot of seedlings," she said. "She is not a gardener and cook is too busy, so they were left to starve on the windowsill."

"Will they survive?"

She shrugged. "Lettuces do not like being moved. If they grow, there will be pigeons and slugs and small children. But the kitchen boy says he will water them, and I am glad they will have a chance."

He stabbed more holes in line with the ones she had made, and trickled in more water. "I think I've made a bit of a mess of everything," he confessed. "We did all that running around in Verulamium to get Metellus to take your name off that list, then when he talked about doing it, I threw him in the river. "

She lowered the next seedling into its new home and pressed the soil down. "I wish I had been there to see it."

"Anyway," he said, "I've come to apologize. You had a right to expect better of a husband."

She looked up. "What do you think I should expect?"

He pondered the question. "Security?" he suggested. "Protection? Enough to live on and a roof over your head. Now the only way I can make sure you're safe is to ask you to come back to Gaul with me, and I know you don't want to live there."

She sat back on her heels. "This is what you think marriage is? Having no enemies and somewhere to put the crockery?"

In the silence that followed, he felt her reach for his hand. "What I expected," she said as the mud squelched and grated between their fingers, "was this man who tries to do the right thing even when it is foolish."

For a few moments they were so still that a robin flew down and stabbed at the soil in front of them before darting off to safety.

"Right." Ruso got to his feet.

"You could stay here and help."

"I'll be back soon," he promised. "You carry on saving lives. This foolish man needs to wash his hands and send out a big pile of letters."

AUTHOR'S NOTE

Verulamium's theater was finally built about twenty years after this story is set, and its remains can still be seen. The site of the Great Hall lies just across the road, but its foundations are buried deep beneath Saint Michael's Church, and with them the putative location of the strong room. Sadly, no details of the town Council's business—unruly or otherwise—survive. The more respectable of the proceedings here are based on bronze tablets recording the constitution of the Roman town of Irni in Seville.

Anyone who shares my delight in obscure facts will be pleased to know that there really was a crackdown on abuses of the transport system in the early years of Hadrian's reign, including a survey of British milestones, although the name of the procurator who would have been in charge of them is not known. Nor is the location of his office, but it seemed reasonable to place such an important man in one of the grandest buildings in town.

A couple of good books for anyone wanting more detailed background are:

Verulamium: The Roman City of St Albans by Rosalind Niblett
The Coinage of Roman Britain by Richard Reece.

Many readers will already have had the pleasure of visiting Verulamium Museum and park, the British Museum, and the Museum of London. For those who cannot make the trip, all have good Web sites, and at the time of writing, the Museum of London's Online Collections include a fascinating microsite exploring Roman London at: http://www.museumoflondon.org.uk/English/Collections/OnlineResources/Londinium/.

Finally, for anyone lucky enough to stumble across something our ancestors left behind, or who wants to see what others have found, www.finds.org.uk is the place to look.

Acknowledgments

Heartfelt thanks to a veritable army of agents and editors, especially Peta Nightingale, Araminta Whitley, George Lucas, Benjamin Adams, Mari Evans, Kate Burke, Stefanie Bierwerth, and Marlene Tungseth.

For their generous advice and recommendation of sources on Roman coinage and Roman law, I am very grateful to Sam Moorhead, FSA British Museum, and Dr. Paul du Plessis. For help with the history of their respective towns, I am indebted to David Thorold, Keeper of Archaeology at Verulamium Museum, St. Albans Museum Service, and Jenny Hall, Senior Roman Curator, Museum of London.

Fellow scribes Carol Barac, Caroline Davis, Chris Allen, Guy Russell, Jan Lovell, Kathy Barbour, and Maria Murphy all slogged through several drafts of the early chapters, and Andy and Stephen Downie nobly read the whole manuscript.

Caro Ramsay kindly saved me from my own ignorance at one point, but all remaining errors, misinterpretations, inventions, and barefaced lies in the preceding pages are my own work.

KEEP READING!

More intrigue and bad luck lie ahead for Gaius Petreius Ruso. Turn the page for a sneak preview of the next installment in the Medicus series,

SEMPER FIDELIS

Ruso, back in service as an army doctor, begins to suspect foul play in the deaths of several British recruits. But who will admit to wrongdoing when the Legion is bracing itself for a visit from the emperor Hadrian? And where do Ruso's loyalties lie—with his legion, with his emperor, or with Tilla and her people?

The new novel by Ruth Downie

SEMPER FIDELIS

Hardcover $25.00
Bloomsbury USA
Available wherever books are sold

1

VICTOR'S LEFT EYE felt as though it were about to burst like a squashed plum. He ran his tongue along the inside of his gum, tasting blood in gaps that had not been there before. He made a tentative exploration of a couple of loose teeth, seeing how far they would move. It was a mistake. He gasped and fell back against the trunk of the willow as pain welled up and flooded the lower half of his face.

This will pass, he urged himself, all the while feeling that someone was screwing a hot poker into his jaw. *Count to ten. Breathe in . . . and . . . One. In . . . and . . . Two. Think of something else.*

But all that came was the memory of Tadius struggling to rise from the floor, and the voices roaring at him to "Get in there, or you'll be next."

As the pain ebbed he crept forward again, peering out between the willow fronds. The trumpets had sounded the hour for the midday meal and there was hardly anyone about. The girl was still alone on the sunny slab that overhung the water, her skirts hitched up and her bare feet dangling in the river. Beside her on the stone sat a wooden platter with bread and cheese and perhaps beer in the cup. She was busy looking at something in her hand. The willow hid her from the guards over on the fort gates. She had no idea that anyone was watching her.

The guards were standing in the shadow of the wall, leaning on their spears and gazing into the distance with the air of men expecting a quiet afternoon. Victor swallowed. There was a time—it seemed years ago now—when he had dreamed that being in the Legion would be a good life.

The girl sighed and flung down whatever she was holding. She pushed a wisp of blonde hair out of her eyes and turned her attention to the platter. The sunlight flashed on a blade. His fingers slid toward his own knife, but she was only cutting the cheese. He let out his breath. He did not want to hurt her, but he had to keep her quiet. If she screamed, the guards would come, and he might not be fast enough to get away with the food.

He would stroll up and try to chat with her. If he said he was hungry she might even offer to share. He ran a fingertip over his injured eye. She might not. If the eye was as ugly as it felt, she might scream at the sight of him.

The guards were still looking vacant and bored. The girl tore off a big chunk of bread and put it into her mouth.

Victor stepped forward. "It is a good day to eat beside the river."

The girl jerked around. Her eyes widened in alarm, but instead of screaming she was convulsed by a choking fit. He reached for the platter, ready to grab the food and run before she could call for help—then saw one hand flapping helplessly toward him as she spluttered and tried to draw breath and thought, *What if she chokes to death?* He changed the gesture into a lunge for the beer. She took it from him and nodded her thanks, still unable to speak.

When she could breathe again without coughing he spoke slowly, trying not to let his swollen jaw mangle his words. "I didn't mean to startle you."

"If you don't want to startle people," she said with the accent of a tribeswoman from further north, "don't creep up on them. Especially when they are eating."

She was older than he had thought: perhaps in her midtwenties, and attractive in a way that would have distracted him on a better day. He took a deep breath. "I was wondering—"

Her gaze shifted past him. Too late, he heard movement.

As he hit the ground, a boot clamped across the back of his neck and rammed his face into the grass. Pain flared from his jaw to his temple. Something hard slammed into the small of his back and a voice said in

Latin, "We've been watching you, sonny."

"Please, sir—"

The meaning of "Shut up!" was reinforced with another blow. "Who d'you think you are, snooping 'round an officer's wife?"

Oh, holy Bregans. She looked like a native. She spoke British. Where were the slaves? The jewelry? The fancy clothes?

There were two of them: one soldier who gave the orders and one who looked as if he would do whatever the other one told him, without question and without mercy. As they wrenched his arms back and lashed his wrists together, the woman began to say something. The senior soldier cut her short. "It's all right, miss, you're safe now."

"But—"

"We'll deal with him."

As if to show how, one of them rammed the pommel of a sword into Victor's ribs. He had no idea why the woman cried out. She wasn't the one being hit. She wasn't the fool who had thrown away an escape for the sake of bread he couldn't even chew.

Half-dragged, half-stumbling, Victor was hustled up through the rough grass toward the fort gates. The officer's wife was hurrying to keep up, still talking.

"Don't you worry, miss," the senior one assured her. "He'll understand Latin when we've finished with him."

"I want to speak to him myself."

The men ignored her. A few paces further on she appeared in front of them, holding her skirts clear of the grass with one hand and clutching a pair of battered boots in the other.

"So!" she said, looking from one to the other of them. "I am worth rescuing but not worth listening to?"

For a moment Victor thought they were going to barge her out of the way. Then the senior one seemed to think better of it, and said gruffly, "The prisoner was watching you, miss. Hiding under the tree."

She said in British, "Were you watching me?"

He lifted his head to look into eyes that were not quite blue, and not quite green either. You could drown in those eyes.

He staggered as a blow landed on his ear, muffling the roar of "Show some respect!"

Victor lowered his head. Trying to focus on the muddy toes poking out from under the woman's skirt, he heard himself mangle the words, "I'm very hungry, miss."

She said, "Have you no family?"

"Not here, miss." None who could feed him, anyway.

Pale curls tumbled forward as she bent to pull on her boots. "You should have gone to a farm."

He averted his gaze, afraid another punch would send him sprawling on the grass. He was not going to explain all the reasons why going to a farm was a bad idea. She seemed to think he was a civilian. If the men thought the same thing, there was a chance they might let him go with a beating.

She finished tying her boots and stood up to address the soldiers in Latin. "I thank you," she said. "Now will you please fetch my husband? He will know what to do."

There was a hesitation, then the senior soldier allowed himself a grunt of disapproval before ordering his comrade to take the message to the gate.

"And ask him to bring his case!" she called after him.

Victor closed his one good eye and prayed that the mighty Bregans would remember the pair of white doves he had promised to sacrifice if he got away safely. He was not to be taken into the fort yet: That was good. But now he had to explain to an officer why he had been hiding under a tree to watch a respectable married woman, who was all alone, untie her boots, hitch up her skirts, and dangle her bare feet in the river.

Of course, the man should never have allowed her to wander the countryside by herself in the first place, but in Victor's experience, officers never took the blame for anything.

His bruised body had already begun to stiffen up by the time more men emerged from the fort. The two big lads in chainmail must be part of the German unit based here. The one in the middle was taller than some officers and scruffier than others, but he had the coloring of a man from a hot and dusty place where they talked too much and thought they were clever. Besides, there was no mistaking that walk. They all had it: The confident stride of a man who knew what to do.

Victor stifled the instinct to stand to attention while the men spoke in Latin about "this native" as if he were a stray dog.

The Germans saluted and marched back to the fort. The officer turned to his wife. "This had better be good," he said.